Lisa Ballantyne is the inte   four
novels. Her debut, *The Gu*   Book
Club bestseller, nominated for an Edga...   slated
into nearly thirty languages. Her second novel, *Good Bad Love*
(previously *Redemption Road*), was a *USA Today* bestseller. She
lives in Glasgow, Scotland.

Praise for Lisa Ballantyne:

'Gripping and emotionally charged . . . Just brilliant'
Clare Mackintosh

'Moving, insightful' *Guardian*

'Sophisticated, suspenseful, unsettling' Lee Child

'Tense' *The Sunday Times*

'Thought-provoking' *Woman & Home*

'Unsettling and compulsive' Rosamund Lupton

'Grips like a vice' *Daily Mail*

'Thought-provoking and clever' Gilly Macmillan

'One of the most readable, emotionally intense novels of the
year' Richard Madeley, Richard and Judy's Book Club

'Dark, intelligent, suspenseful' Saskia Sarginson

'Tense and moving' Rachel Abbott

'Subtle, suspenseful and sophisticated' *Sunday Express*

ONCE UPON A LIE

Lisa Ballantyne

PIATKUS

PIATKUS

First published in Great Britain in 2020 by Piatkus
This paperback edition published in 2021 by Piatkus

1 3 5 7 9 10 8 6 4 2

A CIP catalogue record for this book
is available from the British Library.

ISBN 978-0-349-41995-4

Typeset in Goudy by M Rules
Printed and bound in Great Britain by Clays Ltd, Elcograf S.p.A.

Papers used by Piatkus are from well-managed forests
and other responsible sources.

Piatkus
An imprint of
Little, Brown Book Group
Carmelite House
50 Victoria Embankment
London EC4Y 0DZ

An Hachette UK Company
www.hachette.co.uk

www.littlebrown.co.uk

'Not Proven' Verdict

'Not proven' is one of three options available to a jury or court in Scotland along with 'guilty' and 'not guilty.'

As with a verdict of 'not guilty', 'not proven' means that the defendant will walk free as the case to convict them has not been proved beyond a reasonable doubt. It leaves the accused innocent in the eyes of the law and its supporters say it offers an extra safeguard for defendants.

But critics argue it is confusing for juries and the public and that, although the legal implications of not proven are the same as with a not guilty verdict, it can stigmatise an accused person by not offering full exoneration.

The Double Jeopardy Scotland Act (2011)

An Act of the Scottish Parliament to make provision as to the circumstances in which a person convicted or acquitted of an offence may be prosecuted anew; and for connected purposes.

Prologue

CLARE

August 2019

Clare sat at her kitchen table and picked up her pen. It was late. She had laid out pale-blue writing paper with a thick ply that felt coarse between finger and thumb. It would soak up the ink from her pen. She had thought about it for some time, but tonight she was going to write a letter to Lorraine, about Theo . . . about everything. It was time.

She and Lorraine had not spoken for more than ten years. If Clare tried to call, she felt sure that Lorraine would hang up. Would she feel threatened? Might she call the police? A letter was best. It was non-confrontational and it would allow her to explain her side of the story.

Clare had been silent on the subject of Theo for over a decade. But if she *had* to tell the story, she would have to go way back to before it happened – to before Theo was even born. She would go back to meeting Lorraine at university and feeling that this tall, vibrant woman was the best friend she could ever have. Lorraine with her shiny black hair cut to her jaw, who seemed impervious yet fragile like bone china.

Clare miscarried for the first time the same year that Lorraine's first child, Ella, was born. And now, looking back, Clare could see that something had been set in motion back then, which had led to everything else that happened.

She never wanted to talk about it, did her best to push it from her thoughts, yet what had happened still swelled in her. From time to time it would fill her up, liquid swilling inside her, so that she could taste it in her mouth and memories would come to her unwanted, like gulps of seawater.

No, she *never* wanted to talk about it, but if she had to, she would tell the story in three parts:

The Miscarriage.

The Punch.

The Betrayal.

Some things are too big to understand on their own, and Clare was only ever able to rationalise what happened by breaking it down into those three key events.

She took the lid off her pen and wrote, *Dear Lorraine*.

It felt formal and auspicious to be writing more than a note or a card. She was out of practice. Her handwriting wavered from the tremble in her hand.

So old-fashioned to write a letter. There were so many other means of communication at her disposal. She could text, or WhatsApp. She could Messenger or Tweet. Calling was out of the question after so long, but she could email.

Email was the only other viable option for lengthy, private communication.

But Clare knew that there could never be just one email. Copies would be held in Inboxes, in Sent items, in Deleted items, on servers. Emails could be forwarded to many people over and again. Emails could be found and their content examined long after all trace had been removed from a mail account, or indeed the mail account itself deleted. Emails lived on like electronic fossils, revealing secrets years later.

Letters survived but they were physical things that were subject to the years and the climate, much like human beings. Letters could be shared, but they were often kept close or hidden. Letters yellowed, aged, disintegrated.

Clare pressed her lips together and began:

So long since we've been in touch, but I still think of you every day.

It was true. So long without any contact, but Clare still thought of Lorraine, and Ella and Theo, every single day. She missed them, craved their presence. At the beginning, after the trial, these loved ones had come into her mind like a migraine, sundering her, but now she welcomed them.

Clare looked at the pen in her hand. Why get in touch now? It was weeks since she had discovered the lump in her breast. She had felt it in the shower as she'd soaped: neck, shoulders, chest, armpits. Every day always the same routine and then something hard as a pebble under her skin. A needle biopsy had confirmed it was breast cancer but she was still waiting for the CT scan to determine the spread.

Cancer. It felt like a line drawn. A turning point. She didn't know what the future held but she wanted to put things right if she could. She wanted to at least try. There were things that had to be said.

I've not been well and fear what lies ahead for me and I wonder if, after all this time, we might be friends again, or at least speak, so that I could explain what happened that night, before it is too late.

Clare exhaled down her nose. She crossed out *before it is too late.*

She felt her cheeks flush as she crushed the piece of paper and began again.

Dear Lorraine . . .

She was alone in the flat. She was used to that by now. She had put on some music and planned to listen and write. When her husband had lived here, they'd listened to records, but he'd taken the player away with him. Almost everything in the flat still looked the same since he'd lived here. Still the same white walls, dark floorboards. Sam had taken his expensive designer chairs but even the blanket on the sofa was the same one they used to cuddle up beneath.

It had been hard for her to continue living in the flat after all that had happened. It was an old house, and Clare was sure its walls had witnessed sadder tales through the centuries than theirs. She wasn't superstitious but she wondered if the spirit of a tragedy lingered, absorbed into the pores of the sandstone.

It had been built in 1871 as a flat above a stable for three horses, two carriages and a hayloft. In 1969, the hayloft and flat had been converted into the living area, and when Sam and Clare bought it, it was single storey and covered in pine cladding. As a young architect, Sam had wanted a project of his own. Renovated, it felt more like a house than a flat, with street-level entry leading up a spiral stone staircase to an open-plan kitchen-living room; the hayloft converted into a second floor with three bedrooms.

It was too big for just one person, and cold in the winter, but Clare made use of most of the rooms since she had been living here alone. One of the bedrooms served as her darkroom and the open-plan kitchen-living room was a studio space for her portrait photography business.

It had been Clare's determination to continue living here, but it was also her punishment, a constant reminder of the tragedy that had unfolded within the thick stone walls and her part in that. She regarded it as an achievement that she was still able to call it home.

Clare pressed her pen against the paper, then raised it. There was a black dot where she had hesitated. Part of her wondered if the cancer had been caused by this well of unexpressed feeling inside her, as if the dark memory of that time had burrowed down inside her, turning hard and malignant, rallying, preparing itself to spread.

I've recently found out that I'm not well – breast cancer – and, although I'm trying to be brave, it makes me feel the loss of you all over again. We've known each other for so many years and after all that has happened I still love you like a sister. When we were young we shared so many secrets. We told each other everything. I never thought that anything would come between us.

I am writing now to ask for your forgiveness.

That night was the worst night of my life. The cancer has shocked me, but it has forced me to address things that had been hard for me to face before. I think it will help me to fight this – to get well – if I know that I have your blessing and that you forgive me . . .

Clare stopped. She wanted to add, *as I have forgiven you,* but thought it inappropriate for a first letter. She didn't want to nettle Lorraine. Tears stung her eyes. She knuckled beneath her lid.

Explaining was hard. It was like trying to interpret an avalanche, a tumble of rocks and mud. Clare was not sure how to order it, but she knew that she wanted Lorraine to finally understand.

Again, Clare put down her pen. She swallowed, feeling the liquid swill inside her. So much emotion even after all this time. Her fingers trembled. It was not just sadness that she felt. Even after all this time, she was angry.

She had been angry that night too, all those years ago, and knew her anger had partly caused what happened. She was prepared to admit that now.

Early morning. Clare left her flat and locked the big black wooden door before she headed out to Palmerston Place. The sun was just starting to come up behind St Mary's Cathedral. It was supposed to be a warm day, but this early there was a chill and she wore a scarf over her shoulders and neck. She walked straight to the post box on West Maitland Street.

MS LORRAINE COLLINS printed on a white label, adhered to a brown A5 envelope. First class post.

It had taken Clare several days to finish the letter. It had run to over twenty pages and did not fit into the matching envelope for the notelets, but Clare had already decided against them. She wanted something generic, business-like.

After hand-writing the address, Clare had worried Lorraine would destroy the letter without even opening it. They knew each other's handwriting at a glance. They had been at university together, reading each other's essays and writing in the holidays. No electronic means of communication back then. They had shared a student flat on South Clerk Street with a family of mice. They had been so close their periods had synchronised. Even after all these years, Clare was sure she would still recognise Lorraine's handwriting anywhere: expressive, high reaching 'Hs' and 'Is' and low curling 'Gs' and 'Ys', but the letters thin and close to each other.

And so, Clare had opted for a brown envelope and printed

label. The fatness of the letter didn't seem so strange as part of business correspondence. The letter looked boring, official, innocent.

Before she let it go, Clare held onto it for a few moments – feeling a brief flush of anxiety when its small weight left her fingertips and dropped down into the box. It was done. She had set something in motion.

The letter was signed, *all my love, Clare*, and then she had given her mobile number – which had not changed in all these years – and her email address.

They *could* be friends again.

All Clare had to do now was wait.

Part One

The Miscarriage

1

CLARE

November 2008

Clare squeezed Sam's hand in hers, turning to look into his eyes and feeling the warmth and strength of him. She felt the strain of her smile on her face, an ache in her cheeks.

It took a few moments for the cool smudge of gel and the odd prod of the ultrasound to acquaint themselves with her exposed belly. As the sonographer smeared the gel over Clare's stomach she didn't look at their faces, but at the screen where images appeared, black and white, potent, etched from living fibre, like a computerised wood cut.

Twelve weeks.

After today, they could tell everyone that they were pregnant. Clare was frightened to believe it might happen, although she couldn't remember wanting anything more.

Sam pressed her hand to his lips. Their hands had been clasped for such a time there was a balm of sweat between them.

It was not altogether uncomfortable, as it spoke of their shared anxiety. They had been here before.

This time last year, the sonographer had gone suddenly silent, frowning at the screen before her. 'I'm really sorry; it's not good news. I can't detect a heartbeat. The baby's only measuring ten weeks so it looks as though the heartbeat must have stopped around two weeks ago, but your body still thinks you're pregnant.'

Clare still remembered the swarm in her gut when she heard those words: the panic, the unformed grief. She and Sam had been ushered into a windowless room with a box of tissues on a table and told to wait for the midwife to discuss their options.

'Is this your first?' the sonographer asked, driving the ultrasound over Clare's stomach. The muscular tickle of the prod lurched Clare from her thoughts.

'Yes,' she said, then bit her lip.

Sam rested his lips on her hand again and stroked his thumb along the side of her forefinger. It would be their first child, that was for sure, but they had been pregnant and in this room, or others like it, *so many* times.

'Exciting, huh?'

Clare nodded and smiled thinly at the sonographer. She felt the strain in her arms and neck as she craned to study the younger woman's face, watched the reflection of the screen in her large brown eyes. The woman was smiling at the image and Clare allowed hope to blossom inside her.

Clare felt fatigued by the cycles of hope and despair. Turning up again and again, smiling that this was their first baby, when in fact she didn't tend to get past pregnant. The clinical environment, familiar as it was, always left her feeling exposed, vulnerable, alien, as if all the normal human sentiment that should surround conception and carrying a child had been swabbed away.

She rested her head back on the bed and tried to relax despite her full bladder and her expectation, but it was hard not to feel uptight: she had just turned forty and had had a grand total of nine miscarriages over a period of seven years.

Doctors. Tests. Experimental treatments. She would be able to write a book about it. She was sure that she had tried everything to get to this point.

Vitamins. Acupuncture. Ayurvedic tinctures. Reflexology. Maca. Cold baths. Shatvari. Moonstones. Algae. Wheatgerm. Spinach. No meat; more meat. No milk; lots of dairy. Pelvic physical therapy. Hypnotherapy. Teetotal; very little caffeine. Fresh fruit and vegetables. Clare had even exposed her pregnant belly to the full moon in the hope that it would nurture their growing foetus into a baby. They were not past old wives' tales. Whatever helped. Whatever could bring them a child.

'Have you had much sickness?' The sonographer had a kind face.

'No . . . not yet,' she said, biting her lip to fight back the tears. That too felt like admitting failure. Clare was aware of the school of thought that said bad morning sickness was the sign of a healthy pregnancy. 'A bit of heartburn, that's all.'

Clare heard the quiver in her voice, the strain of trying to sound normal. Sam's grip on her hand was still tight and she knew he was nervous too.

'That's good. Getting off lightly then.'

Pregnancy was so stressful that neither Sam nor Clare

13

could describe it as getting off lightly. They just wanted to *stay* pregnant.

She tried not to think of it as her fault, but Sam had been tested early on and his sperm were active and multitudinous. And they *were able* to conceive. It was hard not to blame herself for being unable to carry the babies to term.

The sonographer suddenly held the ultrasound probe still and kneaded it into Clare's belly. Clare held her breath.

'There we are. I'll turn this screen a bit more so you can both get a better look.'

Clare's view of the screen blurred as she squeezed Sam's hand. When she smiled, the tears she'd been holding back now fell from her eyes.

'Wow, yeah, I see it. The head . . . ?' Sam took a deep breath and turned to Clare.

The technician reached forward and pointed out the head, two legs bent.

Clare raised herself up, staring at the screen, trying to interpret this new life. 'Is it okay? Are you sure it's okay?'

'All looks as it should be. Congratulations. I'll get you a printout.'

'Thank you.' Clare sank back onto the bed. 'Thank you so, so much.'

Back in the car, Clare tried to suppress her joy. 'We made it. Second trimester.'

'I love you,' he said.

'I want to be able to feel it. I want a big belly to wrap my hands around.'

'You will. We will. This is it, this time.' He bent to kiss her, his hand reaching behind her neck.

It was dark outside and wet and the car had not warmed up yet. She shivered under his touch, the cold and her nerves indistinguishable. They had been together so long it was as if they no longer saw each other objectively. Clare was small – just over five foot tall – and Sam six foot four in his socks. One of her earliest memories of him was of reaching up on her tiptoes to stroke his cheek.

She shivered, hands between her thighs. 'Let's go home.'

'Shall we call people tonight?' he asked, turning in his seat as he reversed out of the hospital car park.

'What do you mean? Do you mean *tell* people about the baby?'

'Twelve weeks. We've never got to twelve weeks before, that's the time when it's safe to tell—'

'No.' Clare shook her head once and put a hand on his thigh. 'I just don't want to jinx it, y'know?'

'It's okay, baby. I feel the same.' As he accelerated on the open road he flashed a smile at her.

'I *want* to tell people. I just think, let's wait another week at least . . .'

'We could tell Lorraine? Lorraine's okay; she doesn't count, right? Not like telling our mums.'

Clare sighed and looked out of the window at the houses flashing by in the dark. All those small lit windows, all those illuminated lives. Telling Lorraine was not like telling her mother, but in some ways telling Lorraine was harder for Clare. Babies came easily to Lorraine.

Clare thought of how she would feel if she lost this child. She took the scan picture from her pocket and peered at it, the definition of the image hard to make out in the darkened car.

Traffic lights. Cameron Toll Shopping Centre.

'I just don't think I can take one more,' she whispered, to herself, but Sam heard her.

'Don't.'

'I'm not, I'm staying positive, but I just feel . . . tired, you know. I want this for us so much. I want it for *you* . . . ' Sam would be such a good father – she wanted to watch him in that role. 'I just . . . I don't think I've got another start over, try again in me . . . '

Through the traffic lights, Sam swerved to the side of the road.

'You won't have to. I've got a good feeling this time.'

'You're right,' Clare said, her palm spread open on her belly, under the waistband of her jeans. She tried her best smile and Sam bent to kiss her forehead. She felt the jolt of it; the comfort. 'But let's not tell anyone, even Lorraine – just until next week, okay?'

'Whatever you want.' She felt his warm, large hand reach inside her sweater and cradle her abdomen. 'I mean it. I've got a good feeling this time.'

Clare smiled and said, 'me too', even though she also had a crushing feeling in her chest.

She kissed the lobe of his ear before he withdrew and indicated again to pull out. Staring straight ahead at the white road markings slipping by like beads on a rosary, she willed every fibre of her to hold onto this baby, to nurture it inside of her.

*

Over one week later, Clare and Sam had still not breathed a word about the twelve-week scan. It was Friday night and they had decided to share the news with their families at the weekend. They sat on the sofa watching television, the damp logs on the fire hissing and sparking. The shutters were closed and the high ceilinged room was warm, but they sat close under a blanket, Sam's feet stretched out over Clare's lap.

Clare rubbed her eyes as she watched the shadowy flicker of the flames reflected onto the white wall, so that they seemed to lick upwards towards her framed photographs.

'I think I'm going to go upstairs,' she said, stretching.

'Alright, I won't be long.' He lifted his long legs to allow her to get up.

Standing, she leaned backwards slightly, hands at the small of her back, stretching.

'Your breasts look amazing.'

She laughed. She was naturally boyish-framed, but pregnancy gave her curves. 'Well, they don't feel amazing.' Her breasts had increased in size, particularly in the last month, and ached almost all of the time.

Once upstairs, Clare changed into her pyjamas and washed her face. She watched her eyes in the magnifying mirror – huge startled blue.

She urinated, running a hand through her short hair and wondering whether she would make a chicken pie for the family dinner at the weekend, or if she should make a roast. They were inviting both of their mums and Lorraine and the kids. They were going to tell them all the good news.

When she wiped, there was blood.

Clare stared at it, her mouth drying. There wasn't a lot, just a pinkish spotting, but all her miscarriages had started this way. *Please no,* she whispered.

She was about to go downstairs again, to tell Sam, but hesitated. She didn't want to worry him – they'd had such a relaxing night. And all her years of online chatrooms and pregnancy blogs told her not to be alarmed. *Many women have spotting as part of a healthy pregnancy.*

Clare got into bed, but was no longer tired. She lay still, muttering pleading prayers. *Please let me keep it. Please let me keep this baby.*

She could see it in her mind, this tiny form that was growing inside her although she couldn't feel it. It would have fingerprints, tiny little whorls of individuality. It was their baby, they had made it, and it was asking to be born.

When Sam came to bed, Clare snuggled into him but said nothing. He turned the light out and before long she heard his breathing lengthen and deepen. Clare held onto him, the heat from his body making her feel too warm, but she didn't move away. She thought if she could remain as still as possible, she would stay pregnant.

She wasn't aware of having slept, but suddenly she was jolted awake by a tearing cramp. She sat up in bed, leaning against the bedpost and exhaling through the pain. It came in waves, a drag in her pelvis down to her thighs, and then a sharper pain, which made her squirm.

'Honey ... Sam?'

She reached out and touched his shoulder. Instantly, he was awake. 'You okay?' He sat up beside her. 'What's the matter? Are you in pain?'

Clare nodded, teeth together. 'God. I think I'm starting . . .'

She made it to the toilet, but the blood had already soaked through her pyjamas.

Sam drove them to hospital.

Clare sat curled in the front seat. She was wearing a strange array of clothes – her pyjama top with a thick woollen jumper over it, grey jogging bottoms and white tennis shoes with no socks, even though it was now icy, the tarmac sparkling in front of them. Sam was speeding and the lurch of the car drove the ache into her bones. The pain twisted and cut and pulled inside of her.

It was a twenty-minute drive to accident and emergency at Edinburgh's Royal Infirmary. On Hope Park Crescent, Clare reached out and put her hand on Sam's thigh, as she had done a week ago, in the swell of her happiness. The lights were red. In the glow from the traffic lights he turned to her, his face pale and frightened.

'Clare, your lips are blue. Clare!'

'I'm okay.'

'You're not. You're not. Oh my god.'

Sam drove straight through the red light. He screeched to a halt near accident and emergency, parking the car half-on and half-off the kerb.

'Is this a space?'

'It is now.' He jumped out of the car and ran around to Clare's side.

The rain had started, heavy, chastening. The cold rushed at her when he opened the door. She waited for his hand before she tried to stand, lifted her feet out of the car.

They both stared at her tennis shoes against the tarmac. One was still white but the other had turned almost black with blood.

Clare couldn't walk fast and the freezing rain drenched them. The water soaked her short hair and ran into her eyes. She blinked and blinked again, almost doubled over with the pain.

'I don't think I can make it,' she said.

The door to accident and emergency was fifty feet away.

'I'll get you a wheelchair.' He wrenched his hand from hers.

'Don't leave me,' she cried then, hands on her knees, but he was back and he hugged her, half carried her, towards the door. 'I'm sorry,' she breathed into the warmth of his chest.

'You're alright. You're going to be okay.'

In the waiting room, gasping and feeling the heat enclose them, Clare leaned on the counter as Sam tried to check them in. Clare caught the eye of a man in the waiting room. His newspaper fell slowly to his lap as he stared at Clare's jogging bottoms. Why had she worn pale grey? They were soaked through with her blood.

A drunk man was in front of them, palms on the glass as he mumbled something to the triage nurse. The skin seemed stretched over his skull.

'My wife needs help now.'

The nurse looked at Sam over his spectacles.

'It's okay,' Clare said, 'I can wait,' but spots of light were crowding her vision, nausea washing over her.

'Look at my wife. She needs help now. She's going into fucking shock.'

'Sam, *stop.*' Clare whispered this, bent over, fingertips on the elbow of his fleece. It was hard enough to stay standing without having to pacify him.

A nurse came with a wheelchair and a few large sanitary pads, saying that she would find a bed soon.

Sam sat down beside her in the waiting room, his chest heaving from the emotion as he tried to calm down. Clare knew he found it hard to be vulnerable; anger was sometimes his answer to pain.

'Honey, I need to go to the bathroom. Come in with me, help me. There's a disabled loo over there. I'm scared I'm going to pass out.'

Inside he helped her onto the large toilet. Her thighs were smeared with blood.

Clare felt another stab in her insides. She dug her fingernails into Sam's forearm, so hard that when she took her hand away there were crescent moon indentations on his skin. Clotted blood splashed into the toilet bowl.

She opened her legs and looked down. Sam looked away but she told him what she saw. It was their baby, the size of Clare's small fist.

It was recognisable as a tiny, tiny baby – and then it disappeared.

2

CLARE

August 2019

Clare felt the tension hunching her shoulders and consciously forced them back. She wanted to look confident. As she walked back and forth, she smiled to welcome people, a glass in one hand and a glossy exhibition brochure in the other. Her fingers were moist with sweat and the brochure slippery in her grasp.

All the walls in the gallery were white and the floorboards, although scuffed, had been whitewashed some time ago. The whiteness increased Clare's nerves. It was an unnatural space; it was how she imagined death – a white room with white furniture and no windows.

Her photographs hung on each wall – some black and white, some colour, some abstract. The brochure cover featured one of her favourites: a portrait of her mother in the 1960s – pixie cut and pink trousers, laughing on a rowing boat. Beneath the photograph, in bold, black text read the title of her exhibition:

Clare Richardson: Unearthed

Portraits were a departure for Clare in her art photography, even though she had earned her crust for years doing family portraits.

She had made her name on the local art scene photographing inanimate objects, and had won the Scottish Photography Awards for her abstract of yellow lichen growing on a rusty iron pipe. That had been fifteen years ago, before Theo.

Nearly two hundred invitations had been sent out and it looked as if nearly half of the guests had already arrived. Clare had prepared a speech and would only relax once she had delivered it – then she could circulate properly and laugh with friends. Since her diagnosis, she noticed that she tired more easily, but she still made an effort to seem enthusiastic.

'Hey, great to see you.' Clare stood on tiptoe to kiss Arnold, a fellow artist from the Cockburn Street gallery – where she sometimes used studio space. She kissed him on both cheeks, spilling a drop of her champagne onto his blue, floral shirt as she did so. She touched his chest lightly as if to blot the mark with her fingers.

'This is fabulous,' he said. '*You* look fabulous. Glad you're still in your standard footwear.'

Clare looked down at her baseball boots. They were one of her special pairs, with sequins on them. Arnold lamented that she was always wearing baseball boots, but that was who she was. Clare had worn them since university in the late eighties. High heels of any kind were not for her – although she remembered wearing them at the trial. It was not that she didn't need the height, but heels reminded her of dressing up as a child, clumping down the hall in enormous court shoes with a string of pearls wound around her neck. Clare didn't like airs and graces.

Take me as you find me.

What you see is what you get.

Clare began another circle of the room. Instinctively, she searched for Sam. She hadn't invited him, but there had been a bit of press, a little buzz about the exhibition in Edinburgh – it had been promoted citywide as part of the Art Festival – and she had secretly hoped he would have noticed and come along. They were still not formally divorced, despite being formally separated, and there had been some tentative contact between them over the past few years. They weren't quite friends, but it no longer hurt to see him.

The *Scotsman* had run an article about Clare Richardson and the exhibition, and then some of the smaller papers had picked it up. She used her maiden name, Richardson, for her artwork – it helped to dissociate her from the woman who had stood in the dock all those years ago – but Sam could easily have missed it.

It did feel good to be lauded in the press for once. Back in 2008 the newspapers had not been so kind. The headlines were always accompanied by unflattering pictures of Clare snapped as she left the court, her shoulders hunched, her chin tucked in towards her chest.

Sam had been there too, but the papers had focused on her – because she was a woman? Clare had felt cast as something from a fairy tale – an evil queen, black headdress spiking up like horns, a female incarnation of Lucifer.

Jemima Jones, the gallery owner, swept over, snapping Clare out of her thoughts. 'I think it's going very well. Scott on the door says you have one hundred and twenty already. I thought I'd give it fifteen minutes more, then introduce you?' She gathered Clare into a loose embrace, her bright-red lipstick stretched into a smile.

'Okay. I'll just get a breath of fresh air – calm down a bit before I speak.'

'Don't be long.'

Clare went out the back door into the delivery area. The cold air felt good against her skin. Just a few sips of champagne but her cheeks were burning. She had always been so sensitive to alcohol.

It was dusk and the summer sky was reddening at the corners, taking flame. Newhaven harbour looked quaint, the boats nestling hull to hull, conspiratorial. Clare could lick her lips and taste the place – brine and cobble and sea-soaked rope. The salty air and the high pink sky and she felt almost hopeful again. She had been through so much. Her cancer diagnosis had seemed unfair after all she had survived, but now it steeled her. She had already reinvented herself from the woman she had been – the woman whose husband had left her, whom the press had castigated. It made her feel emboldened enough to believe that she could beat the cancer too.

'Unearthed'. The exhibition had come together quite quickly. Clare had curated the photographs as early as last year, before she found the lump in her breast. Even before she knew she was ill she had been looking backwards. Working on these prints had helped her process a lot of grief. She had physically buried the film in a raised bed outside her flat, then dug up the sheets of photographic film several days later before reworking the images in the studio. The faces that emerged from the degraded emulsion were changed. It was a fresh look at something old, almost forgotten. After everything that had happened – losing Theo, losing Sam, losing her best friend – Clare had felt something like relief.

This new creative project had somehow healed her, made her feel absolved, and then she'd found the lump.

Back inside, Clare took a small piece of folded paper from her pocket – notes for her speech. She glanced at the words she had written to remind herself of key points: *people to thank, inspiration, Dorothea Lange.*

She glanced once more into the gathering guests, wishing for Sam's face. Everyone was animated, shiny-skinned. Everyone's glass was full. Any time now it would be time for her to begin. She scanned the room looking for Jemima.

Just then, she saw a face she recognised in the crowd. It had changed from her memory but she knew it instantly, even from this distance. Immediately, her breathing began to change.

It was Lorraine.

Her hair looked different – blonded or gone grey – but she was also unchanged – that same athletic figure, standing tall among the guests. She loomed, all clavicle and cheekbone and good posture. Swallowing, Clare watched as Lorraine scanned the crowd.

It had been less than a week since Clare had posted the letter to her old friend. She had expected contact – an email, a phone call. Mostly, she had expected no response at all.

She had not thought that Lorraine would turn up at her exhibition.

Suddenly, their eyes met.

It felt like plunging into cold water. For a few seconds, Clare stood trembling from the shock, a lurch and drag in the centre of her abdomen.

'Shall we do it now?' Jemima asked, hand suddenly on Clare's elbow.

Clare didn't look at her, kept her eyes focused on Lorraine. 'Give me a moment,' she said, her voice so quiet, no air in her lungs to carry her words. 'There's someone I need to speak to.'

'Give your speech first. There will be time afterwards to chat.'

'A moment.' Clare walked away from Jemima and straight towards Lorraine, not knowing what to expect. The aching drag in her abdomen was strong now, a painful fist of tension opening slowly inside her. It reminded her of all those miscarriages, the sharp pain and the life seeping out of her.

Holding her gaze, Lorraine stood perfectly still in the crowd. She had come alone.

Clare's mouth became very dry as she walked towards her old friend. The noise of the crowd around her contracted to a dull pulse in her ears – her own heart.

'Hello,' Clare said, offering a tentative smile. 'I didn't expect ... You look great.'

As always, Clare had to look up at Lorraine. It was almost like looking up at Sam – all six foot four of him. Clare had to put her head right back to look Lorraine in the eye. When they were young she hadn't bothered, but now the height difference made her feel threatened.

Lorraine did look great though. The silvery blonde hair was a striking difference and her skin was unwrinkled – only two deep frown lines between her brows showed. Lorraine had always been so dark, and Clare absorbed the change as she looked up at her. It was like looking at a negative of her friend.

'I don't want to cause a scene,' Lorraine said, quickly, eyes darting around the room. 'Is there somewhere we can speak?' There was a prickle of sweat on her upper lip.

All these years, but Clare could still read her friend – the tension in her body, the confrontation in her eyes.

'Shall we talk outside?'

Lorraine nodded once, then turned and headed for the door. Clare followed, her small hands feeling hot and heavy at her sides.

The big white gallery door clacked shut behind them. They were alone in the car park and Clare felt grateful as she didn't want to be overheard, but it crossed her mind to keep her distance. Here they were in shadow and the evening felt cold.

Lorraine was wearing a fitted jacket with a bright-pink scarf tucked into the neck, but Clare only wore a thin blouse. The cool wind sliced off the water and Clare folded her arms to stop herself shivering.

They hadn't stood this close to each other since the night Lorraine left Theo in Clare's care. Even at the trial they had not spoken. The energy between them seemed to crackle and spark.

'How did you find me here?'

'I saw it in the paper.'

Clare nodded, feeling her teeth begin to chatter with nerves. The brackish scent of the water surrounded them.

'I got your letter.' Lorraine's face contorted – visibly holding back tears.

Clare almost reached out to touch her, instinctively wanting to comfort, but then kept her arms folded. 'I hoped you would get in touch. I wanted to see you. It's just tonight's this . . . maybe we could—'

'What do you think you're trying to do to me?' Lorraine was agitated, her fine cheekbones reddening. 'I came here to tell you to leave me alone. And, no, I *can't ever* forgive you, ever . . .' Tears glistened in her eyes but did not spill.

'Look, maybe I didn't express myself very well, but I would love to see you again. I want to talk . . . we could have lunch or dinner . . .?' Clare allowed her question to fade.

Lorraine's eyes widened in response to the suggestion – all the whites showing.

'Jesus, Clare. Lunch? Are you serious? You . . .' She swallowed the words and winced as if they tasted sour.

'I didn't mean it like that . . . it's just now—'

'Just the thought of you makes me physically ill and then to get that letter . . . it all came flooding back to me, every painful second, when I've tried so hard – for Ella – to deal with it, to carry on, and then you just . . .' Tears brimmed in her eyes but still she held them back.

'I didn't mean to hurt you. I just . . . I'm going through some things right now and I thought there were important things that needed to be said between us.'

'You're incredible. I mean—' Lorraine sniffed '—it's all about you. Did you ever think for a moment what this would do to me?' She blinked, then added, 'And to be quite honest, I'm not sorry you're – that you're . . . unwell.'

Clare cast her eyes down to the tarmac. She put her hands in her pockets as she felt the impact of the remark, felt it knuckle under her ribs. She heard a wave slap against the harbour wall.

'And it wasn't just over ten years ago; it was ten years and nine months and . . . ' Then the tears came, heavy, hard – they flashed down Lorraine's cheeks. 'Days, days, and I . . . ' Lorraine used the heel of her hand to catch the tears, a strange gesture, as if pressing them into her skin.

Lorraine couldn't get any more words out, and Clare opened her mouth to speak but the pain in her throat stopped her. She couldn't do this right now – a room full of people were waiting for her – but part of her knew that she had to grasp this chance to talk to Lorraine. After all these years, finally they were face to face.

'I miss him, too,' Clare whispered, her voice so low she felt it taken away by the breeze. The dark lap of the black water against the pier made her feel desperate. 'Don't you think I feel it every day too?'

'You don't get to say that. You have no right. I don't care how you feel about it. I don't want to even *think* about you. I don't want to have any contact with you. That letter was uncalled for. It was like a punch – a *punch* at me.'

'I didn't mean it like that. I didn't want to hurt you.'

'You wanted me to feel sorry for you, is that it? Well, I don't. You do what you have to do, but you leave me alone.'

'Alright. I'm sorry.' The rain started – intermittent hard spots on her scalp.

'You're not sorry. I don't think you said sorry once, not in all those pages and certainly not back then. I could barely read what you wrote.' Lorraine thrust her hands into her jacket pockets. 'Pages of you . . . you, you, you, thinking about yourself.'

'I was thinking about *you*.' Anger flared in Clare, brief as a match struck.

'All those years ago, you insisted you had no memory at all and now suddenly you remember your part. Have you any *idea* what that does to me, what it makes me . . . feel, think?'

'I still don't remember everything, but things have started to make sense . . . I thought from this distance you would see things differently too.'

'Distance? Differently? What you mean . . . the time, the years? It's fresh to me, like it was yesterday. You don't lose your baby and just get over it.'

In her pockets, Clare tightened her fists thinking of all the babies *she* had lost. She looked down at her baseball boots, noticing how the rain was darkening the material.

'Your letter was very different from what you said at the trial . . . ' Lorraine's voice was now steady.

'I wasn't trying to go over that again, I just wanted . . . I thought after all this time and everything we've lost . . . '

'What have *you* lost? *What* have you lost?' Lorraine's voice was full of derision.

31

Clare raised her chin defiantly, as if slapped, but said nothing. 'I lost everything.'

I lost everything too, Clare thought but did not utter.

Lorraine ran a hand through her hair. 'I've done a lot of work on myself over the years, to get myself to a place where I can get through the day without feeling that I might fall to pieces at some point. I didn't need you and your memories and your . . . *paragraphs* on your breast cancer.'

The consonants brought particles of spit that landed on Clare's face. She didn't raise her hand to wipe them away, but just allowed them to settle there with the spots of rain.

Clare inhaled. The cool air of the summer night reached deep into her lungs.

'And if illness has started to make you think again about the night my baby died, then maybe you would be better served going to the police rather than writing to me about how *you feel*. Because, I don't *care* how you feel; I just want you to take responsibility for what you did. You go ahead and have your little photograph party and go for chemo and lose your hair and feel like shit and know that when you are plugged into that drug machine feeding you poison – and you feel like throwing up even though you have nothing left inside you – that is *not the worst* you can feel.' Tears flashed over Lorraine's cheeks. 'That is *not* the worst you can feel.' Lorraine gasped, as if she had no air, or as if her own words had shocked her.

Clare felt the dark swill of the water inside her. She realised, perhaps for the first time, that Lorraine hated her – although she also realised she should have known this for years. 'You've said it already. Your pain is worse. Okay. I shouldn't have written. I just wanted . . . God, to be friends again.' Tears blurred Clare's vision for a moment.

'Friends?' Lorraine wiped the tears from her face with a flat hand. 'How can I be friends with you. How?'

'Oh God, Lorraine.' Clare put two hands to her head, flicking a glance at the doors, sure that someone would be coming to get her. 'I thought you would understand . . . I lied to the police, but that was because it was just . . . too awful. It was the worst thing . . . I wanted you to know that I do now accept responsibility for what happened—'

'Enough,' Lorraine snapped, eyes wild.

They argued then – a confusing lash and slither, like the dark brown seaweed, all pod and mane that clung to the slippery, barnacled rocks. So many words, memories sliding from one of them to the other finding no purchase.

The bone of Lorraine's face was sharp. It was hard for Clare to even look at her.

Winded, Clare began to cry.

'Oh, stop it,' Lorraine said. 'It might be guilt that's made you sick, but at least you've finally admitted that you're guilty.'

Almost of its own volition, Clare's arm rose up and she took hold of the material of Lorraine's jacket. Clare was not sure if she was pleading, comforting, or just asking for their friendship back. Another wave crashed against the harbour wall before Lorraine pulled away.

'You better enjoy this party while you can. Apart from

hurting me deeply, your letter read like a confession. I'm sure the police would like to see it.'

'Lorraine,' Clare called after her, but she was already walking away.

Running a hand through her hair to detangle and smooth it, Clare wondered if she looked as shaken as she felt. Her hair was damp now from the fine smirr of salty rain.

She opened the door to the gallery and slipped inside. She wiped her eyes, took a deep breath. There was a bad taste in her mouth.

'Where did you *go*?' Jemima accosted her. 'Let's do it now.'

'An old friend came to see me.' Clare felt light-headed. Her speech now seemed unimportant.

Jemima teased her fingers through Clare's short blonde hair. 'You're all damp and windswept.'

'I'll give my speech,' Clare said, swallowing, following Jemima through the crowd. The heat of the room wrapped around her. Her fingers felt icy cold.

The salt air still on her lips, she stood at the edge of the stage as Jemima introduced her.

'Welcome ladies and gentlemen.' Jemima was beaming, her bright-red lipstick framing white teeth. 'Thank you all for coming to the opening of this marvellous new exhibition ...'

Clare stood with her hands clasped behind her back. In her mind a shutter opened and closed, again and again, snapshots.

She remembered walking barefoot along the dark floorboards of the hall of her home.

The door to the children's bedroom was closed, although

Clare was sure she had left it open. She couldn't be sure – her mind fuzzy, her tongue thick in her mouth, a sweet dryness at the back of her throat.

Clare swayed, leaning on the door for support, but then she realised that Theo was not in his cot. She rushed over, reaching into the cot to grasp the covers and then holding onto the sides as she checked underneath. She remembered Lorraine's warning that Theo was able to climb out. But where had he gone? The room was spinning slightly, the floor seeming to rise up at an angle and then back down again like the bow of a ship.

She should have been more careful. Trying to conceive had meant it had been years since she had really taken a drink and she had never been able to handle it.

Holding onto the bars of the cot to steady herself, she turned to look around the room. What had she done? She opened her mouth to scream. No sound came, but all the air left her body.

It was like a dream, trying to call out and having no voice. In her memory it was like that: dry mouthed, no air in her lungs, trying to make a sound and not being able.

'Sam! Sam!' His name came out so loud from her lips, suddenly released from inside her. She forgot about Ella asleep and the fright she would give her.

She stood back, waited for Sam. Viscerally she knew what her mind had difficulty comprehending, that Theo was dead.

Suddenly Jemima was saying, 'Please, raise your glasses and give a warm round of applause to the Newhaven Gallery's principal artist for this year, Clare Richardson, and this wonderful collection of "Unearthed" portraits.'

Clare stepped up to the microphone. Her tongue felt thick in her mouth, as if it might choke her. She scanned the crowd for friends – for Sam, again – but faces seemed to blur and morph into Lorraine's face, angry in grief.

Clare cleared her throat. 'Thank you all for coming.'

She tried her best not to tremble, and she remembered her words perfectly. Even more than she had earlier, she wished Sam was here now.

'Some of you might know that I mainly photograph inanimate objects and this collection of pictures is a departure for me . . . So I'd like to start with a quote tonight from the portrait photographer, Dorothea Lange: "*photography takes a moment out of time, altering life by holding it still*" . . .'

She delivered the rest of her speech, word perfect, all the while feeling a split and tear inside her, as if she was freeing herself but exposing herself at the same time, like a moth bursting from its pupa.

'And so, these pictures on the wall are slices of time,' Clare concluded. 'Please enjoy. I look forward to hearing your thoughts.'

She handed the microphone to Jemima, feeling sick, reeling.

3

LORRAINE

August 2019

Lorraine stepped off the bus and smoothed her hair, then walked home slowly, trying to compose herself. Her shoulders were still trembling and so she stood outside the flat for a few moments before turning her key in the lock. The tip of her nose was cold and she cupped her hand to warm it. As she inhaled the smell of her own palm, Clare's words and the argument outside the gallery came back to her. There was a swill of emotion inside her that made her feel physically sick, but Ella would be home now and Lorraine didn't want to go inside upset.

Lorraine had been a single mother for the majority of the time that she'd been a parent. Ella's father had left long ago, returning to Brazil when Ella was just four. There had been very little contact at all, although Pedro was now a Facebook friend. Lorraine knew she had leant on her daughter too much over the years – especially after Theo was born, and after he died. It had been just the two of them since Theo's death, and Lorraine worried that their relationship was less mother and daughter than close friends. But maybe that didn't matter now Ella was nearly grown.

She pushed her key into the lock and opened the door. Home smelled of toast. From the hall, Lorraine could see Ella in the living room, sitting on the sofa. She was just out of the shower, her long hair brushed wet down her back, dampening the T-shirt she wore over leggings. The television was on; Ella wasn't watching it, but rather scrolling through her phone, course books beside her on the couch – *Midwifery Practice, Antenatal and Postnatal Midwifery Care.*

Ella was now at college studying to be a midwife. She had decided halfway through high school that was what she wanted to do. She had studied hard, got the exam results she needed and passed the interview. Lorraine was so proud of her. She had always been such a bright, bright girl.

Lorraine shook off her jacket, smoothed her palms over her face as she checked herself in the hall mirror. She thought she looked okay – no sign on her face of the argument with Clare – no mascara smears or swollen eyes. She looked windswept, but otherwise as if it had never happened.

'Is that you?' Ella called.

'Yeah. With you in a moment.'

Lorraine needed a bath, peace to think, the privacy and the day-stopping relief of immersion in hot water. A chance to cry, to think over what she had said to Clare and what action she should now take.

'How was your day, darling?' Lorraine hoped her voice sounded clean, upbeat, untarnished by the raw emotion that had ripped through her outside the Newhaven Gallery. She had said nothing to Ella about the letter or going to meet Clare. She didn't know how long she would be able to keep it to herself, but she didn't want to burden her daughter, especially when she had college, the pressure of practicals and exams. It would only make her anxious.

Ella stretched, legs lengthening against the sofa and arms raised overhead. Even from this distance, Lorraine could see the silvery criss-cross lines that ran up her daughter's forearms, the violence of them faded now so that the scars were silky smooth. Even as a child Ella had the tendency to turn pain inwards and that had come to a head when she was a teenager. Lorraine smoothed the damp hair on the side of Ella's head. She always wondered if she could have shielded Ella more when her brother died.

'It was okay. We're doing a lot of work on the dummies just now, so that was quite cool.'

'You mean a dummy mother?'

'Yeah, a pregnant torso with a baby inside. I learned about shoulder dystocia – it's when the baby's okay but the shoulder gets stuck behind the woman's pelvis and just can't come out, and so you have to reach in to dislodge it. We all got to practise.'

'Never heard of that.'

'It's quite common.'

Lorraine was always shocked by how *big* Ella had grown. In her mind she was still a child, but here was this young woman who seemed Olympian. Lorraine was five foot ten, but Ella had reached six foot and her build was athletic – strong square shoulders like a tennis player. It was not just her body. Lorraine knew that grief affected everyone differently, but she was relieved that Ella had come through that period of hurting herself, to become stronger.

'Where have you been? Has it been raining?' Ella asked.

'Oh, I … missed the bus. Just decided to walk. Only rained a bit.'

'I made some pasta. It's on the stove.' Ella turned back towards the television.

She often made dinner, had done since she was quite young. Lorraine felt guilty about that too, but also thought that it meant Ella was self-sufficient in ways some other young people weren't.

'I was going to have a bath.'

'I've eaten already anyway. I messaged you. You can have it when you come out.'

'Thanks, sweetheart.' Lorraine kissed her fingers and pressed them onto Ella's forehead, coaxing a smile from her.

'Are you alright?' Ella craned her neck to look up at her mother. 'You look … pale.'

'I just got cold and wet. I'll be fine after the bath.' Lorraine turned quickly from her daughter. They were close and she didn't want her to see the hurt in her eyes.

She went into the bedroom and took off her clothes, then glanced at herself in the wardrobe mirror before she pulled on her bathrobe. Two children and more than fifty years old, but her body was still lithe and strong. The strong straight line of her clavicles, the muscle line running down the outside of her thighs, the ball of her calves.

The words she had said to Clare came back to her now – made her blink at their viciousness. Had she meant them? She was full of hurt, but had she meant to hurt Clare back so savagely?

Lorraine opened her underwear drawer. There, tucked underneath a pile of tights and socks, was Clare's letter, pushed roughly back inside its envelope. Lorraine put the letter in her dressing gown pocket. Even though she knew it would make her feel as if she was splitting open, Lorraine wanted to read it again now that she had seen Clare. Like a finger exploring a scar, she wanted to read it and decide what to do about it. She had an impulse to rip it up, burn it, but her gut told her it was evidence. If Detective Inspector Brookes was still there, she would go to her and ask for advice. As painful as it would be for Lorraine to confront the death of her little son once again, she was prepared to do it if it meant that she could finally get justice for Theo.

While the bath ran, Lorraine poured herself a large glass of red wine.

The water was hot and she had to ease herself into it, but then stretched out, shoulders underneath the surface, feeling the buoyancy of her hips. She blinked in the steamy, dimly lit room, tears flashing from her eyes and into the bathwater. *Now* she could cry. She had shed a lot of tears in this bathroom, with its wallpaper peeling near the skirting and the tap dripping on the sink.

Her hands touched the skin of her belly, found the scar from her caesarean section and rested her palm over it. Theo had been breech and so she had been unable to go through with a normal birth. Ella had been different. Her first child but she had come out so quickly – it had felt as if she knew what to do – her body had known what to do.

Warmth pulsed throughout Lorraine's whole body. All her blood vessels felt close to the surface, her hands floated in the water beside her. She remembered giving birth to Ella – the muscular heat of bringing her into the world; the yawn of her pelvis and then the sheer, shocked, rapture as the new eyes opened to look into hers. Ella had had a head of black hair that was so thick it seemed like a wig. Theo had been bald with a face crumpled like a seed pod and long, long legs. The surgeon had passed him to her, blood smeared, legs sprawling.

Lorraine let one hand rest on her chest, remembering that first weight of the baby, placed right above her heart. She made good babies. Theo in particular had seemed *only hers*, perhaps because Brody had been so disinterested and left so early, so she felt as if she had raised him alone from the start.

She wiped her tears with a wet hand and sipped some wine, then reached for the letter. She read quickly, skimming over the parts that sickened her:

It was like being hit by a wave and taken under. I didn't process what had really happened until after the trial. Theo died and then Sam moved out, and we were interviewed by the police over and over. And I just couldn't remember. I think my mind just blacked it out. It was too terrible to think about. You needed details, but I didn't have them then.

Lorraine narrowed her eyes, taking another sip of wine. *Then.* Now she has the details? *Now* she remembers what she did?

Lorraine hated the passive way that Clare wrote *Theo died*, as if he were an old man who expired in his sleep, not a baby whose life was taken from him before it had had a chance to begin. The arrogance of her – pretending it was just an accident until she was proved wrong.

She took another sip of wine. Clare had been *drunk* the night her baby had died and Clare had never been able to handle her drink.

As Lorraine's wrinkled fingertips dried, and the spots of water on the thick paper evaporated, she remembered those university days when life had seemed like an endless ribbon unfurling before them that they could twist and turn whichever way they chose.

They were nineteen and walking hand in hand along Potterrow. Nearly out of breath, they ran and skipped and sang. The night and the evening before them were cold hands on their faces.

In Clare's room, at their halls of residence, they had drunk vodka with Diet Coke before they headed out for the night and now they were on their way to the student union to see a band. Clare fancied the drummer and Lorraine liked the lead singer. Clare wore leggings with a tartan shirt buttoned on top, and Lorraine wore a loose sweatshirt over a black mini-skirt. Even though it seemed as if the only onlookers were the stars, they were both full of swagger.

The night was clear and there were no clouds and so the

cold wrapped around them. Lorraine's mind was full of electric brightness. She didn't know the time, or feel the sharp winter air even though she had come out without a jacket. Clare linked arms with her as they slowed to a walk, breathing hard after running and singing at the top of their voices. Their breaths clouded before them and they felt suspended in the moment, young and drunk and full of laughter and hiccups. The moment spread out before them, infinite, bright and startling, like the moonlight spilling onto the dark, wet pavements.

As they rounded the corner towards Bristo Square, cars passed, and suddenly a group of lads – ten or twelve of them – spilled out of a pub towards Lorraine and Clare. The boys were singing too: low-toned chants of a rugby song or a drinking song. As they drew parallel, the boys fell silent.

Lorraine hugged Clare into her slightly, as one of the boys whistled across the road at them. She smiled at Clare, snorting a little with laughter. The whistler was unidentifiable but they were undoubtedly the object. The boys were still walking but looking across the road at them.

Just then, Lorraine felt Clare's arm slip from hers. The brief loss of her friend's arm caused Lorraine to lose her balance, but she regained it quickly, pivoting on the pavement to look for her. Clare was clambering onto the bonnet of a car.

'What the hell are you doing?'

Clare's baseball boot caught the wing mirror and the car alarm began to screech and pulse, causing the group of boys to stop and cheer.

'Clare!' Lorraine tried again.

As if she was completely unaware of Lorraine and her pleas to *come down now,* Clare climbed onto the roof of the car and – legs spread wide like a surfer – shakily began to stand.

Lorraine folded her arms, shivering now, looking over her shoulder in case the police or the owner of the car were coming. The flashing hazard lights illuminated the dark, icy puddles on the ground turning them red and orange.

Her mouth open and her eyes shut, Clare grabbed her open collar with two hands and burst her shirt open. Even above the throbbing, wailing noise of the car alarm, Lorraine was aware of Clare's black shirt buttons pinging off the car bonnet and onto the road.

The boys began to chant again, but this time directed at Clare. The group of them ruptured and two or three began to edge out into the road, narrowly missing a passing car.

Under her shirt, Clare wore a black tank top. Laughing now, letting out a whoop, she lifted up her top.

For a second, Lorraine stood open-mouthed as she saw Clare's small white breasts, then went to the side of the car and grabbed her friend's calf, causing Clare to wobble and slide down. Clare fell into Lorraine's arms, light as a child.

'What's the matter with you?'

'Don't be boring.'

The boys across the road were cheering and whistling. Lorraine did her best to fix Clare's clothes, although she kept flopping onto the bonnet. Her own high had evaporated and she felt suddenly, brutally sober and responsible.

Smiling so hard that her eyes were almost closed, Clare

turned again in the direction of the group of boys. Lorraine put an arm around her and turned her around.

'Where are we going? You're making me dizzy.'

'I'm looking after you, because you obviously can't look after yourself.'

Lorraine shifted in the bathwater. She used her toe to nudge the hot tap on and then off when the warmth of the hot water reached her back. Clare had never been able to handle her drink. She became unrecognisable.

Lorraine remembered that the next morning Clare had not remembered a thing about that night – not the student union and throwing up in the graffitied toilets, Lorraine holding her hair; not the band – Clare had been too far back to see and had stood on a table dancing; nor crawling on top of the car and taking her top off before running away across Bristo Square.

'Don't be ridiculous. I'd never do that.' Clare had been appalled, almost angry at Lorraine for suggesting it – indignant even when Lorraine showed her the popped and missing buttons on her tartan shirt that had come undone when she'd torn it open.

'But *you did*, don't you remember?'

Lorraine brought her glass to her lips.

Blackout.

In their first and second years, before Lorraine had her year abroad in Portugal, they'd learned that Clare reacted differently to alcohol. They had both drunk too much, but even after a small amount – two glasses of wine – it was as if a switch had been flicked: Clare would change, and the next day she just wouldn't remember.

Mortified every time Lorraine reminded her of it, Clare had learned to be careful and drank much less, even while she was still a student, fearful of waking up and finding pieces of her life missing.

'I hate it,' she'd told Lorraine. 'I wouldn't mind so much being embarrassed – but I don't like *not knowing*. Thank god I have you to look out for me!'

Lorraine set her glass on the bathroom floor and returned again to the letter.

In the years since Theo died, and in the last couple of years in particular, things have come back to me that I think I tried very hard to forget.

Lorraine let the letter fall to the bathroom floor. She splashed water on her face and wiped her eyes again and again, bathwater and tears all mixed together. She sat up, a hand cupped over her mouth.

Years later, Clare could not remember climbing onto a car and flashing a group of students – complete memory loss. But somehow what had happened to Theo was now retrievable? It made no sense.

The cancer has shocked me, but it has forced me to address things that had been hard for me to face before now. I think it will help me to fight this – to get well – if I know that

I have your blessing and that you forgive me. I still can't remember everything, but I remember enough to know that I must have caused Theo's death.

Lorraine pressed the back of her hand against her teeth. Thinking about all of this again brought a sharp pain underneath her diaphragm.

For Ella, Lorraine had tried so hard to move on, to be strong, to face each new day afresh, even though for such a long time she had only been acting. She had watched people laughing, in bars, at work, on the street – all those small interactions, the crinkling of eyes, the teeth flashing and the mouths opening in laughter. For so long it had been hard for her to understand that simple human gesture – to smile, to laugh. It seemed impossible for so long, out of reach. She felt such devastation inside she had thought she would never manage such a simple thing again. And yet she *had done*, for Ella. She had lost a child, but she still had a child – a beautiful, wonderful daughter – and so life had to go on.

Lorraine made a little sound, indulgent as the tears came. She bit into the skin on the back of her hand.

The steam from the bath hung in the air, water droplets swirling like a cloud of small flies. Lorraine ran her fingers through her wet hair trying to calm herself down. For years she had tried so hard to move past the pain of losing Theo and now here she was again, deep, drowning in it. She nudged her wrist against her nose, trying not to cry again; not wanting to make a sound in case Ella heard her.

Lorraine had known that Clare had been fragile when she'd asked her to take Theo and Ella for the sleepover weekend – she had just had a late-term miscarriage, her worst. At the time, Lorraine had been grateful, knowing that she, too, needed a break. Since that weekend she had wondered if Clare's state of mind, fresh from trauma, had put her children in danger.

Two words that Clare said outside the gallery resounded again and again in Lorraine's mind.

'I lied.'

Lorraine sat up and splashed water over her face. She was going to lose her mind if she didn't do something about this – speak to someone.

There was a brisk knock on the bathroom door.

Lorraine turned, startled.

'Mum, are you okay?'

'What?' Lorraine wiped her face with a wet hand. 'Yes, yes ...?'

The door opened a little and Ella's face appeared. 'You were making noises. I didn't know if you were crying or coughing or ...'

'I'm fine, I'm just getting out.' Lorraine flashed a smile. 'I was just choking a little bit. My wine went down the wrong way.'

The door closed.

Lorraine watched the clouds of steam swirling heavy above her and then stood up. She towelled herself roughly and put on her dressing gown. When she picked up the letter to return it to her pocket, she saw that it was damp – she must have splashed water onto it – and that the ink had run.

4

DETECTIVE INSPECTOR PAMELA BROOKES

August 2019

Pamela Brookes pulled into her driveway, turned off the engine, and rested her head on the steering wheel. It had been a long day, but she was finally home. She felt so tired that she could have stayed where she was, in the driver's seat, and fallen asleep.

Brookes climbed out of the car, sighing as she rose to standing. Her work bag felt heavy. As she approached her front door, she noticed again that one of the outdoor lights was broken. There was a long list of household maintenance chores that Brookes was unable to find time to address. The windows needed replacing and there was a slate missing on the roof from a storm last year, or the year before. She had had the garden replaced with gravel but, even so, pernicious dandelions pushed their way through, as if to reproach her.

Her satchel was crammed and heavy with a tablet, files,

transcripts, and she nudged it out of the way as she slid her key into the lock. The terse, gravelly bark of their Jack Russell sounded her arrival on the other side of the door.

'Dermot, let me get in, will you?' The dog sniffed her toes when she took off her shoes. The little dog's tail wagged so frantically it shook his whole body. Brookes leaned down to stroke his bristly fur. Around his muzzle, the brown fur was turning grey. Despite being thirteen years old, his energy was undimmed.

'Hello,' Mike called from the living room.

Brookes shook her ponytail loose as she entered. Her husband was watching the news. She went over to him and leaned on the arms of his wheelchair as she bent to kiss him.

'How are you? What sort of day did you have?'

'Alright. Legs a bit sore today.'

Brookes ran her fingers through his hair. Like Dermot, Mike's hair was greying at the temples. He had been diagnosed with multiple sclerosis three years after they were married, not long after she found out she was pregnant with Jack. The disease had progressed slowly but after Mike's last relapse the wheelchair had become a constant feature of their lives.

'I asked Jack to take Dermot out but he's not done it yet.'

'I'll do it.'

In the kitchen, Brookes shook some dry food into Dermot's bowl. He crunched, watching her move around the kitchen.

She climbed the stairs, not noticing the dog hairs stranded near the skirting, or the threadbare carpet on the top step. The inside of the house needed as much work as the outside, but long ago Brookes had had to learn to prioritise. As she climbed, the sounds of Jack's computer game grew louder – the bouncing synthesiser and helium voices of Super Mario.

Jack's door was ajar; he was hunched at his desk, the glow from his computer making his young skin seem blue-ish.

'You're home,' he said, smiling, rubbing his eyes with the heel of his hand.

'How long you been on there? Time to take a break?'

'Yeah,' he said, submitting as she tousled his hair and kissed his forehead.

He had turned eleven six months ago. Brookes knew it was coming – the laconic teenager that would withdraw from her touch, but Jack was still a little boy at times, at least when his friends weren't around. She relished every moment of it, knowing it wouldn't last.

'Why don't you go have a shower and I'll make us some supper after I've taken Dermot out.'

'Dad asked me to take him out and I forgot,' Jack gasped, jumping to his feet.

'It's alright. You get washed.' She ran her fingers through his hair again. 'You been playing football today? Your hair's all greasy.'

'I played in the morning.'

'Well, you smell, so hurry up.'

'*You* smell.'

Brookes chuckled at him as she went into their bedroom. She moved one of Mike's walking frames out of the way so that she could open her wardrobe, then changed into tracksuit bottoms and an old grey sweatshirt.

'Come on, Dermot,' she called from the hall. The dog stretched dramatically, front paws out before him and rear in the air before he went to the door, standing obediently while she attached the lead.

Her dog-walking jacket was a big waterproof parka and into this she transferred her house keys and work phone from the tailored jacket she had worn to work. There was no need to take the work phone on the dog walk, but Brookes wondered if her colleague, Sergeant Rory Hendry, would text. There were a number of ongoing cases and Brookes found it hard to switch off her work brain.

She and Hendry had just finished compiling and submitting exhibit evidence on a murdered woman from Barnton. Brookes had been the first detective on the scene when the body was found. Forty-five stab wounds. The blood had covered most of the kitchen floor. Brookes had known right away that the murderer had been someone the woman knew well. When women or children were murdered it was often at the hands of someone close – usually a man. The crime scene manager had recommended a chemist to work up the slight footwear impression in the driveway and the case had now been handed over to the procurator fiscal who had issued a citation for the woman's estranged husband.

On the doorstep, Dermot paused and sniffed the air, as if assessing the evening. A fine mist of rain had begun and it wet Brookes' hair before they reached St Margaret's Park where she let the dog off the lead. Summer, but it felt like an April shower. Brookes pulled up her hood and put her hands deep in her pockets. The tiredness was still with her, but now she felt shivery, wired, an aftershock of leaving work.

Inside her pocket, the phone vibrated. She didn't look at it straight away. If it was Hendry, she would speak to him, but it was just as likely to be another colleague.

Dermot was sniffing at a discarded glove and she whistled to him. She glanced at the phone but because of the rain had difficulty reading the display.

The display read: 'Missed call, Lorraine Collins.'

'Dermot,' Brookes called sharply.

The little dog returned to her side and bowed his head as she leaned down to put him on the lead again. Normally she gave him free rein in the park, but if she was talking on the phone she might lose him.

Lorraine Collins.

Only the other day Brookes had wondered about her – how she and Ella were now. In truth she thought of them often. The Collins case was always fresh in her mind. It was over a decade ago, but she remembered absurd details about it – like the little panda sleepsuit Theo had been wearing when he died. Just thinking about it still brought a tightness to her throat.

Theo Collins had been Brookes' first murder case after maternity leave. She had interviewed Sam and Clare near midnight after Theo was found, her breasts still leaking milk underneath her blouse as she took their statements.

Brookes considered only a moment, and then called Lorraine back.

'Lorraine?'

'Oh, Detective Inspector Brookes, I was just after leaving you a message. I'm sorry for calling this late. It's Lorraine Collins, you were in charge of . . .'

'It's good to hear from you. I think of you often. How are you? How's Ella?' Dermot tugged forward, a scent or a vole driving him. Brookes felt the jar in her shoulder as she remembered Ella, the precocious little eight-year-old with the short dark curls and huge brown eyes.

'We're fine, we're fine. I wasn't sure you'd remember me. It's been such a long time, it's just . . .'

'Of course I remember you.'

Brookes waited, listening to the sound of her boots against the grass. The rain had stopped now. In the approaching darkness, she could smell the wet soil.

'Something's happened. I didn't know whether to call or email and then I thought to call because . . .'

'You know you can call me any time. What happened?'

'Well, I'm calling for advice, I suppose. Clare wrote me a letter – Clare Armstrong – which was—' Brookes heard Lorraine inhale sharply '—well, it was a big shock as you can imagine. The letter is very long, but she asks my forgiveness. She said she can now remember some things that she didn't . . . back then . . .'

'A confession?'

'I wondered what you'd think. It is a confession of sorts. I went to see her and we spoke briefly. When I met her, she told me that she had lied . . . *lied to you*. And the letter, asking my forgiveness . . . it's written very carefully, but in it she takes responsibility.'

'Responsibility?'

'She has cancer. She thinks she's going to die. She might be dying for all I know, but whatever the reason, I think she's finally ready to admit that she killed my son.'

Brookes stopped suddenly and Dermot turned to look at her.

Pamela Brookes closed her eyes and rubbed her eyeballs with finger and thumb. She was glad that she was out on a dog walk taking this call. 'I'd like to see the letter. Perhaps you could hand it in to my office or send me a scan?'

'I'll do that. Will you speak to her?'

'After I've seen the letter, I can let you know what I think.'

'I just thought ... does it matter, if she confesses? We can't take her to court for the same crime, is that right?'

'Well, no; in fact, there's been a change there since Clare was tried.' Dermot stood sniffing the air, his black nose twitching. Brookes' mind was crackling again, back in work mode. 'Previously in Scots law, once you had been tried for a crime, you couldn't be retried for the same one again, even if new evidence came to light implicating you. In 2011, you might have seen it on the news, the Double Jeopardy Scotland Act was passed ...'

'I didn't see it. So ... you're saying now she can be retried?'

'It's not that simple. With double jeopardy, usually we are talking about a new witness coming forward or new forensic evidence ... The Crown also have to petition the court to allow the new prosecution to take place.'

Lorraine sighed audibly on the line. 'Is Theo's case regarded as a cold case now? I was just thinking about how to get that new evidence?'

Brookes inhaled. The end of the day's light on the horizon

still glowed munificently. The sun had set now, but embers glimmered behind Corstorphine Hill and surged through the trees. 'We're trying to get away from the term "cold case" as it sounds like nothing's happening with an investigation. We're always hard at it, Lorraine.' There was a bench and she sank down onto it. Dermot considered the jump up to sit beside her, but then decided against it. 'We never give up on a homicide investigation. They *never* stagnate, and there's always a process of review. But I won't know if we're in that situation ... a review situation ... until I've read the letter.'

'Thank you, Detective Inspector Brookes. I've just been so obsessed since I got this letter. I didn't know what to do. And deep in my gut I've always known she was ... that it was her fault. You know that. She was my friend and I loved her, but I always knew ... I knew ... ' Lorraine's voice became high-pitched and then broke.

'It's alright.'

Brookes let her head fall back and watched the last rays of the sun catching the dark green leaves. She remembered the first time she met Lorraine, which had been not long after she had found out that her little boy was dead. She had liked her from the beginning. There was a messiness to Lorraine, but Brookes had always felt kindred with her as a single mother. Even though Mike was wonderfully emotionally supportive, his condition meant that Brookes often felt on her own.

Blinking at the darkness consuming the daylight, Brookes remembered little Ella with her crumpled, un-ironed school shirt and her mismatched socks – as if she had dressed herself.

By the time Brookes had hung up, Dermot was lying in the

grass by her feet. He had been just a puppy when she'd begun work on the Theo Collins case.

'Come on, Dermot; let's go home.'

The little dog began to trot ahead of her. Brookes wondered how many murder cases she had worked on since Dermot had been a puppy. *Twenty?* Perhaps three had been child homicides. Her colleague, Rory, had come into CID from child protection. But in all those murders Theo Collins had been the youngest, at just two years old.

Sometimes, when she went to sleep, Brookes could still see his chubby curled fingers. Curled as if he had been clutching at life when it was stolen from him. When a child is born, it is born in hope. A child is potential itself.

Back home, the warmth of the house comforted. She kicked off her boots in the hall, listening to Dermot eagerly lapping water in the kitchen. She hung up her coat.

Cases came and went and Brookes did her best to leave them at work and to move on when they were finished. However, something about Theo's case had always felt personal.

When she had returned from maternity leave, her detective superintendent had questioned whether she should lead on the Theo Collins case. Bill Joyce was a string bean of a man, with a grey moustache that yellowed at the tip. Every Christmas there was a charity request for him to shave it off, but he never did.

'A two-year-old?' Joyce had said, smoothing his prize moustache with the forefinger and thumb of his right hand. 'None of us can approach that objectively. I'm not singling you out.'

'I think you are.' Her breasts hard with milk inside her shirt, Brookes had felt as if she had to defend her role, make sure she wasn't side-lined when she had just returned to work.

'When the deceased are so young, it affects us all.'

'Boss, I'm committed. I can be objective . . .'

'I know you're objective: you're a detective inspector . . . but you're also a mother. A *new* mother. I have a responsibility not just to see this case through, but to make sure you're okay. I don't want you suffering psychological effects and stress . . .'

'I'm alright. I'm—'

Joyce had held up his palm, and Brookes had known to stay silent.

'Ultimately that's not for you to say. As a manager, I have to find the most appropriate staff for the case. What would you do in my position? If a member of staff's just had a baby, is it appropriate to deploy that person to a child death?'

Brookes had cleared her throat, tugged her shirt down. 'There's an argument that that detective – the one that's just had the baby – is *exactly* the right person to deploy to that enquiry; have you thought of that?'

Joyce had smiled.

Brookes had known she'd convinced him when she'd seen his hand on his moustache again, teasing a tiny hair towards his mouth.

Brookes took out the frying pan and cracked eggs into a bowl. She called on Jack that supper would be ready soon. Omelette sandwiches and a film; it made her feel warm inside.

She heard Jack's feet on the stairs. As she dragged the

edges of the frying egg to the centre of the pan, Brookes wondered what Clare had written to Lorraine and if it was enough to allow her to finish what she had started all those years ago.

5

CLARE

November 2008

Clare hung up the phone as she sat down on the bed. Elbows on her knees, she rested her head in her hands. The call had been from the consultant's secretary at the hospital, confirming that there was an appointment available at the clinic, this Friday, for Manual Vacuum Aspiration. Clare had accepted immediately. She just wanted it to be over.

As she lifted her head out of her hands, she noticed that the tall, thin mirror that was normally by the window had been moved, so that she could see her reflection. Her complexion was doughy pale, her lips almost the same colour as the skin of her face.

She stood up and lifted the mirror back to its usual position. Turning, she saw that the mirror had been hiding a massive dent in the plasterboard wall. She reached up and ran her hand over it, paint and plaster flaking onto the floor. It was about five feet off the ground, exactly where her face would be, if she were to put her nose against the wall. The dent was shaped like a fist. Sam had obviously tried to hide it.

She heard Sam in the bathroom and sighed. Lashing out – it was how he dealt with pain. He had never once directed this anger at her, but she knew it was how he processed it. When they had first got together, he had trusted her with the broken pieces of him. His father had been hard on him and it had driven him out, to the boxing gym, cycling, always a physical response. He was such an intelligent man, but he found it hard to articulate hurt.

And now this. Clare picked one or two pieces of plasterboard from the wall and a little shower of grey dust rained onto the floor. The whole wall would need re-plastering. Clare thought she could move one of her framed photographs and cover up the hole.

Hole in the wall.

Empty womb.

The pregnancy, the miscarriage – it happened inside Clare's body, not Sam's, and sometimes it felt as if it was only happening to her, but she knew that he felt each loss as keenly as she did. Considering the brutality of what they had been through, maybe punching a wall was as good a response as any.

Clare had heard it happen, she realised now. Last night, he had read her mind as he often was able to – tried to comfort her when she was turning it all over again in her mind.

Sam had tried to comfort her, and in doing so – she knew – comfort himself, but she hadn't wanted to be held. She had turned away from him gently, unable to stop the image of their tiny baby, heartbreakingly recognisable, disappearing. It was loss in its most physical sense, and it was her loss as well as *his* loss, but somehow they found it hard to share and communicate their grief. They had been together for so long, but somehow this failure – her failure – breached them.

And so when she was closing the shutters, she'd heard the clack of the wood against the window frames overlaid with a bang from upstairs. The bang had startled her and she had looked over her shoulder before locking the shutters into place.

He felt so sad, and so he had punched a hole in the wall.

'Who was that on the phone?' he said, coming into the bedroom, stepping into his jeans.

'It was the hospital. She said Friday.' She sat back down on the bed, admiring the ripple of his stomach muscles as he bent and straightened. 'Are you alright?'

'Sorry,' he said, seeing the hole exposed. 'I'll get it fixed.'

'I know it didn't just happen to me. It was your baby too.'

'Our baby.' He smiled, pulled on a T-shirt.

'I love you,' she said, needing reassurance as much as giving it.

'Love you,' he mouthed back, casual as a button loosening on its thread and falling to the floor.

Not for the first time, Clare felt the tenuousness of their decades-old love, as if, after everything, they could still come undone.

'Friday? Well, maybe you should say to Lorraine … cancel the kids?'

Since Lorraine's boyfriend, Brody, had left, Lorraine had

been struggling to manage the two children on her own. Brody had left about a year ago, walking out when Lorraine was still breastfeeding Theo, something Clare still found callous. Since he'd left, however, and now with Theo toddling, Lorraine always seemed harried, the children in mismatched clothes or dirty, as if they were taking care of themselves. Clare had said she and Sam would take Ella and Theo for a sleepover weekend, to let Lorraine get away with her mother.

But the offer had been made before the miscarriage, and now the procedure would be on Friday, just a day before the children arrived.

It wasn't the best time for them to have Ella and Theo to stay, but, despite the freshness of their grief, they wanted to help Lorraine.

Clare sighed. 'I don't know . . . I don't want to cancel. I think she's booked a hotel.'

'Clare, have you taken a look at yourself?'

'I'm fine.'

'You're not,' he said, quietly, rifling through his drawer for socks.

Clare looked up at the fist-shaped hole in their bedroom wall. 'Are *you* fine?'

'Sure.'

Clare had had so many miscarriages, but this one had made her wonder if she had the strength to try again. Just the thought fatigued her, yet at the same time she couldn't bear the thought of another birthday or Christmas or New Year to go by without *being pregnant*. She would have to wait until the bleeding stopped and then wait for her period to return before she could start testing for ovulation. Her whole life now was pregnancy tests, and ovulation tests and making sure that she was eating and drinking the right things to boost her fertility, over-analysing her physical symptoms throughout the month, in case she was pregnant.

It was exhausting.

Her first positive pregnancy test had come when Lorraine was just about to give birth to Ella. As soon as they found out the news, Clare had called Lorraine to tell her. '*This is so perfect that we'll be first mums together,*' her friend had said. Lorraine had been enormous then, Clare remembered – ankles swollen to twice their normal size.

And then, just after Ella was born, Clare miscarried for the first time, but she always remembered that first pregnancy: the feeling of knowing what it would be like to become a mum. It had been taken away and Clare was back in the waiting room, with the box of tissues, waiting on the midwife.

Each subsequent pregnancy hadn't felt like that – even this last one. But the sense of being in limbo, shut in a waiting room, remained. Somehow it felt as if her whole life was in that waiting room, paused, as she went over and over the stages: ovulation, conception, missed period, positive pregnancy test, physical symptoms of pregnancy and then loss. Like a game she would have to start all over again; *they* would have to start all over again.

Of course they had talked about adoption, but that was also a long painful process with little chance of getting a new-born;

and with each pregnancy their own baby felt within touching distance.

'Do you ever think . . .' Clare said, holding her breath a little, almost afraid to ask Sam the question '. . . that we should stop trying?' Their eyes met. Clare bit her lip as she felt her eyes sting. She didn't want tears to sway him.

He sat down on the bed beside her and she smelled the scent of his freshly washed body. He put an arm around her and pulled her gently into him. 'No. We'll do what we always do: we'll pick ourselves up and keep going.'

'But—' Clare looked up into his face '—it's so hard, on us both. I know how much you want it, and you'd be *such a good dad*. I know that . . .' She nudged a tear away and looked up at the hole in the wall. 'I just wish I was better.'

He drew her into him and she inhaled the warm wool of his sweater, the smell of him underneath it, nourishing. 'You can't be better. You're already the best.'

She sat up, wiped her face with her hands, laughing a little at the compliment.

'It'll happen for us,' he said, with such assurance she almost believed him. 'Next time.'

'That wall's ruined, y'know?'

'Nah, bit of Polyfilla . . .'

6

LORRAINE

November 2008

'Theo, *please*, will you get up off the ground?'

'No.' It was his best word, often his only word. He said it quietly, but with authority.

'He's getting dirty, Mummy.'

Lorraine took a deep breath in and out. They were trying to catch the bus to the museum to meet Sam and Clare and so far they had made it three feet from the bus stop, where Theo had thrown himself onto the pavement.

The museum had been Clare's idea – a chance for the kids to play unfettered despite the awful weather – giving the adults space to talk. Just three days ago, Clare had had a miscarriage that had taken them to A&E in the middle of the night. It had been second trimester, her worst so far. Clare had called the morning after and Lorraine had heard the loss right away in the tremble of her voice.

Now, she just wanted to hug her friend and listen to her story, but she hadn't expected to be so tired today, so fraught. She had been up four times last night with Theo and then, just as she'd drifted off to sleep, Ella had wet the bed. Brody had left months ago and now Lorraine felt determinedly alone. A single parent. Again.

This weekend, Lorraine was due to go on a spa break with her mother. Clare and Sam were going to look after the children. For weeks Lorraine had been dreaming of it – not the spa or even dinner with her mother, but just the chance to sleep in a bed uninterrupted. It had not been mentioned, but Lorraine was no longer sure that Clare and Sam would be fit for babysitting after all they had been through. She would talk to them about it today.

'We're going on the bus, Theo,' Ella tried to reason with her brother, squatting down and turning her head to try and look him in the eye, but he had his face planted square on the pavement. 'Bus ... don't you want to go on the bus?'

Theo liked buses, and things with wheels in general, but today he didn't seem interested.

'Get up, now, Theo,' Lorraine tried again.

'No, no, no.'

He had so few words, but that one was perfect. Now that he had mastered it, he didn't feel the need to learn any others.

Frustrated, Lorraine grabbed Theo and roughly set him on his feet. He immediately buckled at the knee, ready to fall face down on the pavement again, next to the cigarette butts, chewing gum and dog urine.

'For God's sake.' Lorraine lifted him and carried him,

screaming and kicking, to the bus stop. She had deliberately decided against the pram. Theo didn't like being secured in it, so either screamed constantly in protest as if he was being kidnapped, or else he would stand up on it, or slide out of the straps. Lorraine often ended up carrying both the pram and him.

There was a queue of people at the bus stop: two young people, both wearing headphones, and an older woman with a polka dot shopping trolley. After jostling Theo for a few moments, Lorraine set him down so she could count out coins for the bus fare.

'What's the matter with you, wee one?' the older woman said, bending down towards Theo. 'You're not very happy today, are you?'

His face reddening, Theo screamed louder. He kicked the plastic glass of the bus shelter so that it shuddered.

The woman raised her eyebrows at Lorraine. 'That's just temper, you know. Not a tear in his eye, do you see that?'

'Thanks … sorry,' Lorraine said, trying not to hear the implied criticism, straining to see the bus in the distance.

'You need to show him who's boss.'

Lorraine stared blankly at the woman, the sound of Theo's cries making her temples throb. Tears stung her nose and, for one terrible moment, Lorraine wondered if she was going to cry. Certainly, she felt like throwing herself onto the pavement with her toddler.

Suddenly, Theo's cries stopped, muffled, and then began anew, angry, louder. As the bus pulled up, Lorraine saw that Ella was pressing her hand over Theo's mouth, literally stifling his screams.

'*Don't do that*,' Lorraine said, poking her toward the bus, scooping the screaming Theo up and holding him under one arm. 'You could hurt him.'

The bus smelled of wet bodies. Hanging onto Ella's wrist, Lorraine forced her way up the aisle to a seat. She slipped in first and let Theo kneel on her thighs so he could look out of the window. The new environment and the dirty window cheered Theo immediately. Gurgling with a mixture of tears and laughter, he slapped his palms against the glass.

'Bus, bus.'

Relieved, Lorraine turned to Ella, who was now sulking, her thin shoulders curved over. She was wearing flowery leggings and Lorraine rubbed a hand along them. 'Come on, you're alright.'

Ella looked up into her face, real tears glassing her eyes. She seemed so *wronged*. 'I was only trying to help you.'

Still holding onto Theo, Lorraine bent right down, so close to her daughter that they were almost cheek to cheek. 'Darling, thank you, but you could have hurt your baby brother.'

'I didn't; I just wanted him to be quiet. It was making you upset.'

'Listen to me. You've not to do that again, and *I know* you were trying to help, but I can manage him myself, alright?'

Ella was still sullen although Lorraine could see her coming around.

'Alright?'

She nodded.

*

70

The bright, cavernous space of the museum opened up before them and Ella and Theo ran towards the children's hands-on exhibits. Rain rattled on the high roof.

Lorraine saw Sam and Clare and waved. It was a good place to meet – they could talk without distraction, and then eat when the children were worn out playing.

Clare was incredibly pale and even thinner than usual, her cheeks grey and hollowed. They had talked on the phone, and so Lorraine knew that she'd lost a lot of blood. Sam was all smiles but his face also seemed drawn.

Lorraine felt Clare's shoulder blades through her shirt as she hugged her. On the phone, Clare had said that her ordeal wasn't quite over. The scan had showed she still had some tissue inside her that would need to be removed. She wasn't sure if they would be able to speak about all of this today, with Sam there, with the children, but the sight of her pale, weakened friend cleaved Lorraine despite the fact that they had bickered over the last few months. Before her miscarriage, Clare had been dropping in unannounced and trying to take over. Lorraine had wondered if it had been the pregnancy hormones. Nesting by proxy.

'This was a great idea,' Lorraine said, linking arms with Clare as they walked in the direction of the children. Inside, Lorraine still felt scorched by tiredness and the bright light and white space of the museum accentuated it. She felt on the edges of a migraine, off-kilter, nerves shrill.

'*Are you alright?*' she whispered to Clare, leaning into her, squeezing her small arm. 'It sounded horrific.'

'It was,' Clare said simply.

'And the fact that you still need to go back for more.'

Clare sighed. 'Well ... yeah, that's the worst of it. But the appointment's tomorrow, so I'll get it over quick.'

'Are you sure you're up to today?'

'Yeah, better to get out. Otherwise I'm just moping around. That's my tenth, you know? Miscarriage.'

Lorraine swallowed, knowing that she had to choose her words carefully. 'But this time you nearly did it. It'll happen, I know it will. Next time.'

Lorraine felt the almost imperceptible tugging of Clare's arm from hers.

It should have been a time when their long friendship came into its own, but somehow *this pain*, this specific *kind* of pain separated them. Because however much Lorraine tried or empathised or listened, she could never fully understand what it was like to lose a baby. Clare had never outright said this to Lorraine, yet it was always there, ever-present, full-throated in their friendship, like a peony in early summer, so heavy with blossom that its own head bends the stem. And so Lorraine felt that she too had to hang her head – not only because she had babies, but because she had babies easily.

'Well, let me know if I can do anything. Do you want me to come with you to the hospital tomorrow?'

Clare shrugged. 'Sam'll come. You've got enough on your plate.'

Up ahead Ella and Theo were screaming with laughter as bubbles exploded from a machine. They ran left and right and jumped to catch the oily spheres that rose out of reach.

'Well, I'd drop everything if you needed me, you know that.'

'I know, thanks.'

Lorraine heard the weariness in her friend's voice. She watched Sam up ahead, picking Ella up and turning her over his shoulders.

'A fireman's lift,' she heard Ella say.

'Is *Sam* alright?'

Clare sucked breath in, but Lorraine didn't hear its release. 'He's ... I dunno, it's hard. It's hard on us both. It kind of uses a lot of oxygen, y'know ... in your relationship, and then you feel like it's all about one thing and ...'

Clare trailed off.

'I know,' Lorraine said, wanting to sound supportive.

Clare didn't continue, as if Lorraine wouldn't understand. 'Relationships' was another thorn in their friendship. Clare was good at them, because of *Clare and Sam*; they had been together forever, since right after university – while Lorraine 'couldn't keep a man'. Most of the time, Lorraine didn't mind being cast as 'the fun one' who couldn't do long-term relationships, but right now she was still raw after Brody. When it had just been her and Ella, Lorraine had felt fine, but two kids on your own was hard for anyone.

Lorraine was never able to talk to Clare about how hard it was – because it would mean moaning about little children when Clare couldn't have any. She couldn't speak about the repetitive boredom, no sleep, no time to wash herself or even go out for the night. There was no way Lorraine could complain about any of that to Clare.

73

If Clare opened up, Lorraine was ready to listen about the miscarriage, but she absolutely could not say what was on her mind. She wouldn't dare say how sick to the back teeth she was of feeling how she felt *right now*, which was so tired she could lie down anywhere, in the stark bright sunshine, on the marble floors and fall sound asleep. She loved her children – of course she did – but often she remembered the time before they came along with great fondness.

Sam set Ella down and turned to face them. He and Ella were hand in hand and Lorraine thought they looked so good together – both skinny and dark and relaxed. Lorraine knew Sam would be a great dad. Even though he didn't show it, she knew the miscarriage had hurt him, this last one in particular. She could see it in his face. 'Let's get something to eat, eh? I'm starved.'

As they walked towards the restaurant, Lorraine said: 'Considering the week you've had, maybe the sleepover's not such a great idea.'

'Sleepover, yay ... this weekend. In my special bed,' Ella chimed, jumping up and down, still holding Sam's hand. She had her own bed in Sam and Clare's spare room.

Lorraine rested a hand on her daughter's head as she looked seriously at Sam and Clare in turn. 'I mean it. I can cancel the thing ...'

'It's fine,' said Clare. 'We've been looking forward to spending time with them.'

Lorraine was about to say that they both looked so weary – but kept quiet for now.

Theo was stamping along by Lorraine's side, but suddenly froze. Lorraine felt his sticky little hand slip from hers. His face began to redden as it assumed a look of great concentration.

'Uh oh, you guys go on ahead, will you? I'll need to change Theo.' Lorraine picked him up and turned, scanning for the nearest toilet.

Ella had found a leaflet about dinosaurs and began to tug on Lorraine's skirt. 'Mum, Mum, Mum—'

'Hang on, love.'

'But look . . .'

Clare gently took Theo from Lorraine's arms. 'The toilet's just over there. I'll change him. Have you got the bag?'

'Oh, thanks, you're great,' Lorraine said, passing over her backpack that was filled with nappies, snacks and juice.

As Clare walked off with Theo in her arms, Lorraine was struck by how suddenly energised and purposeful she seemed.

The restaurant was busy, but they found a table and a high chair. By the time Clare came back with Theo, lunch had been ordered.

Clare passed Theo to Sam and then bent at Lorraine's side, catching her elbow. 'I couldn't find any cream in the bag. He's got *really bad* nappy rash.'

'He's a bit red, that's all,' Lorraine said, waving at a waiter who seemed to have their food.

'He's *raw*, Lorraine. Have you seen it?'

'Of course.' Lorraine knew that Theo was a bit red, but she hadn't thought it was serious. The rash came and went.

'I think we should get some cream for him . . .'

'I'll have some at home; calm down.' Lorraine almost smiled. Clare's face was intensely serious.

'I think he might need the doctor.'

The judgement on Clare's face was stark and Lorraine felt affronted, as if she was being accused of neglect.

'I'll change him again when we get home. I've got the stuff there.'

'But—'

'Come on, sit down. We ordered for you.'

Clare took off her jacket and sat down.

Lorraine felt half-starved, but pushed her panini back and forth on her plate as she watched Sam struggle to put rigid-legged Theo into a high chair.

'Just give him here,' Lorraine said. 'He's stubborn. He'll sit on my lap.'

'Then you can't eat your lunch.'

'What's new? It's fine.' Lorraine held out her hands.

Now Clare leapt to her feet again and tried to put Theo into the high chair. It was painful to watch. He was heavy for a just-two-year-old and Clare really looked as if she had lost three pints of blood. Her skin was pale as marble and Lorraine worried that she might faint.

'No, no, no,' Theo began again.

'He's probably uncomfortable,' Clare offered. 'He must be so sore.'

'Enough. Give him to me.' Lorraine held out her arms.

Lorraine jostled Theo on her lap and fed him chips, letting her own sandwich cool, the cheese turning to plastic.

'Hey, you want to try some cucumber?' Clare said cheerily, holding up a pale-green disc.

Theo didn't react, too absorbed by the fat chip he was sucking.

The weight of her son in her lap made Lorraine shift in her seat.

'What about a piece of chicken? Would you like some chicken, Theo?'

The way Clare spoke to her son irritated Lorraine. She took a bite of her cold panini, knowing that she was irritable because she was tired.

'He's alright,' Lorraine said to Clare, her mouth full. 'Leave him.'

'But he's only having chips. He should—'

'Look—' Lorraine shifted Theo on her thighs '—it's not like he eats chips all the time. We're out for lunch. If he wants chips that's fine. He's quiet. Are we not here to spend some time together . . . ?'

Clare's small thin fingers thrust a little plate of coloured vegetables forward and Lorraine despaired.

'I know, it's just good to give him a choice, that's all. I bet if he sees all the colours, he'll eat what's good for him,' Clare said.

Through the blur of her weariness, Lorraine was aware of Sam putting a hand on Clare's thigh, rubbing, pacifying, asking her to leave it. Particularly since Theo was born and since Brody left, Clare had seemed almost rabid with concern for the children's welfare. The irony of it was not lost on Lorraine. If Clare could only have one of her own, she would understand the way things were.

Just then, Theo tired with the whole idea of lunch and Lorraine had to release him onto the floor. She finished her sandwich hungrily, in a few bites, as he tore between the tables. Clare kept getting up out of her seat and sitting back down again, trying to catch Theo's hand.

'Just sit down. He's not doing any harm. They're used to kids in here,' Lorraine said, her mouth full.

'Sorry about this,' Clare said to diners nearby, more than once. 'Please excuse us.'

Just then, Theo bumped into one of the tables, and caused a drink to spill.

Before Lorraine could do anything, Clare was on her feet, scooping Theo up. 'I'm so sorry. I should have him in the high chair. I'm sorry he spilled your drink. Can I get you another one?'

The table was several feet away, but Lorraine saw the woman smile and shake her head, saying it was only water. Even though she felt it was petty, irritation flared in Lorraine's stomach; Clare was acting as if *she* was Theo's mother.

'Give him here,' Lorraine said, choking on her last mouthful of food. She snatched Theo from Clare and he began to cry again, his activity curtailed. 'Will you just relax?' Lorraine coughed, feeling her face redden. 'I asked you just to leave it.'

'I was just . . .'

Lorraine didn't want to hear any further justification. For months now every time Clare had turned up at the house she had seemed to suggest that Lorraine was lacking as a mother. Only a few weeks before, Clare had turned up with photos of the children and ended up trying to bath Ella, claiming that her hair was dirty. 'Look, just don't apologise for my kids. Alright?'

Clare sat back in her chair, her face hardening.

'Hey,' Sam said, suddenly, reaching out across the table with his long arms so that he held both Clare and Lorraine's arm. 'Hey, it's not a big deal, is it? He's just a little kid; that's what kids do and no damage was done.'

'Exactly,' Lorraine said, waving a cold chip before Theo, which he took, tears frozen on his face as he thrust it into his mouth.

'I think we've all had a hard week, eh? Let's just have a nice lunch.' Sam grinned. 'The five musketeers.' He seemed pleased with himself, as if he had just thought of it. 'All for one ...'

'You're right,' Clare said, shoulders sagging, lips colourless.

'I'm sorry,' Lorraine said. 'I've had about two hours' sleep. Didn't mean to go all psycho on you.' It was true; her temper was worn and she knew that Clare might feel similar. It was easy to take it out on those that were close.

Clare smiled thinly but Lorraine thought she saw something in her eye, as if she was keeping score. Suddenly, Clare's eyes started to brim with tears. She had never been a crier. All through their university years, Lorraine had seldom seen her cry.

'I'm sorry,' Clare said, nudging the tears that fell, and fighting the gulps of breath. 'I just want you to look after them properly. They're so small and ...'

Lorraine smiled, sighing, trying to understand. She thought that Clare was probably physically and emotionally traumatised by what she had been through, and so over-reacting. 'I think he'll survive having a chip or two,' Lorraine said, attempting a joke. 'It's not like I'm feeding him smack for breakfast.'

'Smack . . . ' Ella sat up in her chair.

'It's not just that, you know it isn't. You need to—'

'Look, I know you've been through a lot recently and I know you've probably got all the hormones still going on, but just stand down, alright?'

Knowing something was wrong, Theo put two hands on Lorraine's face. She felt the cool, damp stickiness of them on her cheeks.

'Okay, okay.' Sam dragged a chair around so that he was sitting between her and Clare.

He put an arm around Clare and Lorraine felt the heaviness of his arm on her shoulders and then smelled the salty, olive cleanness of him.

'Let's not do this now, okay? We've got two little ones here. Isn't that right, Ella – you don't want any arguments, do you . . . ?'

Full of seriousness, Ella shook her head vigorously.

'That's right and it's also true that you've had no sleep, Lorraine, and . . . me and Clare have been to hell and back, so let's . . . I dunno . . . maybe let's just enjoy each other's company.'

Lorraine felt the squeeze of his hand on her shoulder. He leaned over and kissed Clare's temple.

'I'm sorry,' Clare said again, wiping her face with both hands. 'I don't feel very well.'

'It's alright,' Lorraine said, reaching out to touch Clare's wet cheek.

Clare's breath was ragged in her throat. 'I was looking forward to seeing the kids, but I'm worn out.'

'I don't think this weekend's a good idea,' Lorraine said. 'You need to get your strength back and two kids is full-on. Especially Theo.'

Hearing his name, Theo sat up in her lap and looked Lorraine in the face. She could smell his sweet breath: potato and fruit juice. Sam seemed to agree with Lorraine that it might be too much, but he looked to Clare to decide.

'Don't worry, I'm fine,' Clare said, clearing her throat. 'We'll have fun together.'

7

CLARE

August 2019

Clare sat in a hospital-issue backless robe, her short hair tucked inside a paper cap, as she waited to speak to the anaesthetist. She was wearing paper underpants and a pair of inelegant white compression stockings. Her belongings were all in a tagged plastic bag by her side. Despite everything she smiled to herself, imagining how she must look. Her face was clean of make-up. She had no phone and only a book to accompany her – an autobiography of Martin Parr – but Clare found that she couldn't concentrate on it and, instead, listened and daydreamed.

There were other patients near her, women like her. She could hear but not see them, as they were each curtained-off from the other. The surgeon was talking to one woman about how he would carry out a double mastectomy. The persistent sniffs that began as the surgeon described the operation and its accompanying risks suggested to Clare that the woman was crying.

Clare had never liked hospitals. The smell reminded her of miscarriages, A&E waiting rooms and lying on her back with her legs in stirrups, waiting for all manner of horrors to be visited on her womb.

All through those procedures, Sam had been with her, but today Clare had come to hospital alone. She had taken the bus, would stay overnight and when it was over, she would get the bus home again.

She clasped her hands on top of her book, feeling nervous about the anaesthetic. She didn't like the sudden blackness, the loss of control, but she knew it had to be done. The consultant had said a lumpectomy and then radiotherapy alone, if she was lucky.

It felt as if whatever luck she had had in life had rolled away from her, but she had sold two large prints since the 'Unearthed' exhibition launch. She might have looked a mess and had a screaming argument with an old friend in the car park, but she had sold two photographs. *Every cloud.*

The night of the exhibition came back to her and the fight with Lorraine in the car park. Lorraine had said she would go to the police and the thought of this now made Clare's chest constrict, as if there was a weight on it.

No, Clare told herself. Lorraine wouldn't want the whole matter dredged up again – that was why she had been so angry about the letter.

Within her curtained, antiseptic-smelling enclosure, Clare looked up at the too-bright hospital lights. Her fingers were trembling and she brought her hand up to her face to watch the tremor. Blinking, she remembered something she'd forgotten.

Lorraine's face was very close to Clare's as she leaned in to apply black liquid eyeliner. The smell of sweet cherry lip balm as Lorraine's thumb pressed into Clare's eyebrow, to hold her lid in position. Looking downwards, Clare could see Lorraine's knee poking through the rip in her jeans. They were going out later – the student union and then a club – and Lorraine always did Clare's eyeliner for her beforehand. She had a steady hand. 'Are you going to wear your red top?' Clare asked, being careful not to move her face as she spoke.

'Nah, I think it makes me look pregnant.'

'No, it doesn't; it looks great.'

'There you go.'

Lorraine passed Clare a mirror so she could examine the eyeliner on her upper lid.

'Amazing, thank you.'

Lorraine flicked through clothes on the rail in her bedroom – a makeshift wardrobe.

'Help me find a top that doesn't make me look like I'm about to have a baby.' She laughed, deliberating bloating her belly and rubbing it gently, as if she was 'with child'.

As she held up tops in front of herself before the long mirror, Lorraine said, 'Do you think you'll ever have kids?'

Clare was sitting on the bed and now fell back onto it, so that she was looking at the ceiling. 'Yeah, probably. I think maybe three . . .'

'You can't have three. One always gets left out. You should have two or four.'

'How many are you going to have?'

'Two probably. Boy and a girl.'

Clare smiled, watching dust motes swirl on the ceiling light.

The pressure stockings were digging into Clare's calves and she adjusted the elastic. She thought how naïve she had been, at eighteen or nineteen, imagining her future was there to be plucked at will, like ripe fruit on a tree. She had wanted three children back then, and as she grew older she would have been grateful for even one, but here she was now, in her fifties, with none. She accepted that now. She was content. But she remembered the feverish grief of each loss as keenly as if it was yesterday.

The curtained bay where she sat felt warm and the sweet antiseptic smell lulled her. She remembered visiting the hospital the day Theo was born. Lorraine had always said she wanted two children and she had done just that.

As she entered the ward, Clare heard the sound of a new baby crying. She swallowed hard and looked down at her red baseball boots as she walked along the corridor. On either side there were bays with new mothers, either breastfeeding or leaning over cribs. Visiting hour and there were children of all ages meeting new brothers and sisters. She and Sam were trying to conceive again, exhaustedly, with an almost Sisyphean resolve.

Around her neck was her camera. She also carried a gift bag with a present for Lorraine's new baby: a small, velvet-eared elephant.

Clare saw Lorraine up ahead – she stepped into the corridor and waved in her dressing gown and slippers. Theo was in her arms, dressed all in white, the size of a rugby ball.

'Oh my God, he's just perfect,' Clare whispered, touching the white crocheted cap on Theo's head before she looked up into Lorraine's face.

'Isn't he just.' Lorraine pulled Clare into her arms, squishing her up beside the baby. 'Great to see you. Thanks for coming.'

'God, he smells good,' Clare said, sniffing Theo and kissing his tiny hands, curled like fern fronds. He smelled of nutmeg and milk. 'You look fantastic.'

It was true. Lorraine was wearing no make-up and her hair was unwashed but she glowed with energy, her skin luminous.

Clare had imagined this experience in advance – rehearsed it. She had visualised entering the maternity ward and passing all the babies in cots, seeing Lorraine and her new baby boy and telling her that he was perfect. The real thing felt less painful than she had imagined, but she felt somehow out-of-body, looking down on herself.

'This is just a wee thing from me and Sam,' Clare said, as she handed over the present.

Lorraine immediately took the elephant out of the bag and scrunched up her nose. 'Oh, he's cute. Thank you. Nelly the elephant.'

'I checked. It's got the label on – safe from birth upwards.'

'Och, don't worry; it'll be fine. It's great. Here—' Lorraine thrust Theo into Clare's arms '—I know you want a cuddle.'

Clare put her camera down and folded the baby into her. His left lid opened for a second, then both, a blue-eyed frenzy to focus on her. His right fist began to unfurl as she stroked it with her finger, skin so thin she could see the tiny blue veins beneath. 'Hello, Theo.'

Her own pain at being unable to carry a baby to term wasn't there at that moment. The warm weight of the little body against her chest, the mesmerising smallness of his fingers and nails, the pinkish skin of his scalp, the softness of him.

Clare was always so busy, so frenetic, but just now, she felt stopped, halted, by this baby in her arms.

Lorraine's mother Rita came in then, hand in hand with Ella who'd turned six only a few weeks before. She hid behind her grandmother's hip as she was led into the room.

'Hey, sweetheart.' Lorraine held out her arms to her daughter.

Slowly, Ella went to her mother, watching her brother in Clare's arms.

'Is this the first time you've seen your baby brother?' Clare asked.

'No, I saw him before,' Ella replied, using the bars of the hospital bed as steps so that she could climb up. She sat on the bed with her hands clasped.

'And what do you think?' Clare cupped Theo's head with her hand.

'He's cool.'

Clare raised Theo up, resting his head against her shoulder.

The movement caused Theo's face to twist and redden. His small tongue appeared.

'I was just about to feed him.' Lorraine took the baby from Clare.

He was so small in her large hands and yet she handled him with such confidence, turning his body this way and that. They were all silent for a moment while Lorraine arranged herself in the chair and began to feed Theo.

'Nice to see you again, Rita,' said Clare, getting up to give Lorraine's mother her seat. The baby had felt so warm and snug against Clare's chest, and now her arms were suddenly empty. She picked up her camera.

'You too, my love.' Rita looked tired, the skin under her eyes blueish-brown.

Clare took some snaps of Ella and Lorraine's face pressed in towards the baby, then sat beside Ella on the bed.

'How are you managing, Rita? Are looking after Ella just now? Me and Sam can take her – you know that Lorraine, any time.' Clare stroked Ella's hair as she spoke, as if to acknowledge that she was being spoken about.

Rita's face creased into smile. She had warm eyes. She was smaller and gentler than Lorraine. 'The wee one's no bother, are you, pet?'

Ella shrugged exaggeratedly. She began to swing her legs back and forth, so that they intermittently clanged against the metal sides of the bed.

Lorraine said nothing, two fingers guiding her nipple between Theo's lips.

'It's just … I know Brody works nights. Sam and I are here if you need us.'

Brody. The name hung suspended in the astringent hospital air.

Clare had been wary of asking about Brody, Lorraine's boyfriend and Theo's father. She was both surprised and *not* surprised that Brody was absent from the hospital. Lorraine had been terse on the subject of Brody since halfway through her pregnancy. The baby had come as a surprise to him. Lorraine had even let slip that she had been on birth control when she got pregnant. Clare tried not to think about it, but the irony of it was intense: that Lorraine could conceive even on the pill, and hapless, unsuspecting Brody could be a father when Sam was denied the chance.

'Thanks, Clare,' said Lorraine. 'I'm supposed to get out tomorrow, but if it's longer, I'll take you up on it. It's the back and forth to school that's hard for you, Mum.'

'No, it's not hard; it's only down the road. I enjoy the walk.'

Lorraine's mother had bad arthritis and Clare knew that she was being polite.

'Well, the offer's there, even if you do get out. You'll probably have your hands full with Theo.'

The whole time she had been speaking, Clare had her hand rested on Ella's warm back, wanting to include her in a small way, even though the talk was of adult organisation.

Suddenly, Lorraine lurched forward. 'Ella, stop banging the bed with your legs like that. People are trying to rest.' Theo was still attached to her as she reached forward, finger pointed at Ella.

Clare had been only vaguely aware of the clatter and squeezed Ella's shoulder in comfort. Her face dark and brooding, Ella curled into Clare.

'Hello, Clare, my name's Dr Opong; I'll be your anaesthetist today.'

Clare gave Dr Opong one of her best smiles. He was good-looking and she wondered what he thought of her in her surgical cap and support stockings.

'I've read your file. Is there anything you want me to know about?'

'I don't like going under. Maybe I'm a control freak or something but I don't like that blackout moment. I panic. Any time I've ever had an operation it's gone badly. When I had my wisdom teeth out I remember five people in blue surgical scrubs pinning me to the table.'

He laughed – casual, slightly uninterested – in that way of detached engagement that doctors seemed to affect. 'I can make sure you're relaxed beforehand. Thank you for telling me.'

Sooner than she expected she was being wheeled along a corridor, the white plastic bag containing her belongings at her feet.

As the trolley trundled along, and she watched the strip lights on the ceiling flicker past, she thought again about meeting Theo for the first time.

Theo's warm, new-born weight in her arms was still tangible, yet she had blacked out those important hours on the night that he died. Just to think that she had been driven to hurt that vulnerable little boy filled her with shock and self-loathing.

That was what she had been trying to explain to Lorraine in the letter. Whether it was the fact that she'd been drinking the night that Theo died, or some perverse action of her mind to protect her from the truth, the moment when she hurt Theo was not available to her, although she now considered that she had to have been responsible. She needed forgiveness from Lorraine in order to forgive herself.

Dr Opong leaned over her, his hand warm over hers. The nurse had fixed a needle in her arm, and Opong was about to inject her with the anaesthetic drugs. He was so close to her, Clare could smell the coffee on his breath.

'You're going to feel a tingling – some people say it feels like a coldness creeping – but that'll only be for a second or so, and the next thing you know you'll be on the ward having tea and toast.'

Blackout.

8

CLARE

November 2008

The doorbell rang.

'It's them,' Clare called out to Sam as she took a deep breath in and out. She was just out of the shower and her hair was still damp, but she had managed to childproof the flat.

They had been to the hospital yesterday for the procedure to remove the remaining tissue from her womb. Sam had held her hand tightly throughout, as he had at their twelve-week scan. The procedure had been painful, but no more painful than the miscarriage itself. Clare was still bleeding a little, but she *felt fine*, as she had told Sam at least five times since they got up this morning.

The only thing she couldn't shake was the emptiness. She felt hollow, scooped out.

The children would keep her busy, she knew – no time to think of herself.

'Hello! Hello!'

As soon as the door opened, Ella crashed into Clare's thighs, wrapping her hands around, causing her to sway for a moment, almost losing her balance. The little girl's jet-black hair felt soft as Clare ran her hands through it. Theo was in Lorraine's arms, his two-year-old cheeks enflamed from teething and his mouth clamped onto the shoulder of Lorraine's jacket. He turned suddenly to watch Clare, all eyelashes and big blue eyes, leaving a trail of saliva on his mother's suede-clad shoulder.

'C'mon up and see the kids' room,' Sam said to Lorraine when they were all upstairs and she had taken off her coat. 'See what we've done to it.'

Lorraine stood in the small bedroom, hands on her hips, sweat misting her skin from the effort of getting the children off the bus and into the house. Clare and Sam's spare room now seemed like a finished nursery. It had been painted and decorated for Ella as she stayed so often, but for Theo's first sleepover they had bought a cot and a new mobile.

'It looks great, but beware—' Lorraine pointed at the new cot '—don't think he's staying in there till you wake up. He'll climb out of that in two minutes flat.'

'The side goes up,' said Clare, and Sam went to demonstrate, but Lorraine laughed.

'He's quite a climber – you'll see. Don't worry, it's the same sort we have at home – side up or down, he'll get out of it if he wants to, so don't say you weren't warned.' She laughed as she left the room, hooking her jacket on the multi-coloured coat pegs in the hall.

Downstairs, Theo stamped on the wooden floorboards, as if enjoying the reassuring sound of them. He had learned to walk a year ago but still had a swagger over short distances. Over longer distances – from the fireplace to the cooker – he would pick up speed, head down, hands out to the side, like a speed skater. Ella had just turned eight years old and skipped into the living room. Her leggings were baggy at the knees and she wore a sparkly top that seemed a size too big.

Lorraine sank onto the couch.

Sam had made coffee and now placed a small cup of espresso on a side table near Lorraine's elbow.

'Thank you. I haven't stopped all morning. I hope I've remembered everything,' she said, swiping the bobble hat from Theo's head as he passed.

'Well, the kids are here; that's the most important thing. Just go and enjoy your weekend.'

Lorraine and her mother were going to a spa outside Edinburgh.

Lorraine sipped her coffee. 'This will be my first night away from Theo.' Almost wistfully, she watched him as he tore back and forth, shoes battering on the wooden floors.

'Really?' Clare frowned. 'Did you not go away with ... down to Newcastle?' She had almost said Brody's name but checked herself just in time.

'No ... remember that got cancelled because Ella had a fever?'

Theo was now bent over the big bag that Lorraine had brought. Clare held up a teething ring that was near the top, but Theo didn't want it.

'He wants his yoghurt.' Lorraine made Theo sit on a small footstool, and handed him his yoghurt and spoon. The spoon had a large metal tip and a plastic grip in the shape of a frog.

Theo spooned yoghurt into his mouth.

'He's good, isn't he?' Clare said. 'Doesn't miss that mouth at all.'

Lorraine visibly swelled with pride. 'Yeah, he's got great hand-eye coordination . . . but his words are still few and far between.'

Clare remembered Ella being almost chatty at that age. 'But when he does speak, they're very clear words,' she said, smiling supportively at Lorraine. Clare was consciously aware of pacifying Lorraine, since their argument.

'Yes, he does speak clearly,' Lorraine said, smiling at her son.

'In his own time,' Sam said, from the kitchen. 'Man of few words, after my own heart.'

As if he resented being spoken about, Theo suddenly cried out and threw the spoon. It flew out of his hand and hit Ella's chin. Yoghurt streaked on her cheek.

'Theo!' Lorraine grabbed him and pulled him towards her, leaning down to speak to him close to his face. 'You've *not* to do that. You could've hurt Ella.'

Chastised, Theo put his two chubby hands between his knees and hung his head, lower lip protruding. It was such an overt display of shame – endearing in so little a person – that Clare felt for him. She put a hand on his head. 'It's okay.'

'No,' Lorraine said, one eyebrow raised, 'he has to get into trouble for that. You can't throw things at people.'

Ella wiped the yoghurt off her face and returned the spoon to her brother. 'That was quite naughty, wasn't it, Mummy?'

'Yes, darling.'

Sam stood up. 'I got a cool new beanbag for your room – want to see it?'

'Yes!' Ella said, jumping to her feet and taking Sam's hand.

'Bean!' Theo followed them out, his hard-soled shoes stamping against the wooden floors.

Alone for a few moments, Clare put her hand on Lorraine's arm. 'How are you? Things any easier? You looked shattered the other day.'

Lorraine broke eye contact, obviously remembering the argument in the museum. 'Yeah, it's all good. Theo's a nightmare but it's just his age.'

'Does he miss his dad?' Clare asked, feeling brave.

Lorraine shook her head once. 'He doesn't know he's gone. He might not even remember him.'

Brody was a folk singer from County Armagh, who Lorraine had met in a bar. Clare had struggled to like him right from the beginning, as he had seemed very pleased with himself. He and Lorraine were together for a year or so before she fell pregnant and he moved in, but Clare had sensed that children were not part of Brody's plan. He would take his guitar and sing songs to Ella, but Clare knew from Lorraine that Brody didn't get up for nightmares, or breakfast, or the school run. As far as Clare could work out, Brody had done what he felt like, when he felt like it.

And so, it wasn't necessarily a bad thing if Theo had already forgotten Brody.

'Is he still in town?' It was a year since Brody had left Lorraine but as far as Clare knew he was still in Edinburgh.

'No, he's gone back to Cork. He texted a few months ago. Did I not tell you?'

Clare was silent. Information sharing was the currency of friendship, but this had been withheld; there was no way Lorraine would have forgotten to mention something so big, so not telling her must have been deliberate. Clare wondered if Lorraine thought of the break-up as a failure.

'Anyway, more importantly, how *are* you? How was your ... *thing*? How did it go?' Lorraine raised her eyebrows ominously.

Clare looked at the floor, rubbed her palms along the thighs of her black jeans. Her turn to deflect now.

'It was, you know, it was okay. It was over quickly.' She found a piece of lint on her jeans and brushed it off. *Over.* Instinctively, her two hands moved up over her stomach. She couldn't describe how empty she now felt. *Foetal matter.* The violence of the words they used fitted the horror of what she'd been through. She remembered her knees, bony and blueish in the stirrups, the nurse stroking the back of her hand as she tried not to cry.

'I know,' Lorraine said. 'It's actually alright, isn't it? You think it's going to be *horrendous*, but then it doesn't hurt as much you think. Like a kind of period pain.'

Clare looked at her friend, blinking, unable to respond. Her lips parted to answer but no words came out. Clare suddenly realised Lorraine was talking about an abortion she had had – before Ella – when she had gone through a similar procedure. That she should equate the two caused hurt to swirl inside Clare, formless and angry.

'You'll be pregnant again in no time,' Lorraine said, nodding affirmatively, as if she was able to decree such things.

Clare had to get up and turn away. She was so sick of hearing that. She put the kettle on even though she didn't want tea, feeling her cheeks flush. She heard Sam and the children on the stairs and felt relief at the thought that Lorraine would be going soon. She didn't want to talk about it any more.

There was the sound of Theo shaking the safety gate in the hall and then Sam growling, as if pretending he was some kind of animal. The children squealed and Sam chased them into the living room, bent over and swinging his arms like a gorilla.

'Right. Mummy's got to go now.' Lorraine threw her arms out.

Ella ran to her mother, hugging her and nuzzling into her neck.

'You be good for Uncle Sam and Auntie Clare.' Lorraine kissed the top of her head and then held out her arms for Theo. She pulled him onto her lap as Ella continued to hang on her arm. 'I'll call you both tomorrow afternoon.' Lorraine licked her thumb and wiped a smudge of dirt on Theo's cheek before kissing the side of his head.

Ella sagged back on the couch, tired from her exertions with Sam or flat because her mother was leaving. She played with the sequins on her jumper, chin to her chest.

'Do you want us to call you at bedtime?' Clare said.

'Only if you want to. I know what it's like. If they're all settled, I'll speak to them tomorrow.'

Sam opened the shutters and placed a chair in front of the big window, so that Ella could stand on it and wave goodbye to her mother as she left the courtyard.

Clare held Theo, waving his chubby little hand as Lorraine walked backwards on the cobbles waving and then blowing kisses. Theo leaned forward and kissed the glass with an open mouth, leaving an 'O'-shaped mark on the condensation.

Clare turned to Sam and pressed her lips into a smile. Lorraine was gone and they were in charge.

9

DETECTIVE INSPECTOR
PAMELA BROOKES

August 2019

I don't like to think about what happened. But lately I've had a lot of time to think and some of the things that I had blocked out – to protect myself? – have come back to me. I don't remember everything, but I remember leaning into Theo's cot, crying. I had drunk far too much. I remember the evidence from the trial and I can't think of any other explanation for what happened to him, except that I must have accidentally hurt him somehow. I can't imagine I would have done to him what the police suggested. I don't think I'm capable of that violence but I know it makes sense that I must have hurt him. To admit that to myself causes me more pain than you could imagine.

Brookes laid the letter onto her desk. Clare's handwriting was clear and careful, but the word *hurt* had been splashed or wet, so that *hurt* was an explosion of ink.

At Clare and Sam Armstrong's trial, both had insisted that Theo's death was accidental. As the evidence had accrued, Pamela Brookes had formed a theory that Clare had murdered Theo, and her husband, Sam, had helped her to cover it up. Brookes still believed that to be true, but the evidence presented at the trial had not convinced the jury.

But perhaps the letter, even though not a true confession, suggested that new evidence could be found now, all these years later, that would bring Clare to justice. Double jeopardy trials were not just another spin at the wheel. Brookes knew that the procurator fiscal would need more than contrition to retry the case.

It was time for her meeting with the detective superintendent. She gathered the letter into a file and walked down the corridor to the meeting room. Bill Joyce was already there, and he had bought her a machine coffee that was steaming on the oval table.

'Thanks, boss. Did you remember the sugar?'

'Of course; if there's anyone needs sweetening, it's you.' He smoothed his moustache with finger and thumb.

Joyce was due to retire next year. There was a chart on his office wall and he used a black cross to mark off each day until February 18th, when he was due to leave.

'So, you want to review the Collins case?'

'Yes, I think it merits it. There's been some recent contact between the deceased's mother and the female accused from the trial.'

'Armstrong?'

'She calls herself Richardson now. She wrote to the child's mother asking for forgiveness. It's not a clear confession, but I think there's something there. It's been over ten years, so I want to see if there's something we missed . . . '

'I had a look at the letter. It might be worthwhile pulling the exhibits and letting forensics have another crack at it. See if there's enough for a reinvestigation.'

'Thank you, boss. That's what I was thinking. I don't want to raise the mother's hopes, but I wanted to look into it again.'

Joyce took an audible sip of his tea. The paper cup seemed too small in his large hands, like a cup from a child's tea set. 'Remember, if you want double jeopardy it will have to be—'

'——new evidence,' they spoke at the same time. 'Yes, I know,' Brookes added.

'Keep me updated.'

'Of course.'

Once back at her desk, Brookes picked up the phone and called Sergeant Rory Hendry's number. They had worked Theo's case together and he had said he was willing to help again if Joyce agreed a review.

According to Lorraine, after receiving the letter, she had confronted Clare outside the Newhaven Gallery where she had confessed again and admitted that she had lied to the police. Brookes didn't doubt Lorraine, but she wanted to verify her story.

'Hendry.'

'Hey sarge, I got the green light.'

'The DS approved review?'

'Not a full re-investigation, but I can pull the evidence and resubmit to forensics, so we'll see.'

'I wondered what he'd say. I didn't think the fiscal were keen on confession-based double jeopardy applications.' Hendry was from up north, a fishing village in Aberdeenshire. His accent still had the clipped tones and short vowels.

Brookes swung back in her chair.

'So we bolster the apparent confession in the letter with objective evidence of Clare Armstrong admitting to the crime and lying to the police.'

'So . . . ?'

'So, I'm going to pick up and resubmit the production from the trial for testing. Can you contact the Newhaven Gallery about getting their CCTV for the night of the fifteenth of August. I'm looking for two women meeting up around eight to eight thirty p.m. in particular but if we get video for the whole night I'll go through it. Also, the gallery's near the harbour, but there might be other premises with CCTV.'

'When do you want it?'

'Soon as you can. Call my mobile? I'm heading out to the vault.'

Before she left her desk, Brookes opened a database and checked the location of the forensic evidence from the trial of the Crown vs Armstrong and Armstrong. The production from the trial was now held in the evidence vault within Edinburgh's

Central Police Headquarters. Brookes noted the number of the aisle and shelf where the Collins case evidence was stored.

Outside was unrecognisable as a summer day. The sky was white and the rain seemed unrelenting. Brookes turned up her collar as she ran towards her car. Inside, slightly out of breath, she smoothed her hair, straining to see herself in the rear-view mirror. Her pale, freckled face looked back at her. Along her hairline, her red hair showed strands of grey. During the original investigation into Theo's death, Brookes' hair had been longer – auburn and shiny – or at least that was how she remembered it.

In the storage vault of Edinburgh's main police station, Brookes walked along the gloomy, dust-smelling aisles of evidence storage. The numbered location on a piece of paper in her hand, she craned her neck to see the numbers on the file boxes higher up.

The police officer who maintained the vault had been here for years injured on the job and now corpulent – a police officer turned librarian. He sat with his back to the shelves, doing a tabloid crossword, a pencil behind his ear. Brookes heard his radio playing 'If I Could Turn Back Time' as she continued her search.

Sometimes evidence was mis-filed, particularly when the cases were very historic. Brookes was impatient. There were ladders around the other side, but she used the shelves themselves as steps as she squinted at the numbers on the edge of the metal shelving units.

'Here we go,' she whispered to herself, standing on tiptoes to haul down a cardboard box, which was surprisingly light. The evidence from Theo's trial was spread over four filing boxes, stacked in a row.

She rested the box on her leg and then placed it onto the floor. On the side, it read: *Procurator Fiscal vs Clare Armstrong and Samuel Armstrong.*

Opening the lid, Brookes flicked through a series of brown, evidence storage envelopes. She lifted out the last one. Through its clear window she could see it was the blanket taken from Theo's cot in Clare and Sam's apartment. She dropped it back into place and looked at the envelope next to it – recognising Theo's sleepsuit.

Through the clear plastic window on the brown envelope, she saw the black belly of a panda bear and two small, black ears. In the dusty aisles, Brookes took a quick intake of breath. She remembered seeing Theo for the first time on the floor of the bedroom in Clare and Sam's flat, his tiny hands cast up beside his face. He might have been asleep were it not for his blue lips and eyelids.

Back at her car, Brookes put the file on the front seat. She checked her messages before she turned on the engine. As soon as she got back to the office, she would send the forensic evidence from the first trial to CID to be reanalysed. A lot had changed in DNA processing since 2008. Perhaps Theo's blanket or panda sleepsuit had kept a secret all these years – a secret that would help launch a retrial.

10

CLARE

November 2008

Lorraine had left with her mother just before lunch and had already texted to say they had arrived at the spa. Clare and Sam headed straight out with the children into the wintry, wet darkness of Edinburgh in November – the park and the petting farm and then a cold walk home with the promise of hot chocolate.

Finally inside, Clare saw how tired Sam was – that look in his eyes so they seemed glassy, opaque. She wanted to put her arms around him, but instead she hung up their coats and chased Theo so that she could take off his wellington boots before he covered the whole flat in mud.

'Cup of tea?' Sam said, hands in his pockets and shoulders raised.

'Yes, please,' Clare said, setting Theo's yellow wellies side by side and then snatching a moment to put her arms around Sam's waist.

She felt his hand on her head and another at the small of her back. She breathed him in.

'You alright?' she asked, looking up at him. 'You look tired.'

'Shattered. Are you not?'

Clare grinned as she broke free from him. She had been tired before the children even arrived. The weather, and Theo's tantrums, and Ella self-consciously trying to help out all of the time had meant the afternoon had been testing. 'Totally, but it's nearly bedtime, right?'

Clare peeled Theo's muddy suit from him. All of today's tantrums were now evidenced in the shiny, all-in-one suit that he wore. Anything that had been suggested that was disagreeable, Theo had thrown himself down on the ground, and because they had been at Gorgie Farm in the rain, he was literally covered in mud. The worst tantrum had been over a stationary tractor. Sam had lifted him up into the seat and helped him pretend to steer, but then the rain had come on again and Theo had been adamant that he stay in the driving seat.

Sam turned the heating up to take the chill from the front room, then began to open the games on his phone for Ella. She had been good all day – patiently helping them to navigate her brother's moods. She leaned into Sam's hip, craning to see what games he had found.

'Here you go,' he said, standing as Ella slumped back into the chair, propping the screen between her knees.

'You feeling alright, Elle Belle?' Clare asked, thinking the little girl looked pale. Ella nodded once but did not look up as Clare felt her forehead. She didn't have a temperature, and Clare decided that she was probably just chilled like the rest of them.

A pot sounded on the stove as Sam began to prepare hot chocolates.

Now on her knees in the centre of the living room, Clare watched Theo's swagger around the room. He was bare-legged now, nappy sagging. 'He's exhausted too. I think I'm going to put him in the bath.'

Sam pivoted to look at her.

'I dunno, Clare. Let's just cut our losses,' he said, running a hand through his hair. 'He's quiet for now.'

'Look at the state of him. He's all spattered with mud, and he's still got beetroot on his face from lunch, and ... his hair feels almost greasy.' *He hasn't been washed for days,* she thought but didn't say. For months she had been tackling this issue with Lorraine.

'Who cares if he's dirty ... '

'*I* care.' Clare locked eyes with Sam. She was aware of Ella's watchful eyes suddenly focusing on her. 'Just a quick one. He's tired so a bath'll probably settle him for bed.'

'In my day we got bathed once a week,' Sam said. 'Never did me any harm.'

Clare rolled her eyes as she picked up Theo.

In the bathroom, she tugged off his remaining clothes while the water ran, thrusting a little boat into his hands as a distraction. It was one that Ella often liked to play with in the bath. Clare had brought up some baking soda to add to the bath water to help soothe the nappy rash. She had noticed during the day that Theo's skin was still inflamed.

The clean scent of the bubble bath filled the room. Clare closed the door so that Theo couldn't escape. She tested the water as he squatted naked on the bathroom scales. When Clare turned to lift him into the water, she saw that he had bruises down his right arm.

Clare picked him up, balancing him on her hip as she inspected him. There were three dark-blue coin-sized bruises on his arm as if he had been grabbed, and then a mark on one of his shoulder blades.

Frowning, Clare lowered Theo into the water. The sensation of the warm water registered on the little boy's face. He opened his mouth, tightening his grip on the boat and splashing it into the water, soaking Clare's shirt and his own face.

Clare dabbed his face dry with a cloth. He coughed and focused his attention on the boat, his eyelashes long and heavy with water. Clare remembered the tantrum at the farm and how Sam had lifted him off the tractor and dragged him onto his feet. She felt a sudden constriction in her chest as she wondered if the bruises had been made by Sam. He was such a big, powerful man. He didn't realise his own strength and anger was often his first response to emotional situations.

As she washed Theo's little body, Clare thought that the rash had died down a little and she was relieved. She wondered if the scene she had caused had made Lorraine take it more seriously. The baking soda she had added to the bathwater would help to clear it up.

With care, Clare washed Theo, thinking how beautiful he was: large head, fragile nape. Chubby shoulders and fists splashing. She placed her thumb into the delicate groove behind his neck. He had been so upset earlier, but now he was content.

For a moment, brief as one of the bubbles that floated, Clare imagined how she would feel if Theo was hers. The feeling swelled, glorious, spherical, iridescent, so that for a second – soapy water enclosing a hollow sphere of air – he belonged to her. Just for that moment, Clare felt buoyant with happiness.

Theo slapped the water with an open hand. It splashed them both; the bubble burst. Theo turned to look into her face, his big blue eyes seeking a reaction.

Clare shampooed his hair, being careful to keep the soap out of his eyes, even as he kept looking down at the boat – submerging it then watching it explode to the surface. Such fine delicate hair and such a pleasing round head. She rinsed him off and tried to lift him out.

'No, no,' Theo said, casually, as if talking to the boat.

As Clare lifted him out of the water, he began to scream. 'Noooooo.' On her knees it was difficult to get leverage and his wet body was heavy, the water pulling him back into the bath.

Suddenly, Theo slipped out of her hands like a seal and slid down the bath, his face submerging as his heels kicked into the air.

'Oh my God.'

She grabbed him and pulled his wet body out of the water, right against her shirt, fully drenching herself. He blinked and coughed, water clumped on his eyelashes. His shock was visible for a moment, his large eyes trying to comprehend what had happened. He stared wide-eyed around the bathroom and then, to Clare's great relief, began to scream again. The noise was amplified in the small, tiled space.

Sam poked his head around the door.

'What the hell is going on?'

'He slipped from my hands.' Clare set Theo down and sank to her knees beside him, draping the hooded baby towel over his body. He sobbed, holding onto the edge of the bath. She took hold of the front of her shirt and held it off her chest. It was so wet her bra was shining through.

'It sounds like you're murdering him. The neighbours'll be on the phone to social work.'

Theo reached into the bath to save his boat from the pull of the plughole. The towel fell from him.

'What happened there?'

Clare looked up into Sam's face and saw he meant the bruises on Theo's body.

She picked up the towel and put it around Theo's shoulders, sitting up on her heels. 'I worried it was today – in the park when you were picking him up.'

'You thought *I* did that?' Sam leaned on the door frame, eyes widening.

She sat on the toilet seat and began rubbing Theo dry. He stood, absorbed by the toy boat in his hands.

'By *accident*. I just thought by accident. I mean ... just there I had to grab him hard when he went under. So easy to hurt them ...'

111

'Hurt,' said Theo, the single word echoing in the steamy bathroom space.

'Jesus,' Sam said.

Clare shushed him. 'Do you know if we still have that Calpol from the last time Ella stayed? Can you check if it's okay for him to take?'

'Why does he need Calpol? He's not sick.'

'Well, I just wondered ... no, you're right; he's not sick.' Clare rubbed Theo dry. He was smiling now, babbling a story about the boat.

'No, he'll be fine.' Sam looked harassed.

'Would you get me his sleepsuit? I think it's in the bag downstairs.'

Theo put the boat on the edge of the empty bath and watched it slide down inside. Clare scooped a handful of bubbles from the bottom and blew the suds in his face.

Theo took hold of her face suddenly, laughing. She felt his warm chubby hands press her cheeks together and kissed his forehead.

Sam returned, putting Theo's pyjama suit onto the toilet seat.

'Oh, this is cute,' said Clare, holding it up. 'It's a little panda.'

'I think when the bruises are blue like that, it means they're older,' said Sam, his voice low. 'So probably not from today.'

Clare let Theo hold the boat while she dried him and put his nappy on, even though the boat was still wet and dampening his pyjamas. She put him into his sleepsuit one limb at a time, then turned him around so that Sam could see. The hood was close to his head and on either side were two panda ears. To help the hood stay up, Clare tied the bow at the neck.

She wrinkled up her nose as she lifted Theo up, snuggling him in her arms for a moment before setting him down again. 'Isn't that just the cutest suit ever?'

The bathroom door was open. He set off like a speed skater again, a panda cub on the run, heading for the stairs.

11

DETECTIVE
INSPECTOR BROOKES

August 2019

DI Brookes and Sergeant Hendry were side by side before a large computer screen as they scrolled through the CCTV footage they had acquired from the Newhaven Gallery. Hendry was slumped down in his chair, eyes unblinking as the frames moved, occasionally taking a crisp from a packet and slipping it into his mouth. Brookes sighed, elbows on the desk, face propped on her hands, her eyes starting to burn. This was detective work: endless, mindless boredom, combing through grains of sand. They didn't show you this on television.

The counter at the corner of the screen showed that it was footage from just after eight o'clock. The gallery doors opened and cars drew up, headlights on even though it was not yet dark. Brookes rubbed her eyes as she scanned the attendees.

At 00:20:36:09, when most of the guests had already entered, a single woman walked into the car park. Brookes sat up and blinked. She recognised the posture of the woman on the screen – tall and angular – the way she walked with restrained confidence. Without a doubt it was Lorraine, but her hair was different. The grey scale of the CCTV meant that Brookes had to guess at the colour – platinum blonde or silver? She would be in her fifties now, of course. She was dressed smartly, in a fitted jacket and scarf. She strode straight up to the gallery door and opened it. One of the frames showed her face clearly, as she looked up into the camera. Those same luminous eyes.

'That's Lorraine Collins,' Brookes whispered, intent.

'Yup. Let's see what happens now.'

For several minutes no one entered or exited the gallery. Brookes and Hendry watched the movement of the waves, the light on the water showing up as grainy silver on the monitor. The time clock scrolled in the corner of the screen.

Just then Lorraine exited, in a rush, striding into the car park. She was followed by a petite woman wearing wide-legged trousers and a blouse. Brookes sat up immediately.

'That's them. Pause it.'

Hendry hit the mouse with his finger, still slumped in his chair. Brookes enlarged the picture, focusing in on the faces. Clare, remarkably, looked the same as she had in 2008. It was windy by the shore and Lorraine's fringe – a long quiff – whipped back and forth. They were the same age, these women, Brookes remembered. They had been friends since university.

'You sure it's them?' Hendry squinted at the screen.

'Without a doubt.'

Hendry noted the frame times as the video continued. The two women walked to the centre of the car park and then began to speak. Lorraine was pitched forward, aggressively so, but it could just have been the difference between their heights meant that she had to bend over to be heard. Yet to Brookes it seemed as if Lorraine was shouting – her mouth opening wide and the tendons in her neck becoming visible.

After a few moments, Clare wiped her eyes, let one hand rest over her mouth.

'I think she's crying,' said Rory.

Brookes nodded, attention focused on the image of the two women.

Clare was speaking, her small lips moving quickly. She reached out and held onto Lorraine's jacket – just as Lorraine had described – and after a moment, Lorraine wrenched her arm away. Their conversation became intense before Lorraine turned and walked out of the car park.

Clare stood for several moments, on her own, looking in the direction Lorraine had gone, and then she went back inside.

'Okay, let's save that section,' Brookes said.

'What do you want to do with it?' Hendry said.

'Did that look like a confession to you?'

'Could be – particularly when Clare hangs onto her jacket.'

'Remember that lip-reader we used for the Coulson murder?'

Coulson was a teenager who had been involved with crack cocaine gangs that operated out of Edinburgh and Glasgow. He had been shot in the head at point-blank range with a sub-machine pistol. CCTV footage of the attacker confessing to the killing outside a pub in Duddingston had helped to seal the case after a lip-reader had successfully transcribed what had been said between the two men.

'I think we get her to take a look at this – give us some more objective input on what's being said. Lorraine said when she met Clare she admitted lying to the police. I'd like to see the transcript for that exchange.'

Hendry went to fetch coffee, as Brookes checked up on forensics.

Janice Barker headed up the lab and Brookes had asked that the Collins production – Theo's panda sleepsuit and blanket – be looked at promptly.

'Janice Barker.'

'Janice, hi; it's Pamela Brookes. I was just chasing up those DNA results.'

'We're still working on those.'

'Sorry to hassle you. I just wondered if it was turning up anything new?'

'It is, but that's what's taking the time. We're using some new techniques and it means running it a few times.'

Brookes sat up in her chair and leaned over the desk, putting her thumbnail between her teeth.

'I don't want to pre-empt but we are likely to be able to work up one of the old samples on the sleepsuit.'

'I see . . . '

'I'm re-doing some samples and then I'll compile everything and email it over to you. The hood of the sleepsuit, in particular, has some areas that we can now develop. There are very small amounts of DNA concentrated in particular parts of the suit, and in 2008 it wasn't sufficient to identify a profile, but now it is.'

'I see.'

'I'll work it up some more and run it past your suspects' samples from 2008 and then I'll be in touch.'

As Brookes hung up, Hendry put a steaming cup of coffee on the desk in front of her. 'Milk and three sugars as usual?'

'Thank you,' she said, not looking at him.

'It's a wonder you're not diabetic. Forensics come up with anything?'

'They're still working it up, but Janice Barker says the hood of the sleepsuit might produce a new profile.'

'New as in clearer information about the previous suspects?'

'I don't know, but I'm as keen as you to find out.' Brookes raised her eyebrows. She took a sip of her coffee, looking at Hendry. 'The hood of the sleepsuit was very important ... if you remember ... ' The milky sweetness of the coffee comforted.

'I *do* remember.' Hendry's freckled forehead wrinkled slightly as he raised his eyebrows. 'Do you think the Collins case will come alive again – double jeopardy? Can you see it happening?' Hendry asked.

'I hope so.' The first trial had been a miscarriage of justice as far as Brookes was concerned, and she knew that now was her time to prove it: how one friend helping out another ended up with a toddler murdered.

'You just want it to happen so you can say you were right, from the start?'

Hendry was teasing but Brookes was suddenly serious. She

stood up, whipped her jacket over her shoulders ready to step outside. 'No, it's not about me, Sarge; it's about that little boy.'

'I know; you've said it before. We're working for the ones who can't tell us what happened.'

'That's right.' Brookes winked and clicked her teeth. 'I know it's not a popular view around here, but I still think that the majority of murders are not premeditated. We live in a world of mostly good people, who sometimes do bad things. Most murders are spontaneous acts that trigger violence and aggression. That's what happened in the Armstrong house all those years ago, I'm sure of it.'

'Yes, boss,' Hendry said, grinning at her.

12

LORRAINE

November 2008

Lorraine had never felt so relaxed. In the corner of the bar, she kicked off her shoes and curled her feet up underneath her. It was dark now, and the large Victorian windows reflected their happy faces. The room was lit with fairy lights, and there was tinkly piano playing somewhere out of sight. Lorraine and her mother both had a half-full glass of Prosecco before them.

'I feel wonderful,' said Rita Collins, leaning right back against the leather seat. 'I don't feel tired at all; I just feel really, really relaxed. It's such a strange, wonderful feeling.'

'I know what you mean. I feel so rested.'

They had both spent the afternoon by the pool, finishing up with an hour-long massage in a darkened room with scented candles. Pore clean and moisturised, they had eaten dinner: lamb chops with mint sauce.

There were few other guests in the large bar and Lorraine

and her mother said little, each of them gazing up at the crystal chandelier. It was so quiet in their corner of the big room that Lorraine could hear the Prosecco bubbles bursting near the rim of the glass.

The Prosecco, the peace and quiet, and Lorraine felt guilty. She hadn't been away without the children in years – had never spent a single night away from Theo. She took another sip of her drink, knowing that she had to savour each moment. Theo had been able to climb out of his cot for months now, and Lorraine was often woken before six a.m. with his sticky little palms pawing her face. Ella was even more direct. She would lift up her mother's eyelids. *Wake up, Mummy. Wake up.*

Tonight she could go to sleep and know that no little fingers would be tugging her hair to rouse her. It was kind of Clare and Sam to take the children, despite the awful week they'd both had. Lorraine hoped that the children had been well behaved, and were asleep already.

Thoughts of Brody came into her head and then were erased, like a wave smoothing over a sandy beach. A year since he had gone and Lorraine now felt differently about him. She thought she'd be fine if she never saw him again.

She took a deep breath in through her nose and out again, still tingling from the spa. She felt rolled out, like a piece of dough, pliant, accepting. Nevertheless, a worry puckered her thoughts. She hoped that Brody would make no claim on Theo. Her son had just turned two and she was defiantly sure that he had no memory of Brody whatsoever.

Warmth pulsed throughout Lorraine's whole body. She

thought she could still smell the eucalyptus oil that had been used on her skin and raised the back of her hand to sniff it. She felt a muscle-deep serenity that seemed to have intensified since she drank the champagne. All her blood vessels felt close to the surface, her hands weighted at her sides. Blood-deep joy.

It was almost how she had felt after each of her children was born, waves of love and contentment radiating even as her bones felt unhinged.

'I don't think I want to move my arms and legs ever again,' she said to her mother, giggling as she let her head rest on the leather booth behind her.

Her mother smiled 'Shall we just ask that nice waiter to carry us up to bed?'

Nevertheless, after a moment, Lorraine reached forward and lifted her glass.

'Cheers.'

'Cheers,' Rita replied, lifting her glass but not taking a sip.

The Prosecco tasted tart and Lorraine sat up a little, her eyes moistening. She gave a small sigh. The piano seemed to have stopped, and classical music began, very softly, its source invisible – piped from the corners of the room. Lorraine listened intently and then as the building violins were joined by ecstatic brass, she raised her eyebrows and turned to her mother.

'Mahler!'

'Hmm?' Rita had let her eyes close and now opened them wide, as if startled. 'Ah yes, "Resurrection".' She reached for her glass. 'I'm not sure if that's appropriate or not.'

Lorraine laughed. Just then, her phone began to vibrate in

her handbag. She had turned the sound off, but she could still hear it buzzing against the leather, making the bag's silver catch chatter like teeth. Still smiling, she reached into her bag just as the phone went to answerphone.

'Who is it?'

'Brody.'

Her mother suddenly pitched forward.

Lorraine squealed with laughter. 'Only joking. I wanted to see if you would stay Zen. It was just Sam.'

'You're a besom!'

Lorraine put the phone on the table, waiting to return the call in case Sam was leaving a message. When there were no further notifications, she called him back.

'Way past their bedtime. Hope they've been good,' Lorraine said to her mother as she waited on Sam picking up. 'I hope everything's okay.'

'My grandchildren are always good as gold,' Rita said, pressing her lips together.

It was Sam's work phone, which he often used to call her, and Lorraine frowned, listening to the familiar message:

You've reached Sam Armstrong at Maitland McConnell; please leave me a message.

'I think I've called him back too quickly,' she said. 'It's just going straight to answer.'

'I hope Clare's taken more photos of the wee ones while they're staying over.'

'She probably has. You know what's she's like: always camera in hand.'

'She takes such nice, natural photographs.'

'Well, they are beautiful children, if I say so myself.'

'They are, aren't they? We're not even biased.'

Lorraine hung up without leaving a message, knowing that Sam would call back, and finished her Prosecco. 'I hope they got the kids in bed early. Last time Ella stayed she kept them up for hours playing Monopoly. And Clare'll be tired, what with . . . '

Lorraine had told her mother about Clare's miscarriage. She glanced at her watch. It was nearly midnight. The bottom of her glass sounded against the table as she put it down. The slightest vein of worry snaked through her. She stared at the phone, expecting Sam's name to flash up again, or a text.

'I think I need my bed,' her mother said.

'Me too.'

Fifteen minutes later, Lorraine was struggling with the key card entry to her room when her phone sounded again.

'Hey, Sam.'

Lorraine held the phone with her shoulder as she waved the card back and forth over the entry scanner.

His voice was changed – hoarse, rasping. He sounded as if he were running at full pelt.

'Are you alright?'

'You have to come. They're trying hard but I don't think . . . '

There was so much background noise and Lorraine couldn't hear clearly. She straightened up and listened, pressing the phone to her ear.

As Sam gulped out words, Lorraine felt all the warmth in her body replaced by a sudden, icy chill. Even before she heard the words and understood the meaning, cold penetrated her so that her teeth began to chatter. Her key and her bag fell to the floor.

13

DETECTIVE INSPECTOR
PAMELA BROOKES

November 2008

Brookes was on her way home when her radio crackled.

'*Male infant found dead, suspected SUDI, SIO attendance requested.*'

It was late, raining heavily. The car rocked slightly at the traffic lights, buffeted in the wind. Brookes was just finishing duty. The address was Haymarket, on the way to her home in Corstorphine, in the west of the city, so Brookes radioed in that she would respond. SUDI. Sudden Unexplained Death in Infancy – what used to be called cot death.

St Mary's Cathedral was floodlit, dark elms stripped of their leaves reaching up into the stormy sky like skeletal hands. At first Brookes couldn't find the location, then saw the blue oscillating light of the ambulance emanating from a cobbled side road off Palmerston Place. Brookes drove the car into a courtyard.

Her phone vibrated in her pocket and she took it out as she turned off the engine, looking up at the two- and three-storey eighteenth-century properties that rimmed the courtyard. Most of the buildings were converted into flats, with skylights illuminated.

Expensive homes, she thought, as she glanced at her phone. Mike had sent a message – a photograph of their new puppy, Dermot, and the words *foot fetish*.

Brookes smiled and texted a reply before she stepped out of the car: '*What's he done now?*'

As if having a new baby wasn't enough disruption, they had decided to get a new puppy at the same time. They had reasoned that a Jack Russell was a small dog and probably not too much trouble. Dermot had fitted into the palm of her hand when they got him, but was now almost full-sized and had ruined three pairs of leather shoes.

When she stepped out of the car, the wind whipped up her ponytail and sent it into a swirl around her face. She ducked her head down and ran to the door of the flat, which was wide open despite the weather. She put one arm over her breasts as she did so, the weight of them painful. It was her first week back to work since giving birth to Jack. She smoothed her hair in the doorway, glancing up out at the courtyard and the faces of neighbours watching the drama unfold.

Brookes stepped inside the flat, where she saw a muddied road bike leaning against the wall. She took hold of the iron railing and began to ascend the spiral stone staircase, wiping the rain drops from her jacket.

One of the paramedics stood at the top of the stairs in her dark-green uniform. She was a middle-aged woman with her hair roughly plaited to one side. Brookes nodded in greeting. The open door and the high ceilings meant that the hallway of the flat was cold. Brookes felt the chill on her throat as the top button of her shirt was undone.

'The child's in here, detective. Sadly, he was gone by the time we arrived. I recorded time found as eleven forty.'

Brookes had lost count how many dead bodies she'd seen, but the sight of Theo, flat on his back on the nursery floor, his panda sleepsuit burst open to access his chest, cleaved her. The little body was so vulnerable and small, his face turned unnaturally away from his body.

The sight of Theo made her think of Jack.

Brookes took two pairs of latex gloves from her pocket.

'You attempted resuscitation?'

'No. He was dead when we arrived. The godparent was performing CPR.'

'Godparent?'

Brookes looked over her shoulder. She could hear a child crying.

'The deceased's name is Theo Collins. His godparents were babysitting. They're in the front room with his sister. They found the child in his cot, unresponsive.'

'I see.' Brookes pulled on one pair of gloves and then the second.

A younger male paramedic was putting away equipment and Brookes knelt beside the body. The sight of the little boy up close, spread out on the floor, caused Brookes to take a sharp intake of breath.

'This is how you found him?' Brookes asked the paramedic.

'Yes. There was nothing we could do.'

'Do you have any observations about potential cause of death?'

'Breathing difficulty – there's slight haemorrhaging in the eyes.'

'We'll get a post-mortem. You think accidental suffocation?'

'It would seem so. They both seem pretty shaken up.'

'Can we arrange for the body to be taken to the City Mortuary within the hour?'

'Very well.'

Brookes took in the small room, painted lemon, rainbows and stars on the wall. She peered inside the cot at the coil of white blanket, the thin pillow. The little girl's bed with the duvet thrown back, the white chair with the old teddy bear.

She looked into Theo's face. His eyes were closed, the eyelids tinged blue.

Sudden Unexplained Death in Infancy was more common in younger babies. Theo looked to be about two years old.

Brookes stood, removing her gloves. Just then a tall man appeared at the door. He almost filled the doorframe, his shoulders shaking, his blue eyes reddened. Brookes stepped into the hall with him.

'I'm Detective Inspector Brookes.'

The man nodded. He was well over six foot tall and Brookes had to look up at him. She could see he was in shock, the skin on his face ashen and visibly trembling. 'Sam Armstrong.'

'The child was in your care?'

'My wife and I ... looking after both the children, our god-children.' Sam coughed, attempting to clear the emotion from his throat. 'What will happen?'

Brookes spoke quietly. 'I'm sorry for your loss. The ambulance team will take Theo to the mortuary ...'

'But his mum's on the way from the Borders. She'll want to see him.'

Brookes nodded. 'We'll need a post-mortem. There will be a chance for the mother to see him after that.'

Brookes looked over her shoulder. The sound of the child crying had stopped. The rain rattled against the glass of the big window in the hall – the force of the gale making it sound like thrown grit. 'There's another child here?'

'Ella. She's eight.'

'The sister?'

Sam nodded.

'You have children of your own?'

Sam shook his head.

'It's just the room looks as if ...'

'We look after them often.'

'I'll need to take witness statements from you and your wife.'

Sam nodded and led the way. Brookes paused again at the nursery door as she saw the young paramedic zip Theo into an oversized body bag. Despite all her training and experience, the sight curdled her insides.

In the living room, a small, blonde woman sat on the sofa comforting a dark-haired girl, who was curled into her, thumb in her mouth.

Casually, Brookes cast her eyes around the room – the high ceilings and walls covered in art photographs, hardwood floor and chic, minimalist furniture. The room was beautifully decorated: simple, uncluttered. White walls and kitchen, lights in burnt orange; it looked like it should be in a magazine. There was a box of toys stacked by the fireplace. By the coffee table, shining like dropped diamonds, Brookes saw a glass had been shattered, no attempt made to pick it up.

'Here, I'll put her back down in our bed.' Sam reached out and lifted Ella, carrying her out of the room like a much younger child.

Brookes saw how the little girl instantly cuddled into Sam, thumb still in her mouth and her eyes pressed shut.

'It might take me a few minutes to settle her,' he said to them both.

Taking her notebook from her pocket, Brookes nodded.

'I'm Detective Inspector Brookes,' she said again, introducing herself to the woman, as she took a seat on the other end of the sofa.

'Clare.' Her face was pale, eyes blurry with dark smudges around them.

'Clare Armstrong?'

She cleared her throat. 'Yes.'

Brookes nodded, making a note. She was sitting nearly a metre away from the woman, but even from this distance she could smell the alcohol on her breath. It hadn't struck her when speaking to Sam and Brookes wondered about this.

A gentle knock on the ajar living room door, and the senior paramedic entered. 'That's us leaving, detective.'

'Thank you.'

Brookes glanced at her notepad, hearing the shuffle and clank of the paramedics on the stairs as they negotiated the spiral staircase, the stretcher and the body.

'I realise that this has been a very difficult night, but I need to take a witness statement from you, Mrs Armstrong. Are you alright to continue, or do you need a glass of water?' Brookes watched her, the woman's gaze wavering. She heard the gentle thud of the main door closing.

'M'alright.'

Clare nudged her face with her fist, leaving a red mark on her cheek. She had the sleeves of her sweater pulled over her hands.

'Shall we wait for Sam?'

'I need to take your statements separately anyway.'

'Would you like a cup of tea, detective ... ?' Clare said, a slur in her words and a flush spreading along her cheekbone.

'Thank you, no.' Brookes imagined that Clare needed the tea. She would be sobering up, thirsty.

'I'll just get ... ' Clare got to her feet suddenly and went to the kitchen.

Brookes watched the heaviness of her gait, balance regained with a hand on the kitchen bunker. At the sink, she poured a glass of water and drank it with her back to Brookes.

Sam's gentle knock at the living room door sounded and he entered, standing with arms folded, hands clutching his elbows. 'She's asleep. I think she's exhausted. She's been crying since ... '

'When is her mother expected?'

'An hour or so.'

'I just explained to your wife that I need to take witness statements from you. I wonder if you would mind waiting upstairs until I've spoken to Mrs Armstrong?'

'Of course.'

Sam left and, through the windows overlooking the living room, Brookes could see him take a seat on the landing of the second floor. Again she was struck by the fact that he seemed sober while Clare was clearly drunk.

As she returned to her seat on the couch, Clare wiped her nose with the knuckle of one hand. 'When Lorraine gets here, what will happen? Theo's gone. She'll want to see him.'

'We'll invite the mother to a formal identification as soon as possible. I'll give her the details for a family liaison officer who will guide her through the next steps. The family liaison officer will be available to you too.'

Clare nodded.

'Why don't you tell me what happened?'

As she hesitated, Clare looked down at her nails, picking at a sliver of skin near the thumb and then smoothing it down.

'We put the children to bed, and—'

'Both of you, together?'

'Yes, we both read and sang to them and then came downstairs, and it was later, I don't know what made me, but I decided to check on them . . . '

'What time was this?'

Clare scratched her head. 'I can't . . . it might have been after eleven? It wasn't long before we called nine-nine-nine.'

'Go on.'

'Ella was asleep and Theo was . . . ' Clare raised her trembling fingers to her mouth. 'He didn't look right, he just . . . ' Brookes watched her swallow, turning her attention to the side, as if recalling.

'Where was Theo?'

'He . . . ' Clare's eyes flicked up to the right, to the windows on the upper floor corridor, where Brookes could see Sam's back. 'He . . . was in his cot.'

'Did you try to wake him?'

Clare shook her head; a tear that had been balancing on her lid flashed over her cheek and chin.

'I called for Sam. I could see that Theo was . . . ' Clare pressed the knuckles of one hand into her temple. 'He wasn't breathing. I was frightened to touch him. I don't know how it could have happened, that he just . . . died in his sleep.'

Clare cleared her throat, then turned to face Brookes, eyes bloodshot, flicking back and forth as if still trying to comprehend. 'He had just . . . ' She opened the fingers of her hand and then brought it over her mouth, as if snatching away her words. 'Sam came and he . . . he tried very hard. And then we called the ambulance.'

'Sam tried to resuscitate him? So he lifted him out from the cot?'

'Yes, he . . . must've. He lifted him and put him on the floor.'

'Must've . . . did you see him do it?'

'I saw him. He lifted Theo from the cot and onto the floor and tried to make him breathe again.'

'And what about Ella while this was going on?'

'Well, Ella was asleep in our room. Theo took a while to settle and so Sam took her in to our bed. She was sound asleep but she woke because she must have heard me. I think . . . I screamed. I shouted to Sam. She—' Clare looked to her left and then met Brookes' eye. 'We shouldn't have let her see, but she came out of our room. She burst into tears. She cried and cried. We've only just got her—'

'What is your explanation for what happened to Theo?'

Clare took a deep breath. 'I don't know. Was it the blanket? The pillow? Was his suit too tight?' Tears flashed down her cheeks. She sucked in a ragged breath.

'And you've looked after the children before?'

'Yes. We look after them all the time. That's why the room is all set up for them – decorated the way it is. But this was Theo's first overnight. Ella has stayed countless times, since she was really small.'

'And Theo . . . did he have any allergies or other illnesses?'

'No, he's a healthy little boy.'

'And how did he seem when you put him to bed?'

'He was just like normal . . . he was laughing. He liked being read to . . . ' Clare began to sob, her face reddening. She curled her thin legs up into her body, hugging them into her.

Brookes was aware that Clare was close to becoming hysterical.

'You were drinking tonight?'

'What?' Clare's wet eyes opened wide, a frown crinkling her brow. Her broken breaths made her small chest heave.

'You were drinking alcohol tonight?'

'I . . . had a glass of wine.'

Brookes nodded. 'One glass of wine?'

'A few.'

'I see. I notice some broken glass on the floor.' Brookes indicated with her pen the shards near the coffee table. 'Did something happen there?'

Clare dabbed at her nose with the tissue. She tucked wisps of hair behind her ears, shaking her head. 'I can't remember . . . if Sam knocked something over. Did I? A glass or . . . I'm sorry, it's just so much has . . . Maybe when I called on him to help me.'

'Is there anything else you need to tell me?'

'I don't think so.' Clare gave a stiff smile before she covered her face with her hands.

Brookes flipped her notebook closed. She went upstairs to speak to Sam, leaving Clare shivering on the couch, and found him sitting with his head in his hands. The paramedics had left the door to the nursery ajar, and Brookes glanced again at the white teddy on the chair inside. It was similar to one that Jack had been given.

Sam suddenly started and jumped to his feet.

'I'll take your statement now, if that's okay?'

'Here?'

'Here's fine.'

'I'll get another chair.' Sam opened the door to the main bedroom and crept inside to get a chair. Curled asleep on top of the duvet, covered in a blanket, was the little girl.

Gently, Sam placed the chair in the hall and closed the bedroom door.

As Brookes glanced down at her notebook, and started a fresh page for Sam's statement, she felt a sensation in her right breast – the lobes contracting and leaking milk through the nipple. Since she had returned to work, she'd noticed that it sometimes happened when she thought of Jack. She shifted in her seat, pulling closer the lapels of her jacket.

Sam was still pale but his trembling had stopped, his eyes locked in an unfocused stare. The shadows under his eyes were delicate as bruises. The visible grief from earlier had been replaced by a tense weariness and he sat up straight, clasping and unclasping his hands in preparation for her questions. Nipples still tingling, Brookes began.

'The paramedics confirmed that there were no signs of life in Theo when they arrived on the scene. We will get a post-mortem, to get a more accurate idea of how and when Theo died, but can you tell me how you were alerted that something was wrong and how you dealt with it?'

Sam spread open his fingers. Brookes watched his Adam's apple bob in his throat.

'Well, I heard Clare call. She had gone to check on him, and ... I rushed upstairs and Theo ... wasn't breathing ...'

'Where was he? How did he look?'

'He was ... he was ... in his cot, his head was turned to the side, I think ... I can't remember the sequence. I just panicked. I started to give him mouth to mouth.'

'So you lifted him out of the cot and placed him on the floor?'

'Yes.'

'What did you do exactly?'

Sam raked his hair. He held out both hands, palms upwards. 'I picked him up, and laid him on the floor and then . . . I tried my best.' Sam's eyes began to shine. 'I was desperate. I just wanted to save him.' He hung his head.

'What did you do to try and save him?'

'What's it called? I put my mouth on his and breathed. I pressed on his chest—' Sam put one hand over another in demonstration then stopped suddenly, looking up at the ceiling. 'Ah, oh God,' he said, pressing both fists into his eyes.

Brookes was chilled with tiredness, her stomach nauseous with the need for sleep, but she gently prompted him.

'I know it's very upsetting, Mr Armstrong, but your statement is very important. Did you know what you were doing – have you had training in resuscitation?'

Sam exhaled, cheeks wet. He sniffed.

'I, well, I did . . . no, not really. There was one time at work, but it was a while ago. I guess I thought I knew what to do.'

'Where do you work?'

'I'm an architect. Maitland McConnell, down in Leith.'

'After you began CPR, did you observe any change in Theo's condition?'

He shook his head, eyes vacant again.

'You're tall, aren't you?' Brookes said.

'Six feet four.'

'And so you must weigh, what, about fourteen stone?'

'Thirteen ten. Why?' Sam pitched forward, eyes imploring. 'I didn't hurt him, I didn't . . . '

'It's just that open-palm heart compression is often used on adults, but babies are different. Normally compressions are done with fingers.'

'I didn't know. I didn't ... but you know—' Sam's shoulders began to shake again '—I can't bear to think about it, but I think it was already—' he met her eye '—too late. It was too late. He was gone already, before I even started.'

Through her tiredness, Brookes believed him.

As if suppressing a sob, Sam choked and coughed suddenly and snot exploded from his nose. He wiped it away with the back of his hand.

Brookes waited for him to compose himself.

'What about the little girl, Ella?'

'She was asleep in our room, but she woke up when she heard us trying to bring Theo back.' Sam waved his hand and then touched his forehead, as if struggling to remember.

'Why was she in your room?'

'She was finding it hard to settle in there with her brother. He was fussing, taking a while to get over, so I moved her into our bed.'

'What time did you move Ella into your bedroom?'

'Oh, early. It must have been about eight thirty or so. Maybe nine.' Sam's breath was uneven and he hiccupped breaths in and out.

'Before Clare alerted you, did you hear either of the children cry out?'

Sam shook his head.

'Did Theo seem unwell at all, when you put him to bed?'

Sam hesitated. 'No, he was fine. He fussed a little at first but then when we put his mobile on, he went to sleep. We thought he'd be tired out. He's at that age, tantrums ... he'd been difficult in the afternoon, but when it came to bedtime he was happy. He seemed ... fine.'

'And again, Clare went to check on the children – just on instinct – not because there was a sound that alerted you?'

'Instinct,' Sam repeated.

'Were you listening to music?'

'No.'

'Television?'

'No.'

'What were you doing then, when Clare had this instinct?'

'Talking. We were talking.'

'What about?'

As if the question caught him off guard, Sam looked at Brookes, and blinked twice.

'Um ... we were talking about the day, what we were going to do tomorrow. We'd taken the children out, to the farm and the park. We were thinking ... about plans for tomorrow.'

'And were you having a drink with Clare while you talked?'

Sam sat back in his seat. Brookes watched the question register in his eyes. He wiped a hand across his mouth.

'No.'

Their eyes met. Brookes waited in case he would expand, but he didn't. She made a note. There was no crime in having a glass of wine in your own home, but his reaction to the question, the broken glass and the fact that one partner was drunk while the other was sober niggled at her. On the face of it, this was a terrible accident and each of them seemed truly traumatised, but there was something that didn't sit right with her, an asymmetry.

'Is there anything else you think I need to know?'

'That's everything,' Sam said, nodding his head.

Brookes closed her notebook and Sam sat back in his chair, audibly exhaling.

'Oh, just one more thing,' she said. 'How did the glass get broken?'

'The glass?'

'Yes, there's broken glass on the living room floor.'

'Is there?'

Brookes pressed her lips together, waiting on his answer.

'I don't know. I mean, we were in a panic, one of us could have knocked something over. Maybe Clare ... I don't know what happened to the glass.'

Brookes nodded. It seemed conceivable. 'Thank you.'

Just then there was a loud thud, a pounding on the main door. Sam leapt to his feet. 'Lorraine.'

'The mother?' Brookes asked, standing.

'The mother.'

14

LORRAINE

August 2019

Lorraine was stacking the dishwasher when she heard the doorbell ring. She and Ella had eaten at six sharp – spaghetti bolognaise that had been batch-frozen for midweek dinners. She finished early on a Friday and Ella got home from college at about the same time.

Through the spyhole, Lorraine saw a woman wearing a black jacket but her face was hidden from view. Dusting her hands on her work trousers, Lorraine opened the door.

It was Detective Inspector Brookes. Years since they had met face-to-face, but Lorraine thought she had barely changed.

Smiling, the detective stepped inside. 'I was just in the neighbourhood and I thought I'd drop by instead of calling,' she said, smiling.

'Thank you. Come in. It's so nice to see you again.' Lorraine's chest swelled with emotion. She was full of gratitude for this woman, who had led the investigation into Theo's death and now seemed keen to help her again, but seeing Brookes also took Lorraine right back to the time when Theo died.

'Good to see you too. You look well.'

As she shook her head to deflect the compliment, Lorraine noticed that the detective's hair seemed darker than she remembered. Her face was the same: open, warm, no make-up, only slightly wearier.

'Would you like a cup of tea?'

'Only if you're making one.'

In the kitchen, Lorraine hurriedly cleared away the rest of the mess from dinner. She put a pot to soak in the sink before she filled the kettle. Detective Brookes had not followed her, but was hovering outside the living room where Ella was sitting with a laptop, watching videos.

Lorraine set up a tray to take through – mugs, milk and sugar – but then thought twice. Whatever Brookes had come to discuss, Lorraine didn't want to talk about it in front of Ella.

'Do you remember Detective Inspector Brookes?' Lorraine said, stepping into the hall, wiping her hands on a tea towel.

'Is it Ella?' Brookes smiled, and took her hand out of her pocket. 'You were only about that height when I saw you last.'

'Stand up, love, show the detective how tall you are now.'

Shy, Ella shook her head, laughing.

'She's taller than me. Nearly six foot,' said Lorraine.

'I'm envious.'

'She's studying to be a midwife; aren't you, love?'

'That's interesting,' said Brookes. 'What made you want to do that?'

'Well—' Ella's head fell to one side '—I guess I'm quite good at sciences – biology, anyway – and then, I heard about it and I thought I would like it. I want to have children one day and I want to help other people have theirs. I think it's even more hands-on than normal nursing . . . I guess . . . '

'Impressive.' Brookes nodded, slipping her hands into her pockets.

'I've made the tea,' said Lorraine, suddenly feeling awkward. 'Do you want to sit in the kitchen?'

'Sure.'

At the kitchen table, Brookes cupped her hands around the mug of tea.

'I just wanted to update you on developments.' The pale skin on Brookes' forehead wrinkled. 'After I got your letter, I sent away some of the physical evidence from the trial – Theo's clothing and bedclothes – to forensics, to see if anything new could be found.' Her eyes cast down towards the pottery sugar bowl with its blue stripes. 'Since the trial, they've developed a new DNA profiling technique. It's much more sensitive and we can get results from very degraded samples and from DNA deposited by the slightest touch. I don't have the report yet, but if it comes back with something substantial – something that can be deemed to be new evidence – I will take it to the procurator fiscal and ask about a retrial.'

Lorraine suddenly felt nervous and drew a breath in, feeling the backs of her arms goose pimple. 'DNA . . . ' She frowned, rubbing her arms as if suddenly chilled. 'I suppose I just thought Clare had more or less confessed in the letter and again when I saw her. Can't you just go and speak to Clare again? Arrest her again – see if she's changed her story?'

'Procedurally, no; we can't speak to Clare again – or Sam for that matter. If this is to go to trial, it'll mean an application to the judge to approve it under the Double Jeopardy Scotland Act.'

'Double jeopardy, yes,' Lorraine whispered. 'You told me about that on the phone.' The kitchen door was ajar and she was aware that the tinny noise of Ella's YouTube videos had stopped. She still hadn't spoken to Ella about her contact with Clare and hoped that she wasn't listening.

'I want a new trial,' Lorraine said slowly. 'I want it to be clear that there was a miscarriage of justice before. My son's dead and she's still walking around . . .' Lorraine pressed her lips together and closed her eyes as she struggled to compose herself.

Brookes kept talking, but Lorraine didn't open her eyes, frightened that she would cry. 'For my part, I want to see this through. You don't need to do anything. I'll let you know when I get the forensic report and then we go through the next steps.'

Lorraine felt Brookes' smooth, cool hand slip over hers and opened her eyes.

'Thank you.'

Brookes pushed her mug away gently and stood. Lorraine smiled, hands on her hips as they went out into the hall. Ella got up from the couch to say goodbye.

'My goodness, you *are* tall,' Brookes said, leaving. 'You're like a model.'

When the door closed, Ella said, 'I remember her.'

Lorraine smiled sadly, tidying up the shoes that were scattered by the door, as if the activity would release the yawning pain of loss that she felt, deep down in the marrow of her bones.

'I remember she interviewed me, back then. I remember it was at the police station and you were sitting outside.'

'That's right.' Lorraine put a hand on her daughter's cheeks and then pulled her into her arms. She loved her so much. She was so precious. She had always felt like that, but somehow, after Theo's death, Lorraine had felt a stronger need to protect Ella, who had always turned all of the sadness in on herself. Lorraine still remembered finding a scalpel slid like a bookmark into the pages of her daughter's teenage diary – the blade she had used to cut herself. It had taken all of Lorraine's strength as a mother to get her daughter through that period. For a sister to lose a brother was just as hard as a mother losing a son. It was still losing a piece of self.

'Why was she here?' Ella said as Lorraine released her.

'Detective Brookes? I think she was just in the area. I called her for an update recently. She was just dropping in . . . kind of her . . .'

'An update? You mean about Theo? After all this time?'

'Well—' Lorraine rubbed her hands together, as if to muster an answer. She felt a responsibility to protect Ella from this news until it was time. 'I think the police always have cases that they review from time to time, that's all.'

That seemed to satisfy Ella and she turned back to the living room.

'I'll clean up and be right with you,' Lorraine said, feeling tension running up the tendons in her neck, towards the base of her skull. She would tell Ella what was going on if the retrial went ahead.

In any case Lorraine didn't have the strength to speak about it now. The chance of Theo's case being reopened filled her with hope, but it also revealed another level of loss. It meant going to that place in her mind that she tried to avoid.

She began to wash the dishes, as memories came to her unwanted. As she scoured the bolognaise sauce from the pot in the sink, she watched the dishwater redden. She scrubbed harder and harder, as if to erase the image of Theo from her mind.

The taxi stopped outside Edinburgh City Mortuary and Lorraine and her mother got out of the car. They held hands as they walked towards the tired 1960s building. It was a damp, cold day and the rain was light but coming in blasts. Lorraine felt it spray against her face, hard as sand, but did nothing to shield herself from it. Her mother wore a hat and walked with her head down.

Inside they saw the reception desk and walked towards it, their shoes making no sound on the grey linoleum.

Her mother's fingers in hers felt cold and clammy in her hand, and Lorraine swallowed. The place smelled airless and therefore stale, overlaid with the waxy sweetness of floor cleaner.

At the desk, Lorraine opened her mouth to say Theo's name but for a moment it stuck in her throat and tears pricked her eyes.

'Theo Collins.'

The receptionist was older, in her fifties. She wore a white coat over a cream polo neck. 'Your names and relation to the deceased?'

Lorraine cleared her throat loudly. 'Mother and ... grandmother.'

'Please sit and wait a few moments.'

They sat side by side on the plastic seats, not speaking. The place had a hospital-like stifling warmth and Lorraine felt sweat prickle at her hairline.

She was trying to think of other things, to lift herself out from her physical surroundings. Sometimes, when she was at the dentist having her teeth scaled or drilled, she would try that – focus on the stark light above and imagine herself rising up and out of her body, unable to feel the pain.

Now Lorraine searched for something to distract her from the fact that she was going to see her baby son. She and her mother had to identify the body, and then there would be a post-mortem, to find out why Theo had stopped breathing.

In the kaleidoscope of her memories, she remembered when Ella was small, only two or three years old. They were sitting out in the communal flat garden having lunch, eating tuna sandwiches.

It was quiet, only the distant sound of the traffic on Leith Walk – a low growl – like white noise in the background. The day was hot and humid, the roses along the wall had gone to bracken and were a tangle of thorny stems and blowsy heads.

Suddenly there was dull thud and Lorraine turned quickly to see – a bird, it was no more than a fledgling, and a coal tit at that – a tiny, tiny bird, had flown straight into their kitchen window and was now stunned on the hot slab, one wing out – broken? – and flat on its claws so that they reached out before him, seeming too big for him, like a clown's feet.

Lorraine took Ella's hand and they drew closer. The bird's black eye watched them, feathered breast heaving. Lorraine imagined the tiny heart, small as a pine nut, rapidly pulsing inside.

'Is it okay?' said Ella. 'Is it hurt?'

'I don't know, maybe.'

'It's sitting on its bum.'

'I think it's shocked.'

Lorraine was sure the wing was broken but after a moment the tit folded it back towards its body.

'Let's leave it in peace and not frighten it.'

'But we'll stay close,' said Ella, 'in case someone else hurts it.'

A magpie. A cat. She was right – it was vulnerable.

'It could get trodden.'

They moved their blanket nearer the bird, but just as Lorraine turned back to their sandwiches – thinking of tossing it a crumb – it flew, in a sudden whirr of recovery, to the Rowan tree next door.

Lorraine remembered Ella's delight – she got up and danced on the lawn, waving goodbye to the coal tit.

The little bird was absolutely fine. Newtonian mechanics. Lesser mass and so a lesser momentum – smaller things survive impacts better. It had been like a resurrection.

'Mrs Collins?'

Ella and her mother startled. They were both Collins, but only her mother was a 'Mrs' as Lorraine had never married.

Nevertheless, she knew that the 'Mrs Collins' the receptionist referred to, was her.

'We're ready for you now.'

Lorraine stood, the muscles in her legs trembling. She tried to remember the groan of the traffic, the moisture on the roses and the way the stems lifted in the breeze. She thought about the little bird, sitting on its behind with its heart beating so hard that she could see the pulse of the soft feathers on its chest.

The room was stark: metal and white tile. A man in a white coat was standing with two hands wide open before a metal table. Lorraine didn't look at him, or the table. She looked up at the too-bright strip lights that ran along the ceiling. She felt her mother's cold fingers slip into hers.

The attendant in the white coat pulled back the sheet. Lorraine wasn't watching but she felt the breeze of the action against her face. She looked down – yellow spots in her eyes from staring at the lights.

Theo was so small, tiny on the metal table and so cold and exposed.

'Oh, darling,' Rita said at once, 'my wee darlin'.'

Lorraine saw him clearly and then he blurred as her eyes filled with tears. She put a hand on his head, cupping his skull as she had done so many times when he slept. His skin was so smooth, like the skin of a mushroom.

Lorraine bent to kiss him and her tears fell on Theo's face. They splashed onto his closed lids that had a hue of blue, as if his own bright-blue eyes were shining through the skin. Thumb trembling, Lorraine wiped her tears from his face.

'You confirm that this is Theo Collins, your son, your grandson?'

'It is,' said Rita, putting an arm around Lorraine's waist.

Lorraine saw what was before her and spoke. 'My son,' she said. She bent to kiss his small, cold lips.

Like the coal tit hitting the window and just sitting in the middle of the concrete path, vulnerable now to everything, Lorraine stared at Theo, breaths tugging in and out of her chest, just waiting for him to surprise her, to sit up and reach out to her with his cool, damp, chubby hands. *Mummy*, with that smile that dimpled his right cheek.

They left the room and Lorraine tried to think again about the little bird getting up and flying to the tree and sitting there looking down on them, unharmed after all. It no longer brought her any comfort.

15

CLARE

November 2008

Through her hangover, she watched him frantically stuffing things into boxes and bags. She had woken up to find him in the bedroom, pulling drawers open with such force that they crashed onto the floor.

She was face down on the bed and still in her clothes. He had not slept or even lain with her. She had been awake all night, her mind bright and sparking and yet confused, a scattering of broken glass. She wasn't sure when she had gone to bed.

The wardrobe door slammed shut and Clare sat up in bed.

When she opened her mouth to speak to him, her tongue peeled from the roof of her mouth.

'What are you doing?'

'I'm leaving.'

'Where are you going?'

Sitting up, the pain in her head was debilitating, as if she had a knitting needle stuck in her crown.

'I'm leaving you.'

The words were awful. She lay back down, rolled onto her side and pushed her face into his pillow, his side of the bed. The smell of him there was delicious, but it did not comfort her.

She tried to remember what had happened last night. There had been an ambulance, paramedics, and then the female detective. Clare remembered giving a witness statement although she had been so drunk she had no idea what she had said. Lorraine and her mother had arrived and Clare had no idea what had been said then, but she thought she remembered standing in the living room holding Lorraine, knowing there was no way to console her. Lorraine and her mother had taken Ella and then she and Sam had been all on their own. He wouldn't even look at her, and so Clare had had even more to drink.

The latter part of the night was available to her, as a blur of images, but the first part – the important part – the part where Theo died – was out of reach.

She heard Sam's footsteps leaving the room, the creak of the floorboards in the hall under his weight. Clare rolled onto her back, feeling a lurch of nausea.

Her brain, two dehydrated hemispheres, struggled to comprehend what was happening. Theo had died and Sam, her partner of nearly twenty years, was now leaving her.

She chose the most immediate problem and put her feet on the floor, before carefully standing. Her bare feet found the warm rug by the side of the bed. Spots of light encroached her eyes as she made her way out of the bedroom, looking for Sam.

He had stacked his belongings at the top of the stairs. It was clear that he had been at it for some time. All night? While she had been lying down, stuporous, he had been carefully packing. That thought cleaved her.

She wavered at the threshold of the hall, watching him stack boxes and cases at the top of the stairs and then go into the spare bedroom where the children had slept.

Blinking, Clare tried to swallow. Her throat was sore. She wanted to brush her teeth. The floorboards smooth against her bare feet, she walked to the door of the children's room, dared to look in.

Theo's cot and Ella's bed were as they had been. Ella's fairy duvet cover was still turned down.

The cot with its white bars. The animal mobile above it, no longer turning. They had bought it just for Theo coming, hoping it would help him sleep, as it lit up and played a tune.

The room seemed contaminated, wrong. The paramedics had cleared a space on the floor, tossing the sheepskin rug aside so that they could work on Theo. The rug was still curled at the edge of the room, and so the space on the floor exaggerated the absence.

Clare watched as Sam opened the white wardrobes along the back wall of the children's bedroom. He used the storage in this room for all his sports gear. Inside the cupboards were rails of cycling jackets, helmets and cycling shoes, gloves, watches, lights and reflectors. The boxing gear was here too: lace-up boots and padded gloves.

Sam took equipment from the cupboards and tossed it into a crate and a box in the centre of the floor. Sweat dampened the under arms of his T-shirt as he worked. He ripped electronic equipment right out of the socket. At first she thought it was his phone charging, but then she realised it was his Go-Pro camera and his bicycle lights. The cords whipped in the air as he threw them towards the box and then forced them inside. He picked up the box – his red and black cycle helmet balanced on top – and pushed past her.

Her headache began to differentiate; she felt a throb behind her right eyebrow.

At the top of the stairs, he put the box down, and rested both hands on her shoulders. Leaning on her, he bent down to look her in the eye.

Clare blinked. Her eyes felt hot. She felt self-conscious suddenly, with him so close to her. She just wanted him to hold her, to say that he hadn't meant what he'd said, about leaving.

'I will always stand by you. You know that. But I—' his eyes filled with tears '—I just can't be around you. I . . .'

Even through her hangover, Clare couldn't bear to see him upset. She reached up to touch his cheek, but he pulled away from her.

'It's just . . . such an awful thing.' He covered his eyes with one hand for a minute. 'That precious little boy. I can't believe. I can't believe . . .' He sniffed, wiped his face with his hands. His voice was changed, somehow cold. 'I lied to the police.'

'What do you mean?'

'I just . . . can't be here any more.' The expression on his face was strange, conflicted, at once loving and accusing. 'I just can't bear to think—'

'Why did you lie to the police? What happened here?'

She needed a glass of water. Her mouth was so dry it was hard to get words out. There was a look in his eye that made her quake. It was a strange, disbelieving but desperate look, as if, after all these years of seeing the best in her, he now saw the worst. 'Please don't go.'

He looked at his feet.

Clare struggled to swallow. She remembered feeling angry and hurt and wanting to drink. She had wanted to be drunk.

Just the thought of that impulse now made her think she was going to be sick. She put one hand over her mouth, turned towards the bathroom door. Saliva flooded her mouth. By the time she turned back again, Sam wasn't there.

She ran downstairs after him, the stone stairs cold on her bare feet. She watched him load all his things into the van. She shuddered with cold in the doorway. The sun was trying to come out and the white sky hurt her eyes. She waited for something more from him, a kiss, some words of comfort, news of when he would be back – but when the last box was loaded up, he got into the van and drove away, without even a wave or a final glance in her direction.

Shattered, Clare sat on the bottom step, looking out into the cobbled courtyard.

Part Two

The Punch

Part Two

16

SAM

August 2019

Princes Street was a glassy mile of wet pavement. Taxis and buses worked their way along it, windscreen wipers waving. The park and the trees that lined it were verdant, leaves heavy with rain. Sam sipped his coffee as he scanned the scene. He had a good view from here, second floor looking onto Princes Street Gardens. The castle, darkened by rain, rose above its black crag as if shrugging indifference. The coffee was bitter and the coffee shop was warm and noisy, and so he leaned closer to the window.

Near the gothic spire of the Scott Monument, Sam watched a father with a little girl. They were hand in hand. The little girl was wearing bright-red wellington boots and she was deliberately sliding on the wet pavement and the father was yanking her arm just before she fell, often lifting her right off her feet. Then she found a puddle and jumped into it, splashing, still holding her father's hand. Sam was too far away to see their faces but the way the little girl moved, with acrobatic abandon, was extraordinarily lovely.

Sam smiled, then swallowed, a knot in his throat.

The man seemed so ordinary, casual jacket and jeans, neither old nor young, yet Sam envied him for grasping that tiny hand. So simple, so mundane, but it was all that Sam had ever wanted: to hold a little hand in his, to be the protector.

The drenched summer scene outside and the air-conditioned, furred noise of the coffee shop made Sam feel between worlds. He drained his cup, picked up his jacket and briefcase, and headed out into the throng.

It was festival time, so Sam hunched his shoulders as he navigated the crowd. He hated the festival, not because of the art but because of the annual possession of his town by millions of incomers.

It was only a few blocks from here to *home*, although he was not headed home, but to his flat in Leith. He still thought of the house at the other end of Princes Street – where he had lived with Clare for more than fifteen years – as home. It was so close. Turning to look over his shoulder, he could almost pick it out from the uniform blocks of New Town sandstone townhouses in the distance.

He and Clare were occasionally in touch now, but he hadn't been back inside that house since the day he left it – a fluster of cardboard boxes crammed with random objects that were the sum of his life with her. It seemed absurd, that those belongings were what he had wanted to salvage from the disastrous end of his one great love. He should have walked away with nothing. He had felt stripped bare and so it would have been appropriate.

Part of him wanted to check on the place again – open the fridge to make sure that Clare was eating right. (Left to her own devices she would eat cheese sandwiches every night for dinner.) Maybe he would clean out the grate or do another of those tasks that had been his, and his alone – let her know he was still there and thinking of her. He still had his key, after all – Clare had never asked for it back and he doubted she would have changed the locks.

Either way, Sam knew it would be too painful standing on the threshold of his old life, knowing he couldn't walk back into it. He turned and trudged in the opposite direction, down Leith Walk, towards The Shore, his flat and his office. Over ten years had passed since he'd left Clare – yet it didn't seem that long. Thinking about it, as he often did, he no longer considered that he had *left* Clare. They had split apart like atoms, compelled by forces beyond them.

Again, he felt between two worlds. One home and another, one image of himself and another. He was used to being an outsider – had been outside looking in since he was a boy. He was that rare thing: an architect from a working-class background. Just walking around each day, he existed between two worlds. After passing only two Highers in Technical Drawing and Art, he had enrolled at Telford College to do a Computer Aided Design Course. He became a technician in an architect's office in South Edinburgh and then went on to study architecture part-time. After he'd qualified, he was hired by one of the top architect firms in Scotland – Maitland McConnell – with the best studio space in Edinburgh: a twenty-first century conversion of an historic building in Leith.

His business card had read simply, *Sam Armstrong, Architect*. When he passed it over the table to clients, they didn't see what had gone before. They didn't see the teenager he had been, with his spray paint and stencils, tagging the pockmarked concrete of Pilton. His colleagues were all graduates from top art schools, but he had still led on projects. Even though success wasn't everything, before Theo, and before the punch, Sam had been very successful.

The rain had been incessant this summer, and the pavement was dark and wet as he walked downhill. It was a fair walk from here to The Shore and he missed his bike. Sometimes he would take the bus, jump on the number ten if it passed, but tonight he was in no rush. He walked, lost in his thoughts, not seeing the blond sandstone tenements or grocery stores, unaware of pubs wafting warmth and cheer out onto the pavements.

He didn't cycle at all these days. His dark leather Converse splashing into the puddles, Sam was almost unaware that it was right here – *right here* – at the junction of Albert Street, where it had happened, on a dark November morning in 2008: The Punch.

It had exploded out of him. He had felt such release.

As he walked past the spot where it had happened, he remembered it casually, a memory snagging.

Right foot, left foot, right foot.

Just this spot, this unimpressive, uneven patch of tarmac.

Right here Sam's anger had exploded out of him, because Theo was dead and he had just left his wife. It was the junction of Albert Street and Leith Walk – coincidentally not far from Lorraine's flat – the spot where everything he had been keeping tight inside of him burst out. The private made public. He hadn't realised it at the time, but it had changed the course of everything that had happened.

On his bicycle, Sam navigated the roundabout by London Road, feeling the heat emanating from the flank of a double decker to his right before he headed down Leith Walk. It was after eight in the morning, but the sun was still tentative and wary on the edge of the horizon.

Morning rush hour and he was headed to work, after spending the night in his mother's house, in the box room where he had slept as a child.

The white light on his handlebars sent a cool strobe finger out into the morning darkness. Until he got caught up in traffic, he had been cycling hard. His heart thumped in his chest and his breath clouded in front of him. He wore a hat under his helmet, but he felt the cold on his cheeks and his nose. The oncoming traffic had headlights on full-beam, dazzling him. When Sam blinked, the inside of his eyelids flashed red, as if he was seeing blood.

There had not been any blood. The little one was dead, but there had not been a single drop of blood. As he cycled, the shock of Theo's loss shuddered through him. In the blizzard of their argument, Clare had gone upstairs and then after a while screamed for Sam to help her. He cycled faster as if to escape what had been done.

It felt much better to be on the bike, in motion, digging in – feeling the almost enjoyable toxic strain in his muscles. The piston action of his legs helped him cope with the images that replayed in his mind, projecting unasked for onto the back of his forehead. But he was deep in traffic and unable to go as fast as he would have liked. Cycling helped, but at this speed – creeping forward – it didn't stop him wanting to *hit* something, someone.

He craved a punchbag. Tonight maybe, he would go to the old boxing gym of his youth, over in Pilton. He still sparred there sometimes – that stinky pit where he had gone as a boy because of his need to fight back. Back then, every opponent had taken on his father's form.

Sam dug into the pedals. Now, he didn't know who or what he needed to hit. The desire was strong in him, to fight, to hit back, but it was no longer his father's face he saw. Maybe he wanted to punch himself? He remembered fervently packing, unable to stay in the house any longer, unable to even look at Clare.

A car horn and a skid on the tarmac up ahead, but in Sam's mind it turned into that scream Clare had unleashed when she called him to come upstairs and see Theo – an unnatural sound, low-pitched – the volume of a scream but guttural, like a moan or a cry. Even now, in the heat of his movement, it made the fine hairs stand up on his exposed skin. He blinked rapidly, trying to erase the image of the little boy.

He was wearing trousers tucked into his socks and a sweater underneath his cycling jacket. He hadn't been able to locate his

Lycras, or his winter cycling gloves. The van was parked outside his mother's house, full of boxes that he had taken from home. He would have to rent a flat, he supposed, but he didn't know when he would feel able to begin that process. His packing had been erratic and he found that his cycling gear was spread over several boxes. There were so many pieces of kit that he normally used on his commute that he had been unable to lay his hands on. He had found his cycling shoes and his helmet and that was enough to get him on the road.

He didn't know why he was even going to work. When his father died there had been bereavement leave available that he hadn't taken. Could he take that now? *I need a week off because a child that I loved very much died in my care.*

Blink. Blood curtain. The windowless bedroom the children had shared and its sweet, slightly cloying smell.

Blink. With Clare in the disabled toilet at accident and emergency a week ago. A week ago and it seemed like a year. Holding her hand as she sat there, blue lipped, red smears of blood on her thin thighs.

Blink. Theo's pale lips and his tiny swollen tongue.

The traffic thickened. Sam balanced on two wheels as he stopped and started again, the toxic smell of exhausts irritating him. He wove in and out of the cars but his progress stalled as he neared traffic lights, or cars pulled out from the side of the road.

For a stretch of five or six blocks he got his speed up. The forward momentum helped to ease the images in his mind, as if he was actually leaving them behind. Then the traffic slowed and

Sam felt again the weight of Theo in his hands. He tightened his grip on the handlebars. His pulse throbbed in his temple. A horn honked. A car on the left looked as if it might pull out from the side of the road, but the driver wasn't indicating.

Sam started forward. At the last minute, the car that he had thought wanted to pull out, *did* pull out, cutting in front of Sam, still not indicating. Under his breath, he cursed, shaking his head as he overtook the car from the inside. He didn't think any more of it, only wanting to get his speed up, to escape the roll of pictures in his mind.

The car, a red Rover with rust on the panel, cut in front of him, and the side window went down.

'I saw you shaking your fucking head.'

Sam dug deep into the pedals. Three seconds went by when he was convinced that he would just ignore it. *One, two, three . . .*

'Aye, well, fucking indicate . . . arsehole.' Sam threw the insult and then pedalled hard. The flash of temper gave him a sudden injection of energy.

There was the rev of an engine behind and shouts of abuse probably meant for him, but they were carried backwards, downwind, up towards town – he couldn't hear and he didn't care. The traffic lights were still at green and so Sam stood up and cycled hard to get to them before they changed, but as he approached, the lights turned to amber and then red. There was no cross-over traffic and he could have gone through anyway, but he wasn't that kind of cyclist.

Chest heaving, Sam waited at the lights, hip jutted out to let his right foot find purchase on the road. The lights took a while, pedestrians meandering over, sullen on their way to work, chins down and shoulders rounded.

Again, the red Rover drew up next to Sam.

'Don't think you can call me an arsehole and just ponce off on your stupid tricycle. Try saying that to my face.'

Sam kept his focus on the lights. Even amber would have been enough for him to go through, but the traffic light stared back at him, an angry red eye.

'Not for talking now, huh? Ya pansy. All ballsy in the passing, shaking the heid, but face to face you don't have the guts, eh?'

Amber. Green. Sam thought he might be able to will the lights to change. They stayed red.

The winter air, which had been gratifying on the cycle from town, now seemed polluted, germinating. The exhaust fumes lay low against the tarmac, trapped in the damp air – rank, invisible, toxic.

'Not such a big man now, eh, lanky Lycra prick.'

Not such a big man now, eh?

Sam had heard it before, from his father, who had been a tyrant.

Was it that – the familiar taunt? Was it the last three sleepless nights, the dark anxiety in his gut, his panicked realisation that life as he knew it was over. Theo was dead, he had left Clare and nothing could ever be the same again.

Later, Sam would try to excuse his response, articulate his anger. There had been something primal about it – a trigger. Something that overwhelmed him so that he couldn't pull back from it.

It had been about Theo – his pure anger at being unable to make him *undead*. It had been about Clare and the loss of her; the heartbreak of all their nearly children. The anger had been waiting in him for so long, asking to be unleashed.

One two, *upper cut*, the swing of the punch bag, the stench of the gym.

Humidity, heat, spores airborne and finding purchase.

The lights still at red, Sam got off his bike and leaned it against a parked car at the side of the road. He walked – that strange clip-clop swagger in his cycling shoes – to the driver's side of the Rover, just as the lights turned amber.

'Alright, I'm saying it to your face: "you're a fucking arsehole".'

Green light.

The driver of the Rover didn't seem keen to get out of the car now, but Sam tugged on his sweater as car horns sounded in the queue of traffic behind them. The man got out of the car, but he was holding an ice scraper, with a red handle and an angled black head. He held it up like a weapon. There was a significant height difference between the driver and Sam. The Rover driver was barely taller than the height of his car. He was overweight but it didn't make up the weight difference between them.

The physical properties were loaded against Sam so that he was, on paper, the most likely aggressor, despite the brandished plastic weapon. Sam was a tall, fit, muscled man who weighed nearly fourteen stone and had been a boxer since he was fifteen years old; the driver of the Rover was short with a beer belly and a heart condition.

Sam slapped the ice scraper to the ground and slammed

the driver against his Rover, holding him by the scruff of his sweatshirt.

'Is this in your face enough? Is this what you wanted?' With each word, Sam slammed the man against the car.

Just that would have been enough to quell the argument, but it was no longer about that to Sam. There was a need for violence in him, a hunger to hit something in order to lance his rage and his hurt.

Car horns sounded, and Sam was aware of them, despite the alarm of nerves and cortisol that flushed and throbbed in his body. The small man did not seem threatened.

'You think you own the road, but you don't. Go fuck yourself.'

Sam hit him. It felt good . . . a bite of relief.

He hit him again, at least twice. Maybe three times.

The adrenalin rushed in his veins – the rage rising up and releasing from him, like loaded spores. He wasn't aware of who he was hitting and why, but it felt so good.

Sam didn't even feel the impact of his fist on the man's face.

It was the blood that stopped him – on his hands – and the dark spatter on his blue and white cycling jacket. The curtain of blood he had been seeing since he set out that morning was now real before him, fresh and wet as the sun began to rise and shine through a flat grey sky.

Green light.

The sound of cars honking their horns was suddenly overlaid by the wail of sirens. Sam stood, chest heaving. His hands were bright red, theatrically so. The Rover driver slid down the side of the car and then onto the road, still conscious but spitting blood, moaning. Sam stood back, red knuckles hanging by his side.

Some drivers were sly and managed to sneak around them when the lights changed. Most cars were backed up for two blocks on Leith Walk, as drivers tried to do U-turns or got out of their cars to watch. One woman got out of her car and ran to the Rover driver. She took off her jacket and put it under his head – felt for a pulse, began to talk to him, holding up three fingers.

Sam stood alone, bloodied, staggering, like a gladiator. The cars began to crawl past. He felt the stares, saw his bike had fallen over onto the road, abandoned, wheel spinning. He hung his head, the perspiration cold on his skin. He wiped his mouth with the back of his forearm, unaware that he had smeared the man's blood over his face.

The siren drew closer and Sam saw that it was the police.

The punch. He hadn't felt it that day, but all these years later, Sam still felt the impact. He had regretted it instantly, while the blood was still drying on his hands, but it had been months later before the consequence of his actions became clear. The day he had punched the Rover driver, the police still thought Theo's death was an accident. When he dragged the small man from his car, Sam already felt as if he had lost everything, but after punching the man, Sam lost more.

Late afternoon but already the moon was visible, thin and diaphanous in the early autumn sky. As he approached his flat, he looked up at the sky and thought he could see two moons: the real one and then another, reflected in the illuminated clouds. A second moon was like a second chance, another slice of time. It was like one of Clare's old photographs, the exposed paper rocking in the developer, coaxing a picture, the eye of another witness at another time and place.

Time was not constant, Sam thought. It was a dimension.

Light particles could be in two places at the same time.

Physics was no comfort to him now. It helped him design buildings but it didn't help him understand why every day he woke up remembering the precise weight of the child in his hands. He scanned his key fob and entered his building and then began to climb the stairs. The carpeted stairwells were stained.

He had lived in this flat since the year of Theo's murder trial. An uninspired contemporary block, it was his office now as well as where he lived. His old firm, Maitland McConnell, had terminated his employment after he was brought before a professional conduct committee and punished with a suspension order that stopped him practising for nearly two years. When his suspension was over, Sam had gone into private practice – Sam Armstrong, Spiral Architects. He was still trying to rebuild his name.

Every day he woke up hands out, as if still holding Theo – one hand under his shoulders another under his bottom. Taking him down. Placing him on the floor.

Every morning he woke with palms turned upwards, as if asking for grace.

As his muscles felt the strain of the climb on the stairs to his flat, he felt a strange disconnection. His body was going up but his mind was spooling backwards. He was like a man with his head on back to front, going forward but always looking behind, trying to understand what had happened – to piece it together so that it made some kind of sense.

Sam's phone vibrated in his jacket pocket. He unlocked the door to his flat and shouldered it closed behind him before he answered it.

'Well, this is a surprise,' he said. 'How are you?'

It was Clare. Clare. *Clare*. He had felt so down just then, remembering, but at once she cheered him. 'I was just thinking about you.'

'Really? I was thinking about you too. Obviously.'

Somewhere deep inside of him cleaved. He could construct a thousand memories around the sound of her voice. He had last seen her a year ago, or maybe two. He still felt close to her, as if some part of them had stayed together. After the tragedy, they hadn't spoken for a year or so, and then they had gravitated to each other again, tried to navigate a friendship but it had been too difficult.

'This'll sound out of the blue, but I didn't know if you wanted to get a coffee this week?'

'Sure. Coffee would be great.'

Sam put his keys and the change from his pocket in a dish on a table by the door. Still holding the phone, he shook off his jacket. She must have some news, he thought. A thought darkened the cheer he had felt when he took her call. Over a decade and they were still not divorced. He wondered if she wanted that now.

'It's just I've got some down time at the moment, so I thought . . .'

'Well, great. It would be good to see you. Any news?'

As he waited for her to answer, Sam looked at himself in the mirror by the door. He raked his grey hair, which was longer now, brushing his collar.

She sighed. Sam was suddenly aware that all was not well with her. All these years but his body still felt conditioned to react to her emotions, or how he perceived those emotions. He had seen a flyer a few weeks ago, for her art exhibition.

Clare Richardson: Unearthed.

She had always dreamed of having a solo exhibition, and he had swelled with pride for her. Now he heard the resignation in her voice and felt deflated.

'Everything alright?'

'It's . . . well, I guess that's why I wanted to meet. Something . . .'

Sam bit his lip.

'We could have lunch if you want, any day next week?'

Lunch. Lunch was safe. Lunch was friendly. He was sure he hadn't seen her in the evening since he had lived with her – *since that evening* – the night that Theo died.

'Sure, Wednesday?'

They made arrangements, putting each other on speakerphone so that they could check their calendars; opening restaurant websites to book a table.

'Clare, are you alright?' Sam pressed again.

She was silent.

'Hello, are you still there?'

'I'm still here. I'm okay. It's why I wanted to see you. I suppose it's not worth dragging out. I've got breast cancer. I've just had surgery. I . . . '

'Oh, God, Clare, are you . . . do you need me to do anything?'

'I'm fine. I'm on the pills. Thank you. I'm sorted. I had a lump taken out. I still have my breasts, at the moment anyway. Don't worry. I see the consultant in a month or two. She's left me to get on with it. I feel alright, actually.'

'But, are you having chemo? Do you need me to take you anywhere?'

'Thank you. You're so lovely. There's no chemo right now. I caught it early, I hope. I don't know, I just . . . I wanted you to know.'

He was aware of his heart beating harder, as if he was still climbing the stairs. He couldn't countenance anything happening to her, even after all this time and despite the fact that he saw her so rarely. Clare had to be alright. Even if she had met someone and wanted a divorce, that would be fine, but he didn't want anything to happen to her.

'There was something else too. I mean, I'll go into it when I see you, but . . . '

He heard her intake breath and he waited. He remembered holding her hand at countless ultrasound appointments – the way she would gasp when the cool ultrasound prod touched her bare belly.

'Well, I did a stupid thing and I wrote to Lorraine.'

Lorraine.

'You . . . wrote to Lorraine?'

'I don't want to talk about it now. I can tell you at lunch.'

'I know but . . . what . . . why?' He stood in the hall, hunched, one hand over his mouth.

'It was a mistake. I don't know if you saw, but I had an exhibition in Newhaven.'

'I saw, I was . . . '

'You saw? I wondered if . . . '

'I was going to come, but I had a work thing.' That was a lie. He saw the advert and had felt proud of her, but he never had any intention of going. That would have been his old life. He would have felt between worlds again, looking in on what could have been.

'Anyway, after I wrote to her, Lorraine turned up at the gallery and she was very angry. I'm not sure, but I have this horrible feeling that she's gone to the police.'

'Jesus, Clare. Forward me what you wrote to her.'

'I can't. I wrote her a letter. I sat down in what used to be our house and I wrote her an actual letter.'

Our house. Sam felt a complicated flush of emotion at the words.

'God. Well, maybe we should meet tomorrow then. I don't know if I can wait until Wednesday.'

She laughed, and it raised his spirits. He walked into his main room – a combined kitchen and living room – so that he could look out of the window onto the Water of Leith.

There was an alcove off the living room, which Sam felt sure had been meant for a table in the architect's design. He had filled the space with boxes. All the boxes he had taken from *our house* were still stacked there, unopened most of them, even after all this time.

He knew lifestyle gurus would advise he throw them all out, since they had been untouched for years, but dealing with the boxes in any way depressed him. Whenever he attempted to sort them out, he became instantly dispirited and gave up.

'Monday then?'

They checked their diaries. Lunch was rearranged.

'It's a date,' Sam said.

He hung up. He didn't know why, but he felt a strange sense of foreboding. He glanced at the wall of cardboard. It reproached him. He had a sense that his old life was enclosed in those boxes and until he unpacked them, he would never be able to move on.

17

DETECTIVE INSPECTOR PAMELA BROOKES

November 2008

Brookes parked in the heart of the Cowgate, in Edinburgh's Old Town. As she got out of the car, she took a deep breath, glancing through the side window at Edinburgh City Mortuary. The soot-blackened Victorian sandstone of the building seemed apt, but Brookes was headed to the crude 1950s annexe at the back, where most of the serious business took place.

Today was dry but cold, and Brookes flipped up the collar of her jacket as she waited to cross the road. She braced herself, not just against the weather, but for what she would see when she went inside.

She was here to attend Theo Collins' post-mortem.

Brookes had met the lead pathologist, Brendan McKay, on countless occasions, but she was no closer to understanding who he was outside of his vocation. More than any pathologist she had known before, McKay seemed to fully inhabit the role. He was a tall, thin, clean-shaven man with clipped speech and a passionless intensity presumably cultivated over years spent in the isolated study of corpses. His limbs moved in an almost mechanical way that reminded her of insects.

She found him in the theatre, pulling on a pair of latex gloves. The theatre lights reflected off the lenses of his small glasses so Brookes couldn't see his eyes.

'Afternoon, detective,' Brendan McKay said. 'Here we are again.'

'Yup.' As the senior investigating officer, she attended every post-mortem when there was an unexplained death. Brookes had never been squeamish – the only girl in a family of five boys, she had seen a variety of grisly injuries up close long before she joined the police force, but she knew today would be hard. Brookes had steeled herself for this moment, yet was surprised about how uncomfortable she felt. She had never attended a post-mortem of a child so young.

The mortuary was clean and metallic, a vague smell of astringent preservative in the air, and crowded with the usual suspects: a second pathologist, technicians, forensics and a photographer, although McKay was the only one that Brookes knew.

Theo Collins' small body was lying on the metal table that had been sized for adults. Brookes swallowed, her saliva acidic. She frowned as she looked at the little boy. He was still dressed in his panda suit and it was very difficult to stay objective. The skin of his face and hands was now a bluish grey. So much of her job was compartmentalising moments like this – so that she could remain professional, detached. As she looked at Theo, she couldn't help but think of her son, Jack.

Breathing through her teeth, she put on a blue, polythene apron. The action calmed her – a task.

Theo's eyelids had been closed when she saw him last, but now one lid was slightly open, showing a crescent of blue iris beneath.

Again, she thought of Jack asleep, eyes closed but rolling under the blue-veined lids, watching a dream, savouring a scene again that he had experienced for the first time today. A smile teasing that precious face. A good dream. The lips closing and opening, tasting something and smiling again. The wonder of that living, breathing, dreaming child. Even asleep, she could watch him for hours.

Theo was not asleep and would no longer dream. As she waited for the examination proper to begin, Brookes rubbed one hand over the other.

'Sudden Unexplained Death in Infancy,' McKay said, his voice clipped, 'What we used to call cot death and still largely unexplained.'

The photographer took shots of the body as forensics carefully cut the panda suit and nappy from Theo, leaving him exposed. Brookes had a strange instinct to cover Theo, as if he might be cold.

The photographer, a petite young woman who worked with silent intensity took several pictures of Theo's chin and neck and then, when the body was turned, photographed the other side. Brookes was used to watching the cumbersome shifting of corpses on the post-mortem table and sometimes she would be asked to help. The ease with which McKay flipped little Theo cleaved her.

'Contusions are clearly evident on the body, particularly on the neck but also on the upper arms and backs of the arms. Bruising on the arms is consistent with fingermarks,' McKay said, to no one in particular.

Brookes blinked as the camera flashed again and again.

She put her hands in her pockets, knowing the first cut would come soon and she braced herself for it, as if she would feel it on her own skin.

McKay spoke into a recorder, describing Theo's body in detail. He picked up his scalpel.

Brookes pushed back her shoulders. The scalpel paused over Theo's small chest. 'Are you alright, detective inspector?' He glanced over his spectacles at her.

Brookes cleared her throat and said, *yes*, but she felt herself tremble as McKay made the Y-shaped incision then cut open Theo's chest to expose his organs. Brookes felt an inexplicable urge to protect the little boy.

When Theo had been roughly stitched, McKay removed his gloves and turned to Brookes.

'Death *was* sudden for this infant, but it is no longer unexplained. It is clear that the child was asphyxiated: blood in the lungs, which indicates suffocation, and retinal haemorrhaging.'

Brookes nodded, the trauma of what she had seen now replaced by an urge to understand. 'Yes, the paramedics had flagged the haemorrhaging, but the couple who were looking after the child said they found him unresponsive in his cot. What's the likelihood that he accidently asphyxiated or was suffocated by his clothing or bedding?'

McKay's head turned slightly as Brookes spoke. He looked at her, yet did not meet her eye. 'It is clear that asphyxiation occurred as a result of constriction of the neck, probably by ligature. The bruising around the neck and the angle of contusion shows where pressure was applied . . .' Very faintly, McKay licked his lips. 'It is highly unlikely that this pressure could have happened accidentally by blankets or clothing or whatever.'

'So . . . you think deliberate strangulation?' Brookes clarified as she gathered her thoughts – comparing what had been known on the night Theo died with the information now.

'Yes, asphyxia due to strangulation with a ligature.'

'And is there any indication what kind of ligature was used?'

McKay's long forehead wrinkled. 'The skin samples might provide some information, but I am going to conclude that this was not an accidental death.'

'What about the bruising on the arms and body?'

'The bruises on the arms and upper body are older. The colouring is distinct, so I would place them a few days to a week before death. But the contusion on the neck is consistent with strangulation and the time of death.'

Brookes nodded. 'Okay. So just to make sure I have this right – it's murder. Theo was strangled with a ligature, and the bruising on his body was inflicted some days before his death.'

'Sharp as ever, detective.' With a snap, McKay removed his surgical gloves.

Outside, the rain had started and Brookes walked head down back to her car. Inside she put the key in the ignition but did not start the car. She pulled her notebook from her bag and glanced over Sam and Clare's witness statements. Both Sam and Clare had said that Theo had been found unconscious in his cot.

Brookes started the car. She was shivering – not cold but nervously recycling energy from attending the post-mortem. It was clear to her now that either Clare or Sam – or both of them – were lying, and if they had lied about *how* they'd found Theo, it meant that one of them, or both, had been responsible for his death.

She would be late home to her husband and baby son. She took out her phone ready to call Scenes of Crime officers and the forensics team. She would need them to go into Sam and Clare's Haymarket flat today and then Brookes wanted to interview them formally at the station.

Back at the station, Brookes saw that Sergeant Hendry was at his desk.

'Scenes of Crime are inside the West End house,' Hendry said, his pale eyebrows raising. 'Clare was at home, but it seems that the husband has left.'

'Left . . . what do you mean?'

'They've separated, apparently. The husband has officially moved out.'

'Interesting timing.' Brookes sank heavily into a swivel chair next to Rory's desk.

'How did they seem to you?' Rory asked, resting an ankle on his knee. He had a blue biro tucked behind his ear. 'When you first took their statements?'

'Odd ... now that I know he's moved out, it makes more sense. They were strange, even given the fact that the child they were looking after had just died. They were both clearly in shock but—' Brookes leaned back in her chair, hands clasped as she shared her thoughts '—I believed them at the time, though something still didn't sit right with me.'

'So who do you think did it?' Rory asked. There was a small framed photograph on his desk, of his partner and their three-year-old daughter.

Brookes began to bite her thumbnail, distracted, almost forgetting that Rory was there. 'I don't understand why *either of them* would hurt that little boy. I mean, she was drunk but they're both professional people with no criminal records and they only had the child for one night. It's not like either of them had a history of violence and were driven crazy with a baby crying night after night.'

Hendry took the biro from behind his ear and pointed it at Brookes. 'I wouldn't be so sure about that.'

'What do you mean?'

'I just got a message from the duty sergeant. Your man was brought into a station in Leith just yesterday, charged with assault to severe injury. He's been bailed and his plea hearing's on Monday.'

183

'You're kidding, Sam Armstrong? Who did he assault?'

'An older man. Some random, road rage incident. But it was serious stuff – fractured the guy's eye socket and he might lose his sight. Your nice civilised architect, eh ... and if that's what he does to a stranger ...'

Brookes snatched the biro from Hendry's grasp. 'Let me see the charge sheet.'

Hendry typed Sam's name into the database and the police custody record appeared.

Brookes shook her head slowly, staring at the startled photograph of Sam on screen. She read the recorded comments by the arresting officer. Sam had been splashed in the victim's blood when he was arrested and several eye witnesses had said the attack had been unprovoked.

'I didn't see that coming, I'll admit that,' said Brookes. 'If I had to put my money on one of them acting violently out of control, it would have been her.'

'Mrs Armstrong. The photographer.'

Brookes nodded, biting the skin around her thumb again.

'So, we're bringing them in. How do you want to play it?' Hendry asked.

'Bring them in, but let's get feedback from Scenes of Crime as soon as possible. I need more. What evidence is in the house, what's on their phones, their computers – who were they communicating with and what about? What do forensics have to say about what happened in the children's nursery? Skin samples from the post-mortem about the ligature type will take forty-eight hours or so, but let's get what we can. I still don't understand *why* they would hurt that child. No motive I can think of . . . Arrest, but ideally we need more information before we question them.'

'Yes, mam.'

18

SAM

August 2019

Clare had booked a casual French restaurant off Randolph Place and Sam caught the bus there from his office in Leith. When he arrived, she was sitting at a table outside. From some distance away he saw her, shades on and reading a menu. It had been a couple of years since he had seen her in the flesh and he felt a surprising bristle of nerves as he walked towards her. They were strange, conflicted nerves, a mixture of excitement and regret.

'So good to see you,' she said, standing.

The smell of her comforted him as he bent to kiss her cheek.

'You look great,' he said, meaning it. He was greying with a belly that was creeping over his belt, but Clare never seemed to age.

'Did you get the bus? No bike?'

Sam put a hand on his belly. 'I need to get back into it. I

stopped cycling a while back. I'm unfit now. I'd need to ease myself into it.'

'Stopped cycling? You always loved it ...' Her voice drifted off, as if realising too late that she was referring to that time.

The punch, Sam thought; *Theo*; *You*. That's why I no longer cycle.

Besides, all of his cycling equipment was still buried in the cardboard boxes that lined the alcove of his flat, and he hadn't actually ridden his bicycle since the day he had been arrested for assault. Cycling for him was associated with that time.

Sam tried a smile, looked over his shoulder for the waiter. 'I work from home now, so it's not like I need it to commute any more.'

'Of course.' Clare's tiny fingers, small as a child's, toyed with a corner of the menu. They had shared the dock at the trial and she knew then that he had lost his job at Maitland McConnell because of his criminal conviction. He had told her about his new company, Spiral Architects, when he set it up but he had never really shared this part of his life with her. It had all happened when they weren't speaking. 'Still, it's a shame.'

She seemed uncomfortable, drawing the scarf she was wearing around her shoulders.

'Shall we eat inside? Is that okay?'

'Sure.' He followed her upstairs to the main restaurant, watching the neat curve of her hip. Her hair was still short and he could see the fine bones of her spine above her collar. Some part of him still wanted to reach out and touch her.

They sat near the window and ordered fish and Sam ordered a beer, and in the noisy warmth of the room, Clare relaxed.

'I was so sorry to hear about your illness, but you seriously look fantastic. I mean it.'

She laughed. 'I look terrible, but thank you.'

He loved that way she had of deflecting any praise. The bright sunshine from the window made her hair shine like butter.

'I feel fine, but I've not had any of the nasty treatments, just the operation and some radiotherapy, so we'll see.'

'Let's hope that's it then.'

'The consultant said it will depend on the spread; I can never pronounce that *meta-whatever* word that they use.'

She smiled – her teeth were small, with a gap between the front incisors. Noticing these little things again, when they had been together for so long and then apart, roused him.

'Metastasis.'

'That's it.'

The waiter brought their drinks and, when he had poured his beer, Sam put his elbows on the table and leaned towards her.

'So . . . you wrote to Lorraine?'

As Clare began to talk, Sam watched the tension return to her body. He regretted bringing the subject up so soon. The name *Lorraine* fluttered between them, awkward and blinded, like an injured moth at a bare bulb.

'What makes you think she's contacted the police?'

'When Lorraine came to the gallery, she was *incensed*. I mean she was . . . We were outside, alone in the car park and I just felt . . . I don't know . . . threatened maybe? But she did clearly say she would go to the police and that she wanted me—' Clare turned from him and looked out of the window, resting her chin on her fist '—to go to prison.'

Sam noticed a pulse in the hollow below her throat. It made her seem more vulnerable than he knew her to be, and he was filled with a flush of protectiveness towards her. He was still conditioned to react to Clare's emotions, as if on some physiological or emotional level they were still partners. The heavy, white tablecloth, the small crystal salt and pepper shakers on the table, the art on the walls and the middle-class, middle-aged diners – all offered decorum, distance. But Sam still felt intimate with her: aware of the small pieces of chewed skin around her thumbnail, the forgotten fleck of mascara on her eyelid, the tiredness under her eyes.

He had wanted to have a child with this woman – who he had been with since he was a young man from Pilton from a rough family, with ideas above his station about architecture and design. This fun, creative woman who had always supported him and encouraged him. He had let her down when she'd needed him most.

As their meals arrived and they set about unwrapping napkins and asking for condiments, Sam remembered the bathroom in accident and emergency and the bright-red blood on Clare's thighs. He remembered the rusty, female smell of their loss.

He tried to remember what had really driven them apart – Theo – or all those miscarriages?

Ten miscarriages.

Sam couldn't remember them as single experiences. It was

like a fight in the ring, ten rounds. He couldn't remember the blows he'd taken or the punches he'd thrown, but he knew that both he and Clare were wounded.

They had married in their twenties. They had travelled, and bought the house and done it up together. They were both creative and wanted to *make things* together. He still remembered them knocking down the wall that separated the living room and the kitchen, both wearing masks to protect them from the swell of dust. He had to help Clare swing the sledgehammer as she struggled to lift it.

Until their early thirties, they didn't worry that Clare never got pregnant. But somewhere around then came the first of many doctor's appointments, intervention that began the attempt to calibrate desire. Passion was the antithesis of science, Sam learned.

Now, he could not remember why having children had been so important. He still craved that human experience, to be a father, to be the protector, to hold a little hand in his – but he didn't understand *why* it had eclipsed their relationship. Who had been the driver – who had wanted it more?

He had wanted it more, he supposed. And Clare had then wanted it *for him*, and all of their combined frustration had isolated them. It had driven them apart, like two electrons with a negative charge. They had become alone, together.

He remembered arriving home one rainy night. Dark outside but not late in the evening, so it must have been winter. He had cycled to his parents' house in Pilton after work, because his mother had called to say his father had fallen over and couldn't get up.

His father had been on his hands and knees in the bedroom, unable to stand. Sam had lifted him with ease, the old tyrant's body feeling light and fragile, as if his bones were porous like a bird's. Afterwards, sitting in his chair and breathing hard, his father had reached for Sam's hand and held it, thanking him.

Sam wasn't sure he'd ever held his father's hand before. The back of the old man's hand was speckled with liver spots and the knuckles were red.

Finally home, Sam pushed his key into the lock of the black, wooden door and rested his forehead against the wood, tired but somehow resisting going inside.

Sam didn't know what he felt about it. He felt something, but it was distant from him, ungraspable. He didn't want to think about it any more and he didn't want to talk. He *needed* something. He needed to lose himself. Needed touch. Needed to feel home.

He turned the key in the lock and slipped inside, stood for a moment waiting at the bottom of the stone staircase. His senses were alert and full of want, hope: dinner cooking, music playing, the sound of Clare's voice laughing on the phone. Instead there was no sound, no smell he could distinguish.

He climbed to the top of the staircase and opened the living room door. In the kitchen, teabags were squeezed of life and drying out on a saucer. Clare was at home – her photo screen and lights were in position by the window. The ominous silence told him that Clare was either in her darkroom, or she was in bed. He had come home from work early two weeks ago to find her there, curled under the duvet, bereft because her period had come early.

He opened the bedroom door. Clare sat up in bed, beaming.

'What you doing? Don't you want some dinner?'

'I'm ovulating. I thought we could do it now and then again in the morning?'

'Yeah, I'm just ... shall we have some tea first?' He wasn't hungry.

She looked away from him, began to pick her nail. They could negotiate, he realised, but it would only weary him further.

As he unfastened his belt and let his jeans fall to the floor, he tried to remember what he had wanted a moment before. The recollection was fleeting, imperfect, like the memory of an old friend.

Under the covers, the smell of her folded over him and the comfort of it made him want to curl behind her and pull her in close. Inexplicably, he tasted tears at the back of his throat. He felt so hilled, so disappointed, but he forced himself to continue, willed himself hard.

'It's alright, you can come now,' she said after a while.

Sweat broke at the small of back as – lethargy sliding into panic – he thought he wouldn't be able to complete.

Desire

That was what he had needed. He had wanted fun, oblivion, to be taken out of himself.

He shuddered inside her and then lay on his back, trying not to watch as she shunted herself round to rest her hips on the pillow, legs right up the wall. She crossed her ankles. Her tiny little feet looked pale.

Not for the first time, he felt distant from her. He felt alone lying in bed beside her. It was no one's fault, but something was coming undone between them – the give in a seam, thread loosening.

'Was your dad alright?' she asked, finally.

He looked at her, but her face was upside down and he struggled to make sense of it, eyebrows where her mouth should be.

'This is a nice little place,' said Sam, as he cut into his fish. The restaurant was on Clare's side of town and he couldn't remember it from the time when they lived together, but it didn't seem new.

At once he felt the strangeness of sitting having lunch with her, as if nothing had changed and it had only been a week or so since they had sat down together. He still felt close to her. He avoided thinking about what had driven them apart – the loss of all their *nearly* children punctuated by Theo's death.

Before the trial, the lawyers had sent Clare to a psychologist, who had diagnosed her with post-traumatic stress disorder as a result of the compounded loss of miscarriages. The prosecution had argued that PTSD gave Clare a predisposition to act out violently. Sam had not been sent to a psychologist but he felt sure that he too had been traumatised.

He remembered the morning after Theo died, standing in the living room alone, looking around at the home he was about to leave, a burnt-out tiredness making his body feel heavy but alert at the same time. The heating had come on, and the warm room brought condensation back to the old window panes. The breath had stopped inside him when he saw the 'O' made by Theo's lips return to the glass.

Sam remembered leaving and telling Clare that he would stand by her, but he couldn't be with her any longer.

Outside of the window there were tall trees that reached higher than the three-storey buildings around them. Sam didn't know what kind of trees they were, but their branches, green with leaves, swirled and waved in the wind.

'Lorraine wouldn't go the police after all this time,' Sam said, decisive, cutting the flesh of his trout and carefully removing the backbone, which he set to one side. 'I mean, I don't doubt she's still hurting ... of course she is but ... she wouldn't.'

'*I'm* still hurting,' said Clare, fork in one hand, blinking at him across the table.

'We all are, but bothering the police ...'

'I think I said too much.' Clare put down her fork and rested her face in her hand, elbows on the table.

Sam tightened his grip on his cutlery.

'I told her I felt responsible. The diagnosis, you see – the cancer, it made me remember ... things that had always been too painful to even think about. When you're told you've got cancer, naturally you think about dying.' She ran a hand through her hair. Her blue eyes were elsewhere, looking out of the window, at the trees whipping in the breeze. 'I think I wanted to write to her *for me* – to make me feel better – and now I think that was a mistake.'

'Well ...' Sam picked at his fish.

'I wrote a lot – about twenty pages.'

'Jesus.'

'I know. And I did say that I remember things now that I didn't at the time.'

'Do you?'

'I think so, yes. Not everything, but more . . . '

They looked at each other. For a moment, they were back there, together, navigating a horror so awful neither of them could articulate it. It had changed them as individuals and as a couple, irreparably.

Clare began to eat, carefully built forkfuls of fish, vegetable and potato. He felt a deep love for her, sudden, suffocating, just because of that habitual little gesture that he knew so well and it disoriented him. That he still loved her, after everything that had happened, seemed preternatural.

'And it all came to a head at your event . . . Congratulations again, by the way.' His mouth was full and he nodded until he swallowed. 'I went along, the other day.'

'You've seen it?' Her spine straightened, mouth and eyes turning up at the corners.

'Quite a lot of your pictures have sold.'

She shrugged, looking out of the window again, at the square, the grey tenements still blackened by soot from Victorian times, and the green swirl of trees above.

'Yeah, I was pleased.'

'I saw you had . . . ' Sam inhaled the words he was going to say and swallowed them. He turned his attention to his plate and then, deciding he was finished, set his cutlery to one side.

195

'Had what?' Clare dabbed her mouth with her napkin and put it on her plate.

Palms on the table, Sam looked up into her eyes.

'Well, I recognised some of the photos. You took them from our old snaps.'

'That's right.'

'It's so effective – that technique you used. They look like paintings. There was one, of a baby and, for a moment, I thought it was . . .'

Clare's eyes opened wide.

'Theo,' he exhaled.

The name settled on the tablecloth, now marked with crumbs and stains – a tiny, potent chrysalis of years and lies and secrets between them, which had finally driven them apart.

'That baby *was me*. That was *my baby photo*. You've seen it before.'

'Yes,' he said quietly. 'I realised that, of course.' He noticed her cheekbone reddening and felt his stomach muscles tighten.

'Of course I wouldn't use a picture of . . . that would have been . . . awful. Creepy.'

She was defensive and he wanted to change the subject – didn't want their time together to end on this note. Yet, going around the gallery, the grainy picture of the baby – which *was*, of course Clare, in that dated, white lace baby gown – it had stopped him in his tracks. It had been like a spectre of little Theo. 'Unearthed' was the title of the exhibition, and the dirty grainy prints were striking.

Mistaken as he had been, that Theo's face was one of the portraits, the shock of that thought reminded him of that first, sickening glance when he realised Theo was dead, and then, seconds later, that giddy, punch drunk moment, unable to see straight, when he realised they would need to come up with a story.

'That was a stupid thing to say. I'm sorry.' He raised his hand for the waiter.

19

DETECTIVE INSPECTOR
PAMELA BROOKES

August 2019

Brookes was on hold. She nudged the receiver into the space between her neck and her shoulder to allow her to reach over and tease a biscuit from a packet on a colleague's desk. It was late afternoon and she hadn't eaten since breakfast. She was waiting to speak to the specialist lip-reader who had viewed the CCTV footage of Clare and Lorraine outside the gallery. In her inbox, and open on her desktop, was the new forensics report on DNA samples retrieved from Theo's clothing. Brookes crunched as she flicked through the paper copy on her desk, and the open documents on screen.

Brookes had read the report last night, in bed, Mike asleep at her side. It had been nearly one o' clock when she turned out the light and only realised on her way to the bathroom that Jack was still on his computer. She had chased him off to bed.

The principal forensic scientist had returned a number of positive results based on techniques that weren't available at the time of the 2008 trial. Previously invisible cellular material had been found on Theo's sleepsuit. Degraded deposits that had returned only a weak DNA profile in 2008, had now been reworked with improved results.

These results had identified Clare's DNA on specific, targeted areas of the sleepsuit – the underside of his panda hood and the tie of the drawstring cord on the neck of the panda suit.

Brookes was preparing to submit her new evidence to the procurator fiscal, in the hope of gaining a retrial.

'Detective Brookes … It's Joanna Curran here. Are you still there?'

Brookes swilled down a gulp of lukewarm coffee. She had drunk far too much coffee today.

'I'm still here,' she said, again shouldering the phone so that she could type. She had been waiting on the line for so long that she had been automatically logged off her computer. She logged in again and brought up the lip-reader's transcript of the CCTV footage of Clare and Lorraine meeting at the Newhaven Gallery. Brookes had received the transcript only a few hours before.

'I'm so sorry to keep you waiting. I was on another line. I understand you wanted to chat through some of the things in the transcript?'

Joanna Curran's accent was English, clear and crisp.

'Yes, thank you. I've only had a chance to quickly read it, but it was more than I'd hoped for.'

'Yes, it was very successful. The picture quality was excellent. There were only one or two places where I've indicated that sentences were indecipherable because the target was turning away, or touching the mouth area. Overall, I was able to get the transcription, which you have there.'

'I think what I wanted to understand was . . . how reliable is the transcription?'

'Unless I have added a note, then what I have transcribed is what was said.'

Brookes felt emboldened. 'There is a section of the video, towards the end, around the five-minute mark, where the subjects appear to be arguing. There is a quick exchange of words. Your transcription is one hundred per cent reliable during this section?'

'I believe there is one sentence or two, within that area of video you are talking about, where I have noted a difficulty identifying some words. If not noted, then what is transcribed is what was said.'

'And what difference does accent make? I note that you are not Scottish, but both of the subjects are . . . ' Brookes changed the phone from her right ear to her left. 'Forgive me, I'm just anticipating how the evidence would be tested in court.'

Curran laughed awkwardly. 'Well, I *am* Scottish even if I don't sound it, but in terms of the report, none at all. As I've said, if I had any indecision about a word or exchange, I noted in the margin, even where I couldn't see the mouth of the subject but was able to piece together from context.'

'Thank you,' Brookes said, pursing her lips. 'That's great.'

During the argument scene, when Clare and Lorraine had seemed to lean in towards each other, apparently shouting, Joanna Curran reported speech that would help Brookes' application for a retrial: new and convincing evidence.

Clare said: 'I do now accept responsibility for what happened.'

And Lorraine replied: 'It might be guilt that's made you sick, but at least you've finally admitted that you're guilty.'

Together with the new forensic evidence, it would be vital to the application for a retrial. It was evidence, together with the letter, of a confession.

Just as Lorraine had reported to Brookes, the lip-reader going through the CCTV footage had noted that Clare had clearly said the words, 'I lied to the police.'

Of course, Brookes had known that back in 2008. Clare and Sam said that Theo was found unresponsive in his cot, but the pathologist had been clear that the baby had been asphyxiated with a ligature.

Brookes hung up the phone and continued to flick through the new evidence, comparing it with the results of the earlier investigation. She found an electronic copy of her written notes taken when she interviewed Lorraine's little daughter, Ella.

Brookes steepled her fingers as she stared at the screen. The office was open-plan, and, on the far side of the room, two detectives were talking about football.

Visiting Lorraine's flat the other day, Brookes had been pleased to meet Ella again. So tall, yet still something there of that little girl she had known all those years ago.

Brookes remembered meeting Ella for the first time in the

high-ceilinged flat in Haymarket where they had found her brother, dead. She had been crying convulsively when she'd arrived, before Sam had put her back to bed.

She remembered her decision to interview eight-year-old Ella. Although she had been asleep in the other room when her brother had died, Brookes had wanted to make sure that Ella hadn't seen or heard something. Sam and Clare had lied to her, but Brookes remembered the scene she had entered on that rainy night – one partner drunk, another sober – a glass smashed and a baby dead. Ella had been with them all day and night and, although she was barely eight years old, Brookes had thought she might be able to fill in the gaps in their story.

Things had been different in 2008. Now, Ella's statement would be recorded on film with her mother or another responsible adult present. Back then, it had been acceptable for Brookes to ask Lorraine to wait outside, and the interview had only been noted as a hand-written statement, not recorded at all.

Brookes opened Ella's witness statement from the original crime file. The statement had been transcribed using her own notes. Re-reading, Brookes remembered holding out her hand and feeling Ella's cool, slightly sticky palm slide into hers.

'Thanks for coming, Lorraine.' Brookes put a hand on Lorraine's elbow. 'You can sit here and I'll bring her back shortly.'

'If she gets upset . . . ?'

'We'll do our best not to upset her. It's just routine – make sure we haven't missed anything. You don't need to worry.'

Brookes hunkered down so that she was face to face with Ella. The little girl smiled at her from behind her mother's hip.

'Ella, this won't take long. I just want to ask you some questions and then you'll be right back with your mum. Do you want to hold my hand?'

Brookes felt the little girl's palm slip into hers. It had been just over a week since her brother had been found dead.

The room was small, with a table and two chairs in the centre and another couple along the wall for observers.

Ella sat on the plastic chair in the centre and began to swing her legs. She was wearing her school uniform. Her white shirt was wrinkled, as if it had dried unhung. The button over her belly was undone and her vest showed through. One of her knees had a yellowing bruise on it. She wore two odd socks, one white and patterned and the other grey and smooth-knitted. Her white sock was halfway down her shin. Hands on the edge of the chair, Ella sniffed as she looked at Brookes, her eyes flicking to the woman sitting in the corner of the room.

Brookes sat down facing her. 'Hello, Ella. We just met properly outside, but my name is Pamela Brookes. I'm a police officer and this person here—' she pointed at a woman sitting in the corner of the room with a pad and pencil '—is Samira, and she's a social worker.'

'Hello, Ella,' Samira said.

Samira Siddique was nearing retirement, but Brookes knew her well as she regularly assisted in interviews with children and vulnerable young adults. Her role today was to observe and ensure that Brookes adhered to the Joint Investigative Interview rules.

'Hello,' Ella said, very quietly. Her lip quivered. Her eyes moved from Samira to Brookes.

Brookes smiled, trying to make her relax. 'Part of my job is to listen to children and young people. Sometimes they have things that they want to tell me. Today I want to talk to you about the night that you spent with your Aunt Clare and Uncle Sam. I want to hear about your memories in your own words. Is that okay?'

Ella nodded, huge dark eyes unblinking.

'I'm mainly here to listen to you. If you don't understand something I ask you, or if you don't remember, it's fine to tell me that you don't know, or don't remember. Okay?'

'Okay.'

'That's great. When I ask you a question, it's important that you tell the truth. Do you know the difference between telling the truth and telling a lie?'

'Yes.'

'Do you think you can explain to me what the difference is?'

'The truth is what really happened and a lie is what didn't.' Ella's voice was clear. She sniffed when she had finished speaking and licked her top lip with her tongue. Brookes saw that her nose was running.

'Right, we can get started. I wanted to ask you first, if you liked watching television?'

'Yes.' Ella half-smiled, nodding her head vigorously.

Brookes found a clean tissue in her pocket and passed it to Ella, who took it but held it in her hands on her lap. Brookes smiled to herself. She had passed the tissue so Ella could wipe her nose.

'And what do you like to watch?'

'I like um ... "Drake and Josh" ... and "Tracy Beaker" ...' Ella half smiled, her new adult teeth seeming too big for her small mouth.

Brookes knew 'Tracy Beaker' – Mike's niece and nephew watched it.

'Tracy's very naughty, isn't she?'

'Yes, but mostly she's good.' Ella wiggled in her seat as she spoke. She sniffed again, and pulled up the sock that had wrinkled down her leg, but didn't use the tissue in her hand.

'Did you watch television the last night you stayed at your aunt and uncle's house?'

Ella looked upwards, considering, and then shook her head.

'Can you tell me what happened when you went to your Aunt Clare and Uncle Sam's – right from the beginning?'

Ella took a deep breath, then nodded, pressing her lips together.

'Well, my mummy was going away with my grandma and so Mum took me and Theo over to Aunt Clare and Uncle Sam's. And we were late. And it was Theo's first time to stay over and so ...' She took a breath in, but didn't exhale.

Brookes pitched forward onto her elbows, making sure her head was the same height as Ella's. She nodded to encourage her to finish her sentence. It was the first time Ella had said Theo's name. Brookes wondered how the little girl processed what had happened to her brother. 'Go on ...'

'Well—' Ella smiled suddenly, looking up at the ceiling before flicking her eyes back to look at Brookes '—Theo was excited to be staying over, and he was running all over the floor. And Uncle Sam hadn't fixed up the gates yet, so he kept running after Theo and picking him up in case he fell down the stairs.'

'The gates? Do you mean baby gates?'

'Um ... yeah.' Ella seemed unsure. 'The gate goes over the top of the stairs. Theo might just run down the stairs, because he's little and doesn't know he could hurt himself.'

Brooke noted that Ella was speaking about her brother in the present tense.

'And what happened when your mummy left?'

'We had lunch and we went out to the park ... only it wasn't a normal park, there were animals there. There was a tractor that Theo liked and I liked the goats a lot—' she giggled, hand over her mouth '—'cause they were coming right up to us. And one had a beard and you could feed them the grass.'

'That sounds fun. Then what happened?'

'Well, it was getting cold and dark and so we went home to have dinner. And Uncle Sam was playing with us. He lets you go on his back like he's a horse.' Ella giggled, showing her teeth and Brookes smiled back at her.

'I'm listening. Go on.'

'And Aunt Clare took Theo for a bath and he was crying because he doesn't like baths.'

'I see and what were you doing?'

'I was downstairs with Uncle Sam who was making dinner but he burned the fish fingers—' she put a hand over her mouth

'—and then we went to bed and Aunt Clare and Uncle Sam told us stories.'

'What stories did they tell you?'

'I can't remember. But I remember Theo was standing up in his cot and trying to get out because he didn't want to go to bed.'

'Could Theo get out of the cot by himself?'

'Yes, he can get out of all cots. He's good at climbing. And he's good at going up stairs. If you don't watch him, he'll climb right to the top of all steps.' Ella stopped and sniffed loudly, wiping her nose with her forefinger. 'But he can't go downstairs yet, only up. So you have to make sure you get him when he gets to the top, otherwise he could fall down . . . It's okay at home, because we don't have any stairs.'

'And what happened when Theo tried to get out of his cot that night?'

'I went downstairs and told Aunt Clare and Uncle Sam. I said he was trying to get out and keeping me awake. Aunt Clare said I could go into her and Uncle Sam's bed if I wanted and I said I did want to and so Aunt Clare got Theo to lie down again. I stayed with her while she rubbed his back, and then she tucked me into the big bed where her and Uncle Sam sleep.'

'So you were in your aunt and uncle's bed and Theo was in his cot . . . what happened then?'

'Um . . . we went to sleep.'

An expression came across Ella's face – cheeks pinched – as if a dark thought passed over her mind.

'What else do you remember?' Brookes took care to ensure the tone of her voice was even and soft.

Ella was suddenly sullen. She held one hand in the other.

'It's okay, Ella; I'm still listening to what you have to tell me.'

'I woke up and ...' A frown puckered the perfect, unblemished skin on her forehead.

'Can you tell me what you saw or heard?'

Ella touched her lips, literally pinching them shut with finger and thumb, then she tweaked her eye, tugging at the eyelashes. It was hard for Brookes to watch this. She glanced at Samira in the corner, whose face was impassive. Brookes had an instinct to reach out and take Ella's hand away from her eyes yet waited, not wanting to distract or control her.

'What did you see or hear?' Brookes said, aware that the nature of the interview meant that she couldn't repeat or press questions. Ella stopped pulling at her eyelashes and began to answer.

'I woke up. I got out of bed and went along the hall. Theo was on the floor and Uncle Sam was ...' Ella made a fist with her hand and let it fall to her knee.

'What was he doing?' Brookes prompted.

'He was—' again Ella beat the side of her fist into her leg '—hitting Theo on his front.' Looking Brookes right in the eye, she placed her fist in the centre of her own chest.

Brookes saw that Ella's eyes were moistening.

'Uncle Sam was crying.' Dimples appeared in Ella's chin and Brookes wondered if she, too, was going to cry. 'And Aunt Clare gave me a hug and she smelled funny. And she took me back into their bedroom, but I wanted my mummy and I was crying for her.'

Brookes bit her lip. 'What do you mean, she smelled funny?'

Ella shook her head and shrugged. 'She took me to her bed, but I didn't like her smell. She smelled ... not like she normally does.'

Brookes nodded. 'Okay, thank you. Ella, is there anything else about that night that you would like to tell me? Is there anything else about what you remember, something you saw or heard?'

'Theo died.' Ella's face was now calm, no sign of distress. Her legs, which had swung throughout most of the interview, became still.

'That's right. Do you know how that happened to him?'

Ella looked past Brookes at the wall and cocked her head to one side. 'I think he was being naughty. Maybe he made Uncle Sam and Aunt Clare upset.'

'What makes you think that?'

'He was being naughty most of the day. Theo always has tantrums, but especially when Mummy goes away. Theo likes it when Mummy is there, and plays with him.'

'What makes you think your aunt and uncle were upset?'

'They were arguing about Theo. I heard them say his name. Uncle Sam was shouting and Aunt Clare told him to calm down ...'

'When was this?'

'When I was in the big bed, Uncle Sam and Aunt Clare were arguing downstairs and they were saying Theo's name and shouting.'

'What were they shouting about, can you remember?'

'I don't know, but maybe it was about Theo and how he was so naughty.'

'Can you remember any words they said?'

Ella looked up to the right. There was a long thin, horizontal window at the top of the interview room. The sun suddenly cut through it, and Brookes could see the rectangular reflection of the window in Ella's large black eyes.

'I think they said—' Ella's lips moved without sound '—bad words. Swearwords.'

'Both your aunt and your uncle were swearing?'

'Yes, both of them. They were saying Theo's name and swearing, and I think Aunt Clare was also crying.'

'You're doing very well, Ella. Just a few more questions. I want to make sure I understand. You went to sleep after the story, and then you woke up to hear your aunt and uncle arguing?'

Ella nodded.

'And then, what you said at the beginning, about waking up again and seeing your Uncle Sam hitting Theo on his front . . . do you remember what happened in between?'

Ella looked down at her scuffed school shoes. 'No, I think I maybe went to sleep again. They stopped arguing. They stopped. I remember trying to listen, but they were quiet. And then I think I went to sleep and when I woke up Theo was on the floor and Uncle Sam was trying to make him breathe.'

Brookes nodded. 'Samira – do you have any other questions you would like to ask Ella?'

'No, that's fine,' Samira said, still scribbling notes on her pad.

'Thank you, Ella. Thank you for coming to talk to us today and for your effort.'

Ella clasped her hands on her lap and smiled. Brookes stood and opened the door.

The little girl wiped her nose on the sleeve of her jumper just before she left the room.

Brookes inhaled and stretched. It was hard to superimpose the memory of Ella as a little girl with the young woman she had met just a few days before.

The light from the computer was hurting her eyes; Brookes knew she needed a break and to eat something. She felt full of nervous energy as the case was on the brink of being heard again. She had sufficient evidence to go to the procurator fiscal to request an application under double jeopardy to retry Clare Richardson for the murder of Theo Collins. In a matter of days, Brookes would know the result. For her, it wasn't about DNA profiles or lip-readers, or confessions from a murderer more than a decade later. It was about justice for Theo.

20

CLARE

November 2008

The doorbell went, and then a sudden pounding on the door.

Clare wasn't sure if the noise was echoing from the stairwell, or coming from the inside of her head. She was in bed. It was afternoon, perhaps evening, and she had been in bed since Sam left. She was alone in the big flat and her heart was broken. Along the hall was the children's bedroom, with Theo's crumpled blanket and Ella's duvet thrown back. All Sam's things were gone. Nothing felt right. It was as if Sam had taken pieces of her flesh with him, or one of her vital organs – a kidney or a lung. Despite being under the covers, she shivered and twitched.

Within the duvet nest she had made for herself, she was sure that she heard the word, *police*. Whoever was banging on her door was saying *police*.

Clare righted herself in the bed. She pulled a cardigan around her and trod barefoot along the hall and down the stairs; the banging hurt the space between her ears. The stone steps were cold against the soles of her bare feet.

She opened the door and stood back, confused, blinking at the grey canvas of flat, bright sky.

A female officer stepped through the open door and unhooked a pair of handcuffs from her belt. 'Clare Armstrong, I am arresting you for the murder of Theo Christopher Collins on the twenty-first of November.'

'What? I don't understand.'

The cuffs were heavy and cold on her wrists.

There was a police van in the courtyard with *forensic services* printed on the side.

As Clare slipped on shoes – but no socks – and was led away, she saw people in white paper suits getting ready to enter her home.

At the police station on Gayfield Square, Clare caught sight of Sam for a brief second. *Was he here as a witness against her, or had they arrested him too?*

The duty officer led Clare into an interview room and removed her handcuffs. As she waited, Clare rubbed her wrists where the handcuffs had pressed, then clasped her hands tightly on the table, watching the sinews rise on the back of her hands.

Brookes entered with a male police officer, who started a recording device as the two took their seats. Clare felt thirsty, tried to swallow but didn't have enough saliva. Unsure of what was coming, she felt afraid to ask for a glass of water.

'Twenty-first of November 2008, time is eighteen forty-two; Sergeant Rory Hendry and Detective Inspective Pamela Brookes interviewing Clare Armstrong, date of birth second of March nineteen sixty-eight.'

DI Brookes flipped her notepad onto the table and faced Clare, mirroring her posture by clasping her hands. 'You have the right to remain silent, but anything that you do say will be noted – sometimes video recorded – and may be used in evidence against you.'

Clare's breath was rough and uneven in her throat. 'I um ... I spoke to the duty sergeant. My lawyer is on his way?'

'You have the right to have a solicitor informed of your arrest and your lawyer has been notified. You don't get to see a lawyer at this stage, or seek legal advice before the interview, but you *are* entitled to have one notified, and that has been done.'

Clare blinked at Brookes, realising that she had no choice but to accept what she said.

'The last time we spoke, I took a witness statement from you in the early hours of the morning after Theo Collins was found dead in the house you share with your husband. We now have the results of the post-mortem on Theo. Scenes of Crime officers are currently in your home.'

Clare stared unblinking at the detective.

The man, Sergeant Hendry, had something in his hands. Clare frowned when he produced it.

'Before we begin, I need a buccal sample from you.'

'Um, what?' It looked like a takeaway spoon for stirring coffee.

'Can you open your mouth, please?'

As the officer leaned in towards her, Clare realised the stick was a swab to collect her DNA.

'A little wider. That's it.'

Clare felt the stick run along the inside of her cheek. Hendry capped the sample and Clare stared at it for a moment, before he put it in a bag and passed it to someone outside the door. She watched the door for a second before turning back to the detectives. She wondered what would happen now – if the cells they had taken from the inside of her cheek would somehow betray her.

'What is it you do for a job, Clare? You're a photographer?'

'Um, yes.'

'And have you been working since I saw you last?'

'No.' She shook her head, feeling it sore. She was dehydrated. 'I ... wonder if I could have some water?'

'Of course, we can get you that.' Brookes nodded to Hendry who left the room and returned a moment later with a small plastic cup.

Clare sipped the water. He had brought so little, and she felt so thirsty.

'Not working. What have you been doing?'

'I ...' Clare looked around the blank walls for inspiration, finding none. 'I suppose I've been too upset to work. I haven't done much. Such a shock.'

'A stressful time, I see.' Brookes flipped open the notebook on the table. 'I have some questions for you about the day and evening when you found Theo dead.'

Clare nodded, a ripple of panic passing through her. 'I didn't hurt him. If that's what you're . . . I didn't . . . '

'Let's start at the beginning, shall we? I'd like you to talk to me again about the hours after you put the children to bed. What were you and Sam doing during this time?'

Clare sighed. She looked up into the left corner of the room and saw the red eye of a camera watching. She didn't like being on this side of the lens.

'We . . . put the children to bed and we were . . . just talking.'

'Just talking? Explain that to me again. You were drinking alone and a glass was smashed. Were you arguing?'

'I can't remember everything. I had a few glasses of wine like you said, and . . . it was such a terrible thing. To find that Theo was . . . ' Clare sucked her lower lip. She picked up the cup to take a sip, squeezing it too hard so that a little spilled. Her hand trembled and she set it down again without drinking.

'But before that, before you found Theo, what were you and Sam talking about? I mean I'm just a police officer, but if I was a stage director and I found a broken glass and an empty wine bottle that only one person had been drinking, I would say there had been something amiss.'

'We weren't arguing. We've had a hard time of late. We've been trying to have a baby, and I've . . . had a number of miscarriages.' Clare leaned forward as she said this, wide-eyed, although she couldn't imagine that the detective had children and so didn't expect her sympathy. Brookes seemed too hard to have children, freckles trapped in the creases around her eyes.

'We weren't arguing, but we were talking through … what we've been through.'

'The glass?' Hendry's deep voice intervened. 'How did that happen?'

Clare cleared her throat. 'I don't remember how it got broken.' This was a lie. There was a lot that Clare could not remember, was still struggling to piece together, but she clearly remembered about the glass.

It had been almost empty, a centimetre of white wine swilling at the bottom. She had hurled it at him. Perhaps she had thought there was more wine and simply meant to soak him with it, but the glass left her fingers. Sam ducked. The glass hit the wall and pieces rolled under the coffee table.

'It could have got knocked over when we found Theo. How can we be expected to remember about a broken glass when that … tragedy happened?'

'But *you* found Theo, did you not? When you went to check on him? That's what you told me before. The glass was broken in the living room and you were the only one that was drinking.'

'Maybe I dropped it when Sam called the ambulance.'

Flints in Brookes' quartz eyes began to sparkle. 'Okay. Let me ask you this. The post-mortem reported a number of bruises on Theo's arms and upper body. Do you know how he got those?'

'I saw those bruises too, when I was bathing him. I've no idea how it happened. Only that, with a little boy his age … you have to grab him sometimes to keep him out of trouble.'

'Really? You have to grab him?'

'Don't make it sound like that. I saw those bruises too. I was concerned by them too.'

'I'm not making anything sound like anything, Clare, I'm just trying to understand what you're telling me.'

'Well, Theo's very boisterous . . . he wants to get his own way. He's prone to tantrums. We struggled that day but Lorraine has been having trouble with him for weeks, months.'

'But what do you have to say about the bruises?'

'I'm just saying that Theo was very wilful and sometimes you would have to grab him to keep him out of harm's way . . . the bruises you talked about, I saw them too – they were on his arms, as if he had been grabbed.'

'Out of harm's way,' Brookes repeated. She sat back in her chair, her body half-turned from Clare so that part of her face fell into shadow. 'I know little ones can be a handful. I have a one-year-old.'

Clare sat up a little. The personal detail surprised her, but she wondered why Brookes had told her this. Was it to empathise, or was it, like Lorraine, an attempt to frame Clare as *not* a mother.

'Let's leave the bruises for a moment; I want to ask you again about bedtime. You bathed Theo before bed?'

'Yes.'

'After the bath what happened?'

'I got him dried and into his sleepsuit. We had a bit to eat and then we put the children to bed. We put Theo in his cot and I put his mobile on – we'd bought it especially for him. It lights up and plays a tune. We got Ella into bed and read to both of them until they started to drift off.'

'Did either of the children wake up at all, after that, while you and Sam were . . . talking?'

'Yes. Theo didn't settle and Ella got up and came downstairs. She said her brother was keeping her awake and so Sam put her to bed in our bed, while I settled Theo down again. The mobile we'd bought him – he liked it. It worked. They were both asleep again.'

'And what time was this?'

'About eight thirty, certainly before nine.'

'And were you having a glass of wine by that time?'

'No, I had some wine later, after I knew the children were asleep.'

'So, from that time, until you checked on the children at—' Brookes referred to her notes '—eleven forty-five, you hadn't heard a peep from them?'

'That's correct.'

Brookes slapped her notebook onto the table.

She leaned in, so close that Clare could smell the milky coffee on her breath.

'I think you're lying to me, Clare. I want you to stop it and tell me the truth.'

'I'm not lying.'

'You are. I spoke to Ella. Little Ella, your god-daughter. She said that after you and Sam settled her in your bed, she woke up because you and Sam were arguing. Shouting and swearing at each other, she told us. *Shouting and swearing.* Not discussing miscarriages over a Chardonnay.'

Clare felt a flare of heat rise from her chest, right up her neck to her cheeks.

At once, she felt guilty and angry. She had been called out for lying – of course she and Sam had been arguing that night. And Ella was right – they had been swearing too. But Brookes' tone was dismissive: *miscarriages and Chardonnay*. It reminded Clare of that time when Lorraine had equated her abortion to the procedure Clare had to undergo to remove tissue after the loss of their thirteen-week-old baby. Clare picked up the flimsy cup and drained it, as if consciously trying to douse her anger.

'I don't think we were shouting and swearing. That's not how we communicate.'

'That's what Ella said. Are you saying *she's* lying?'

'Of course not, but I don't think she heard correctly.'

'Come *off it*, Clare. One minute you're lying through your teeth; the next minute you're saying you can't remember.' Brookes picked up her notebook and slapped it on the table. 'I have a *dead child*. I have a child that the pathologist just confirmed was murdered. And he was murdered in *your house*. I want you to tell me what happened to him. I want the truth, *now*.'

Brookes' eyes were unnaturally pale, so that the blue of the iris seemed to leach into the whites. The eyes loomed large in front of Clare, even though Brookes was no longer invading her space with her coffee-smelling breath. Clare's throat felt sore.

Just then there was a knock on the door. Another officer stepped inside and passed a note to Hendry. He read with one eyebrow raised and then passed it to Brookes.

There was the thinnest trace of a smile on her lips as she read the note.

'We have your husband next door.'

Clare blinked twice.

'Sam told us – not only that he agrees with Ella, that you were arguing on the night that Theo died ... '

Clare could hear the beat of her own heart in her ears.

'Sam also told us that you have split up. Is that right? He's moved out already. You're officially separated.'

Clare toyed with the empty cup and it toppled onto the table, making a swift, tinny drumbeat as if mirroring the sound of her heart.

'Could I have some more water?'

'Answer the question.'

'Well, if that's what Sam said ... '

'Oh, Clare ... ' Brookes sat well back in her seat, crossing her legs to set her ankle on her knee. 'Don't mess me around, or I'll have you here all night. I want you to stop it right now and come clean. What were you and Sam arguing about that night, and why are you no longer together?'

Brookes slapped the table with the palm of her hand. 'And that's the easy question. The big one's coming, so cut your teeth on that one. And before you start with the *"can't remember"*—' Brookes mimicked her, a whiny voice '—don't forget that I spend my life with murderers and thieves and extortionists. I know all the tricks.'

Clare swallowed. She wanted to ask again for water, but decided it was best to offer some information first.

'Okay, we weren't just talking, we were arguing. We started to argue and I had a drink, but I ... don't drink. I don't *often* drink.

221

It makes me—' Clare scratched her face, feeling it flushed '—lose time. Lorraine would tell you I've never been able to handle my drink, since university, since I started drinking at all. I drank that night, because—' her hands were under the table now, and Clare picked at her cuticles '—Sam and I weren't getting on so well. We'd been through too much. I'd miscarried at thirteen weeks just days before we had Ella and Theo to stay. We were under a lot of strain.' Clare felt tears stinging her eyes but willed them away. 'It's hard on a marriage. It's hard when you're more than three months pregnant and then you just—' she clenched her fist and then opened her palm '—miscarry again. It's hard to hang onto hope. It's hard to be with a man who wants desperately to be a father and not be able to *give that to him* . . . '

Despite her best efforts, Clare began to cry.

Brookes nodded at Hendry. He got up and fetched tissues from another room. Clare took one, balled it up and nudged it into the corners of her eyes.

Like some kind of machine, Brookes continued, unfazed.

'Tell me again what you saw when you went to check on the children after eleven?'

'It was like I said. I checked, but Theo looked wrong and I screamed for Sam.'

'How did he look wrong? Where was he?'

'I told you before he was in . . . his cot.'

'What position was he in?'

Clare hesitated. 'On his back.' She wondered now if it was better to say on his front or side. She thought she remembered that babies were more likely to suffocate in those positions.

'You're quite sure?'

'I ... yes.'

Brookes tapped her notebook with her forefinger.

Clare wasn't sure what she was meant to take from the gesture, but it seemed to assert power, foreknowledge, as if Brookes knew something that she had not yet shared.

'We now have the results of the post-mortem and they *also* show that *you are lying*.'

Brookes' white-blue eyes were intense. Clare had to turn her face away.

'The post-mortem told us that Theo could not possibly have died passively lying in his cot. He didn't get wrapped up in the blankets and suffocate. Someone deliberately choked him to death. He was strangled, with a ligature. That's not something that you'd miss, I'd say – even after a few Chardonnays. What do you say to that?'

Brookes' face, with its wide smile, off-white teeth and the shadows of tiredness under her eyes, made Clare want to turn away. She touched the skin of her face and felt it puffy. She wondered if she was getting a migraine because she had a sense of being somehow altered, not herself. 'I don't ... know how that could be.'

It felt as if the room was spinning and her jaw felt slack, as if she had taken a punch to the face.

21

DETECTIVE INSPECTOR PAMELA BROOKES

November 2008

In the back office, Brookes and Hendry sat side by side watching the tape of Sam's interview under caution. Rain rattled against the window pane and dark clouds obscured their partial view of Calton Hill.

'I don't care what you say,' said Brookes. 'Something's going on with them that they're not telling us.'

'I hear you.'

The duty sergeant who had booked Sam in had highlighted his recent charge for assault to severe injury. Forensics were still combing through Sam and Clare's Haymarket flat, focusing their attention on the child's bedroom for evidence to support the pathologist's report that Theo had been strangled.

'There's a missing link,' Brookes muttered, almost to herself. 'Sam and Clare both tell us the *same lie* – that Theo was found unresponsive in his cot. That means either they're both guilty, or one is covering for the other.'

'I know what my money's on,' said Hendry.

Brookes cut her eyes to look at him and then turned back to the screen. 'They have a screaming argument and a glass gets broken; they lie to us about the position of the body, Sam moves out and then gets done for violent assault the next day . . .' Brookes put her pen in her mouth and resumed chewing its blue plastic lid.

She used the mouse to rewind the video of Sam's interview and start it again. She leaned in closer to the screen.

Sam seemed paler under the bright lights of the interview room. He raked a hand through his hair and wiped a hand across this mouth.

Sergeant Hendry had his back to the camera as Sam confirmed his name and address, frowning, eyes flicking around the room.

'So, you've moved out?' Hendry began.

'Yes.'

'What's the reason for that?'

'Clare and I have separated.'

'Was that a mutual decision?'

'I think so. Pretty mutual.'

'Strange that this should happen just hours after your godson was found dead in the home you share,' Sergeant Hendry said, raising an eyebrow. 'Don't you think?'

'It's not related.'

'Not related, I see. We spoke to Clare. She said that you were having an argument after Theo went to bed. What were you arguing about?'

Sam's Adam's apple bobbed up and down in his throat.

'We've had a lot of bad news lately. We've been under a lot of stress. We've been trying for a baby . . . '

'Yes, we heard that.' Hendry sifted pages in a file before him, seeming bored. 'But it seems you're the argumentative sort anyway, stressful times or not.'

'What do you mean?'

'Well, you're certainly keeping the criminal justice system in business.'

Sam was silent, staring slack-jawed at the sergeant.

'Charged with assault to severe injury yesterday and today . . . arrested for murder.' Hendry whistled dramatically.

'Yes,' Sam hissed.

'You're not having a good week, are you?'

'It was an accident.'

'This is ringing a bell.' Hendry swung back in his seat, crossing his foot over his knee. 'There's a dead baby in your flat, and *that's* an accident. You hit someone in the face so hard you fracture their eye socket and that's . . . *an accident.*'

Sam slid his hands under the table and looked down.

'I want to ask you a question about Theo. You gave a statement to say that Clare shouted to say she had found Theo unresponsive. You ran upstairs to help. Tell me again *where* Theo was when you saw him.'

'He was—' Sam indicated with his hand, as if Theo was there in the interview room '—lying in . . . his cot.'

'As if asleep?'

'Yes, he had been peacefully asleep, but immediately we real-ised something was wrong.'

'Something was wrong. Theo was strangled. The pathologist has confirmed that Theo was asphyxiated as a result of a ligature around his neck, choking him. We know he wasn't lying snug in his cot when you found him.'

'He was, he was—'

'Either Clare was lying to you, or you're both lying. Which is it?'

Sam wiped a hand over his face.

'We've spoken to Clare and faced with the evidence from the post-mortem, she's now told us the truth. It's better for you if you do the same. You said it yourself that you're separated now. You're on your own. Best just tell us what you know.'

Sam's face twisted. '*It was an accident*, but—' he panted, back of his hand over his mouth '—you're right. When we found him he wasn't in bed.'

Sam's chest heaved, then he placed both of his hands, palms upward, on the table. 'I lifted him down.' He gasped, a single ragged breath. 'I lifted him down and tried to make him breathe again.'

Brookes reached over and stopped the video. Sam's face was frozen on screen. She tapped the screen with her pen. 'That gesture, his hands turned up – he's showing us how he took him down.'

A door opened and closed behind them. 'Mam, I'm sorry to interrupt.'

It was a young constable who was working on the Collins case since it had become a murder investigation.

'Don't worry, have you got something?'

'Yes, thought you would like to see this.' She passed a few sheets of paper. 'It's the transcript from texts we found on Sam Armstrong's phone. From Scenes of Crime.'

'Oh, you have that already?' Brookes put the transcript on the desk between her and Hendry. She stood, stretching her lower back.

'Yes, after arrest we got phones and a computer.'

Hendry had already begun to read. One of his eyebrows arched and he passed the file to Brookes. 'Surprise, surprise.'

Brookes scanned the transcript. She clicked her teeth, thanked the constable and then dismissed her.

'There we go, huh. I told you we were missing something,' Brookes said, resuming her seat beside Hendry.

'Motive,' Hendry said, a smile beginning on his face.

'Book them.'

22

CLARE

August 2019

Adjusting herself on the white crepe paper, Clare lay back on the examination bed and unbuttoned her shirt, taking deep breaths in and out.

'Forgive me. My hands are a little cold,' said the consultant, Dr Raner, his flint-dark eyes looking upwards at the ceiling as he felt around the scar tissue on her breast. 'That's fine. I'll give you a moment to get dressed and then we can have a chat.'

The consultant was a very tall man – long-back and long-legged. Even sitting down, he towered over Clare. He smiled thinly at her then turned to his screen.

'It's very good news indeed. The wound has healed well, and the last ultrasound showed no further masses in the breast tissue. Combined with the CT result and blood test, it is very encouraging indeed.'

'So—' Clare pushed her glasses up into her hair '—I don't have cancer any more?'

Dr Raner swivelled to face Clare. 'You don't have cancer any more.' He slipped his hands between his knees. 'We'll still need to monitor you. We'll schedule a follow-up scan in six months, but right now, no further treatment is required.'

'*Thank* you. Thank *you*.'

Raner's long face blurred.

Trembling with joy, Clare boarded the Number 33 bus and dropped her coins into the slot. She took her ticket and headed upstairs, sitting right at the front so that the whole of Edinburgh lay before her as the bus lurched from Little France back to the West End. She had been so anxious about today, almost making herself physically sick as she considered the verdict. Now she had been given a reprieve. She held onto the bar that crossed the big window before her, feeling its reassuring red-painted steel as she looked out over the Pentland Hills. It was the most beautiful day – glorious – the distant green of the hills fading to blue.

The bus turned onto South Clerk Street – the street where she and Lorraine had shared a flat when they were at university. They had met in halls of residence in first year, and then shared a flat together until their final year. Just the two of them and the family of mice. The flat was still there – a dark-red painted door between a Chinese restaurant and fish and chip shop marked the entrance to the close.

Clare couldn't help but turn to look; she always looked any

time she passed, as if watching her life in the past. Now she actually pressed her forehead against the bus window to look down at the red door – as if it was a photograph from her old life. She could still remember the smell of the place – the stale dampness of the stairs overlaid with Chinese spice.

She remembered Lorraine's big smile, chin resting on her knee and a mug of cereal with a teaspoon in it by her side as she recounted a story from her day. A guy she liked. A professor who forced her to re-sit her Spanish oral; whether or not she should try and get a part-time job with the Tourist Board.

Clare pressed the bell for the bus to stop, and made her way downstairs.

Once home, Clare shut the door and then leaned back against the black wood of her front door, feeling it hard against her shoulder blades. *Thank you*, she said again, out loud.

She skipped upstairs and hung her jacket in the hall. She opened the shutters in the living room and let the daylight stream inside. She wanted to *tell someone*. She wanted to celebrate being cancer-free. She wanted to hit the town.

She reached into her pocket for her phone. She would tell Sam. Seeing him the other day had nourished her. He would be happy for her; he would be relieved.

On the lock screen of her phone, she saw that Sam had already texted her. She had been so distracted by her thoughts on the bus she hadn't noticed.

How did it go today? Thinking about you. X

He had remembered about her appointment. It felt good to be in touch with him again, as if they might even manage to be friends.

Leaning against the shutter, the bright sun through the Victorian glass casting dappled ripples onto the hardwood floors, she began to type a response.

It went well. U free tonight? Fancy a . . .

There was a knock at the door, a playful *rata tat tat* and Clare stood up straight. She put a hand to her chest – was it possible? Had he dropped by on his lunch hour? She skipped down the spiral steps and opened the door with a huge smile on her face.

It wasn't Sam at the door, but instead two police officers, a man and a woman, both so young and clear-skinned that they seemed like children dressed up.

'Can I help you?' Clare asked, frowning.

The police officers were both unsmiling. Clare pressed her lips together.

'Are you Clare Armstrong of this address, ten Palmerston Mews?' the female officer spoke.

'I am . . .'

'What's your date of birth?'

'Oh God.' Clare felt suddenly nauseous. She had been here before, almost exactly eleven years ago. Suddenly, she realised what was happening.

'Your date of birth, madam?'

Clare swallowed. 'The second of March nineteen sixty-eight.'

The male officer handed Clare a brown envelope. 'It's twelve thirty-five on the afternoon of Friday the twenty-ninth of August. You must appear at the high court at nine a.m. on the morning of the twenty-first of October twenty nineteen.'

Not once did the officer make eye contact. Clare took the envelope then watched as the police officers turned and made their way back out into the courtyard. Trembling, she tore the mouth of the envelope and read the letter inside.

TO: MRS CLARE ARMSTRONG (02.03.68) (*10* Palmerston Mews, *Edinburgh*)

A CRIMINAL CASE IS BEING BROUGHT AGAINST YOU

A document has been prepared which sets out the criminal charges against you.

That document (the 'indictment') is attached to this notice.

YOU MUST APPEAR at (*Edinburgh High Court*) High Court of Judiciary (*Parliament House, Parliament Square, Edinburgh EH1 1RQ*) on (*21 October 2019*) at (*09:00*) for a preliminary hearing at which you will be required to answer the criminal charges against you in the indictment.

You are indicted at the instance of Her Majesty's Advocate and the charges against you are that, on 21st November 2008, at 10 Palmerston Mews, you, CLARE ARMSTRONG, did murder THEO CHRISTOPHER COLLINS.

IF YOU DO NOT ATTEND THE COURT, A WARRANT WILL BE ISSUED FOR YOUR ARREST

The words swarmed in front of Clare's eyes, the black type seeming to break free from the words and disintegrate, marching over the page like ants. The cold air reached inside her shirt and her skin goose-pimpled. The letter fluttered from her grasp and out into the courtyard.

Her neighbour, Jan, got out of her car and moved to catch the letter for her.

'It's okay,' Clare called, one hand in the air to suggest that Jan step back. The letter took the air and turned, taunting her. Clare snatched it near the wheel of Jan's car and turned, smiling, a frozen mimic of a real smile. Just then, her foot twisted on the cobble and Clare fell full length.

'Oh, Clare, are you alright?' Jan squeezed Clare's elbow.

'I'm fine.'

Jan sucked air through her teeth. 'You've hurt yourself.'

The heel of Clare's hand was bleeding.

'No, I'm fine. Thank you. Thank you. I'll be alright.'

Clare shouldered the door shut. She used the iron railing to pull herself upstairs. A sob spasmed in her chest. At the top of the stairs she turned to the corridor with the bedrooms and threw open the door to the spare room – the room where Theo had died. Its beige emptiness mocked her.

She crumpled the letter in her hand, leaning against the wall as she stared into the windowless room. What had happened in this room all those years ago refused to leave her alone. Just as clumsily as she had toppled in the courtyard just then, an incomplete memory came and took her off balance.

Clare flushed the toilet and splashed water on her face. She shook her head once, hoping to clear it, but lost kilter. To stop herself falling, she reached out for the shower curtain. The weight of her ripped two eyes from their hooks. She left the curtain hanging like that, ragged, and lurched into the hall. She would check on the children.

One hand on the wall, she swayed – fingertips steadying herself as she lilted from the bathroom. The door to the main bedroom was ajar, and Clare saw Ella asleep on her back, one hand up beside her face. Unsteady, Clare used the wall for support as she worked her way along the hall. She touched the door to the children's room and felt the unnatural weight of the door.

In the syrupy swell of her drunkenness, the changed weight of the door gave Clare pause, but she pushed harder and finally it opened to her. Her tongue stuck to the roof of her mouth.

She crept into the room, on the balls of her feet, socks against the thick pile of the blue carpet.

Tippy-toe, tippy-toe. Shhhh.

She watched the soft, multi-coloured lights of the animal mobile turn. Its lullaby tune had stopped, but the nightlight kept spinning. The dark shadows cast on the wall rose and fell, lions and elephants, enlarged and umber, like shadow puppets.

Clare grasped the wooden spokes of the cot, holding on with two hands for support. The room reeled. Gripping the handrails, Clare looked down into the cot.

Theo was missing. She had wanted to be alone with him – to find comfort – but now he was gone, escaped. She tried to smile.

She would make it a game. She would find him and hold him, rock him to sleep.

There was a sound – brief, high-pitched, like a keening. The door creaked as it returned to its frame, the strange heaviness creating momentum.

All the air left Clare's lungs. Suddenly she was on her knees, panting as if from a physical effort and Theo was staring her in the face.

He was hanging before her – eyes wide open. Huge blue eyes hiding pinprick explosions of red – blood vessels bursting as he choked. She put one hand over her mouth. What had she done? She hadn't meant to hurt him.

Clare backed out of the bedroom. She sat down at the top of the stairs still able to taste the horror of that night. In her hand, crushed into a paper ball, was the indictment. She opened her hand and it fell from her grasp, bounced and rolled down the stairs.

Part Three

The Betrayal

23

LORRAINE

May 2009

May was often fine on the East Coast, but today was the first properly warm day of the year. Lorraine had taken the week off work and walked from her flat up the Bridges towards the Mile. On North Bridge, she looked left to the Crags and then right to the castle and Waverley Station. She had lived in this city for most of her life now, but she didn't tire of this view.

The elevation here, and the fact that there were few buildings to break the wind, meant that a breeze swirled and tugged her cardigan off her shoulder. She took it off, because already, despite the wind on the Bridges, she was perspiring. It was supposed to be eighteen degrees today, but the city centre always felt hotter. She took a deep breath, trying to steady her nerves as she turned onto the cobbled High Street. The day smelled both refreshing and toxic at the same time – dry air blown in from the volcanic rock of the Crags mingled with bus diesel and the sweet dough of cheap, chain restaurants that lined the Bridges.

Ella was at school. A part of Lorraine had wanted to keep Ella out of school and bring her along, so that she could experience today. She wanted her to see and learn, feel involved in this important moment in their family, but also, so that she could hold her little daughter's hand and take comfort from it. When that thought had precipitated in her mind, becoming solid, real, Lorraine had felt it was selfish and that she needed to protect Ella from this. No mother or sister or grandmother should have to experience this, but Lorraine steeled herself for it, alone.

Being a single mother had never been easy, but she felt sure that sitting through her son's murder trial would be her hardest test.

By the time St Giles' Cathedral came into view, Lorraine had to stop, feeling herself breathless with anxiety. She stood in the dank shadow of Advocate's Close, the steep leer of the steps leading down onto Cockburn Street. As the damp air funnelled up the close, Lorraine realised she was sweating. She brushed a forefinger along her upper lip, finding it wet. She could just make out the weathered bronze statue of David Hulme outside Edinburgh High Court. Her limbs were shaking, as if asking her not to go forward, but Lorraine took a deep breath in and out and then proceeded up the hill towards the courthouse.

Lorraine's lawyer had decided not to call her as a witness at all during the trial and so she was free to attend the full trial. Just the thought of being in the same room as Sam and Clare made Lorraine feel nauseous.

There was a throng of people outside the court. Lorraine slid her sunglasses over her eyes and kept her head down as she pushed inside. She had been warned that there would be reporters outside and sure enough she heard a male voice somewhere in the crowd:

That's the Collins boy's mother.

Anger and hurt flared inside her at the words they used. *Collins boy.*

Theo, his name is *Theo.*

Lorraine turned her back on the reporters and made her way to court number eight.

The advocate depute for the procurator fiscal, Brian Peterson, was pacing in the corridor as he talked on his mobile phone, fully robed and wigged. He would present the Crown's case against Sam and Clare and was representing Lorraine. Holding one hand in the other, Lorraine waited to speak to him.

There was seating outside the courtroom and, as she was waiting, Lorraine saw Clare sit. She just wandered into the high court and took a seat in the lobby, as if she was not a criminal. The clothes she was wearing were the only sign that she was not just passing through or attending for jury duty. She was dressed in clothes that she would never wear – a skirt and court shoes – although the crisp white shirt was one Lorraine had seen before.

Quickly, Lorraine turned away from Clare – not wanting to catch her eye – just as Peterson finished his call and deposited his phone into a pocket in his black robes.

'You're here. Good to see you.' He took both of her hands in his.

'I can go in now? It's court eight?'

She didn't want to be anywhere near Clare. There had been a hearing earlier in the year and Lorraine had been shocked that both Clare and Sam had been given bail. Peterson had expected at least Clare to be sent to prison on remand. Clare's lawyer had argued that she was not a danger to the public or a flight risk and that imprisonment on remand would serve no purpose.

'Yes, go in, get a good seat. I have a couple of calls to make beforehand. The clerk of court will get things rolling as soon as the case is called. We can speak again at lunch.'

Lorraine opened the heavy door to the courtroom and stepped inside, choosing a seat near the front of the gallery. At the small of her back, her T-shirt was now damp with sweat, yet in the large, windowless room she felt a chill. The room held a disorienting, furred silence, interrupted only by the slap of a door to the front of the court. A suited and wigged middle-aged woman entered and began to use the computer in the centre of the room. Lorraine guessed that she was the clerk of court.

Turning at the sound of the door again, Lorraine watched as Clare and Sam were led in by a security officer. They took the dock, sitting apart, leaving one chair empty between them. Lorraine knew that they had separated since Theo died, and wondered if the spare seat between them was deliberate. Husband and wife together in the dock, but not on speaking terms. She watched them furtively, eyeing them without turning her head to look. Seeing them both in the flesh was painful and Lorraine felt her chest tighten with anxiety, yet she steeled herself. It was six months since Theo had been killed – six months she had been waiting for this moment.

'Court. All rise, please.'

Lorraine stood as the judge entered. The preliminary hearing had been presided over by a man, but for this trial the judge was a woman – the Honourable Judge Stevenson. A woman was better, Lorraine thought, for this type of case. The judge might be a mother, like her.

Sam and Clare had their backs to Lorraine. Most of Lorraine's hatred was directed at Clare. Hers was the greatest betrayal.

Detective Brookes had not shared with Lorraine a lot of the detail that would be the subject of the trial, but she had shared her theory that was the basis of the Crown's case.

'Clare Armstrong killed your son, and her husband helped her cover it up.'

That was how Brookes had explained the trial to Lorraine and it was only then that what had happened made sense to her.

They had never acknowledged it in their friendship, but there was a thick, red pulsing vein of competition between Lorraine and Clare. Looking back, it had been there since university – marks, popularity, coolness. When they had grown up it had turned into children and jobs. Lorraine had won with children, and Clare – she supposed – had won with jobs. Her work as a photographer was much more interesting than working for the housing association. Clare managed such creativity while being unable to procreate. She had been jealous of Lorraine's children and jealous of her fertility. Lorraine remembered telling Clare that she had conceived Theo when she was on the pill and now she realised how that must have galled her. Clare had won the competition for a partner, with Sam. He was a good man. Lorraine had had boyfriends, lovers, but she had never had a real partner.

Now Clare had lost Sam. She had almost never known what it was like to be single. She would experience that now.

Jealousy, spite – was that what it had been all about? Was that why her little boy had lost his life?

The clerk stood up and addressed the court.

'Case number three-four-zero-seven, the Crown versus Armstrong and Armstrong. Malcolm Power for accused number one, Clare Armstrong; and Judy Miller for accused number two, Samuel Armstrong. There is a joint minute agreeing certain matters in this case – which will be produced and referred to in due course – but there are no other preliminary matters so the case can proceed to trial.'

Judge Stevenson gave her assent.

'May I empanel the jury, my lady?' said the clerk, glancing at her notes and adjusting her wig.

'Very well.'

The G4S officers remained in the dock with Sam and Clare. Lorraine wondered if it was common practice to guard the accused in the dock, or if the security officers had been drafted in just to keep husband and wife apart.

Judge Stevenson seemed elderly. She sat low on the bench as if weighed down by her robes and wig. She was petite, with a round face and a florid complexion. She leaned in towards the microphone and turned to address the jury.

'Ladies and gentlemen of the jury, you are about to hear the evidence in this case. Please listen carefully. You may take notes if you wish. This is a criminal case – which involves a prosecution by the state. Accused number one, Clare Armstrong, is charged with the murder of two-year-old Theo Collins, and accused number two, Samuel Armstrong, is charged with attempt to pervert the course of justice in relation to the death of the same Theo Collins.'

Lorraine swallowed. Hearing her son's name, tears flooded her eyes.

'Please keep an open mind until you have heard all the evidence. At the end of the trial you, and you alone, will be asked to decide upon a verdict and answer the issue. The advocate depute will now address you.'

Lorraine reached into the bag at her feet for a tissue. When she sat up, she saw – across the court, but sitting on the same row as Lorraine – Clare's mother. She was in her seventies now and Lorraine hadn't seen her for years – not since university had finished – but she knew from Clare that her mother didn't keep well. Mary was her name. She wore a bright purple suit, her hair was fresh from curlers and she was sitting very straight with her hands clasped in her lap. What was she feeling now, seeing her daughter tried for murder at a time when she might have expected grandchildren or weekend car trips down the coast? Lorraine had asked her own mother to stay away from the trial, and to look after Ella instead.

The courtroom, Lorraine realised suddenly, was layers of mothers. Lorraine sat in the gallery as the mother of a dead child, Clare stood in the dock, a murderer, but someone who had strived to be a mother for almost as long as Lorraine had known her. Her mother was in the courtroom to see her tried, and then there was the judge, Sam's advocate, Judy Miller, the clerk and the women in the jury. How many of them were mothers? Everyone had a mother, after all.

Silence fell on the courtroom. The room was filled with static electricity as everyone's expectation focused on Lorraine's lawyer.

Peterson stood, adjusted his gown over his grey suit and opened a heavy ring binder file on the lectern.

'The Crown calls Detective Inspector Brookes.'

24

SAM

May 2009

The judge took her seat and then, in a unison of coughs and shuffling, everyone else in the court sat down. There was a pane of glass in front of the dock and Sam felt brutalised by it, as if he were an animal that needed to be contained. He could smell Clare and, even though they weren't speaking, it comforted him. He had missed the smell of her with an almost physical craving. They hadn't even said 'hello', but they were now in the dock together for what Sam's advocate, Judy Miller, had approximated would be two weeks at least. *Most murder trials take that long.*

Sam didn't know what was more surreal: that he was in the dock on a murder trial, that he might go to prison when it was finished, or the fact that he was standing so close to his wife that he could reach out and touch her, yet they were now separate entities.

Only three months before, Sam had stood in another dock,

this time in the sheriff court, to answer to the charge of assault to severe injury with permanent disfigurement, for punching the driver of the Rover. He had pleaded guilty on his counsel's advice, to avoid a trial, and had been fined and ordered to do six months of community service.

As soon as he had been sentenced, Sam had received a text from work – asking him to attend another hearing – this time a professional conduct committee.

The committee hearing was held in the boardroom of the offices of Maitland McConnell. Sam wore a suit and loosened his necktie slightly as he listened to Harry Maitland summarise the committee's decision. By his side was a man in a black polo neck from the architect's registration board.

'You have been a valued member of the core team at Maitland McConnell and we acknowledge how the projects you have led on during nearly fifteen years of service have helped to build and maintain our reputation as leading architects in the field.

'Today we are here to consider a disciplinary order against you, as you have been convicted of a criminal offence, which has relevance to your fitness to practise as an architect.

'You pled guilty in your recent court case to assault to severe injury with permanent disfigurement.

'The committee notes the judge's remarks on sentencing you, which I now will read: "*Mr Armstrong, I make it clear that a reason for going down the route of community service order is that I am acutely aware that the next thing that will happen is that you will have to self-report to your professional body and they may penalise you further or indeed strike you off as an architect. All of those features I have taken into account in sentencing you today, but the saddest thing is that you have lost your good name."*

'It is therefore clear to the committee that you have already been punished for the offence of which you were convicted. However, the judge's sentencing remarks revealed the expectation that a punitive sanction would be imposed by this committee and bore that in mind when sentencing.

'As the committee, we are unanimous that your recent conviction requires a disciplinary sanction and that the matter is too serious for a reprimand. We take into consideration your obvious contrition before the sheriff court and before the committee today. We have been convinced that erasure from the register is not required, but we do impose a suspension order on you for one year.'

Under his jacket, Sam felt sweat course between his shoulder blades.

'As you know, a suspension order is publicised for the period of suspension and a subsequent two years from the date of reinstatement.'

Sam swallowed and nodded. He thanked the committee and stood, banging his knee hard on the metal rim of the table. The pain jarred him but he took care not to show it. He left the room.

He was suspended for one year, but he knew it might be three years or even more before anyone was willing to hire him again.

*

Sam was aware that his conviction in the sheriff court and the fact that he had recently lost his job might go against him in this high court trial. He had asked Judy Miller, his advocate, what might happen if he were found guilty. He and Clare were charged with different offences but their sentences could be the same or similar.

An attempt to pervert the course of justice in relation to murder carried a maximum penalty of a life sentence, although Judy had said it was more realistic to expect five to ten years.

Five to ten years.

Ten years was half the length of his relationship with Clare. He had been with her for half his life. He turned his head just a little to look at her. He could tell she felt afraid because the tendon on her neck was tensing. She would have pain there later, running down her neck to the space between her shoulder blades, and he would not be able to massage it for her.

He hadn't seen her for months and the absence of her had eroded him somehow, so that he felt as if he were crumbling from the inside. They stood together now, but they were no longer together, and that was his fault. He wanted to reach out and hold her hand, but she was sitting straight-backed, eyes forward.

He wanted to tell her he was sorry. She was facing a mandatory life sentence and he knew she wouldn't be in this position were it not for him.

There were no windows in the courtroom, but he knew it was a fine day today, blue sky, a gentle breeze. It was a day for cycling. As he sat in the febrile, static atmosphere of the courtroom waiting for their trial to begin, Sam thought about being outside. He remembered years ago, the fine, soothing heat of the sun on his skin.

Summertime. The sandstone tenements seemed to absorb the rays – their light stone taking the sunshine and then giving it back – so that the streets felt warm and dusty even in the late afternoon. Cycling up Leith Walk, he saw Lorraine walking home from the delicatessen. She was by herself, no Ella in tow, and carrying a big Italian loaf and a pot of fresh olives.

'Hello, stranger,' she called to him when he was twenty or thirty yards away. He weaved out of the traffic queue he was in and skimmed the edge of the pavement until he was able to pull up beside her.

'Fancy meeting you here.' Still straddling his bike, he leaned over to kiss her cheek, self-conscious of the sweat on his face.

Lorraine and Ella lived on a nearby street, on Sam's bicycle commute home, but they rarely ran into each other. Usually, Lorraine was picking Ella up from the childminder around the time that Sam made his way up Leith Walk from his office, towards home.

'You not working today?' he asked. He was surprised to feel his heart thumping against his ribcage. He hadn't been aware of exerting himself as he negotiated the traffic.

'No, I'm off today. Have you bunked off early?' It was not quite five o'clock.

'I was going stir crazy in that office. It's such a lovely day. I just wanted to ...'

'Escape.'

'Exactly.'

'Well, c'mon in for a bit. Sit in the garden with me for half an hour. Aperitif and some Italian snacks?' She held up the bread and olives she was carrying.

Knowing he should get home, Sam glanced over his shoulder. He and Clare were locked in a cycle now: trying for a baby, failing to have a baby, recovering, and then starting over. Starting over was never such a bad place to be, but Clare had just got her period two days ago and so the mood was sombre. And their home in the West End had no outside space. Italian snacks and sunshine sounded like just what he needed.

'Where's Ella?' Sam said, as he entered Lorraine's cramped little two-bedroom flat with its low ceilings that made him feel too tall. He wheeled his bike inside and leaned it against the wall in the hall.

'She has a sleepover. Fancy a beer?'

'Alright.' He sniffed, aware of the film of sweat on his skin and the acrid heat under his armpits. In the living room, washing was drying on a clothes horse, and Sam took a seat on the sofa. Ella's brightly coloured clothes were on the bottom rungs, and Lorraine's blouses and underwear hung at the top. The house was messier than his own, Ella's toys on the floor near the television, and the couch strewn with newspapers, plates from lunchtime still on the coffee table. Sam sat in the armchair waiting for Lorraine to return.

He wasn't sure why he felt nervous. He had known Lorraine for years and they saw each other regularly when she dropped off

Ella at their house. When they were younger the three of them would go out together: Clare and him, Lorraine and a boyfriend if she was seeing one, or by herself if not. He realised that he felt strange because he had not been *alone* with Lorraine for many years. Lorraine had been single on and off over the years, but Sam had always been with Clare. He had always been part of a couple and they had met, almost always, with Clare present.

Clare had told him that Lorraine had started someone new – a musician called Brody – but Sam was yet to meet him. She always went for those types – artists, musicians, people who were travelling. It was as if, subconsciously, she didn't want to settle down.

Lorraine came through holding a beer for each of them in the fingers of one hand and the olives in a little bowl in the other. She was wearing a loose skirt with a vest top and her limbs seemed so long.

'Cheers,' Sam said. The bubbles fizzed on his tongue.

Lorraine pushed the newspapers out of the way and sat at the corner of the sofa near to Sam. He put his beer down, staring straight ahead, noticing and then trying not to stare at one of her bras among the laundry – a sheer pink lace – hanging from one of its straps from the corner of the drying rail.

His skin was cool now but clammy, and he took a long sip of beer. After cycling, it seemed to hit his system fast and he felt a brief buzz.

She held up the bowl of black olives and he shook his head.

'Go on.'

'No, I'm not daft on them.'

'These are gorgeous; they're not like supermarket ones.'

'I dunno.'

'Go on.'

He acceded, biting hard on the stone before chewing off the waxy flesh. He spat the pip into his palm and sat it on the edge of the table.

'Try another.'

He shook his head.

'You need to have another. The second one is always sweeter.'

Sam wasn't sure he trusted her on that, but took another and set the stone on the table again after he had finished, just as she opened the big window onto the garden. Sam smelled freshly cut grass.

'How's Clare?'

'She's okay. A bit down at the moment, but yeah, she's fine.'

Lorraine knew about them trying to conceive but Sam knew Clare guarded some of the details from her friend. He felt the need to change the subject in case he said something he was supposed to keep to himself. 'How's work been?' Lorraine worked at the housing association. It was good, meaningful work, but he often thought Lorraine could have done better – she was bright and spoke two second languages – but for the last few years she had been a single mum and work came second.

'Oh, the usual.' She put a hand to the tendons on the back of her neck, as if she felt strain there. 'It's always quite full-on. It's hard when I have to turn away single mothers with kids. I always think that but for the grace of God it could be me and Ella. Shall we go outside?'

'Sure.'

It was a shared garden, but no other neighbours were outside, even though the patch of grass with slabs along the building wall was drenched in sunshine. Lorraine had some wooden chairs, which she unfolded for them to sit on. She set the olives and their beers on a large, upside-down terracotta plant pot repurposed as a table.

Sam sat back in the chair letting the nearly empty beer bottle rest between his legs. He had drunk it so quickly that the bottle was still cold and he felt the chill against his inner thigh. It was after five, but the heat of the sun was strong. It felt like midday. Sam let his head fall back and felt the full force of the sun on his face.

'This is lovely,' he said, eyes closed looking up at the sun.

'Lucky I bumped into you then. We come out here a lot. I love your place, but it doesn't have a garden. When the sun finally comes out, it's nice to have someplace ...'

'Mm hm,' said Sam, opening his eyes and draining his beer. A large bumble bee, seeming cumbersome, attempted to enter the long purple blossom of a foxglove. There were roses along the far wall, and the grass was covered in daisies. A tree was shedding white blossom, but he wouldn't be able to say what kind. 'It's great.'

'Do you want another one?' Lorraine pointed at the beer bottle between his legs.

'Um ...'

'They're only wee ones.'

As she went to fetch the beer, he felt a reluctant relaxation ease into him. It felt as if the frantic claustrophobia of his life at the moment – work, hospitals, trying to conceive – had paused and he was outside, free from it, smelling the grass and looking up at the high blue sky.

Lorraine brought a new beer and set it on the plant pot with more olives. He thought of saying that he could text Clare – see if she wanted to come along – but something stopped him.

Lorraine sat with one foot on the chair so that her skirt spread out. She ate one olive and then another, licking her fingers after each one. The muscles flexed in her long, thin arms. She had the body of a tennis player.

'Sounds like Ella's doing really well at school.' He and Clare had looked after Ella the weekend before last, so that Lorraine could have some time to herself. It was then that Clare had mentioned Lorraine was seeing someone called Brody. *Think he's just a bit of fun,* Clare had warned him, *don't say anything to Ella.*

Sam wondered about asking Lorraine about Brody – if he was someone she was planning to introduce – but again he thought better of it.

'She's doing *so* well. They've got her on these advanced readers already. Her teacher told me she's starting primary two on a primary four reader. Who knows who she got her brains from.' She waved away a hover fly.

'Well, *you,* clearly,' he said, indulging her.

She laughed outrageously, combing fingers through her hair. 'I don't think so.'

The laughter, the bright sun, the beer and the scent of the

flowers and he felt lighter than he had in a long time. He took a deep, deep breath as if the air itself nourished him.

They reminisced about fun they'd had years ago – Sam getting a flat tyre when he was running Lorraine to the airport. He had changed the tyre with Formula One speed and she had made it to the gate with just a minute to spare. They talked about Ella's baby naming ceremony when Lorraine's mum had fainted and Sam had caught her, dropping to one knee so that it looked as if they were about to kiss. They talked about the long year when Sam was refurbishing the Haymarket flat. On weekends, Lorraine would drop in with cakes and tea and they would drink it sitting on makeshift stools on the newly stripped hardwood floors.

They laughed, loudly, tears pricking their eyes, as they remembered when Ella had been a baby, and Sam had been left to look after her by himself one evening. She wouldn't settle and Lorraine and Clare had come back to find them both asleep in the playpen.

'I mean—' Lorraine knuckled a tear from her eyelid '—I could hardly lift *you* up and put you to bed, could I?'

'Did you wake me up? Did you just leave me there?'

'I was going to put a cover over you and then you woke up. Can you imagine if you'd stayed asleep and woke up in the morning in the playpen . . . you were out for the count.'

'It was hard work.'

Lorraine touched his arm briefly. 'It's not easy, but it's worth it,' she said, as if acknowledging the struggle he and Clare were having.

Sam felt the coolness of her fingertips. Her hand was so much larger than Clare's. Long, thin fingers, like a pianist. His gaze drifted to the makeshift table, realising that the energy of her touch had made him lose his train of thought.

As if in synchrony with his mind, the sun slid behind a cloud and the heat was replaced with shadow and chill.

'Well . . . ' Sam wasn't wearing a watch but he wondered if it was time for him to go. He had only meant to drop in and now the sun had shifted.

'Do you want another beer?'

Sam looked at his bottle and was surprised to see that it was empty. He had been drinking quickly.

'I should go. Clare'll be—'

'Is she not teaching tonight?'

'Oh yeah, she is.' He had forgotten completely. Clare had recently started teaching a continuing education class in photography at Edinburgh University. It was just one evening a week but she wouldn't be back until after nine. He felt better, remembering that she wouldn't be waiting for him.

'So . . . do you wanna get something to eat?'

Sam reached forward and gently put his bottle onto the plant pot. The glass against the terracotta made a pleasing sound.

'I dunno. I have some work to finish off,' he said, standing up and stretching. 'Thanks for the beer though. Come round with Ella at the weekend?'

Lorraine picked up the bowl of olives and ate one. 'Sure,' she said, her mouth full.

'You've got such a nice spot here.'

'It's different when the sun shines, huh?'

They had to go back into the flat to pick up his bicycle. Lorraine had been wearing flip flops, which she now kicked off as she followed him into the hall. Her toenails were painted a bright turquoise and she had silver rings on each of her middle toes. She was still holding the bowl of olives and now presented them again to him.

'One for the road?'

'Nah, I don't think you managed to convert me there.'

'Here . . . ' Despite his protestations, she picked an olive from the bowl and brought it to his mouth, so that the salt blackness touched his lip. She thumbed its dark ovalness right into his mouth. He chewed slowly, confused as he felt a twitch in his cycle shorts. He spat the stone out into his hand.

He gripped the handlebars of his bike, waiting for Lorraine to open the door. 'Thanks for the beer. Not so much the olives.'

She smiled. 'Anytime.'

Lorraine moved forward to kiss him goodbye but they didn't choreograph it well. They missed each other's cheeks and their lips touched.

They both laughed.

'Sorry.'

'Bonus, eh?' Sam said. He tried to withdraw but the bike prevented him. He was close to her face and she was wedged between the handlebars and the door.

'You take care.' Lorraine reached up to touch his cheek.

Sam tried to reverse his bike so that she could open the door but they collided again, gently. In the shadow of the hall, her blue irises seemed black as the olives. He felt his heart rate increase.

It seemed that neither of them leaned forward, and yet their lips met again.

Against his will, he felt himself harden. A ripple of anxiety and excitement sank to the pit of his stomach.

He kept one hand on the handlebars, as if he was headed out of the door. It was easy to kiss and be kissed. They were similar heights. All his life he had had to bend down to kiss a woman. He felt Lorraine's fingertips on his stomach. She tasted of sugar and hops and vinegar. The sensation was gentle, tingling, and it meant he didn't think about it beyond itself. It was wrong, but in that moment it was only unfamiliar, disorienting.

When he finally let go of his bicycle, he was already lost. He was plummeting downhill, the wind whistling in his ears and gravity pulling him down, down. Volition was there only in the effort he made to stay in the present, not to think about *who* he was, only what he was doing. He opened out his palm to touch her and the olive stone fell silently to the floor.

Everything happened quickly, action before he had a chance to consider. For so long sex had been timed and regimented: ovulation charts, pillows under hips, temperatures, conception positions. For so long sex had had a purpose beyond himself and his body.

This was different: the heft of her in his arms, the weight of her above him, the sweat that trickled from her neck down between her shoulder blades, the tattoo at the base of her spine that curved into the dimples on her buttocks. At first he let her just crash over him like waves and then he took charge, rolling on top and cupping her breast. The joy and shock of the full breast and he squeezed each one until the nipples perked and then he worked his way down her body, to her thighs, making her moan. He stopped then, thought about it for a moment, perhaps for the first time, but realised he had gone so far already.

It was everything he remembered sex to be, until the regret came a second after the final shudder of his orgasm. He hated himself, the hatred fast and quick and drenching, filling him up, so that he felt both full and empty as he wheeled his bicycle back outside Lorraine's flat.

She didn't kiss him goodbye this time, but instead stood with one hand over her mouth. She looked as if she might cry. He hung his head.

High summer and it was still so bright outside, no dusk afforded him as he got on his bike feeling tender, drained. The heat of the day had swelled and he felt it on his skin as he cycled back, the taste of Lorraine and the olives still in his mouth.

Neither of them would speak of it, but both of them would know it had happened. He knew from the way they had parted that they were both full of shame.

By the time he reached home, guilt coated his skin as the sheen of his sweat. He put a hand over his face, just imagining the hurt Clare would feel. He tried to remember *how* it had happened. He hadn't meant to, but all the same he had *chosen* to sleep with Lorraine. When had that choice been made? Had it been the moment he'd walked into her flat, after the beer or when he'd smelled the subtle scent of the flowers in the garden?

The salt of his palm smelled different. His fingers smelled of Lorraine. Just imagining the hurt Clare would feel ripped at his insides.

She was still at her class. The emptiness of the house was a relief but also reproached him.

He showered, washing all the traces of the betrayal from his skin. Fingernails, toenails, teeth. He soaped up and rinsed, watched the whirlpool of the drain between his feet.

Sam inhaled, fingers over his mouth, as he watched Detective Brookes take the stand, raise her right hand and swear to tell the truth. He was still reeling from the memory and felt ashamed again, for that, for everything. Sitting in the dock, he still felt the dizzy downward momentum, like cycling from the top of Arthur's Seat – that point when he's going so fast that braking is dangerous. Sitting in the dock separated from the woman he loved, his life felt like that now – plummeting downwards, out of control. He had no idea where it would end.

25

CLARE

May 2009

Clare glanced at Sam as Brookes took the stand. He was pitched forward, elbows on his knees and one hand over his mouth. She knew him so well and could tell he was frightened.

She had accepted that Sam would not be in the dock with her if he had not decided they should lie to Detective Brookes about finding Theo in his cot. Sam had his own advocate and so Clare did not know how she had counselled him. Clare's advocate, Malcolm Power, said that Sam could only be found guilty if *she* was found guilty. Their fates were entwined.

When they met to discuss their strategy for the trial, Malcolm Power had asked Clare why she thought Sam had lied.

'You were drunk, but Sam was sober. You say it must have been an accident, so why would he lie about how he had found the body?'

'Sam believes I did it,' Clare had told Malcolm Power. 'He wanted to protect me.'

'And now? Do you think he'll say in court that he thinks you're guilty of murder?'

Clare sucked her lower lip and bit it gently. She understood what Malcom was trying to say: her fate was entwined with Sam's. If Sam told the court he believed she had killed Theo, then the jury were more likely to find her guilty.

Now, Detective Inspector Brookes rested her hands on either side of the witness box. Her red hair was loose and pushed behind her shoulders, instead of tied in a ponytail as it had been every other time Clare had seen her.

Brookes' evidence began, and the video interviews with Sam and Clare in the police station were played back in court. Clare was shocked at the pallid-skinned, swollen-eyed image of herself that appeared on the monitor. She glanced at the jury – nine women and six men – wondering what they saw. Did they see someone capable of murder?

As the video played in court, Brookes' questions could be heard clearly, but the angle of the camera, shot from the corner of the interview room, only captured the back of her head.

'In your witness statement, and in your first interview under caution, you asserted that when you discovered Theo not breathing, he was unconscious in his cot. Now you know the results of the post-mortem, and you have changed your story. Tell me, Clare, why did you lie?'

'I didn't ... lie. I was in shock when I found Theo and I couldn't remember exactly the chain of events. I'd been drinking.'

'You appeared heavily inebriated, but even so the sight of that baby hanging must have been hard to forget.'

One of the women in the jury seemed distressed as she listened. She leaned forward and put her fingers over her mouth as she watched the video. An older man at the end was sitting back in his seat, arms folded as if sceptical of what he heard.

Clare turned again to the monitor, hearing her voice.

'It was an accident,' she heard herself say. 'I don't know how it happened, but it was an accident. Theo must have got out of his cot. He must have been running to get to us and got himself caught somehow.'

'I'm less interested in your theories and more interested in the reason why you lied in your initial statement about the position of the child's body.'

Clare swallowed, watching the messy, confused image of herself on the monitor begin to break down and cry.

The clerk of court cued up the sections of Sam's interview with the police and Clare saw her husband appear on the screen. He looked tired, hunched over the table with hands clasped. She felt a confusion of bitterness and guilt. He had stood by her with the police, and so he had been arrested, but he had also abandoned her, walking out on her just when she needed him most.

'You lied about how you found Theo – the position of his body before you tried to resuscitate him.'

'I shouldn't have – I'm sorry. I think I panicked . . . I was . . .'

'You shouldn't have lied, but you did.'

Sam sat up, raking his hair and then reaching out over the table towards Brookes. 'Theo is a climber. He could climb out of the cot – Lorraine warned us about that the minute she

265

saw the bed we had bought for him. "*Don't think he's staying in there*," she said. "*He'll climb out of that in two minutes flat*", and I think he did climb out just as she had warned – I think he ran towards the door, to find us and got caught, that hood he was wearing hooked him.' Sam sighed and looked down at his palms that were turned upwards on the table. 'It's the worst thing that could ever happen. The worst thing, but it was an accident.'

'You didn't tell me that when I took your statement at the house. You lied to me instead. But now I know that's who you are – you're a liar, Sam, aren't you? You lied to me, and you lied to your wife—'

The clerk of court paused the video and Brian Peterson, the advocate depute, resumed his questioning of Detective Brookes. The video evidence had been slow and pedantic and Clare had watched two or three members of the jury stifling yawns, but the place where the clerk had paused Sam's interview – about him lying to his wife – seemed to stimulate their interest.

'Detective Inspector Brookes, what electronic devices belonging to the co-accuseds were taken into evidence?'

'At the time of arrest, we took into evidence personal mobile phones . . . also a laptop computer was removed from the property by Scenes of Crime officers following the post-mortem.'

'And what was found on these electronic devices?'

'Mr Armstrong's mobile phone provided personal correspondence that we have submitted into evidence as it appeared to show a motive for the murder.'

Peterson briefly turned towards the jury.

'The jury has a transcript in their bundle of a text message received by accused number two, Samuel Armstrong, on the night of the murder. Detective, please can you read this text message to us now?'

In the dock, Clare closed her eyes. This was the reason Sam had lied for her and why he could no longer be with her. This, she could remember.

As the detective read out Sam's text, the night at the flat came back to Clare, bleached and ghostly like film negatives. She watched the reel turn in her mind.

Clare sank onto the couch in the living room. For the first time in what felt like hours, there was silence. Theo was no longer crying, there were no children's footsteps stamping over the hardwood floors. Theo was asleep, Ella was asleep in their bed and Sam was upstairs showering.

Clare laid both hands on the skin of her belly. It was flat and smooth. Pregnancies swelled her up – she would bloat even a few weeks after conception. The miscarriage and the procedure had left her feeling so empty.

It was just after nine. The old pipes clanked as Sam turned off the shower and Clare picked up the remote, about to turn on the television – sound down low in case it woke the children. Sam's phone sounded. He had left the phone on the coffee table and Clare saw Lorraine's name flash on the lock screen.

She smiled and reached to pick up the phone. The message just disappeared from the screen as she drew it towards her, but she entered his password to retrieve it. She expected that

Lorraine wanted a call now or at least wanted to find out if Ella and Theo were asleep.

When the message opened, Clare couldn't read it at first, or rather she read and re-read – disbelieving. Was it sent in error – meant for someone else? One of Lorraine's boyfriends? It wouldn't have surprised Clare if Lorraine was back in touch with Brody or seeing someone new.

The meaning seeped into her slowly.

'I drank too much Prosecco and I've been thinking it's funny how things worked out with us. I know I shouldn't but I want you here now to hold. Give our boy and Ella a kiss from me. X'

The message had to be meant for Sam and whoever Lorraine was texting was with Ella.

Our boy.

The full impact of the text's meaning burst around her suddenly, like mushrooms blooming on time-lapse photography. A lurch in her gut. Clare made two fists with her hands and covered her eyes.

The phone fell to the floor. She stayed like that for long seconds that seemed like minutes. Patterns of light radiated where her fists pushed into her eyes. It wasn't true. It couldn't be true. It was a mistake. She had read it wrong. She ran upstairs to tell Sam, wanting to hear it from him that it just *wasn't true.*

*

Detective Brookes read Lorraine's text out to the court-room: *our boy.*

'The jury will find the transcript from the mobile phone on page nine of their bundle,' Peterson directed. 'Detective Inspector Brookes, we now return to your questioning of accused number one in relation to the evidence obtained from accused number two's phone.'

Clare's interview again flashed up on the screen.

'You've been trying to have a baby for some time, have you not?'

Brookes' face was still off camera, but her voice sounded suddenly kinder.

'Yes, for many years.'

'And how many miscarriages have you had so far?'

'Ten.' Clare cleared her throat and pinched the tears from her nose.

'That's an awful lot of loss. Ten miscarriages?'

'Yes.'

'I'm a mother and I know what it must feel like to lose a child.'

Clare's eyes were startled, wary.

'So let me recap—' Detective Brookes' voice became harsher, more business-like '—the night Theo died you've admitted that you were drunk and fighting with your husband. The text message we have from Sam's phone tells us *what* you were fighting about . . .'

The skin on Clare's face visibly trembled.

'How did you feel, Clare, when you saw that text? You and your husband had been trying for a baby all this time – *years* – suffering miscarriage after miscarriage. You had just lost a baby at thirteen weeks, and now you find out that Sam has not only been unfaithful to you, but *had a baby* ... with your close friend, and that baby is sleeping in your house.'

Tears flooded from Clare's eyes. They shone on her face under the harsh lights of the interview room.

'It was awful. It was the worst thing ... ever ...'

'The worst thing ever,' Detective Brookes repeated. 'So how did you feel – angry?'

'Yes, angry, and ...'

'It made you *so* angry you smashed a glass, didn't you?'

Clare parted her lips, staring at the police officer. She nodded.

'You found out about the affair and you were *seething*. You smashed a glass. What else did you do? Did it make you want to hurt Theo, knowing that he was Sam's son?'

'No, of course not. How could you even suggest that I *killed* Theo? I couldn't do that ...'

'I'm suggesting you have a motive for murder.'

As the video continued, Clare watched the jury's faces. They were all intently watching her image on the screen. She wondered what they were thinking. She glanced at Sam and he half-nodded at her. She thought she saw kindness towards her in the light of his eyes. Understanding.

'So, Detective Inspector Brookes,' advocate depute Peterson continued, 'during the interview, Clare Richardson admitted that she had discovered this text on her husband's phone the night that the children were staying?'

'Correct.'

'And accused number one also admitted that she became

intoxicated and had an argument with her husband about the paternity of the deceased, Theo Collins?'

'Correct.'

'Did you attempt to corroborate that Theo Collins *was* the child of accused number two, Sam Armstrong?'

'We did. A paternity test was conducted, comparing post-mortem DNA from the deceased and DNA extracted from a buccal sample provided by accused number two, Sam Armstrong – taken after initial arrest.'

'And the result of the paternity test?'

'Probability of paternity was ninety-nine point nine-nine-eight per cent.' Brookes sighed. 'Sam Armstrong is the biological father of the deceased child, meaning that Clare Armstrong had a clear motive to murder Theo Collins.'

Clare's lawyer, Malcolm Power, leapt to his feet, black gown ballooning behind him. 'M'lady, please can the witness wait for questions to be asked before answering them herself?'

Judge Stevenson leaned in towards her microphone. 'I agree. Detective Inspector Brookes, if you could restrict your answers to the questions posited by the advocate depute and his colleagues. It is unhelpful if you offer conclusions without first being asked.'

'Yes, m'lady,' Brookes replied. 'Sorry, m'lady.'

In the dock, Clare glanced over at Sam. He was facing forward, completely still. The only movement was the gentle rise of his stomach as he breathed. Clare swallowed and began to knead her temples with her fingers. The fight from that night began to play in her mind.

*

'Our boy? Oh my God, Sam, *our boy*?' Clare had his phone in her hands. 'What does it mean? What can it mean?'

'What are you talking about?' His hair was sticking up and wet.

Her voice sounded breathless, as if she had been running at full pelt. 'Lorraine just texted you. I thought she just wanted an update on the kids but then I read ... What does it mean, Sam? Tell me it doesn't mean what I think?' She pressed the phone into his hands.

He was silent. He took the phone from Clare and stared at the text message for the longest time, his face impassive.

'Are you?'

'What?'

'Are you?' It seemed impossible. This couldn't be happening to them, to her. This only happened to *other people*. 'Are you ... sleeping with *Lorraine*?' The words choked from her throat.

Clare felt desperate now, but still disbelieving – she was ready to be told that she was mistaken. She had staked so much of her life around him. Two decades, their life had shared a course.

'It wasn't what you think ...' He avoided her eyes, still looking at the damn phone. She wanted to take it from his hands and smash it, dash it into pieces. 'It wasn't an affair or anything. It just happened and I didn't know ...'

Clare bent over as if punched. Her mouth was open and she couldn't take in any air.

'What? Are you?' She looked up, hands on her knees. 'Are you really serious? After all this time? After all we've been through?'

Tears sprang from his eyes. 'It was only once. Oh my God, I

wouldn't do that to you, but it was once, just once and then she told me ... that Theo was mine. I couldn't believe it, I didn't dare think—'

'Oh my God,' Clare cried too loudly.

He grabbed her elbow and she wrenched it away from him.

'Clare, please, let's not talk about it now. The children—'

'So when are we going to talk about it? What – you think this is a keep for tomorrow? Seriously?'

She wasn't crying yet. The tears were there, waiting, a swarm of them inside her.

'*Our boy?* Jesus. He even looks like you. I see it now. He looks *like you.* Oh my God, my God, God ...'

Clare turned and went downstairs, hearing Sam behind her, feeling him so close, the energy of him disoriented her. All of the comprehension she had been trying to hold at bay suddenly came at her, a wave, making her lose kilter.

It was the worst thing, the worst thing in the world.

You'd be such a good dad, she had always told him, and – now – he *was* one. After all those years and all those miscarriages, one fuck with Lorraine and Sam was a father. Just like that.

Clare bent over and screamed. It was a visceral, physical sound, as if she was in labour. Sam ran to her and tried to press her into him. 'Be quiet, *be quiet.*'

She broke away from him, the tears now streaming down her face. She beat his chest with her fists, feeling the power in them lessen with each blow. He took it from her – pushing back his shoulders as if asking for more – but she pushed him away.

She didn't want it to be true. She didn't want to take it in.

273

She opened the fridge and took out the wine that had been in there for months. She didn't care about anything any more, but she was going to drink it. She wanted to be numb, for this not to be happening. She needed to blackout, wanted to be lifted out of herself. She just wanted the pain to go away.

Clare opened her eyes. Detective Inspector Brookes was still on the stand.

'Further examination of the laptop revealed relevant Internet searches made on the night that Theo Collins and his sister, Ella, stayed at the co-accuseds' property.'

Mr Peterson glanced at his ring binder. 'The jury will find a transcript of the Internet search in their bundle. Detective Inspector Brookes, can you read for us now the significant searches?'

'Yes, the first was for *Calpol Six Plus for infants*, followed by a search for *how much Calpol can overdose two-year-old*.'

'We will hear from the pathologist shortly, but from your knowledge of the post-mortem examination, was Calpol present in the body of the toddler?'

'It was not.'

Clare's advocate, Malcolm Power, took to his feet at the same time as Sam's advocate, Malcolm Power.

'The toxicology for the deceased showed no drugs were present in the toddler's system at all – not only an absence of Calpol. Is this not correct?'

Brookes cleared her throat. 'Yes, the toxicology results were clear, but I considered this Internet search could have been the first evidence of premeditation. Clare Armstrong had motive to murder Theo Collins and she was considering ways to carry it out—'

'I see, evidence of premeditation. There is no way to tell who – which of the co-accuseds – made the search?'

'No, it was a shared computer. During the interview, Mrs Armstrong said she could not remember making the search and Mr Armstrong denied it, but one of them certainly did.'

Judge Stevenson reached for the microphone and pulled it towards her. 'I think, in consideration of the hour, we shall begin cross-examination of this witness tomorrow.'

All rise.

The security guard opened the gate of the dock for Clare. She glanced at Sam, but he was still seated, staring straight ahead, the muscle in his cheek twitching. Clare shouldered her handbag and left the courtroom as quickly as she could, then slowed her pace in the lobby. Lorraine was just ahead of her, passing through the metal detector.

Clare went into the bathroom and waited for a few moments, catching sight of herself in the bathroom mirror and thinking that she looked ill, aged.

Stepping outside the court, Clare thought she was safe, but just as she turned onto the Royal Mile she heard the shutter of a camera sound. She turned to look and a flash flared, bringing spots to her eyes.

26

CLARE

August 2019

'So, you've not been indicted?' Clare asked.

'No.' Sam reached out and touched her hand briefly. 'Not this time.'

She liked being near him. Even though they had only met to speak about her retrial, it felt comforting to be in his presence.

They were in Princes Street Gardens. *Good news and bad,* she had texted him: the cancer had gone away but that November night in 2008 had not. Only he could really understand how she felt and so she had asked to meet again.

She still remembered the lurch inside her when she learned that he had been unfaithful. That he had slept with Lorraine hurt more. *Anyone else* would have been better – a colleague on a drunken night out, even a random affair would have been easier to take, but soon the pain of his betrayal had merged with Theo's death, and the stress of the trial. She told herself she now forgave them both – Sam and Lorraine – for the sake of her mental health, yet Clare still felt damaged by it. *It just happened*, Sam had said. *It didn't mean anything.* But of course it had meant something: it meant that the man she loved had breached her trust. If she thought about it, which she tried not to do, it could still bring tears to her eyes.

It was the height of the festival and the gardens were seething. The sun was out and hundreds of people were lying on the sloped grass. Children ran back and forth, screaming. Litter rattled along the pathway where they sat on a bench that they shared with two tourists from Italy or Spain. They were surrounded by so many people, so many different languages, yet their meeting felt private because of that. No one's attention settled on them.

'A retrial. How is that even possible?'

'Double jeopardy. Except I'm the only guilty one this time.'

He frowned. 'You've talked to a lawyer?'

'Yes, I called Malcolm Power.'

'I remember him. Solicitor advocate. Good surname.'

'Yes, a good name.' She laughed briefly, feeling hopeless. 'Let's see if he can live up to it again.' She let her head fall into her hands then felt his strong fingers kneading the tendons at the back of her neck. The touch surprised her. It was something he might have done when they were together.

'But that was great about your test results.'

'Yes.' She sat up, took a deep breath. The gardens smelled of a strange amalgam of takeaway food from the nearby caravans and the perfume of roses that lined Princes Street above them. 'I can be healthy in prison.'

'Don't say that. Think positive.'

Clare didn't turn to look at Sam as he spoke. A searing memory came to her suddenly, painful as heartburn, of the look Sam had given her when he'd packed up all his things and left her.

'I asked Malcolm if I had brought this on myself, by writing that letter to Lorraine. He thinks it didn't help, but it's not just that which has led to the retrial. It seems they have new forensic evidence. For double jeopardy there must be new evidence that was not available at the first trial. We don't know yet *what* they have, but Malcolm says it's some new DNA evidence that confirms I—'

Clare couldn't say the word, *murder*.

Sam's face was grave. He had deep lines now around his mouth and the line of his jaw was less firm, and Clare wondered if that was why he had grown a thick layer of stubble. Designer stubble – too short to be a beard. She thought it didn't suit him – partially grey as it was – but knew she no longer had a right to comment.

She stretched her arms, taking a deep breath as she looked up at the sky, its blue encroached by the leaves of tall trees, oak and ash.

'I don't know how I'll plead this time,' she said, speaking to the blue sky and the scant clouds that skirted above. 'In the letter to Lorraine, I admitted I was responsible, and of course I was, but I never, ever meant to hurt him ...'

The truth was, she wasn't certain of that fact. There was, after all, new DNA evidence that again pointed to her guilt. She had been angry, hurting. Who knew what that alcohol fuelled rage had driven to her do? What had happened in the darkness of her blackout?

'I know that,' he said quietly.

She looked him straight in the eye. Despite all the years they had been apart, she knew him so well, and she saw the uncertainty in his large blue eyes. Sadness rose up within her, like warm liquid. She wanted to ask him how he could have loved her, yet still think her capable of such cruelty.

It was overwhelming sitting beside him, navigating their new post-traumatic friendship. She hadn't so much as kissed another man since they had separated. She hadn't even wanted to, but she knew that Sam dated – he could be seeing someone right now for all she knew. Her friend from the studio on Cockburn Street, Arnold, had told her a few years ago that he had seen Sam's profile on a dating site.

To change the subject, and to stop herself from crying, Clare pointed at Sam's thin-wheeled city bike that he had leant against the side of the bench. 'I thought you said that you had given up cycling.'

'I had, but—' he smiled, looking down at the children who had stopped screaming and were now attempting lopsided somersaults down the hill '—the other day, after I met you, I decided I needed to get back into it for my own health if nothing else. I'm so out of practice, but you inspired me. It's still early days.' He ran his hands down his thighs, over his jeans that were still tucked into his socks. 'I can really feel it on my legs, just that tiny bit of cycling up here. To think I used to cycle over a hundred miles a week.'

'King of the Mountain,' she said, remembering all those small cyclist triumphs he had cherished. 'And you just stopped.'

'Yeah, it was just . . . I don't know, partly it was that fight I got into . . .' He still referred to it as a fight, rather than what he knew it had been – him venting anger at Theo's death on some unsuspecting driver. 'I didn't want to cycle any more after it; I'd had enough. But then—' he rolled up the sleeves of his white shirt, one and then the other '—after I moved out, all my stuff was in boxes and it seemed too much effort to unpack.'

She smiled, knowing his tendency for procrastination. He had always seemed to need her to instigate tasks – to point out what needed to be done.

'After our lunch the other day, I finally tackled the wall of cardboard boxes in my flat.'

'You don't mean—' Clare sat up straight, put a hand on his bare forearm '—boxes from us? Our boxes? It's been, like, nearly eleven years. You're not serious?'

Sam chuckled. 'I'm afraid I'm serious. I've not really unpacked since . . . then.' He was coy now, pitching forward, elbows on his knees, glancing at her for only a second before staring down, at the daisies in the grass bracing themselves against the breeze.

Clare was not sure why, but just imagining that wall of cardboard boxes -- the same ones he had carried out of the flat the day after Theo died – filled her with a great swell of feeling.

'Tell me something,' Sam said, stretching his legs and crossing his ankles.

'What?'

'Why did we never get divorced?'

'Um—' Clare put her hands in her pockets '—both lazy?'

He turned to her and after a moment she looked up at him. He shook his head. 'You're not lazy though, are you?'

Clare hung her head, looked at her bright-red baseball boots. One lace was close to becoming undone.

'No . . . I think we didn't do it because despite everything that happened we knew being together was what we did best,' he said.

She felt a great pressure underneath her ribs, something like joy, but she kept focusing on her laces and didn't dare to look at his face.

27

SAM

May 2009

'The Crown calls Dr McKay.'

The pathologist took the witness box. He was a tall, thin man and when he repeated the oath to tell the truth, his eyes seemed small and furtive. Sam imagined him at dinner parties, concentrating on dissecting his meal rather than engaging in conversation.

Brian Peterson nodded briskly as he reviewed notes in the heavy binder that he carried to the podium, then began questioning.

'Please can you state your name and occupation for the record?'

'Dr Brendan McKay, senior forensic pathologist at the University of Edinburgh, offering a specialist on-call service to the Crown in regard to suspicious deaths.'

'Dr McKay, you examined the deceased, Theo Collins; what was your conclusion about the time of death?'

'I fixed time of death at between ten thirty and eleven forty-five at night.'

'How did you come to this conclusion?'

'The attending paramedics noted rectal temperature when they pronounced life extinct at shortly after twelve thirty a.m. This temperature, and the one noted in the Scenes of Crime officer's report on the ambient temperature of the bedroom where the child died, are used in an algorithm to approximate the time of death.'

'And this algorithm, how exact is it?'

'It gives time of death to within an hour of accuracy.'

'Any greater leeway – you do say that it *approximates* time of death?'

'Yes, it gives a window of about an hour when death could have occurred but is exact to that hour. There is no possibility that death could have occurred before or after that point.'

'So just to be clear, Theo could have died any time between ten thirty and eleven forty-five but not before or after that time?'

'Correct.'

'Following your post-mortem examination, what were your findings with regards to the cause of death?'

'The cause of death was asphyxiation. Marks were observed on the child's neck and the area underneath his chin, suggestive of ligature. Retinal haemorrhages were clearly visible in his eyes, and, further to this, tissue samples taken revealed that there was also blood in his lungs. Both of these are consistent with death by asphyxiation with ligature.'

'Thank you, doctor. What were your findings about the

nature of the death? Did your post-mortem examination suggest murder or an accidental death?'

McKay took an intake of breath and pushed his metal-framed glasses further up the bridge of his nose.

'Having examined the body and read the reports by Scenes of Crime officers on the room where Theo Collins died, it was my conclusion that it was significantly *more likely* that death had been deliberately caused. Although it is rare in children above the age of one, suspicious deaths in infants are often ascribed to accidental asphyxiation as a result of becoming caught in bedding or being unable to raise the head off a pillow, for example. Theo Collins was just over two years old and able to walk. He was unlikely to have become entangled in his bedding and therefore asphyxiated, but beyond this, the clear ligature marks around the child's neck suggest deliberate strangulation was the cause of death.'

The courtroom screens projected an image of Theo's small, pale neck – up close – showing the dark line of bruising at the top of the neck and underneath his chin.

'We have heard from Detective Inspector Brookes and listened to police interviews with the co-accuseds, where they recant their original statement that Theo Collins was found unconscious in his bed, and state instead that the child was found hanging by the hood of his sleepsuit from the bedroom door handle. Does this revised statement from the co-accused posit a likely cause of strangulation?'

'Yes, the marks on the neck corresponded with the fabric of the sleepsuit, and fibres from the suit were found on the skin along the area of contusion around the neck. The angle of bruising on the neck, and the fact that fibres from the sleepsuit were so embedded in the skin suggested that the child could have been asphyxiated as a result of being suspended by the neck of his sleepsuit.'

'Thank you, Dr McKay. Reflecting on this likely scenario where asphyxiation occurred, was it your conclusion that Theo's death was accidental or deliberate?'

'I defer to forensic scientists whom I believe conducted modelling, but according to the pathology, strangulation by ligature suggests murder and the explanation the child was hung in such a manner only strengthens that assertion in my opinion. The suggestion that death by hanging occurred accidentally is, while conceivable, highly improbable.'

'Thank you, doctor.'

McKay raised his chin, unsmiling, as he waited for Clare's advocate to cross examine him.

As the advocate depute took his seat, Malcolm Power approached the lectern. Power was short and stocky, with a low centre of gravity like a fighting dog.

'My client, accused number one, made a corrective statement to the effect that she found the child hanging by his hood from the door handle in the bedroom. Doctor, you have stated under oath that an accidental death was – I refer to your wording – *conceivable*. The defence alleges that, on the night in question, Theo most likely climbed out of his cot, and, in running towards the hallway for his carers became caught by the hood of his sleepsuit on the door handle, which caused asphyxiation and eventual death. We will hear shortly from forensic scientists who carried out a recreation of the crime scene using life-sized dummies, but you agree that this is a *conceivable* alternative scenario, which could have resulted in the accidental death of the infant?'

The judge lurched forward over the bench, her red face puckering. 'Please can you ask the question in a way which is not leading?'

'Of course m'lady. I apologise. Dr McKay, what is your opinion of the defence's proposition that asphyxiation occurred accidentally?'

The pathologist shifted his stance in the witness box, causing his tall frame to waver at the front of the courtroom. He frowned deeply. 'While it is in the realm of possibility that death was accidental, and in the manner posited, I find it highly improbable as I have stated already. As I said, I defer to experts in forensic science, but, purely on the pathology, it is statistically unlikely that the hood of the sleepsuit could have risen up and snagged on the door handle in the manner you describe, causing these injuries.' McKay shrugged almost dramatically. 'I would argue that the height of the door handle and the lack of give in the material of the sleepsuit meant that strangulation would have been inevitable had he found himself in that position, but that it was more likely that the child was *placed there* with the intention of asphyxiating him.'

As if he had not heard Dr McKay's last words, Malcom Power added,

'To clarify, the proposition that the child became caught

and asphyxiated on his own, without malicious intent, is still possible?'

'Possible, but extremely unlikely,' McKay said, his jaw tight so that his mouth barely seemed to open in answering.

'And one further thing, there was no evidence of obstruction on the child's nose or face?'

'That's correct.'

'If Theo Collins *had* found himself hanging on the door handle, would he have been able to call out and warn others of his ... predicament? At the time of his death, Theo's sister was sleeping next door and his godparents were within earshot of the room.'

'Regardless of facial obstructions, strangulation would have begun immediately and the pressure on the vocal chords and the lack of air would have meant crying out was impossible.'

'And finally, Dr McKay, a difficult question for you to answer and the court to hear, but in your examination of the body and determination of time of death, were you able to say how long it would have taken Theo to die?'

'It is difficult to say, but it would have been swift, two minutes or three at most.'

There was a communal gasp in the court.

Sam shook his head, trying to erase the image of Theo hanging. He turned up his palms and rested them on his knees.

28

LORRAINE

September 2019

It was Theo's birthday and, as they did most years, Lorraine and Ella visited the cemetery where he was buried. When she finished college, Ella met her mother in town, and together they caught the bus out to Portobello.

It was a double-decker and they sat on the top deck, right at the front to watch the bus winding its way down Leith Walk towards the shore and then out to Portobello. It felt like watching fate steer – seeing things just before they happened. At her feet, Lorraine set down her shopping bag, which contained a bag of mixed bulbs – tulips, daffodils, crocuses – and a trowel. Every birthday they did this, so that Theo had fresh flowers growing on his grave through spring into summer.

Lorraine had taken today off work. She tended to take Theo's birthday as annual leave as a matter of course. She was never effective on this day – it was easy to think too much and get depressed. But this year, she felt more hopeful. This year she might be able to give Theo the best birthday present of all: justice. Detective Inspector Brookes had confirmed that Clare's retrial was set to commence in October. Less than a month away.

Ella pressed the bell when she saw the sea. She was so tall she couldn't stand up straight on the upper deck and so headed down the steps in front of Lorraine. It was still a surprise to her, how the little girl who had once held her hand skipping along the road was now a grown woman. The silvery criss-cross lines on her forearm were still visible but they were all healed. Lorraine thought they would both now be able to heal, if they got justice for Theo.

As they entered the wrought-iron gates of the cemetery, Lorraine linked arms with Ella. They walked past rows of Victorian gravestones – Celtic crosses, faded moss-covered plinths – to a patch of ground where the grass was kept neat and the stones were shiny granite and freshly tended.

At the far corner of the cemetery, in the shadow of one of the four protective elms that marked the circumference of the yard, was a red granite gravestone, still sparkling and seeming new, even though over a decade had passed since it had been placed as a marker.

The stone was cut in the shape of a teddy bear.

Almost immediately, Lorraine got down on her knees and started to clear away the debris: autumnal leaves, faded leaves of day lilies that would come again in early summer, a crisp packet that had blown in from the road. She knelt on her canvas shopping bag as she marked holes in the earth with her trowel and Ella dropped in the bulbs, roots pointing downwards. When they were done, Ella held out her hand and Lorraine took it to help her stand, dusting the trace of soil from her jeans. There was a watering can and outdoor tap near the gatehouse and Ella went to fetch it, leaving Lorraine alone. She stood, hands clasped, staring at the headstone.

Theo Christopher Collins,
18 September 2006–21 November 2008
Died aged two years and two months.
Beloved son of Lorraine and sister to Ella.
Dearly missed.

The words *Dearly Missed* always made Lorraine's throat ache when she read them. She had chosen the wording herself. It had been her choice to name only herself and Ella as Theo's family. When Lorraine had registered his birth, she had made no record of the father. At the time, Brody believed Theo was his, and had offered to go with her to the registry office but Lorraine had said she would go alone. Better to have *no* father than the *wrong* father listed.

Lorraine swallowed. Her feelings from that time had become a hard, calcified lump inside – self-created, like a gallstone. Her pain at losing Theo, her anger at how Clare had made him suffer, was also strangely blended with her own guilt, for that hot summer afternoon with Sam.

Even through the wrenching pain of her loss, the guilt was

still clear, iridescent on the surface, like oil on a puddle. Clare was her friend and Lorraine had hurt her almost without think-ing. It had come out of nowhere; neither she or Sam felt able to navigate it, but it must have been waiting there, an energy between them, for many years. She had not expected what would happen would be a beloved little boy.

There was a strong scent of pine from the evergreens that created a barrier between the graveyard and the main road. Lorraine breathed it in, shifting her attention from the teddy bear grave to the spectacle of colour on the deciduous trees: the different shades of yellow, red and rust.

Lorraine was starting to show. She had said nothing about the pregnancy to Sam and Clare for as long as she could. She put her hand on the gentle swell of her belly and said that she would like both apple pie and ice cream and so would Ella. They were in Sam and Clare's flat, finishing dinner.

'It's piping hot; you'll need to be careful,' said Clare, slicing the homemade pie and placing it, steaming, onto plates.

Brody stood with his hands in his pockets before the fireplace, looking at each of Clare's photographs in turn. It was the first time he had been in their flat and he was irritating Lorraine by commenting every minute or so, on one object or another, saying how stylish everything was, and how he would love to live in a place like this.

It was becoming obvious and so, today, Lorraine had told Sam and Clare that she and Brody were expecting a little boy – even though they had only been together for a matter of months.

'Why did you want to find out the sex of the baby?' Clare asked as she served up the pie. Lorraine heard the forced cheer in her tone.

'Why not, I thought?' Lorraine answered, aware of how painful it had to be for Clare that she was expecting again. 'Why should the doctors know more than me?'

'I suppose. I think I would want to wait.' Clare's voice sounded vague, far away, as if it hurt to put herself in the position of choosing. 'I think I'd want to savour the surprise.'

Lorraine got up and gave Clare a one-armed hug. She wanted to say something in comfort, but knew that there were no words. 'You'll be godmother again, of course.'

'I'd love to be.' Clare was still serving up, but her eyes shone.

'Let me do that.' Lorraine took the pie slice from Clare.

Clare rested her hands on the counter and whispered to Lorraine. 'Why didn't you tell me? Why did you wait all this time?'

'I'm sorry.' Lorraine gathered her into her arms and squeezed her. Her throat ached. She had dreaded this. There was never going to be a good time. 'I'm sorry; it's just that I didn't want to upset you. I know what you're going through.'

'But that doesn't mean I wouldn't be happy for you.'

'I know that.' They hugged again and Lorraine closed her eyes. 'Of course I know you're happy for me. You'll get to watch me blow up like a beachball again.'

They laughed as they let go, each wiping the other's tears.

'I'm sorry,' Lorraine mouthed again, and then louder: 'I'm fat already!'

'You look great,' Clare said, smiling valiantly. 'Sam, can you go upstairs and get the extra chair from the bedroom?'

'Sure thing.'

A minute later Lorraine excused herself to go to the bathroom. Ella was content on the living room floor, flat on her stomach with her heels in the air, leafing through a picture book. One hand on her lower back, the other on the handrail, Lorraine made her way upstairs. On the landing there was a multi-coloured bookcase with framed photographs of Ella when she was a baby, and then more recent prints.

As Lorraine reached the top of the stairs, Sam was coming out of the bedroom with the extra chair. They both stopped on the landing, Sam with the clear plastic chair in his hands and Lorraine with her hands on her hips. They had barely been alone since the afternoon at her flat. 'We thought you might be pregnant,' he said, pausing at the bedroom door. He seemed awkward and his smile was stiff, wary. 'Brody seems chuffed.'

'I suppose he is,' she said, shrugging, turning to face Sam, so that her back was to the window overlooking the living room. She felt a sudden crushing sensation in her chest. It took her breath away and she rested a hand on her belly as if to protect the baby from the strength of her emotion.

'You should have told us, though. You know we'd be happy for you. It's not a competition.' His smile was assured, closed lipped.

They had been carrying on this act for a while – pretending as if nothing had happened between them.

'Of course it's not a competition.' Lorraine swallowed and met Sam's eye. 'That wasn't why I didn't say.' Lorraine began to whisper; not afraid someone would overhear but rather not having the breath to carry the words: 'The timing, y'know ... It can't be Brody's. I'm very sure.' She was going to say more, but tasted tears at the back of her throat.

For the briefest moment, Sam let his eyes fall to gaze at her belly. His lips parted and he inhaled as if about to speak, but said nothing, passing her to return downstairs with the chair. Lorraine went into the bathroom and let her forehead rest on the back of the door.

When Ella returned with the watering can, Lorraine was still staring at Theo's grave.

'You alright, Mum?' Ella's long back curved as she watered the freshly planted bulbs in the earth before the grave.

'I'm fine.' She had known early on that the baby was Sam's. The dates matched and then Theo, when he came, looked so like him. And then Brody had finally left – an afterthought in a shouty argument – *I don't even think that's my child.*

Ella set the empty watering can at her feet. 'Do you want to stay here for a bit, or ...'

'I wanted to tell you something,' Lorraine said, turning to Ella. 'You remember the detective that came to the flat?'

'Yes, Detective Brookes.'

'Well, she's been successful in getting a fresh trial for Theo. It's going start next month. I'll take time off work and I'll go along there each day. You've got college and you should concentrate on that.'

'A new trial? But what does that mean?'

'They have new evidence that Clare killed Theo.' Lorraine felt her chin tremble. She turned towards the red granite teddy bear grave.

Ella was silent, beginning to bite her fingernail. 'Aunt Clare?'

'Don't call her that,' Lorraine said sharply, tasting the salt of the tears in her throat, but also the acidity of her anger. 'I'm sorry. I shouldn't dictate that to you. You're entitled to your own—' Lorraine sighed '—view of things. It's just, she's not family. I don't like pretending that she is.'

29

CLARE

May 2009

Clare was due in court at eight thirty for a meeting with her solicitor advocate. Today was more evidence for the prosecution – the forensic pathologist and then the forensic psychologist. It was hard for her to tell all the expert witnesses apart.

Earlier she ran out to the corner shop in her worn, grey jogging bottoms to buy some milk for her morning cup of tea. Haymarket was quiet at this time and Clare felt relieved, the streets smelling clean in the early sunlight of a new day.

The newsagent's was busy, and she stood in line behind two or three other people buying papers and rolls. They were regulars and Clare closed her eyes – tired rather than impatient – as she listened to the predictable chit-chat: the weather; the price of cigarettes these days; whether or not a twenty-pence-piece dropped between the piles of fresh newspapers could be easily retrieved.

As she waited, Clare looked over the shoulder of the man in front of her, who was reading his newspaper in the queue while he waited to pay. He was a small man, only slightly taller than Clare, with a belly that rolled over his belt.

She wasn't intentionally reading the headlines from the paper that the man held up before him, but she couldn't help but recognise the haggard, washed-out face depicted on page fifteen.

ULTIMATE BETRAYAL:

GODMOTHER ON TRIAL FOR BABY
THEO'S MURDER

Clare scanned the racks of newspapers for the tabloid the man had chosen and almost grabbed a copy, but then stopped herself. Distracted, she paid for her milk, having difficulty counting the change to such an extent that the shopkeeper reached into her purse to help her.

'That's you. Fifty-two pence exactly. No problem. No problem.'

'Thank you.'

'No problem.'

Hoping that no one recognised her, Clare left the shop and ran back to her flat. She put the radio on as she showered and got dressed, but there was no national news about her case. The news was only of swine flu, MPs, expenses scandals and soundbites from Prime Minister Gordon Brown on the fallout from the Lehman Brothers' collapse.

She stood before the long mirror, tugging down on the jacket of her skirt suit. She didn't recognise herself in these clothes, but her lawyer had advised her against jeans and baseball boots as it would give the wrong message. With her wet hair and pale face she looked so similar to the snapshot in the tabloid.

Clare put her hands over her eyes. Broken breaths bloomed in her palms. She didn't want to believe that she had hurt Theo – just the thought took her breath away, opening inside her like dark wings. She didn't want to remember that night because she didn't know if she could cope with the truth. Her hands fell to her sides and she stood, trembling, looking at herself in the mirror, watching her image, unblinking, until her own features began to morph and change. Her shoulders sagged and the shadows in the dimly lit room made her eyes seem hooded, hollowed out, and her nose hooked, like a bird of prey.

She walked to court, feeling terrified of what was to come. Not for the first time, she wondered if she should run away – hop on the airport bus and then get a flight to anywhere. She knew it wouldn't be that easy to escape justice.

Sam was not in the dock when Clare arrived. She took his seat from the previous day, leaving the two available seats next to her free. When he arrived she kept her eyes to the front, smelling the waft of scent from his freshly showered body. It reminded her of the life she had known just six months before – her life with him – and filled her with sadness and regret.

Brian Peterson seemed even more energised today. His gown flapped as he announced his first witness.

'Please state your name and occupation for the jury.'

'My name is Dr Judith Kemp and I am a forensic scientist.'

'You carried out a number of tests on the clothing the deceased was wearing at the time of death and also tested theories on body position during death?'

'That is correct. I initiated DNA testing of bodily and clothing samples recovered from the deceased. We also carried out a number of recreations of the death scene in order to reach a conclusion about how Theo Collins died.'

'We have just heard police evidence in regard to the co-accused changing their statements in regard to the position of the body when it was found, so perhaps we can begin with that ... can you tell us about the tests that you carried out in this regard?'

'Yes, of course.' Dr Kemp cleared her throat and indicated to the clerk, who used the computer on the central desks to project images of testing diagrams on the courtroom monitor.

The court monitors illuminated a diagram of a child's body, showing the height and weight of Theo. The figure was depicted next to a diagram of the bedroom door in Sam and Clare's flat. The height of the door handle and the floor were clearly indicated.

'When the child was found, and prior to the post-mortem, first responders suspected a case of "Sudden Unexplained Death in Infancy", what used to be referred to as "cot death". The post-mortem ruled out passive suffocation as a result of bedding or clothing and confirmed that the child was actively strangled by a ligature. When the police received corroborations from the co-accuseds that the child was found hanging from the door handle, we began to stage recreations to determine two things—' Dr Kemp indicated the fingers of her left hand '—one, that asphyxiation in this position was possible and corroborative of post-mortem findings; and two, whether this method of asphyxiation – the hood of the sleepsuit as ligature, suspended from the door handle – was accidental, caused by the child himself, or a deliberate act caused by another person with the intention of causing harm or, indeed, death.'

'What were your findings?'

'The staging determined that Theo's height and weight and the hood of the sleepsuit worn at the time of death were all sufficient to allow asphyxiation as a result of hanging from the door handle. The diagram to the right shows the weighted dummy suspended from a similar handle, the hood and neck of the sleepsuit acts as ligature. You can see the feet are unable to touch the ground to prevent strangulation.'

The advocate depute interjected, 'I should have noted, m'lady, that members of the jury have these projected diagrams in their bundle.'

'Noted.'

'And what of your second point, doctor – whether the hanging was accidental or deliberate – what did you find?'

Clare watched the jury who were audibly flicking through their folders. When Peterson asked his last question, all fifteen members of the jury looked up.

Dr Kemp rested both hands on the sides of the witness box. 'We found it statistically *unlikely* that Theo Collins was accidentally asphyxiated by – for example – running past the door and becoming hooked, a theory suggested by both co-accuseds. To put it another way, there was no evidence at all *how* the child would have got into that predicament by himself. However, we did find evidence that he was most likely placed there, as a deliberate act.'

'So this is your second point, doctor – you reached this conclusion using the modelling?'

'Yes, in recreating events, it seemed most likely that the child could have become hung in such a manner if he was lifted by his hood and placed there. Further to this, analysis of the interior of the hooded material – the part that would have been held to place the deceased on the door – showed cellular material deposited by touch from which we were able to work up a partial profile.'

'Were you able to identify the DNA at all, or restrict it to a number of individuals?'

'Unfortunately there was not sufficient DNA available to create a full profile and we found it impossible to upgrade the sample. The gender indicator was clear – the DNA had been deposited by a female. There was insufficient DNA to positively identify accused number one, Clare Armstrong, but we also could not exclude her.'

'Did you identify full DNA profiles in other areas?'

'We did. We were able to identify accused number one's DNA at several significant points on the sleepsuit – down the front, around the neck and also on the tie used to secure the neck area. Paramedics undid this knot, but we found Clare Armstrong's DNA inside it, confirming that she had tied the knot.

'We also identified accused number two's cellular DNA on

the underside of the sleepsuit, concurrent with Mr Armstrong's revised statement that he lifted the deceased down from the door handle in order to commence cardio pulmonary resuscitation.'

'So to clarify, Clare Armstrong's DNA was found over the front of the suit, around the neck of the suit and on the knot used to tie the neck area. Her DNA *may* be on the hooded underside that would have been accessed in order to suspend the deceased from the door.'

'The underside of the hood showed DNA from an *unidentified female*. We were not able to link it to accused number one.'

'But the unidentified female DNA *could* be hers, only we cannot be sure. She cannot be discounted.'

'That is correct.' Dr Kemp pursed her lips.

'And to clarify again—' Peterson held out two hands above his folder, palms facing upwards— 'the DNA identified as belonging to accused number two, Mr Armstrong, was on the underside of the suit and the body, we might say the buttock and shoulder area . . . ?'

'Yes.'

'Consistent that he did indeed lift the deceased down and place him on the floor.'

'Correct.'

Clare glanced over at ⬚⬚⬚. He was covering his face with his hands. She wanted to r⬚⬚ ⬚ut ⬚nd to⬚ch him, comf⬚ hi⬚, but stayed still. She won⬚ ⬚ wh⬚t he ⬚as thinking. Th⬚y had barely spoken since tha⬚ ⬚l⬚. ⬚he re⬚embered him l⬚ving, that brutal morning a⬚ ⬚ ⬚e⬚ died. She remember⬚ ⬚ th⬚ disgust on his face, the ⬚⬚ ⬚at he co⬚ld barely look ⬚ he⬚.

Listening to the evidence, she understood that now more than ever. The forensics, the psychological reports and the DNA were laid out before her like pieces of a puzzle. The truth that she had been trying to hold back seemed obvious to her now – that she had hurt Theo and that she might be found guilty of his murder.

Clare's advocate, Malcolm Power, stood up to begin cross-examination.

'Doctor, thank you for your careful explanations. I have two quick questions for you.'

As if bracing herself, Dr Kemp pushed back her shoulders.

'Firstly, the DNA that you identified as belonging to my client, Clare Armstrong, on the sleepsuit would surely have been there because my client bathed and dressed the child before bed. Would you not agree?'

'Much of the DNA found on the sleepsuit could have been deposited as a result of dressing the deceased and putting him to bed.'

'Thank you. And to restate your position, the more incriminating DNA on the underside of the hood of the sleepsuit – which according to your modelling could have been used to hang the child – cannot be attributed to my client.'

'No, it can't. The sample was degraded as there was so little DNA. Our methods at present do not allow us to work the sample up any further.'

'Thank you. Finally, in regard to the modelling you carried out with dummies, do you admit your finding that – and I quote your testimony under oath – *"no evidence of how the deceased came to be suspended from the doorknob*" would therefore beg the question that accidental death is still a possibility?'

'Possible, but unlikely.'

Judge Stevenson excused the witness before addressing the advocate depute for the Crown. 'Mr Peterson, are you preparing to examine your next witness?'

'I am, m'lady; the forensic psychologist is next on the list.'

'Well, I think before we proceed, this might be a convenient moment for a comfort break. We shall reconvene in fifteen minutes.'

Sam left the dock but Clare stayed. She took two deep breaths, stretching a little as she looked around the courtroom. Lorraine stood and looked straight at her. For a few moments, Clare returned her gaze even though it cost all the energy in her body just to hold her head up. She wanted to fall to her knees. Suddenly, in a strange gesture that unnerved Clare, and made her heart thud in her chest, Lorraine pointed her finger straight at her.

Trembling, Clare sat down, fearing that Lorraine would shout out as the jury filed out of court back to their jury room. In the dock, Clare made herself as small as she possibly could and when she glanced up again, Lorraine had left the court room. As Sam had done earlier, Clare covered her face with her hand. Lorraine's verdict was clear.

What terrified her most was that Clare didn't know if she had hung Theo the way the doctors suggested. Her memory, keeper of her conscience, taunted her. She had pleaded not guilty, but the problem was that she just *didn't know* if she was guilty or not. Her belief that she was not a person who would do such a thing was not supported by her memory of the night. She had never been good with drink, and she had been so angry that night and had drunk more than she had in years. Her recollection was degraded, patchy – but parts of her memory from that night were coming together now, bit by bit as each day passed, becoming solid and real, sinking into her consciousness, like liquid precipitating.

The jury were visibly refreshed when they returned – they sat up straighter in their seats and their faces did not contort with suppressed yawns as the psychologist took the stand.

Clare had been compelled to speak to him – be analysed by him – in the run up to the trial. She had been surprised that she liked him, even though she knew he was employed by the Crown. He was older, thick around the middle, with huge brown eyes that she had found kind, empathetic. She had warmed to him, perhaps because right then she needed someone to listen to her.

Prompted by the advocate depute, the psychologist gave his name and position. 'I am Dr Philip Turnbull, and I am a forensic psychologist.'

'You have assessed both the co-accused, Clare Armstrong and Sam Armstrong, in regard to their mental state on the night of November twenty-first last year, is that correct?'

'Yes.' Dr Turnbull seemed eager. Each time he spoke he leaned in close to the microphone, so that his Ps and Ts burst into the courtroom as if his speech was accompanied by snare drum. 'I examined Mr and Mrs Armstrong separately and had two sessions with each of them, which provided the basis for my report to the Crown.'

'What is your view of the state of mind of Clare and Samuel Armstrong on the night in question? Can you speak to their state of mind and their potential for acting out violently, causing the child's death and attempting to cover it up?'

Dr Turnbull nodded and smiled, held one hand out as he spoke. 'Firstly, my report mentions that accused number one and accused number two spoke in detail of their great affection for the deceased. I think that it would be correct to say that Clare and Sam Armstrong *loved* the children in their care on the night in question – both the deceased, Theo Collins, and his sister, Ella. I will speak first about my considered opinion of accused number one, Clare Armstrong.

'Clare has, over the last ten years or so, suffered a number of miscarriages. We discussed this in relation to her state of mind on the night in question, because a matter of days before the children came to stay, Clare had her tenth miscarriage. It was a miscarriage in the second trimester and involved a trip to the emergency room and then further follow-up in hospital only a day before the children stayed over. This event, and the miscarriages prior, are, I think, significant. I diagnosed Clare as having post-traumatic stress disorder – often referred to as PTSD – as a result of the many painful miscarriages she endured.'

Turnbull's hands were expressive as he spoke.

'Now, I would say both clients experienced trauma on the

night of November twenty-first, on finding their godson dead; but my discussions with Clare, regarding her experience of miscarriage, her self-expressed need for counselling, led me to believe that she had been suffering from PTSD on the night when Theo died and many of her behaviours were symptomatic of this.'

'Can you tell us about specific behaviours she exhibited that you think were related to your diagnosis of PTSD.'

'Clare reported feelings of avoidance – specifically avoiding the memory of the miscarriage. She reported feeling withdrawn and numb, and subsequently avoiding affection – particularly with her husband. On the night in question, the night of the murder, November twenty-first, she began to drink heavily. Self-medicating with alcohol is a symptom of PTSD, but Clare reported it was something she tried to avoid because of her own sensitivity to alcohol.

'PTSD normally exhibits as overwhelming feelings of anger and Clare reported feeling that – although much of it was directed at herself. She felt angry at herself for being unable to carry a baby to term.

'PTSD often results in feeling "on edge"—' Turnbull used his fingers as quotation marks '—and often this manifests as aggression, violent outbursts or destructive behaviour. Some of these can be prompted by flashbacks, which Clare also reported. She told me she not only suffered flashbacks about the miscarriage itself – the physical pain that took her to the emergency department – but she also suffered flashbacks about seeing the baby – the foetus – recognisable as a baby, pass from her.

'It is therefore my opinion that Clare was suffering from PTSD when Theo Collins was in her care and that may have explained her behaviour – acting out violently and impulsively in anger and ultimately killing Theo Collins.'

'Thank you, Dr Turnbull. What were your findings regarding Mrs Armstrong's level of intoxication and its impact on her behaviour?'

Dr Turnbull nodded his head vigorously and wetted his lips before answering.

'Mrs Armstrong reported drinking a substantial amount of alcohol on the night in question. After abstaining from alcoholic drink for nearly a year because she and her partner were trying to conceive, she, on her own admission, drank a whole bottle of wine fairly quickly on the evening of the twenty-first of November. As someone who did not drink regularly and therefore had a low tolerance – and who also self-reported a sensitivity to alcohol – it is likely she would have been significantly mentally and physically impaired. It is my opinion that her inebriation may have increased her pre-disposition to impulsivity and would have affected her ability to recall events.

'During our session, Mrs Armstrong told me that, since she was a teenager, she has suffered serious behavioural changes as a result of drinking even small amounts of alcohol. She gave examples of impulsive and outrageous behaviour that she put down to her sensitivity to this drug. She also reported regular memory loss following episodes of heavy drinking – which she characterised as four or more drinks.'

'Blackouts – if that is the lay terminology – does this seem possible to you after four drinks?'

'I think it is consistent with someone who reports a high sensitivity to alcohol as in the case of Mrs Armstrong. During my session with her she consistently reported that she had no memory of the evening of the twenty-first of November, or of her actions in relation to her godson that night. I found memory dysfunction to be consistent with her alcohol consumption, but also her PTSD.'

Brian Peterson chapped the lectern with the knuckle of his forefinger to underline the next question.

'So in other words, when accused number one asserts that she has limited memory of the evening of the twenty-first of November – convenient as that may seem – you find it believable as a result of inebriation and PTSD.'

'I find it not only believable but highly possible. Declarative memory dysfunction is a well-known side-effect of inebriation, but it is also specifically associated with post-traumatic stress disorder. Memory deficits – forgetting – is a proven product of neurobiological abnormalities caused by trauma. Brain regions implicated in declarative memory deficits include the hippocampus – which is a part of the brain involved in emotional responses – and the prefrontal cortex, which is often related to personality and the sense of self.

'In summary, I think that it is entirely possible that Clare Armstrong murdered Theo Collins but has no recollection of doing so.'

'No further questions.'

Clare felt the eyes of the jury on her. The jurors had been shown *how* she could have killed Theo, and also told *why*. The psychologists had depicted her as a victim, traumatised by grief and driven by impulsivity. The horror of admitting to herself that she had done it was too much for her, but she saw now that she could have – heartbroken and angry and shocked by the trauma of all those lost babies. It was logical. It made sense, even if her feelings and actions that night did not make sense. Clare pressed her knuckles to her mouth, hanging her head. She had given up on the belief that she had some inherent goodness in her that would have stopped her from this act of murder. As the procurator fiscal demonstrated her guilt, she felt lost without that belief, shorn. Malcolm Power, her advocate, was yet to present the case for defence but already Clare knew her fate was in the hands of the fifteen ordinary people sitting across the courtroom from her.

30

LORRAINE

September 2019

Thirteen.

Theo would be thirteen years old today, Lorraine realised, as the warmth of a department store door swept her inside. Thirteen, if he had lived.

She still had soil on the knees of her jeans from kneeling by Theo's grave and wasn't sure how she had ended up inside this store, which was too warm and crowded. She found herself on an escalator going upwards.

Ella had gone home to do college work, but Lorraine had said she would pick up something for dinner. There was no food in this store, only furniture and clothes. Her cheeks flushed, Lorraine found herself touching the fabric of T-shirts and sweatshirts, holding them up to check the sizing. She was in the boys' clothing department. Fervently, she found herself flicking through coat hanger sizes, 10–11, 11–12.

Thirteen, she needed a T-shirt for a thirteen-year-old boy. Needed it. Breaths fluttering in her throat as one T-shirt fell from the rail and clattered to the floor. When she bent to retrieve it and place it back on the rail, she saw a little boy standing at the top of the escalator, watching the downward roll of the metal steps. The child's back was turned to Lorraine, a little woollen hat on his head. He seemed to be only two or three years old.

Lorraine swallowed, a sudden smile threatening to spill tears that had come into her eyes.

The little boy put a foot out, as if to step onto the escalator. *Where was his mother? Who was watching over him?* Just as Lorraine stepped forward to save him – from the metal teeth of the escalator, from his own adventurous spirit – a heavy-set woman grabbed him so hard that he was lifted off his feet.

'What did I tell you? You're not to walk away. If you can't stay by my side, you'll go back in the pram.'

The little boy began to cry, clutching his arm where his mother had just grabbed him. It was a sore cry. She had hurt him.

Lorraine put the T-shirts back on the rack and pushed gently past the mother, now trailing her toddler by the wrist. She walked down the escalator as fast as she could, feeling her lungs bursting.

Outside, she huddled into a concave space near the big shop windows, tears wetting her cheeks. She wiped her face with one hand. It wasn't just that she missed him, but it was the thought that she had not been good enough to him in his short life. She had taken him for granted. She had thought he would always be there. Now only her love for him remained.

As she sniffed and staggered away from the department store, towards the whole food shop where she hoped to pick up dinner, she saw, as if for the first time, the Georgian edifice of St Mary's Catholic Cathedral – so big yet almost hiding, tucked between concrete and glass. Her cheeks still wet with tears, Lorraine stepped inside.

Automatic doors closed behind her, shutting out all the noise of central Edinburgh and sealing her inside. She heard her pulse in her ears as she looked up at the stained glass arched windows. In the pews, silent worshippers were on their knees, heads bent and hands clasped, praying.

Her mother, Rita, had been raised Catholic and Lorraine still remembered being taken to chapel as a child – the strange, stiff taste of the host sticking to the roof of her mouth. Lorraine had lost her mother too, five years ago. It was comforting to think she was with Theo now, although Lorraine didn't believe in God or an afterlife.

The wood of the pew creaked as Lorraine knelt, for the second time that day, remembering her son. His loss was so intermingled with guilt – her own guilt. She didn't let herself think on these things normally. Lorraine was not sure if it was because it was Theo's birthday, or if it was because – once again – she was in the wake of a trial over his murder. Whatever prompted them, memories of the first murder trial came back to her as she raised her eyes to look up at the neo-Gothic ribbed vault above her.

In court, Clare had fought back. Her defence lawyer had not only sown the seeds of reasonable doubt in the jury's minds, but presented Lorraine as a bad mother who had hurt her own children. Chilling as she knelt in the stone ribcage of the church, Lorraine remembered the shame she had felt in court, all those years ago. Even though she had not been on trial, it had felt as if she were.

Lorraine's eyes opened wide and she pressed the nails of one hand into the other as she saw Ella's Primary Two teacher make her way to the witness box.

Clare's defence had begun, and her advocate, Malcolm Power, seemed to have a defence strategy that involved protecting his client by casting Lorraine as a bad mother.

'I call Preeti Mukherjee, m'lady,' Malcolm Power said. His voice was louder and clearer than the older lawyers and Lorraine saw that, beneath his wig and gown, he was attractive. She could imagine him in a bar, the centre of attention, people surrounding him, laughing.

Lorraine had only sat down with Ella's teacher once, at a parent and teacher meeting, although they had spoken once or twice at the school gates. She had that chummy, officious air that many primary teachers seemed to possess, but when she spoke into the microphone, swearing to tell the truth, her voice was strong, professional, confident.

'Ms Mukherjee, in what capacity do you know the victim's family?'

'I am Ella Collins's teacher in second year of primary.'

'Ella is the sister of the deceased, Theo Collins. Did you have occasion to meet her brother at all?'

'Only briefly. Mrs Collins brought Theo along to a parent-teacher meeting once.'

'Can you tell us your impression of their home life and if there were any problems at school?'

'Ella did very well at school. She always did what she was told and completed her work to a high standard, but there were some issues that were apparent from the beginning of her second year at primary that caused me some concern.'

'Such as?' Malcolm Power said, the court lighting casting his face into shadow.

'Early on in her second year of primary, Ella began to appear at school in clothes that were unwashed and her hair would be dirty and uncombed. Sometimes she would go several days wearing the same stained shirt to school. She would have odd socks, once even odd shoes, and her jackets would not be suitable for the weather, which sometimes meant that she was soaked and cold after walking to school.'

'Can you outline your concerns about her appearance, particularly as Ella had no academic or behavioural issues?'

'Often in teaching, we are alerted to problems at home by hygiene issues in the children. It can indicate financial concerns, changes in circumstance … At the more extreme end of the scale, it can mean neglect, abuse, but very often it is an early indicator of a family that is struggling.'

'I see. Did you raise your concerns with Ella's mother, Lorraine Collins?'

'I called to speak to her and asked her into school to discuss it, but she said that she was too busy working. I raised the issue over the phone on that occasion and she stated clearly that she disagreed with me.'

'Disagreed?' Power prompted.

'I paraphrase, but she told me I was talking rubbish and that I should mind my own business.' Preeti Mukherjee stiffened, pushing her shoulders right back and raising her chin. 'Except she used another word, instead of *rubbish*.'

'Do you mean that Ms Collins was abusive to you over the telephone?'

'She swore at me, yes.' Ms Mukherjee turned slightly to the judge.

Her cheeks aflame, Lorraine felt her breaths lengthening in her chest as she waited for the questioning to continue. Of course she remembered swearing, but Ella's teacher had called at the worst time. Brody had just left and Theo was playing up and Lorraine had felt so alone.

'And was that the end of the matter?'

'No. Ms Collins came in for parents' evening, bringing Theo as I had mentioned. She was different in person. I remember I was apprehensive about meeting her, in case she was aggressive, but she just seemed tired. She explained that her partner – the father of her youngest child, Theo – had left a year after the birth and she was struggling on her own. She said that Ella was a huge help to her and that she often took care of herself.'

'What was your view of this?'

'I took notes on the meeting. We are required to now, particularly if there is a case that might need referral to social work or other services.'

Slowly, Ms Mukherjee took reading glasses out of a case that she'd placed on the witness stand, put them on and read from a sheet of paper. Even though her voice was still strong, the paper shook enough to be visible to Lorraine at the back of the courtroom.

'Here, I have noted that ... Ms Collins seems to have a warm and positive bond with both of her children, but she is clearly struggling and could be relying on Ella more than might be expected of a six-/seven-year-old child. I asked if Ms Collins had talked to her GP and she had responded that the doctor was "only interested in giving her pills". I took this to mean that she had spoken to the doctor and that perhaps anti-depressants had been offered, but this was only my assumption.'

'What was the conclusion of the meeting?'

'I explained that Ella's hygiene and presentation at school was not an issue at present but that it might make her vulnerable to bullying. I said that I would not take any further action for the time being, but that I had a duty to log issues like this, in case they needed to be passed to social work at a later date. Ms Collins assured me that she would double-check that Ella was appropriately dressed. She said she hadn't noticed any of the issues with hygiene that I'd mentioned and said that Ella tended to take care of herself.'

'Take care of herself, and how old was Ella at this time?'

'Seven years old.'

'And did the hygiene situation change?'

'A little, yes. Ella no longer wore stained shirts that were clearly the same shirt, day after day. But Ella still seemed grubby and tired . . .'

'And was there any further action?'

'I had planned on discussing the matter further at the next parent teacher meeting, but then came Ella's brother's death.'

'Did you consult on Ella's case with a colleague?'

'Yes, I discussed the matter with my head. She shared my view that Ella's case should be monitored but did not warrant intervention at that stage.'

'Did you remain concerned?'

'Of course. It was my opinion that Ella was experiencing low-level neglect at home and being left to care for herself and quite possibly her younger brother as well . . . I would hear Ella telling her friends that they couldn't come over to her house, that she had to make dinner and look after her little brother because her mummy would be lying down. I'm not a doctor but my contact with Ms Collins suggested she was depressed or suffering from mental ill-health.'

As Preeti Mukherjee made her way back to her seat, Malcolm Power called on Clare to take the witness stand. Lorraine was sitting far back in the gallery and folded her arms, feeling her breaths become uneven. What had been said about her, as a mother, left her reeling. Of course she remembered struggling, trying to raise two small children all by herself. But she loved them without question. They might not always have been perfectly turned out, but she had never knowingly neglected them.

Lorraine's advocate, Brian Peterson, had initially told her that Clare was not going to take the stand, but he had recently been advised by the defence that she would testify after all. *Not testifying can seem like an admission of guilt*, Peterson explained to Lorraine.

Already shaken and feeling accused by the primary teacher's testimony, Lorraine waited, dry mouthed, to hear what Clare had to say.

Clare stated her name and raised her right hand, swearing to tell the truth. Lorraine twisted her mouth, expecting nothing but lies. Even from this distance, Lorraine could see that Clare's shoulders were shaking.

'Did you murder Theo Collins?' Malcolm Power began.

'No, I did not.' Lorraine could hear the fear in her voice.

'We have heard from experts in pathology and forensic science, but what is your explanation as to how Theo ended up hung from his sleepsuit on the door handle of your spare bedroom, if you did not place him there?'

'When Lorraine dropped the children off, she told us that Theo would easily climb out of the cot we had bought for him, and I think he did climb out and ran to get us. I think his hood flew up and he was caught there, unable to shout for help.'

Clare's voice thickened, as if from tears. Lorraine held her breath, wondering if she would break.

'Your DNA is on the knot that secured Theo's sleepsuit at the neck. What is your explanation for this?'

'I dressed him for bed after his bath. I tied the knot. I had no reason to think it would be dangerous. He played for an hour or so before we put him to bed in his pyjamas.' Clare took a tissue and dabbed at her nose.

'We have heard from the forensic psychologist about the trauma you suffered from repeated miscarriages. When you had Ella and Theo to stay, how long had it been since your last miscarriage?'

'It had been under a week, and I had had a . . . procedure to—' Clare cleared her throat '—remove the . . . leftover tissue, just the day before we had the children to stay.'

'I ask because I am curious about the timing. Why did you have the children for a sleepover when you had just gone through such an emotionally and physically trying experience?'

'We were worried about them, Sam and I. *I* was particularly worried about them.'

'Who are you referring to when you say "them"?'

'All of them – their whole family. I was worried about Lorraine. I knew she wasn't coping well. I knew that the children were not being . . . looked after properly. I wanted to give Lorraine a break and I also wanted the children to have a weekend to just . . . play and be happy.'

'The pathologist has described bruising on Theo's body that was older by several days than the bruising around his neck caused when asphyxiation occurred. Did you notice this bruising while looking after Theo?'

'Yes, that night, when I bathed Theo, I saw the bruises and pointed them out to my husband.'

'How do you think these injuries were incurred?'

The advocate depute for the procurator fiscal leapt to his feet. 'M'lady, I am not sure this is an appropriate question for this witness – her speculation on the matter is not relevant.'

'I will hear her opinion, but note that it is only that.'

'Theo was going through a phase of tantrums and I know Lorraine found him difficult. I had witnessed her struggling with his behaviour. I also know it's easy to hurt little children when … I wonder if the bruising had been caused by Theo being … grabbed too hard.'

'The bruising was significant as we see from the photographs and the pathologist timed the bruises as having been inflicted before he was in your care. What was your initial reaction when you saw the marks on Theo?'

Clare sighed. Lorraine felt her heart thud in her chest. She sucked in breath, as if ready to scream and then pressed her lips together.

'I thought it was just further evidence of the fact that this was a family in trouble. I was glad that I had offered to take the children for the weekend, to give Lorraine and everyone a break.'

'And how did you feel about the children in your care?'

'Feel?' Clare's voice softened. 'I love them. I've always loved them.'

Lorraine's heart was beating so loud and so hard in her chest that she struggled to hear the testimony.

'And when you learned that Theo was actually your husband's child, did that change the way you felt about the boy?'

Clare paused before answering and Lorraine held her breath.

'No. I was angry, I was very, very upset. I had an argument, with Sam, as I told the police, but that wasn't Theo's fault. My feelings towards Theo were unchanged … are unchanged. I loved him as if he were my own child.'

Lorraine couldn't restrain herself any longer. She stood up with an explosive straightening of her legs. 'Liar. That's a lie,' she shouted, before it turned to tears. As her vision blurred, Lorraine saw each face in the court turn to her. One hand over her mouth, she got up and ran out of the courtroom.

The wood of the pew creaked again as Lorraine got to her feet. If she had been her mother, she would have crossed herself before the statue on the altar, but Lorraine simply put her hands in her pockets and turned for the door.

Through the glass door that sealed the wide stone arch, she could see double-deckers working their way around the roundabout where York Place meets Leith Walk.

Lorraine remembered the headlines after she called Clare a liar and ran out of court.

TODDLER'S MOTHER CRIES OUT IN COURT AFTER EVIDENCE OF NEGLECT AND ABUSE

And then,

I WAS PROTECTING BABY THEO FROM NEGLECTFUL MUM SAYS GODMOTHER

Outside in the fresh air, a gust of wind lifted the hair from Lorraine's face. She put her hands in her pockets, breathing deeply. Clare had been found 'not proven' after that performance in court. And then at her photography exhibition, all these years later, she had the gall to tell Lorraine that she now took responsibility.

Clare should have been an actress. She might have fooled everyone in 2009, persuaded them to believe that she was nothing more than a loving godmother and a caring friend.

Lorraine knew that the trial to come would change things. Theo, who would have been thirteen years old today would finally have justice, and Clare would be sent to prison.

It was now after five. Lorraine felt herself almost blown downhill as she turned towards Broughton Street and the delicatessen where she would find dinner.

31

SAM

September 2019

Sam finished his coffee looking out over the Water of Leith, which today was a grey, wrinkled skin below him. His flat was on the sixth floor and he had a good view. He could almost see along the coast to Pilton – and the housing estate where he had grown up – but not quite.

He drank the last mouthful of his coffee, silt from the bottom making his lips grainy. He thought about the possibility of Clare going to prison, after what she had told him in the park, about new evidence that might be used to prove her guilt.

It was like cracking an egg and finding two yolks inside. Long ago, when he left her, he had internalised the belief that she had done it – that she was capable of such a thing – while still loving her so much. Loving her and believing in her guilt were hard to reconcile but Clare had not acted in premeditation.

He believed that. It didn't exculpate her, but somehow it still allowed him to love her.

Now they were in touch again – almost friendly. He had felt more himself sitting with her on that bench in Princes Street Gardens a few days ago than he had in the last decade. He remembered cycling to meet her and feeling alive for the first time in a long while. He only made sense when he was with her. Perhaps that was even more true now, after all they had been through together, and apart.

Sam put his empty coffee cup on the desk. His living room-kitchen was arranged for functionality. A table in the middle of the room, facing the window, that he used as a desk. A single chair that he sat on – seldom – to relax, watch television, videos. There was a stool in the kitchen where he ate breakfast and dinner, if he ate at home. His now seldom-used bicycle was tucked behind the sofa.

Clare was right: he should cycle more often. It was the person he had been when he had been with her; a cyclist. He had lost her and he had lost himself.

He put his hands on his hips as he stared at the pile of boxes stacked in the alcove that had been there since he'd moved out of the flat he'd shared with Clare. He had been a serious cyclist when he knew Clare, not just someone who had a bike. He had given it all up because of a fight with a motorist, the pain of leaving his wife, and the shock of finding a child – his son, his precious son – dead in their house.

He had taken his bicycle to meet Clare in Princes Street Gardens the other day and it had felt like a liberation. Two thoughts came to him at once – he should cycle again, and he should be with Clare – as if to reclaim his happiness. Of course he was changed, and he could never become who he had been before, but he felt a sense of wonder – that cycling and loving Clare might still be available to him.

The wall of boxes faced him. He wanted to go out for a ride *right now*. His lobster gloves, his lights, his lock, his good helmet. Just thinking about finding his gear, his heart began to palpitate as if he was there already, on the road near the summit of Arthur's Seat and heading down, the whirr of the wheels and the cold air against his face.

He knew that the cycling gear was at the bottom of the pile of boxes. Somehow, after all this time, even though he had packed quickly, shocked and heartbroken, he remembered the vague order of these boxes from his life with Clare.

Breaking sweat, he began taking down boxes and lifting their lids to check the contents. Some of the boxes were heavy: books and CDs. One box even contained a pair of dumb-bells. There was kitchen equipment, drawing materials, framed pictures. Sam didn't stop to analyse the contents. All of these belongings had been entombed the day after Theo died.

He had kept these memories close to him but enclosed for so long and didn't want to acknowledge them now, yet as he worked he remembered seeking out Lorraine after the trial, his friend for years – and the mother of his only child.

'Lorraine!'

He had noticed her walking up ahead, a bag of shopping

in her hand. At first his instinct was to keep his head down and cross the road to avoid her, then he realised that this was his chance. He had wanted to speak to her – to see her. Since the trial he had thought of calling her many times, had once set out to visit her but hadn't wanted to cause a scene if Ella was there.

He was heading back to Leith from town. He had been doing community service, picking up rubbish near the bypass. It was a workday, but Sam had no work to go to any more. He planned to set up on his own as an architect, but that would take time. He would need to wait more than a year until his suspension was complete.

Today Lorraine was on her own, heading towards her flat.

He picked up his pace to catch up with her. This part of the street wasn't busy, yet he worried how she would react if he approached her. They hadn't spoken face to face since the night that Theo died and she arrived to collect Ella. All through the trial they had not spoken, although he had seen her in court almost every day, almost always distraught. He remembered the day when Clare testified and Lorraine stood up and shouted that she was a liar.

Sam jogged gently up to her and touched her on the shoulder. 'Lorraine!'

She turned, but, as if she had been lost in her thoughts, it took a moment for her to realise that it was him. She turned away but then faced him, her lips pressed together. He froze for a moment, anticipating how she would react.

'How are you?' It wasn't what he had meant to say. He hadn't thought it through. Not waiting for her to reply, he continued: 'I'm sorry. I can guess how you must feel, it's just—'

Again she half-turned from him and looked down the Walk. A strand of her hair blew into her mouth and she picked it out with her pinkie nail.

'—I've wanted to talk to you. I didn't want to come round, but then I saw you and ...'

'What?'

There were no tears in her eyes, but he could see she was shattered. She was smartly dressed and she stood tall, but it was there, visible in her eyes, that she was just blown apart. He wanted to gather her into his arms, but didn't dare touch her. He wanted to tell her how sorry he was, and how he knew that everything was his fault. He felt culpable, and he needed her forgiveness. He no longer had feelings for her – that afternoon, hot and feverish in his mind, had ruptured all their lives – but he had created a much-longed-for child with this woman, this dear friend, and he had loved that boy as much as she did.

'I know nothing can make up for what happened, but I want you to know that I'm sorry, and that—' he coughed, feeling his voice break '—my heart is breaking too.'

The breeze picked up again. Lorraine faced it, so that it lifted the fringe from her brow. 'I know that ...' She seemed to smile but then Sam realised it was not a smile but rather her teeth clenched together to stop herself from crying. Her blue eyes shone. 'Well, I mean ... I can imagine.' She put her shopping down on the pavement and held up her hands. 'Look, I'm shaking.'

'Let me help you,' he said, reaching for the bag at her feet.

'No, it's fine. It's not what I meant. I just mean . . . I still don't believe he's dead and then . . . every now and again it blows over me. When I wake up . . .' A tear flashed over her face, and she pressed one palm on her cheek, as if she had been struck. She didn't finish her sentence.

'Maybe it would help if . . . I would still like to see you—' his tongue felt dry and his words clumsy '—and Ella. I just wonder—'

Lorraine shook her head vigorously and picked up her shopping. 'It's too painful,' she said nodding, turning away. 'He was my baby. He was *my* son.'

Sam stood, hands by his sides, as Lorraine went on her way, her carriage tall and elegant, somehow resilient.

Sam felt strain in his lower back as he lifted and laid the boxes, twisting at the waist as he started on a new tower of boxes along the adjacent wall.

He was about to give up when he noticed a blue crate that had been right in the corner, next to the wall, and so obscured. He remembered it from the time when he had moved his things out of the home he shared with Clare.

'Bingo,' he whispered, pulling out a bicycle pump.

The crate was full of his cycling equipment: helmet, cycling gloves and trouser clips, his reliable old pair of cycling shoes that he had worn the day he'd punched the driver of the Rover.

At the back of the crate, packed carefully into its own cardboard box, was the special cycling camera he had bought to film his rides at the weekend, back when he felt like one of those long-legged man-machines on the Tour de France. Sam felt a poignant smile on his lips as he looked at the GoPro camera. The strap was still attached that allowed it to be mounted on his helmet.

The camera did not respond when he pressed and re-pressed the power button. A decade with no power; it might be broken altogether. He took it and its charger to the kitchen and plugged it in; he was relieved to see a small light illuminated on the top of the camera to show that it was charging. It was like a signal flare from his old life. He imagined himself getting up to speeds of fifty-miles-an-hour as he plummeted downhill, recording every moment to watch later.

As the camera charged, Sam returned to the boxes. In the same blue crate, he found his pair of boxing gloves. All the suppressed aggression from his childhood and teenage years had found release in the old gym in Pilton. Sam wiggled his fingers into the right-hand glove and smacked it off his bare left palm.

One, two.

One, two.

Running a hand over the glove, he felt the premium leather, cracked in places from repeated impact. It smelled of leather and his own old sweat.

Again, a memory stroked him tenderly then stung, like walking through nettles.

He was in the dock with Clare, watching the theatre of the court play out before him through a Perspex screen with holes drilled into it.

'The Crown calls Samuel Armstrong,' said the advocate depute, looking at his notes and then over his shoulder in expectation.

Sam stood, opened the gate of the dock and walked to the witness box. His advocate had told him that testifying carried great risks, '*but not taking the stand at all can be viewed as an admission of guilt by the jury. You've pled "not guilty" to perverting the course of justice. I think they need to hear your side of the story.*'

And so, Sam had agreed to testify.

Sam was represented by Judy Miller, a tall woman with very short grey hair and an intense face. When she wore her advocate's wig there was no sign of her real hair underneath it, which gave her a strangely historic look, as if she had been teleported from another century. Her eyes were small and scrutinising and her jaw always seemed to carry tension, as if she was gritting her teeth. '*Stick to the facts,*' Judy had told him when he was preparing to testify, '*keep it simple, but use emotion. The jury need to feel your anguish.*'

Sam rested his hands on the witness box. There was a glass of water before him, a small box of tissues. A shudder took hold in his lower body. He was relieved that the witness stand covered his legs, as otherwise the whole court would be able to see them shaking.

He looked straight at the procurator fiscal, who was sorting his notes, getting ready to begin questioning. Lorraine sat to the right of his peripheral vision and Sam did his best to avoid looking at her.

'Isn't it true, Mr Armstrong,' Brian Peterson said, 'that you are quite accustomed to the position you now find yourself in – moving from the dock to the witness stand?'

Sam parted his lips but did not respond. The aggressiveness of the question blanked his mind.

Judy Miller stood. 'I'm not sure what relevance this has to the matter at hand, m'lady?'

'I'll allow it for now, as it refers to character. Can you be more specific, Mr Peterson?'

The advocate depute leaned forward, as if in attack.

'Mr Armstrong, I refer to the fact that you were charged with assault to severe injury with permanent disfigurement *mere days* after the tragic death of Theo Collins in your care, which now brings us to court. Not only were you *charged* with this grievous, violent offence but you have since *pleaded guilty* ... and been sentenced.' Peterson waved his arms dramatically towards the jury as he uttered the words 'pleaded guilty'. 'Not long before you were called to attend here, at the high court, for attempting to pervert the course of justice in relation to the murder of Theo Collins, you were along the road at the sheriff court to receive sentence. Is that not correct?'

'Um ...' Sam found his mouth dry. He cleared his throat. 'Yes.'

'Enlighten us as to the outcome of the sentencing hearing for your offence of assault to severe injury with permanent disfigurement ...'

Brian Peterson's smile seemed menacing.

Sam felt his hands slippery against the veneered wood of the witness box.

'Um ... I was fined and—'

'Please speak up, Mr Armstrong. You have since been convicted of this offence and fined five thousand pounds . . . and are currently serving a sentence of six months' community service. Is this not correct?'

'Yes.'

Sam glanced at Judy Miller who stared back, hands clasped. She raised her eyebrows at Sam as if to indicate he was in dangerous territory, but she could do nothing.

The judge cleared her throat and intervened, turning to address the jury.

'Accused number two's previous conviction is something that you may take into account, particularly as it occurred in a similar time frame to the offence for which he stands trial today . . . but you may not convict him on the evidence of that alone or mainly on that evidence. You must consider the importance of this prior conviction. The procurator fiscal says that it supports their case because it demonstrates that the defendant's character is that of someone who commits acts of violence and is potentially accustomed to acts of violence. The defence, on the other hand, asks that you pay no attention to this evidence because it is a crime unrelated to the charge of attempt to pervert the course of justice, for which accused number two is standing trial. You can take it into account only if you consider it fair.'

The judge sighed lightly as she sank back into her chair.

'Thank you, m'lady.' Peterson smiled thinly as he focused again on Sam. 'Would you say you have a violent temper, Mr Armstrong?'

Sam frowned. 'No.'

'You lost your temper over a minor traffic dispute and ended up—' Peterson glanced at a note in his file '—inflicting two facial fractures on an elderly man, one of which – an eye socket fracture – caused permanent disfigurement … I don't know about you, but I would call that a violent temper.'

There was a murmur of suppressed laughter from somewhere in the court room, unidentifiable.

Before Sam was able to respond, the judge intervened. 'I asked you to keep your questions specific, Mr Peterson. You are well aware that you are to ask questions, not give statements to the court. The jury should take note.'

'I was provoked,' Sam said, feeling his colour rise in response to Peterson's taunting.

'And is it just traffic disputes that provoke you, Mr Armstrong? Drivers cutting in – or do other things cause your temper to flare, like a toddler crying, perhaps?'

Sam felt Lorraine's eyes on him. Even though she was seated fifty feet away he felt the searing heat of her gaze.

'You're a boxer, aren't you, Mr Armstrong?' Mr Peterson was smiling.

'I box a little. It's a hobby.'

'It's an aggressive hobby. Would you describe yourself as an aggressive person?'

'No. I would not.'

'In the interviews with police, you and your wife both gave statements to the effect that Theo had been *difficult* during the day that you looked after him.'

'He's a two-year-old; it's normal to have tantrums.'

'*Was* a two-year-old, Mr Armstrong,' Peterson corrected, narrowing his eyes. 'He is *not* a two-year-old any longer. *He was* a two-year-old, if you will bear correction.'

Sam felt sick. His mouth was dry. He looked at the glass of water that was within reach, but he knew his hands would tremble if he tried to bring it to his lips, and so he left it where it was, not wanting to show weakness.

'Did you find your temper tested when you looked after Theo?' The advocate's voice was full of derisive scorn.

'I . . . found his behaviour difficult, sometimes. I wasn't used to it. I didn't have a lot of experience. Theo's sister Ella – we had looked after her on many occasions and she had never behaved like that. She was . . .'

'I see. And would you say you became close to losing control when faced with Theo's tantrums – as you had lost control during the traffic altercation?'

Sam swallowed. He had sworn to tell the truth, but the answer to this question would strengthen the case against him. 'I kept myself under control,' he said, hoping it would be enough.

'And you expect us to believe that? That you – a convicted criminal, someone whose pastime is boxing, and who has very recently been found guilty of a violent offence . . . someone who admits being tested by the demanding behaviour of a small child – were able to control yourself? I put it to you that *lost your temper again* on the night Theo died.'

'No, that is not true,' now the anger rose up in Sam. He felt it lift the hairs on the back of his neck. 'I admit when we were out together, I was frightened that I might—' Sam stopped. He was panting, his heart racing. He forced a breath in and out to steady himself. 'I thought I might ... but I would never, ever hurt him.'

Peterson laughed dramatically. 'Might what, Mr Armstrong ... what were you afraid you might do?'

Sam held the sides of the witness stand. He felt a flush along his cheekbones.

'I wasn't afraid, I just ... at one point when we were out, at the farm and he wouldn't stop having a temper tantrum, I did think to give him a tap, but I didn't. I didn't ...'

'I see ... a little tap.' Peterson smiled as he turned to face the jury. 'The last time you "gave someone a tap" you fractured their eye socket, Mr Armstrong. The last time we know you "tapped" someone, you were convicted of assault to severe injury with permanent disfigurement.'

Peterson then turned back to face Sam in the witness box.

'We know that you are a person with violent tendencies. A tap, losing an eye, it's all the same to you. I wonder if you were feeling as if you could hurt someone that night when Theo Collins died.'

'No, of course not.'

'The police found an Internet search regarding overdoses of Calpol for a toddler. Did you make this search?'

'I did not. I don't think so.'

'Which is it?'

'I don't think I made that search, but I can't remember for sure. I might have, but only to make sure we didn't give him too much, not out of any desire to harm him.'

'So you say. Let me ask you this ... we have evidence that

your character is that of a violent man with an uncontrollable temper. As someone who is of that character, I assume you are accepting of this weakness in others?'

'I don't ... understand what you're asking me.'

'You fought with your wife on the night Theo died. Did you both lose your temper during that argument? We have heard testimony that you were shouting.'

Sam cleared his throat. 'I think you could say we both lost our temper. We were shouting.'

'I see. And when your wife, accused number one, lost her temper, and was driven to asphyxiate the toddler in your care, did you find yourself understanding of her rage and murderous actions?'

Sam's face was burning hot, as if he had a fever, and he wondered if the redness was visible to the court. 'No, it was an accident. What happened was an accident – Theo must have got caught on the door handle.'

'So why did you lie to protect your wife?'

'It wasn't like that. It was such a stressful time. Everything happened so fast and it was so awful, so terrible, and to see Theo hanging like that, and have to take him down ... He was my son, my own little son, and it broke my heart—' he stuttered, emotion thick in his voice and he remembered what his lawyer had said about showing feeling '—so much that I couldn't think straight. I think that was why my first statement had ... inaccuracies.'

'Inaccuracies, yes ...' Peterson spoke quietly and then the next words exploded from his lungs into the microphone. 'You

LIED to the police about where you found the body of Theo Collins. You *admitted* lying. We have you on tape agreeing that you lied. So, how do you expect us to believe you now?'

Sam sniffed and wiped his nose with the back of his hand. He tasted the salt of tears on the back of his throat but was determined that he would not cry. 'I'm telling the truth now,' he whispered.

'You say you found Theo unresponsive and then began to resuscitate him. Tell the court what efforts you made in this regard?'

'I put my mouth to his ... I pressed on his chest, to try and make his heart beat again. I couldn't find a pulse.'

'You couldn't find a pulse because Theo was already dead when you pressed on his chest. You did so with such FORCE that you broke his tiny sternum.'

Peterson paused and turned to the jury for effect. Two people in the front row covered their mouths with their hands.

'I wonder – were you really trying to save the life of Theo Collins, or were you trying to cause so much damage to his tiny body that your wife's murderous actions would be hidden?'

'No,' Sam whispered, feeling a tear flash over his cheek. 'No.' He felt his lower teeth jutting out. Anger trembled in him.

'No further questions.'

Sam stepped down. He could barely stand up straight but glanced at the gallery as he walked back to the dock and caught Lorraine's eye. She stared straight at him, her face blank.

Words he had never been able to say to her since Theo's death came into his mind: *he was my child too.*

*

Sam put the boxing gloves to one side. The GoPro camera still flashed charging, although Sam doubted it would come to life. He continued to empty the crate of sport equipment. He began to move more quickly in an effort to shake off the memory of the trial. He put the cycling gear by his bike, which was now in the hall as it always had been in his old life – ready to go – his primary mode of transport. He was about to kneel and pump up the tyres when he heard his phone vibrate in the kitchen.

The photo of Clare flashed on the screen – taken long ago on holiday somewhere; she was throwing her head back in laughter.

'Hey, how did it go?' he said. Clare had been meeting with Malcolm Power about the upcoming court case.

'Oh god. He now has full disclosure, so he knows the basis of the Crown's case against me. He says that they have new DNA evidence from Theo's sleepsuit. In the first trial they said that the underside of the hood was most likely used to lift Theo . . . onto the doorknob.' She sounded out of breath and he knew it was anxiety. 'I don't know if you remember, first time around they only had a – what was it he called it – a *degraded* sample.' Clare tried to catch her breath and he almost told her to take her time. 'Before they were only able to pinpoint an unidentified female – I'm sure I remember that from the first trial. But now, thanks to the wonders of science, that degraded sample is viable and they now have a match with my profile, on the underside of the hood.' He heard her breath and then swallow, almost as if she had been running.

Sam shook his head, disbelieving. 'You need to talk to Malcolm again. There must be some way to undermine that evidence. I mean . . . ' He remembered that first lurch in his gut when he thought it possible that Clare might have hurt Theo. The first sick taste at the back of his throat when he watched her drunk and reeling back from Theo's body, hanging on the door handle. 'There must be something he can do to counter that. It was so long ago and you weren't . . . yourself that night. Remember what the psychologists said . . . '

'I know.'

Sam bit his lip as he moved to the kitchen.

Clare had no memory of the most important moments of that night, but Sam recalled the night that Theo had died with startling clarity. He remembered Clare confronting him over Lorraine and Theo and then the fight they had, how she had screamed at him, and then began to drink with such reckless-ness – huge glasses knocked back in seconds. It had frightened him. They had turned away from one another – him in the living room, her upstairs.

He remembered Clare calling on him, running upstairs and seeing her sway before Theo, her eyes blackened by mascara. He had reacted immediately and taken Theo down, carrying the limp little body in his two large hands and placing him on the carpet.

He had known it was hopeless even as he laid him flat, tilted back his still-warm head, pinched the tiny nostrils and pressed his own frantic mouth against the toddler's small, blue lips. And then the violent pressing on his chest, Sam's big veined hands flat out and placed carefully one over the other, just above Theo's heart.

A tiny new heart in a compact chest that minutes before had been pumping furiously, sending oxygen, vigour, mischief around his sturdy little body.

And Sam had begun to cry – twisting his neck to wipe his tears on his shoulder – keeping going until the siren of the ambulance – without knowing that he had broken two ribs in Theo's fragile thoracic cavity, as he became more and more insistent that the child would be revived.

It was then, when the siren sounded outside, that the truth of what Clare had done filled him. He had betrayed her, and she had responded with this unspeakable act. Had she known she would kill Theo, had she meant to?

'You killed him?' Sam said to her, on his knees, feeling as if the pulse of the siren was inside his own body.

'I didn't mean . . . I didn't think . . .' she had sobbed.

The pain of trying to love her, even then, tore through him. The paramedics pounded on the door.

'Is he? Can you not?'

It was as if she thought he could fix this, as if he could make it undone.

Tears cold on his face, so that his skin felt like clay, Sam said: 'We'll say we found him in his cot, okay?' He was out of breath, sweat along his hairline, on his palms. 'Okay?'

Clare's eyes had been flat, bloodshot. He didn't know if she understood what he was saying. He had struggled to his feet and gone to answer the door.

At the trial the psychologists had theorised about her state of mind on that night – fresh from the grief of miscarriage, compounded by the loss of all the other babies. She had been drunk and in shock, altered by trauma. It had taken time – years – but he had come to realise just how deeply he had hurt her and how his betrayal had caused everything that happened.

Even during the trial the truth of that night had not come to light, but now finally there was proof of what happened.

Clare sighed on the other end of the phone. He didn't want her to despair, even though he knew a double jeopardy trial meant the Crown were convinced of getting a conviction. He didn't think she deserved to go to prison. What would it solve? It wouldn't bring Theo back.

'Well ... don't lose hope yet. You need to speak to your lawyer and find a good line of defence.' As he spoke he picked up the camera, which now showed that it had a full charge. He turned it in his hand. 'Are you alright? What are you doing this afternoon?'

Clare sighed. 'Malcolm has asked me to think about how I want to plead. If I plead guilty, it will go straight to sentencing and avoid another trial.'

'Plead guilty? You can't do that.'

Clare said nothing. Her breathing had changed on the end of the phone. 'By pleading guilty I might get a shorter sentence.'

'You need to talk to him about mitigation. Remember those psychological reports ...'

'The first trial and the length of time that has passed might mean that's no longer available. I think I just want it to be over, even if that means prison, but I don't know if I can find it in me to plead guilty, when I don't fully remember.'

He listened to her soft exhales. More than anything he wanted to be near her. 'Of course you can't plead guilty to something when you don't even remember what you did.'

There was silence on the other end of the line.

'Do you want me to come over?'

'I don't know. I have to make a few calls. I need to get my head round it.'

'Listen, I'm off today. I'm just tidying the flat up, so call me if you need anything – even just to talk some more.'

'Will do. Thank you.'

After he hung up, Sam began to pump up the tyres of his bicycle. It had been years since he had cycled properly and the bike would need work if he was going to go for a long ride again. He would need to strip it down and clean it, give it a full service.

He felt restless, worried about Clare. The boxes, opened and emptied, taunted him and he thought how he would much rather head out for a cycle than stay and sift through the flotsam of his old life.

In the kitchen, he put the kettle on and picked up the GoPro camera. He had worn the camera routinely on all his long cycles. He wondered if it still had footage of his big rides.

Sam made himself a cup of tea, perched on the stool and pressed play. The matchbox-sized monitor lit up.

32

LORRAINE

May 2009

In the courtroom, Lorraine and Rita held hands, as they had when they had visited the mortuary to identify Theo's body. Lorraine had allowed Rita to join her in court only today, because today the jury would return their verdict. It was painful, but seeing Clare and Sam found guilty today would also bring a strange kind of peace.

As they waited for the judge to enter, Rita leaned into her daughter and whispered, 'So if they're found guilty, they'll be sent straight to prison.'

'I think so,' Lorraine breathed.

'But Sam will go to prison too? Even though he didn't do it.'

'Yes, he could go to prison, and for quite some time. He helped her.' Lorraine pressed her teeth together and felt the ache.

The judge entered the chamber, seeming very small when she stood next to the judicial chair.

As soon as the jury were in their seats, Judge Stevenson turned to address them.

'Ladies and gentlemen of the jury, you have now heard all the evidence. We have reached the stage when you will hear closing speeches from counsel – firstly on behalf of the pursuer and then on behalf of the defender.'

Lorraine glanced at the dock and saw that, for the first time since the trial had begun, Clare and Sam were sitting by side, so close that their shoulders seemed to be touching. The thought that Sam would choose Clare over their son caused a flare of pain inside her. She squeezed her mother's small, cold hand.

Mr Peterson clasped his hands as he approached the jury. Lorraine noticed that he was warmer in his address to the jury than he had been throughout the whole trial. He seemed suddenly human, still energised but softened. He was like a politician, she realised, changing tone to get them on side.

'Ladies and gentlemen, some of you are parents. I want you to think about the people you entrust to look after your child. On the night of November twenty-first, 2008, Lorraine Collins trusted her best friends, accused number one, Clare Armstrong, and her husband, Sam Armstrong, accused number two. Ms Collins returned from an evening away with her mother to hear that her little boy, Theo, had come to harm. What she did not suspect was that her friend, Clare, whom she had known since university and who she had previously referred to as a sister, had brutally murdered her son in a jealous, drunken rage.'

Peterson visibly reddened in the face as he uttered the last sentence. Rita tugged her hand from Lorraine's, unsnapped her handbag and took out a tissue.

'You heard from the senior investigating officer, Detective Inspector Brookes, that Clare Armstrong *deliberately lied* in her first witness statement to the police. She said that she found Theo in his cot – leading police to believe this was an innocent case of Sudden Unexplained Death in Infancy. But the pathology told a different story. Only when confronted with the truth of how Theo had died – asphyxiated, hanging – did Clare admit that Theo had not been in his cot *at all*.'

At all, Peterson's hands exploded out at the words, as if exclaiming from a pulpit.

'Clare Armstrong was heavily inebriated on that night, when she found out that her husband of more than fifteen years had been having an affair with her friend Lorraine and that the child, Theo, was in fact *her husband's child*. You heard the psychologist describe Clare Armstrong's state of mind at the time of the murder and the potential for her behaviour to become impulsive and violent. Imagine her *anger and fury* on discovering that after ten years of trying to conceive, her husband had in fact conceived a child with someone else, and not just anyone . . . her best friend.

'I think the evidence presented to you in court today shows that Clare Armstrong acted in a premeditated manner and murdered Theo Collins. She took him from his cot and hung him, strangling him; then she lied about the position of the body to ambulance staff and the police, only changing her story when confronted with the truth.

'Little Theo Collins is not able to tell us what happened to him that night, but the forensic evidence tells us what he is unable to express. His story – Theo's voice told through the forensic evidence – was key in Clare Armstrong changing her story.

'Clare Armstrong had *motive* to kill Theo Collins. It is my assertion that on learning that she had been betrayed she *intended* to kill Theo. She murdered him in cold blood and afterwards tried to cover up her actions.

'The issue before you is simple: if you believe Clare Armstrong's actions were premeditated, then she is guilty of murder. *Guilty.*

'Accused number two told the same lie to police as accused number one about the situation of the child's body when it was discovered. Samuel Armstrong is a man who already stands convicted of a violent crime and he has admitted lying to the police and changing his story in regard to little Theo's death. On the night of November twenty-first, when his wife alerted him to Theo's death, Samuel Armstrong saw that the child had been murdered, witnessed him hanging and lifted him down, but when ambulance staff and police arrived he colluded with his wife to lie about *how* the child had died.

'The cruel murder of little Theo Collins, a vulnerable toddler in the care of people he should have been able to trust, is unacceptable in a civilised society. Accused number one and accused number two colluded in a vile plot to hide the violent manner of Theo's death.

'For the sake of little Theo, who has had no say in these

proceedings, I ask you to convict Clare Armstrong for murder and, for his lies and deceit, Samuel Armstrong, for attempting to pervert the course of justice. Thank you.'

The jury were perfectly still. Mr Peterson's heels sounded as he returned to his seat. Malcolm Power stood and walked towards the jury. He addressed the jurors, palms turned upwards.

'When you go back to your jury room, ladies and gentlemen, you need to consider one of the most important aspects of this trial, and one that my learned friend, the advocate depute, failed to highlight for you . . . Clare and Samuel Armstrong *loved* Theo Collins and his sister, Ella, to whom they were godparents. You heard them both tell how devastated they were that this accident occurred in their home.

'Ambulance staff and police attending on the night in question all agreed that this was an accident – a tragic accident that we all hope would not happen to us and our loved ones on an everyday family night at home. We watched Sam and Clare's remorse over the outcome of that night and we have heard from forensic psychologists who testified on the effects of trauma on memory.

'Finding a child, whom you love deeply, dead in your own home, while under your care, causes severe mental distress. Sam and Clare admit that their witness statements to the police were incorrect, but remember that they had just discovered Theo, their beloved godchild, unresponsive in their home. Sam Armstrong tried hard to revive Theo; his actions show how desperate he was to bring the baby back to life.

'The pathologist has told you that Theo's death could – in

all probability – have been a terrible accident. Considering this situation makes accused number one and two – Clare Armstrong and her husband Sam Armstrong – victims too, of this horrendous family tragedy.

'The truth is, we *cannot* be sure what happened that night. There was insufficient DNA on Theo's sleepsuit to convict anyone caring for him of asphyxiating him. The most potentially incriminating DNA on the underside of the hood could not be identified as belonging to my client, Clare. In determining guilt, you have to base your decision on evidence, pure and simple, and here the evidence is not clear.

'We cannot be sure that Clare, on learning that Theo was Sam's child, became so angry that she resorted to murder. This is an assumption by the procurator fiscal and, I would assert, more than that – a fantasy. It *has not been proven beyond a reasonable doubt.*

'*Reasonable doubt* ...' Malcolm Power paused, raising his voice again, so that the word *doubt* punctuated the silence before him. 'To convict Clare Armstrong of murder, you must find that she acted with premeditation and without mitigation or diminished responsibility, *beyond a reasonable doubt.* There is *clearly* doubt in this case and so I say that the only thing you can do is find Clare Armstrong not guilty, or find that the case put before you has simply not been proven, in which case, you can return a verdict of not proven.

'On the charge of attempting to pervert the course of justice, again we have reasonable doubt. The highly emotive circumstances in which Theo was found dead, the panic and ensuing confusion on finding the child unresponsive may have resulted in Clare and Sam Armstrong giving contradictory information to police.

'Accused number one, Clare Armstrong, and accused number two, Samuel Armstrong, are charged separately. You may decide a different verdict: guilty, innocent or not proven for each of them.'

Malcolm Power stood back and Judy Miller stepped forward, one hand on her hip.

'Ladies and gentlemen, my honourable friend Mr Power is correct. Reasonable doubt is key and when it comes to my client, Mr Armstrong, we find that there is no evidence at all that he colluded in the death of little Theo or that he sought to cover up a crime. Mr Armstrong is clearly innocent of all charges against him, and I ask that you recognise that in your decision today.'

The judge cleared her throat.

'Ladies and gentlemen, you are now retired to consider your verdict.'

33

SAM

September 2019

The screen of the cycle camera was tiny, so Sam stood with his chin lowered on the breakfast bar so that he could watch the ride undertaken by his younger, more athletic self to the top of Arthur's Seat. He heard the whirr of the bicycle chain and the rhythmic splashes of water from the tyres, his exhalations short and quick, the occasional spit and sniff. The camera had been secured to his helmet, and so the video was a view of what Sam had seen on the day, the road ahead, with no image of himself at all.

Sam's eye view. The sky was blue; the summit was in sight.

Watching, he felt energy return to his muscles. He remembered the muscular joy of it, the heat and sweat and cool wind against his face and wrists, the burn of the lactic acid in his thighs. He had lived for that feeling, those long cycles on weekends when he lived with Clare.

He had a strange sense of being between worlds. His right hand rested on his thigh. He remembered how hard his quads had felt back then, muscles like steel ropes in his thighs. When the video was recorded, 2008, he had been at the peak of his fitness.

And then Theo had died, Sam had punched a man and permanently disfigured him, and then he had stopped cycling for good. It had been a great love of his life, but he had left it behind, just like that.

In 2009 the jury had given their verdict. Sam was innocent and Clare they found *not proven*. In a note to the judge, the jury said they considered that Clare had *in all probability killed Theo*, but the case had not been proven by the prosecution beyond a reasonable doubt.

And now, in 2019, Clare was going to enter that world again – go back into the dock, answer the same charges, face prison, but without him at her side.

Two worlds. Like a photograph and its film negative, the image is identical but darkness and light are switched.

It was hard to comprehend how it could happen once in his lifetime, but now it was happening again.

Sam hunched over the small video screen. He remembered the ride so well as he had ridden to and from Arthur's Seat countless times – a steep, short climb and then the thrilling spin to the bottom. So long ago, but just a few frames and Sam felt back there again. His body remembered too. His heartbeat began to increase as he watched his younger self reaching the summit and preparing for that giddy descent.

'Whooooo.'

Sam heard his voice whoop, a click as the gears changed. The black of the smooth road under his wheels, the rock and grass to the side and the blur as he began the high-speed descent. The gradient still so high, Sam watched as he reached cobbled streets, aiming for the drainage line.

Standing in his kitchen, Sam felt every sensation – the shudder of the cobbles through his bones and teeth. He put a hand to his jaw – remembering.

Sun at his back, he saw the shadow of himself on the screen – stretching out ahead of the bike – the oversized wheels, the long back and legs. He looked invincible, lean, a professional cyclist.

On camera, he heard himself whistle, exhale. *King of the Mountain.*

The film of the ride finished and there was a crackly segue into blank film. Sam fast-forwarded, sure that more rides must have been recorded. He could watch this stuff all day.

Suddenly there was movement, figures moving. Sam paused and rewound, then pressed play again.

An image appeared, shaky at first. It wasn't the recording of a ride, but something else.

Sam put the back of his hand to his mouth. His fingers began to tremble.

It was the children.

Theo and Ella were arriving at the flat, charging into the spare bedroom.

And then there he was, such a clown with his dark, floppy yet un-grey hair, Ella on his shoulders and then Theo. *Little Theo.*

Sam watched, transfixed, mouth open and lips drying as he saw the little boy bouncing on his shoulders, his tiny, chubby hands holding onto Sam's forehead.

Sam put a hand to his head. He could remember the giggles, and the sensation of those little hands on his brow. The view of the bedroom continued, but everyone left and so Sam was just watching film of the closed bedroom door.

Sam frowned, winded by the sight of them. He remembered that the spare bedroom had been where he'd kept all of his sports gear, and when the GoPro needed to be charged he had used the socket in that room. Somehow, it must have been recording when he thought it was just charging. He pressed fast-forward, wondering if there was more footage.

Two hours of video passed when the image was the same – a closed white door – the same door that had been the subject of court diagrams because Theo had been strangled, hanging from the door handle. Sam sighed. His thumb was beginning to ache from pressing the fast-forward button, so he switched fingers.

Finally, the door to the bedroom opened. The light from the hall cut inside, a blade of brightness in the room.

It was bedtime. Theo was crying, screaming in fact, from a room nearby, and Sam could hear Clare telling him he had to be clean before bed. She was bathing him.

There was Ella, in pyjamas with ladybirds on them, jumping up and down on the bed, a book in her hand. Sam saw his own legs and slippered feet walk over to Ella's bed, help her get in and then lie down beside her on top of the covers. Clare came and settled Theo into his cot. He fussed for a while and so Clare turned on the mobile with the African animals.

Sam heard the tinkling music of the mobile, watched the turning shadows of the animals on the wall, reflected by the soft light. Sam put a fist to his lips, unbelieving. His breaths fluttered in his throat, like trapped moths.

The sound wasn't good; he couldn't hear the story he was reading to the children, still he watched, transfixed, heart-broken. He could almost smell them, the buttery sweetness of their skin.

After half an hour or so, Theo stood up in his cot and began to cry out. Ella got up out of bed and left the room.

It was as Sam remembered, Clare had taken her upstairs and put her down in their bed. Sure enough Clare came into the room and settled Theo in the room on his own. She leaned over his cot and stroked the hair on his head before she left the room.

The bedroom light went out, yet there was still a parallelogram of light on the floor cutting in from the hall. They'd left the hall light on, as Ella was afraid of the dark.

Little Ella. Sam remembered reading to her and the familiar way she would snuggle against him, hand to his face to pull him closer.

Swallowing, Sam fast-forwarded again until the continuous geometry of light and darkness of the room was interrupted.

The sound wasn't clear but it was just possible to make out the sound of him and Clare arguing downstairs. The words were indistinct but he heard their raised voices.

And then he saw it – a shape rising in Theo's crib. The

shadow of the little boy as he attempted once, twice, three times to get out of the cot. On the third attempt he managed it – the panda bear treads on the soles of his sleepsuit searched for purchase. His feet touched the carpet. Sam felt an odd twinge of pride, sensing Theo's satisfaction at climbing out.

The little boy swayed by the cot, hand on the railing. He seemed uncertain about what to do, now that he had got himself out. He began to cry. It wasn't an urgent, attention-seeking cry, but rather a cry of tiredness, loneliness, fear. Sam touched the small screen as if to comfort – the tip of his forefinger the size of Theo's whole body.

Theo tried again, crying louder now.

Sam shook his head, hatred for himself swilling inside. He knew that neither he nor Clare would hear the little boy crying. They were too busy fighting over their sordid secrets – Sam's sordid secrets.

The shadow of Theo loomed in the centre of the floor. He looked like a little cartoon bear, the ears on the hood of his suit sticking out behind his head, and then that rounded body standing on two wide-set feet, hands out trying to find balance. Theo walked towards the parallelogram of light from the open door and began to cry louder, calling for attention now, as his shadow extended behind him.

Sam was now holding the screen so close that the image was almost distorted. If only he could go back to that time, he thought; he would take Theo up in his arms and protect him. This was his son, his little son, that he had known for so short a time. He had not heard him crying. Shame flushed through him.

Just then, the parallelogram of light increased as the door opened a little. A larger shadow subsumed the smaller umber shape of Theo. Light and dark in the room hung in the balance, crepuscular, disguising the movement, making the shapes indistinguishable.

The small sound of Theo crying was distinctly audible, even though the video resolution was grainy and almost blank. A long shadow lifted Theo up by his hood. The light was restored and at the same time, Theo was quiet. Sam saw the toddler's feet kick backwards and forth, tiny feet trying to find purchase.

Silence. Nothing but a crackle. Suddenly, Sam felt goosebumps prickle all over his scalp, lifting each follicle of his hair.

The shadow on the film found stillness. Sam held his breath. Her bare feet trod over the dark shadow of Theo on the carpet. They were tiny feet and they walked towards the camera.

There were three full seconds when Ella looked straight into the lens and Sam felt as though he had been flailed, skin peeled back so that all his nerves were shrill.

Ella left the room again. The camera shook in Sam's hand. Moments later another shadow cut across the room from the hall. It was Clare. She was crying, staggering as she made her way along the hall to the bathroom.

Still the shape of Theo hung by the door and, in the background, there was the sound of Clare unlocking the bathroom door.

Sam couldn't watch it all. He couldn't even remain standing, but instead buckled onto the kitchen floor. The camera fell from his hands. He dropped it and let it roll away from him as if it were burning hot. He couldn't watch Clare coming to the bedroom door and finding Theo, nor could he watch his own leap into the hall, taking Theo down from his hanging place and beginning to breathe into him – his own frantic mouth against the small, blue lips.

Sam touched his fingers to his mouth and began to cry.

'Oh God,' he said over and over again, 'oh dear God, no.'

He wept as he had that day, over a decade ago, when he'd held Theo's body in his hands.

It took a while for Sam to recover. He wasn't sure how long he spent sitting on the kitchen floor, but after some time he got up and called Clare.

He watched the photo of her on the home screen of his phone as he waited for her to answer, a taste of sickness at the back of his throat. She didn't pick up the call and it went to answerphone.

'This is Clare Richardson, please leave a message.'

'Clare, it's me. I need . . . '

Sam hung up. He didn't have the words.

He fastened his helmet and wheeled his bicycle out onto the landing, then carried it downstairs. He had the GoPro camera in his jacket pocket and he was going to show Clare what he had seen.

He glanced at his watch before he pushed off, realising that it was evening although the summer sun was still shining. The Leith bars around his apartment building were starting to fill up with diners and drinkers.

Sam dug into the pedals. By the time he reached the flat stretch of Princes Street, he was doing at least forty miles an hour. The volcanic hulk of the castle blinkered him to the left. The shops were closing and pedestrians were milling back and forth. Sam went as fast as he could, streaking through the first set of traffic lights at amber. Trams crept on either side of him, their spare, dull clang of warning barely heard as he headed west.

At the traffic lights at the bottom of Lothian Road, Sam stood, one foot on the pedal, one foot on the road, his chest heaving, sweat trickling from his hairline down to his ear.

He waited for the lights to turn, heart pounding. Frasers to his right, now sold, and behind it the bar that had been his and Clare's local when they were together. He remembered pulling her close in the private stone alcoves filled with tweed cushions.

Green light. Sam shot through the T-junction quicker than the buses to his left.

Shandwick Place, Atholl Place.

Sam turned towards St Mary's Cathedral, free wheeled and then dismounted.

Breathing hard, he battered his fist on the black-painted wood of his old front door. There was no reply, but stepping out into the courtyard, Sam could see lights on, and condensation between the window and the shutter. She would be in her dark-room, out of earshot.

Sam called her, but again she didn't answer her phone.

Sweating and out of breath on the doorstep, Sam wondered what to do. He realised that he still had a key to the flat on his key ring. Instinctively, he put the key in the lock and turned it. The door opened. Clare had not changed the locks after all. He hadn't lived in this house for over a decade, yet his key still worked.

He laid his bike against the wall in the alcove next to the front door. When he had lived here, he would have wheeled it inside. Now, he left it outside, unlocked.

Sam stepped over the threshold. 'Clare?' He stood at the bottom of the stone staircase and called upwards.

The smell of his old home was a deep comfort.

'Clare?'

Barefoot, she appeared at the top of the stairs, wet and wrapped in a towel.

'What are you doing?'

She was confused, not angry but puzzled to see him, and he smiled in relief.

'You're not going to believe this,' he said, wiping sweat from his brow with his forearm.

He climbed up the stairs and stopped a few steps from the top so that they were level with each other. Skin creamy pink from the bath, she seemed younger. He felt an overwhelming urge to touch her warm face.

'How did you get in? Did I leave the door open?'

'You didn't answer your phone. I tried knocking. I've something very important to tell you. I still have my key, remember?'

'Your key, oh my god. You just ...'

She touched her cheek, smiling but still unsure.

He wanted to take her by the shoulders.

'You're not going to face another murder trial.'

She tightened the towel around her.

'Don't make it harder than it is. This is something I have to go through.'

'You won't believe it until you see it. I have proof that you're innocent. Proof. Actual proof.'

'What?' Sudden goose pimples on her upper arms.

'Put some clothes on. I'll show you and then we need to find Detective Brookes.'

'What do you mean, *proof?*'

'The camera doesn't lie.'

34

DETECTIVE INSPECTOR
PAMELA BROOKES

September 2019

Brookes parked her car on Albert Street and walked slowly towards Lorraine's apartment block. It was late, after ten in the evening, and Brookes had not called to say she was coming.

It had been a surprisingly hot day, and the dry dusty pavements still seemed to blush from the sun's heat – pinking under street lights that would not be needed until midnight. Pamela Brookes pressed the button to gain entry to Lorraine's close. As she waited, hands in her pockets, Brookes noticed that the privet hedge that led up to the door had recently been trimmed and small green leaves the size of fingerprints were stuck to the path.

The door entry system buzzed and Brookes stepped into the close and knocked on Lorraine's door. Moments later she heard the key turn in the lock.

Ready to apologise for the hour, Brookes inhaled.

Ella stood before her, statuesque, her long hair coiled into a bun on top of her head. She wore leggings and a cropped sweat-shirt, a single wireless earbud in her left ear.

'Ella, I met you recently ... it's Detective Inspector Brookes. I wonder if I could speak to your mother?'

'Um, sure ... she's ...' Ella looked over her shoulder and then opened the door.

Brookes accepted the open door as an invitation to step inside.

'She's gone to bed already. I'll go and tell her.' Ella smiled over her shoulder at Brookes as she tapped on the bedroom door. 'I don't think she's asleep.'

'It's important, otherwise I wouldn't ...' Brookes let her sentence trail off. She closed the door behind her but stayed in the hallway, hands in her pockets.

Coats hung by the door. On the hall table, there was a note by the telephone. The date 21st October was scrawled in red pen. Brookes inhaled sharply, realising it was the date of Clare's double jeopardy trial.

The hall was dark, painted orange, but the lounge was bright and Brookes saw that the window was still open. The alkaline warmth of the late-summer night waited outside, accompanied by the intermittent chirp of birds.

'Detective Brookes?' Lorraine stepped out of the bedroom into the hall, pulling tight the tie on her dressing gown. She was barefoot.

'I'm so sorry to come this late, Lorraine. I have some news. I was passing and ...'

'No, of course, come in, come in.' Lorraine raked a hand through her hair. 'I'm sorry, I was having a bit of an early night. It always seems ridiculous in summer because it's still so light. I just felt tired.'

'Of course, that's understandable. I apologise.'

Brookes was aware that Ella walked with them both into the kitchen where Lorraine put on the kettle.

'Would you like a tea or coffee, Detective?' Ella smiled and raised her eyebrows at the same time.

'Coffee's fine. Black ... only if ... ' she let her sentence trail off. Ella seemed so young, so eager, her face fresh and poreless.

Lorraine and Brookes sat at the round table in the kitchen while Ella fixed the coffee. As soon as Ella set the mug of coffee down, Brookes spoke up, to avoid any awkwardness.

'Ella, do you mind if I have a word with your mum in private, please?'

Ella nodded, brown eyes wide open. Brookes cupped her hands round the coffee and stared into its unforgiving black eye until Ella left the room.

'What is it?' Lorraine said immediately. 'Is it about the retrial?'

'It is.' Brookes gently nudged the hot coffee away from her. She got up and closed the kitchen door and then sat back down.

Lorraine put a hand over her mouth. 'Is there a problem with the evidence? Is it not going ahead after all?'

'Almost.'

'I knew it.' Lorraine's face puckered. 'I can't keep going through this. I can't. I need it resolved. I need her guilty and put away. I can't keep ... ' Tears burst from Lorraine's eyes, illuminating tiny veins on her cheeks as they rolled to her chin.

Detective Brookes reached a hand across the table and set it palm-down inches from Lorraine. 'I'm going to tell you something now that I know will be very hard to hear, but I need you to listen to what I'm going to tell you, so that we can discuss options.'

Lorraine sniffed, nudged tears from her chin and neck with the back of her hand.

'I've been given a video that clearly shows Theo being murdered.'

Brookes waited for her words to seep into Lorraine.

'But how? You have a video . . . .? Of Clare . . . '

'I have, in evidence, a video that shows Theo being . . . ' Brookes felt saliva flood her mouth, as if she might vomit. The images she had watched on the office computer flashed in her mind, frame by frame. 'Lorraine . . . it *wasn't* Clare.'

Lorraine's eyes, glassy with tears, opened wide at the same time as her lips parted. 'Not Sam . . . ' Lorraine's cheeks were wet now.

'Not Sam, no.' Brookes shook her head once, making sure she maintained Lorraine's eye contact. She kept her voice low. 'Sam's cycle camera was filming in the corner of the bedroom the night that Theo died. It clearly shows what happened to him. Sam has now handed the video to the police and we have verified it.'

Lorraine blinked, nodding, prompting Brookes to continue.

'Lorraine, I'm so sorry to tell you this. But it was Ella . . . Ella killed Theo. The video has been corroborated. It is clear to see.'

'Wh ... what?' Lorraine ran a hand through her hair. It had been swept back but now a lock fell forward, wayward. 'What do you mean? How could she ....?'

'The video shows that Theo woke up when Sam and Clare were fighting and began to cry. He got out of his cot, as we all suspected he did, but then – and I think you need to see this video, but I don't think tonight is the time ... you can tell me when you are ready – we see clearly that Ella enters the room, takes her brother by the hood and hangs him on the bedroom door.'

Lorraine's face drained of colour, one hand clasped over her mouth. 'My ... Ella? No.'

Brookes clasped her hands and leaned further over the table, closer to Lorraine. 'I know this is going to take some time to sink in. I wanted to tell you tonight and not wait, but I suggest that we meet again tomorrow or the day after and discuss what happens now.'

'What happens now? What do you mean?'

'I've already contacted the procurator fiscal about this new evidence, and Clare's double jeopardy retrial will no longer go ahead.'

Lorraine wiped at her wet face.

Brookes got up and moved next to her, put a hand on her shoulder, patted the towelling robe of her dressing gown.

'But ...' Lorraine gasped, reaching up to touch Brookes' fingers on her shoulder. 'I wanted this trial. I can't believe that, after all this time, she'll get away with it again.'

Brookes nodded. It was to be expected. It was why she had decided to come round tonight rather than call. It would take time for Lorraine to accept that the woman she had hated for so long – believed to be the killer of her son – was innocent, while her own daughter had taken her son's life.

'Lorraine, there is something else you need to think about.' Brookes put her hand over Lorraine's. 'We can talk again tomorrow, but now that we have irrefutable evidence that Ella killed Theo, the fiscal may want to prosecute her.'

Silence spread over the kitchen. Brookes was suddenly aware of the hum of the fridge freezer.

Lorraine shook her head. 'What?'

Brookes hated this part of her job, but she knew that she had no choice but to tell Lorraine what to expect.

'Lorraine, it's every mother's worst nightmare, I know that—' Brookes nodded once '—but we now have proof that your daughter murdered her brother in 2008. In Scotland, right now, the age of criminal responsibility is twelve, but, in 2008, it was still *eight years old*. And Lorraine—' Brookes dipped her head, found Lorraine's eyes again '—Ella was eight years old when it happened. *Just eight*, barely eight, but still eight years old.'

'What are you talking about? What do you mean?' There were no tears now. Lorraine was pale-faced, her red eyes struggling to comprehend.

Brookes watched as the realisation filled Lorraine's face.

'I will argue, *strenuously*, that it is not in the public interest for Ella to be prosecuted, but it is *not my decision*. The procurator fiscal can charge her with murder now, try her … we need to be wary of that.'

'Wary? What? No, it can't …'

'My hope is that the procurator fiscal will agree that it is not in the public interest to try someone for an offence when they were just eight, as it contravenes modern thinking.'

'Hope?'

Brookes stood but Lorraine remained seated at the table. The mugs of coffee that Ella had prepared for them sat untouched.

'You need to speak to your daughter,' Brookes said. 'I'll call you tomorrow. I'll see myself out.'

When Brookes stepped out of the kitchen and into the hall, Ella was not in the living room. Brookes closed the door behind her and stepped outside.

It was almost dark now, as dark as it would get. There was still a hint of light, so the sky looked navy blue.

35

LORRAINE

September 2019

Lorraine sat at the kitchen table. Her hands felt cold. She heard the front door close as Detective Inspector Brookes let herself out of the flat.

What Brookes had told her settled on Lorraine like a layer of frost, even though she felt warm, almost feverish.

She heard Ella locking up for the night, turning the key and sliding the chain. Her daughter's shadow cut across the kitchen floor and Lorraine looked up at Ella in the doorway.

'Are you alright, Mum?'

Lorraine didn't move. Even the breath was quelled inside her.

'Are you okay? What did the detective say?'

Ella was leaning over the table, the curtain of her long hair swept to one side.

Lorraine parted her lips to speak. There were small crumbs on the table.

As if she thought it would help, Ella started to make tea – pouring the undrunk, cold coffee down the sink. The click of the kettle shutting off made Lorraine flinch. As Ella set a steaming cup of tea on the table before her, Lorraine looked up at her.

'Thank you,' Lorraine said, looking down at the pale-brown moon of the tea.

'Is everything alright?'

Lorraine swallowed. 'The other day, when we visited Theo's grave, I told you that they were going to re-try Clare for Theo's . . .' she found herself unable to utter the word.

Steam from the tea rose in a just-visible spiral.

Ella nodded. She put her hand on top of her mother's and Lorraine felt the heat from her hand, a heat that quickly became uncomfortable, making Lorraine withdraw her hands and set them in her lap.

'The night your brother died, do you remember it?'

Ella frowned. 'Some things.'

'Do you remember if . . .' Lorraine raised her eyebrows, feeling a swirl in her gut.

'I don't like to think about it.'

'No.' Lorraine looked into her daughter's big brown eyes. *No, of course not.* Her eyes were so gentle, so full of warmth. They were the eyes of the father she hadn't heard from in years.

A thought came to Lorraine, harsh, physical but intangible, like a gust of wind. She remembered standing outside the Newhaven Gallery in the swirling summer rain and telling Clare that losing a child was the worst thing anyone could ever go through, ever feel. She realised now that she had been wrong. She had been wrong about so many things.

'Sweetheart.' Lorraine smiled, feeling a hot tear flash over her face. She caught it at her chin with the back of her hand. 'The detective says there is a video. I don't know how. I can't think why . . .'

'A video?'

'She says . . . *you* hurt your brother,' Lorraine whispered.

Ella became very still, then her head bowed suddenly.

'Darling?' Lorraine felt a flare of hope and pain inside. She put her hand on Ella's arm. She wanted to shake a response from her. She wanted to hear her say it wasn't true.

'I don't really remember, but often I see it happen,' Ella whispered. Lorraine couldn't see her face. 'I can see what happened, but it's like a dream – something I imagined, but it's always stayed with me . . .'

Lorraine pressed her knuckles to her mouth.

Ella's eyes became wide as she looked around the room, as if watching again a scene from years ago.

'I just remember that Theo always made everyone upset. I remember when he cried you would just go to bed. You would feel tired and lie down. I felt like his mother. He was my brother, but also *my* baby. I felt I was responsible for him. I wanted him to be good, to be quiet, so that you wouldn't be sad, so that you'd . . .'

Lorraine wiped her face with one hand. It didn't seem real.

'And that night, he started crying and Aunt Clare and Uncle Sam started arguing. It's like a bad dream in my head. I see it but . . . ' Ella's breath became ragged. 'They were shouting and swearing, getting so upset. And I think I thought . . . if Theo would just be quiet, things would be okay.' Ella's face glistened with tears. 'I didn't understand. I didn't think that he'd be . . . I don't think I knew what would happen. I don't . . . '

Lorraine sat back in her chair. The wood dug into her shoulders. She felt weak. Her ankles buckled and her knees fell open.

'Mum, please. I'm sorry.' Ella covered her face with her hands. 'I could never tell you. I didn't want you to . . . '

Lorraine was numb, her nose was running with tears, but she did not lift her hand to wipe them away.

'I'm so, so sorry.' Ella suddenly sank to her knees on the kitchen floor. She put her arms around her mother, squeezed tight. 'I hate myself. Forgive me. Will you ever forgive me?'

Ella's arms linked around her mother's waist, her face was pressed into the front of the dressing gown. Lorraine felt the itching vibration of Ella's voice sounding against the drum of her chest. Lorraine stayed with her back against the chair, let herself be embraced. She didn't push her daughter away, but her arms remained paralysed at her side. The foul taste of this truth was still working its way into the crevices of her mouth.

Ella stopped crying, suddenly. She picked up one of her mother's arms and put it around her, held it there as she again buried her face in Lorraine's chest so that she felt the breath convulsing inside her daughter's body. Lorraine's arms remained limp.

'You were so little,' Lorraine said finally, looking down at Ella pressed against her belly. Her daughter's hair smelled sweet as strawberries. 'So little, but—'

'I didn't feel little. I felt grown up. I felt old.' Ella sobbed.

Lorraine knew that she was supposed to comfort her and felt that – in time – she would be able. But right now she couldn't bring herself to put her arms around Ella and say that it would be okay.

Because she had been wrong, standing outside the Newhaven Gallery in the wind and the rain, telling Clare – poor Clare – that losing a child was the worst thing she could feel. In her heart, loss-layered as with fallen leaves, Lorraine knew now that there was something much, much worse.

Epilogue

CLARE

October 2019

Clare was in her darkroom. She had finished developing all the old film she had found in the loft, and the last prints were dripping on the line before her, drying under the red lamp. Three pictures were pegged to the string line.

Looking at each one in turn, watching the edges curl inwards, become glossy, Clare washed and dried her hands. They were colour prints, but the film had been corrupted a little and she had had to work and rework them to bring out the shadow, and the detail on the features.

The first was a picture of her and Lorraine from university. Clare shook her head as she looked closely at the photograph – so close that she could smell the chemical stop bath.

'What the hell are we wearing?' she wondered out loud. They were arm in arm, laughing so hard that their eyes were almost invisible.

The second picture was one of Sam. He was slim and dark-haired, his stance slightly awkward, revealing how much he doubted himself. It had been taken before they were married, before they tried to have children, back when they simply enjoyed being with each other. The third picture was little Ella, in the hospital, the day that Theo was born. Clare remembered taking the photograph. She was trying to smile, but her face was full of worry, so that she looked so much older than six.

Clare sighed, slipping off the old shirt of Sam's she still wore to protect her clothes and hanging it on the hook on the back of the door. Stepping out into the hall, she wondered how Ella was – how she felt right now. It would be time for her to start a new year at college.

Clare had not felt relief when she saw the film of Ella killing Theo. Instead she had been filled with sadness. The gaps in Clare's memory of that night remained. When the double jeopardy trial had been set, Clare had almost been ready to accept that she had been guilty. She might even have pleaded guilty. How else would they have her DNA? How else would they be so convinced of her guilt that they would try her twice?

Somehow – a combination of what Detective Inspector Brookes had told her, and her own broken memory, she had pieced together what must have happened – how her DNA had been on the underside of Theo's hood. When Clare came back into the room and had found him hanging, she had tried to get him down before recoiling and calling on Sam. It had been so clear to her that he was already dead. She had slid her hand under the hood that hung him, but couldn't lift him off because the horror of it had stopped her. She had called on Sam and he came and saw . . .

Now, Clare opened the door to the spare room. It was still empty. She had never been able to use this room, or fill it with furniture. It was empty, yet full of the loss of Theo. Little Theo, who never had the chance to grow up.

Sam's son.

Clare took a deep breath and closed the door. Life was strange. Everything she had loved had been lost – but then hope had appeared unexpectedly. When she was indicted for murder a second time, Clare had only thought the worst. She had not expected that good would come of it.

Right on time, there was a chap at the door.

She skipped down the stone steps, trailing a hand on the metal bannister. When she opened the door, the cold reached inside. The season had changed sharply and it was almost winter now.

'I thought you would just walk in – use your key.' She put a hand on her hip, mock chastising him.

'I thought you would have changed the locks,' he said, bending to kiss her cheek.

As he leaned close, she felt the cold from the canvas material of his jacket.

'Are you ready?' he asked.

'Of course I'm ready.'

Sam waited downstairs while she put on her coat and wound a scarf around her neck. They were going down to Cramond to walk along the beach.

Since the case had been dropped, they had started to meet up regularly. Once a week, just friends, but Clare had noted that the last two times, when they had said goodbye, he had kissed her on the lips.

Clare locked the big black door to the flat and they headed out together. Around the corner, on Palmerston Place, Sam noticed his shoelace was untied and knelt at the side of the pavement. She waited beside him, hands in her pockets and her back to the wind.

He laughed suddenly, looking up at her.

'On one knee before you like this ... I feel like I should be asking you to marry me or something.'

'Sam,' she said, putting both hands on his cheeks, 'you *are* married to me.'

'Oh yeah ... so I am.' He took the offer of her hand, to help him stand.

He kept a hold of her hand and they walked, side by side for the next block, towards his car. It felt natural, normal, like being home.

ACKNOWLEDGEMENTS

A great many thanks to my editor, Emma Beswetherick, for her patience and thoughtfulness over the evolution of this book. Thanks too, to the Piatkus team, including Hannah Wann, and to my agent, Sophie Lambert, for her continuous encouragement and support.

Any errors of fact or emphasis are my own, but I am indebted to several people who helped me when I was researching this novel. My gratitude goes to Gerry Considine and Eileen Leyden for their invaluable advice on legal and procedural matters. Apologies if I have, on occasion, distorted the information they shared for the purposes of the story.

Special thanks to Juliet McEwan for her enormous generosity and time in sharing her own experiences to help me write this book. Thanks are also due to Anthony Hubbert, Annie McLaughlin, Mary Fitzgerald, Rita Balneaves and Elizabeth McCrone; and thank you to Mark Kobine, for allowing my imaginative property theft of his beautiful home.

Finally thank you, Crawford, for your love and support and willingness to help me at every turn, and to the rest of my family and friends who cheer my efforts.

Read on for an exclusive extract from
Lisa Ballantyne's stunning new novel

The Innocent One

Ten years ago, criminal solicitor Daniel Hunter won a trial
that gripped the nation. He defended Sebastian Croll, an
eleven-year-old boy accused of murdering his playmate.

Now, a woman has been brutally killed in Cambridge and
Daniel receives a call from his old client. Twenty-one-year-old
Sebastian, a student at the university, finds himself a suspect.

As Daniel steps in to defend Sebastian for a second time,
news of the murder sends shockwaves across the country.
The media are keen to see Sebastian convicted, instantly
branding him as guilty.

Can Daniel prove once again
that Sebastian is the innocent one?

Coming in 2022

PROLOGUE

Frankie walked to work, enjoying the early morning air, unaware that today was the day she was going to die. She often went into work this early, when the throng of gawky students were still asleep, but these past few weeks she'd made a point of it because it was the coolest part of the day. She would let herself into her office in the Classics building and plunge into her book on the Macedonian conquest of the Persian Empire. It was due to be published in November and she hoped to present it before then, a keynote speech at Princeton University.

It was going to be another searing hot day and already it was clammy, a film on her skin. She wore a long, loose skirt and flat sandals. It was just over an hour's walk to work from the riverside cottage she shared with her husband, Jon, just off Fen Road; the rooms small and dusty, the back garden long and semi-wild, leading right down onto the banks of the Cam. Early afternoon she would walk home again, let Artemis out, and eat lunch at the bottom of the garden, waving away hoverflies and looking at the gnarl of bramble. Artemis was her blonde beagle, named after the Goddess of the Hunt, but even though she was a pedigree, at twelve years old she no longer showed any interest in hunting. She barely opened her eyes if a squirrel came into the garden, and even a rabbit spied on a walk failed to incite any enthusiasm for a chase. Artemis seemed to have decided that she had run after her last rabbit some time ago; Frankie considered that thought probably came to everyone eventually.

Jon was away with work again – three or four countries in a row this time – Malaysia, Singapore and . . . somewhere else. Frankie couldn't remember the last one. She wasn't inconsiderate, but international travel was a constant thing for Jon and after a while she lost track. She was sure he had been due home last night, but he hadn't appeared, and so she expected he was probably in the air just now, sipping a blended malt from a plastic glass while scanning a journal on quantum electronics.

Jon was Professor of Electrical Engineering, his office just a thirty-minute walk from hers, but he was always away 'doing deals' with one foreign university or another, in the Far East or North America. She was used to him being gone. They had been married for fifteen years and she still loved him, but it was easier to love him while he was away. Jon hadn't always been faithful. He was older than she was, by eleven years, but his energy was expansive. Jon, dark-eyed, dark-haired even in his mid-fifties, burst into any room demanding all attention. He was six-foot two, but seemed to take up an even larger metaphysical space. He had absolutely no insecurities. In that sense, he was quite a good advertisement for the potential of positive self-esteem, or the public school system, whichever way you looked at it. Young women seemed to accept that he was as attractive as he proclaimed; he had risen in the ranks academically – Professor by the age of forty two – and now in the university leadership.

Unless Jon returned, she might have a few friends over later to drink Sangria as the sun went down. Sangria from the Latin, *sanguis*, for blood. They could bring their swimsuits and take a dip in the Cam. It was delicious to swim in the river at this time of year. She liked to swim out to the deepest point and then slip her swimsuit off under-water. It was uniquely liberating.

A group of early rowers passed and Frankie paused to watch them, even though she had seen them many times. This group were all women. There was almost no breeze and so the Cam was grey-brown, ripples catching the new pink light in scales, like snakeskin. The boat cut through it, even and straight. The rowers' easy rhythm set her up for the day and Frankie unconsciously found their timing as she continued her walk.

She would get her work done and then sit at the bottom of her garden and call her mother, which she did every Wednesday without fail. Frankie was from Liverpool originally and her mother, Delia, still lived in Kirkby, Merseyside. She was eighty-three, five foot three, and still went to bingo under her own steam every Tuesday evening. Frankie was one of eight – four sisters, three brothers – and had been her mother's fifth child. When they spoke, Frankie's Scouse dialect unconsciously came back, thick and guttural. When she spoke to Jon, or her students and friends in Cambridge, her accent was smoothed and rounded, like a piece of glass washed by the ocean. She had been in Cambridge since she left Liverpool at the age of eighteen, and it was hard to keep a grasp on her short vowels. They were all but lost now, to everyone but her mother.

While Frankie had felt an oddity at University of Cambridge for a long time – working class in a sea of quaint academics and awkward public school students – she often attested her wish to study Classics here with her background in Merseyside. The noisy pack of her family meant she had all the grounding she needed in Greek drama before she even read *The Iliad*, which she had, on a whim when she was fourteen, while all her friends were drinking in the park.

As Frankie turned onto Turpington Street, the bakers had just opened and the sweet smell of fresh bread stopped her in her tracks. She bought a hot roll wrapped in a paper bag and carried it in two hands, her pace quickening with anticipation, feeling the sweat at the small of her back soaking through the waistband of her skirt.

Frankie used her key to enter the Classics building. It was just after six now and the cleaner would not arrive until six thirty. She took the stairs, fanning herself lightly with her hand. If she could summon the courage later in the morning, she would speak to Dean Winter about the Princeton trip. She was already booked into the conference, but the Dean was begrudging of the funding and it seemed as if Frankie might have to pay for it herself. Jon stayed in five-star hotels wherever he went, and spoke on his return of massages in his room administered by lithe, young women who barely spoke English. Frankie couldn't even persuade her boss to fund her economy flight to Newark and then three nights at a Motel 6.

The arts entertain, but science educates, was one of Jon's proclamations that infuriated Frankie. Jon thought it fitting that the bulk of university and government funding went to science and engineering. Frankie had argued with him countless times. The Ancient Greeks had a dazzling knowledge of the universe, and their intricate theories of physics, astronomy, chemistry, and biology were the very foundation of science. The arts gave birth to science and engineering but now were cast aside as fluff and nonsense.

At the top of the stairs, she paused and touched her moist brow with the back of her hand. It was a relief to be inside, alone and soon to be deep into her book. She would break open her roll and watch the steam rise from the pores of the dough.

She took out her key and, as she did so, the bag with the hot roll fell to the floor. It was only when she bent to pick it up that she noticed the door to her office was already ajar. She might have forgotten to lock it, or else Harvie, the janitor, might have been in overnight – worried about squirrels chewing the electric cables in the roof again.

Bringing the warm paper bag to her nose, she smelled the hot bread and saliva flooded her mouth. She shouldered the door open.

Frankie took a sharp intake of breath. Something was wrong, although she couldn't say what. She pinched her lips together, noticing that the large chunk of ornamental agate that sat on the middle of her bookshelf was missing.

It was her focal point when she was working. She would look up and admire it, with its ancient crystalline structures in brown, green and purple. Hand-sized and heavy as a bowling ball, it only moved when she stood on a chair and took it down to wash it. Dust dulled the sparkle and so Frankie would wash it every now and again, careful not to crack the porcelain sink in the bathroom with its heavy, jagged stone.

Frowning at the bare shelf, Frankie stepped inside. The door fell silently closed behind her and she turned quickly, hearing the lock click.

At first she smiled, but it fell from her lips. She felt the emptiness of the building, heard the electric hum of the strip lights. She thought about running or shouting out, but he was standing in front of the door and there was no one to hear her.

Professor Frances Isabel Owen, who was forty-three years old with not a single grey hair; who was a European authority on Aegean prehistory, who liked swimming in the river at the bottom of her garden. Frankie, who had size five feet and had to speak to her mother this afternoon; Frankie, who needed to be home at two to let Artemis out to relieve herself; who had so much more life to live, looked straight into the face of the man who was about to kill her.

It was a terrible thing to know you were going to die and not be able to do anything to prevent it. She tried anyway, raising up her small hand to protect herself (still holding the paper bag with her warm breakfast roll, as if it was the magic shield of Perseus) until her finger was smashed and her own blood blinded her.

1

He hadn't been sleeping, but as soon as the alarm sounded, Daniel got up and put on his running gear. No breakfast – he liked to run empty, with only his wits for fuel. In his battered trainers, he padded down the stone steps and began to jog around the circumference of Victoria Park. It was going to be another hot day and already he felt the humid weight of it wrap around him.

His body felt light and energetic, despite barely sleeping. The slight breeze blew him along like lit paper and he let it, knowing that when he climbed back upstairs and closed the door on that studio shoebox he would feel like crying. He didn't want to be back here, in his old flat.

When he bought the flat in Bow in the early 2000s, as a young lawyer, this part of the East End had been rougher and he had liked the edge to it. Since the Olympics, and since he had lived here last, it had become gentrified and the whole landscape had changed, so instead of simply looping around Victoria Park, he headed over the canal towards the Olympic Stadium.

Daniel was a runner. Even though he was in his mid-forties now, he could still complete a marathon in under three hours ten. He had been running ever since he could remember. *Fight or flight*; he chose flight. Flight was, after all, often the most logical course.

As he ran, he tried to shake off the feeling of being in the flat. It felt as if it didn't belong to him, like wearing someone else's shoes. For nearly ten years now, he had rented it out; it was just luck that the short-term tenancy had come to an end when he needed it again, otherwise he would have been sleeping at the office.

A day ago, he and Rene had had a blazing row. They didn't often fight, but it had come out of nowhere. As an adult, Daniel tried to avoid confrontation when he could and now he considered this strategy had forced their issues underground. He had been blind-sided by the stream of hurt and anger she threw at him.

I can't take it any longer. I can't be with you right now, she had said, putting on her coat.

It had been the action of tugging on her parka – a warm evening and she grabbed any coat – a winter jacket – to escape him. He had thought he just wanted to walk it out, but she said she needed to be away from him for a few days. Her green eyes stark in the hall, zipping the jacket despite the humid night, as if to show her seriousness, saying she would go and get Billy out of bed.

He had relented then, put his hands on her shoulders and said he was sorry, but it was too late. To stop her walking out, he had said that *he* would go.

Just the thought of that – leaving them – winded him, and

his pace slowed. His dirty training shoes beat into the pavement. It would only be for a few days, he hoped. He would stay in Bow and give her space, but already he missed them and he felt the ever-present intensity of that in the centre of his chest, as if there was a fishbone stuck in his windpipe.

Slowing his pace for the traffic on Roman Road, Daniel thought he could already smell the warming tarmac underfoot. He began a circuit of the public running track at the Olympic Stadium and his breathing evened out, slow and deep in his chest as his pace steadied. His hamstrings were tight, and his right leg felt almost mechanical when it swung forward. Whether it was his hamstring, or the fact that he was so tired and distracted – not lifting his feet enough – he pitched forward suddenly into the red dirt. His forearm and elbow took the weight of his fall. Sitting up, Daniel saw the graze was bleeding a little and he wiped it on his dark shorts. Normally, he would just get back up and start running, but today, as slashes of light cut across the track leaving half of it in shadow, he put his elbows on his knees and let his head rest on his knuckles. He felt the pulse of his blood in his hands. He had been listening to music on his phone and he let it and the headphones fall gently onto the track. He smelled his sweat and the scent of freshly cut grass from somewhere in the distance.

He sniffed, ready to get back on his feet, but just then a call came – lighting up the screen of his phone. It was an unknown number but he took the call anyway.

'Daniel Hunter.'

Silence on the line.

'Hello?'

'Danny ... it's good to hear your voice again. It's Seb Croll.'

Daniel picked himself up. He hadn't heard the name clearly, although it was someone who knew him. The name sounded like *subcrawl*.

'Sorry, I didn't catch your name?'

'It's been a long time, I know. It's Sebastian. Sebastian Croll.'

The name resonated deep inside him and then a sudden prickle up the back of his neck and across his scalp, as if all the follicles had suddenly tightened.

Daniel grabbed a fistful of his sweat-dampened hair. 'It ... certainly has been a long time. Are you ... ?' Daniel was about to say, *grown up*, but stopped himself as it sounded inappropriate. Sebastian had been just eleven years old when he represented him. It had been a high-profile, Old Bailey trial, with Sebastian accused of murdering his eight-year-old neighbour, Ben.

'I'm fine. How are you Danny? You're still ... solicitor?'

'I am.'

'I'm afraid I need your help again.'

Noticing that he had a smudge of blood on the back of his hand, Daniel waited for Sebastian to continue.

'Don't worry, it's not as bad as last time ...' Sebastian laughed lightly and Daniel frowned in response to his attempt at a joke.

'I think it's just an informal interview. The police said they wanted to have a chat with me and I've to go in today or tomorrow ... Perhaps I'm being overly-cautious, but I wanted to take someone with me. With my history ...'

'Informal interview? What about?'

'Well, my tutor,' Sebastian's breathing became audible, as if he too was running, or becoming upset. 'My tutor at Cambridge. It's unbelievable ... it's ...' his voice trembled. 'She's been murdered ...'

Daniel took a slow intake of breath.

'Obviously I ... had nothing to do with that. I was ... I mean I still can't believe it, but I think the police are just speaking to everyone who knew her. I was going to go by myself, but then I thought it might be sensible ... to have representation. Because of my history.'

He pronounced the word *history* very carefully, sounding all three syllables.

'You're in Cambridge then? At the university?'

'Yes. I'm studying Classics.'

'So, it's Cambridge Police then?'

'Yes. I wondered about going to speak to them today. I didn't know if that was convenient ... If you would be able to come?'

Daniel wrinkled his forehead as he mentally ran through his diary for the day. He thought he had a couple of appointments that he could shift, but he knew he would need to catch a train and wasn't sure it was worth it for a routine interview. He and Rene shared a car, but he had left it at Herne Hill. His reluctance was not only because of the inconvenience. Sebastian was not just any old client. To date, Daniel had not represented anyone else so young; but of course Sebastian was no longer a child.

Daniel wiped a hand wet with sweat over his jaw. 'My colleague knows some people up in Cambridge. I could get another name for you – an alternative. To save you time?'

Even as he offered this, Daniel sensed Sebastian would refuse.

'That's very thoughtful, but I would prefer if it were you.'

He looked up at the sky as if asking for guidance and saw a jet drawing a white line across the immaculate blue.

'Is this your number? I need to move a couple of meetings and get up there. I can text you a time later and then you could let the police know?'

'Thank you. Yes, this is my number . . . Thank you so much.'

'I'd need to charge you, of course. If you're not suspected of a crime, it won't be covered under Legal Aid.'

'Of course that's fine. You can just let me know your fee.'

Ready to ring off, Daniel almost talked over Sebastian with his goodbye and confirmation of arrangements. 'It will be wonderful to see you again,' Sebastian gasped.

Daniel hesitated, feeling uneasy as he heard the words, subtle but uncomfortable, like an insect walking on his skin. 'Yeah . . . you too.'

Before he jogged back to the flat, Daniel stood for a moment reflecting on the call. He could visualise Sebastian exactly – as he had been then – the little sprinkling of freckles on his nose, his large eyes. The thought of meeting him again was unnerving.

The Innocent One is available now to pre-order

Don't miss Lisa Ballantyne's other gripping and thought-provoking thrillers

To find out more, visit www.lisaballantyne.com